KT-559-195

4 4 0168196 8

Diamond

JESSIE KEANE

Diamond

First published in Great Britain in 2022 by Hodder & Stoughton
An Hachette UK company

1

A CIP catalogue record for this title is available from the British Library

Hardback ISBN 978 1 529 36304 3
Trade Paperback ISBN 978 1 529 36305 0
eBook ISBN 978 1 529 36306 7

Typeset in Plantin by Manipal Technologies Limited

Printed and bound in Great Britain by Clays Ltd, Elcograf S.p.A.

Hodder & Stoughton policy is to use papers that are natural, renewable and
recyclable products and made from wood grown in sustainable forests.
The logging and manufacturing processes are expected to conform to
the environmental regulations of the country of origin.

Hodder & Stoughton Ltd
Carmelite House
50 Victoria Embankment
London EC4Y 0DZ

www.hodder.co.uk

To Cliff

He who lives more lives than one
More deaths than one must die.
Oscar Wilde, 'The Ballad of Reading Gaol'

PART ONE

I

1909

When the Boer War was going on over in Africa, Warren Butcher and his Butcher Boys ruled the streets around Soho. Everything was fine. Then the Austrian Wolfe crew under Gustav Wolfe came to London and snatched the business out from underneath the Butchers.

It was bad in one way – very bad – but good in another, because Warren was forced to hastily decamp to Paris and there he met Frenchie, an artist's model, who would become his exotic-looking wife and Diamond Butcher's mother. Warren didn't speak French, and Frenchie had only a little English, but they learned from each other, and the language of love soon overcame their differences. Warren fell head over heels for Frenchie and together they settled down to married life.

Prosperity followed. Paris was good to the Butcher family. They started with one nightclub, then expanded. One more. Then another. And so on. Buying, decorating, dreaming, creating their dream. They were happy in Frenchie's golden city. Deliriously happy. And getting rich.

Then came the three children, in quick succession. Frenchie wanted to give her babies French names, but Warren was insistent. He was English, to his bones.

'Diamond for a girl,' he said. 'And she *will* be a diamond, won't she? A little jewel. And Aiden, I've always dreamed of that name if I had a son.'

'And if there are two boys? What then?' Frenchie teased him.

'Owen,' said Warren.

So along came Diamond, then Aiden and then finally – a last hurrah for Frenchie, by then a glamorous grande dame in her forties – Owen.

Diamond loved both her younger brothers. Aiden was a nightmare of a kid, lively to the point of mania, stuffing his pockets with all kinds of rubbish, running everywhere full throttle, jumping off shed roofs and forever getting into mischief. He was always dirty, always covered in mud and blood, but he was sweet too, and smiley, and Diamond loved him very much.

She fussed around after Owen too, who sadly was slow-witted because the cord had knotted around his neck during the birth, poor thing. As a consequence of his disability, Owen was Aiden's opposite: peaceful, almost slothful, happy with his colouring books at the kitchen table, alarmed by loud noises or shouting, needing to be shielded from the world.

'Red and yellow make orange,' Diamond told Owen, showing him with the crayons. 'And look, Owen – red and green make brown. And blue and yellow make green. You see?'

Owen was delighted. He laughed and kissed her cheek and she hugged him, ruffling his dark hair and smiling at his pleasure in such simple things.

Diamond loved Aiden and Owen. She worshipped her dad. And she *adored* her glamorous mother Frenchie, who had taught her daughter to speak her native tongue so that she was fluent in the language, perfect in her pronunciation.

'She could pass for a Parisian,' Frenchie told Warren proudly.

Then disaster struck. Gustav Wolfe – who had previously seized all the Butcher holdings and driven them out of London – expanded across the Channel and into Paris. Sheer force of numbers defeated the Butcher clan. The Wolfe mob descended on them, snatching away their six Parisian nightclubs – the Pompadour, the Miami Beach, thc Metropole, Ciro's, the Lopez and the Cabaret de l'Enfer. Again, Warren Butcher had to run – or die.

'It'll be all right,' Warren told his wife.

But Frenchie didn't think so. What she thought was this: that the hated Wolfe mob would hound them until their dying day. And Diamond, from an early age, believed her mother to be absolutely right.

2

'Maybe we'll try Manchester,' Warren said to Frenchie. 'Or Birmingham.'

'You mean, we will run?' sniffed Frenchie. 'Run away from Gustav Wolfe and his mob of thieves and cut-throats?'

They'd returned to Soho, to Warren's home town of London, with all their belongings – which included a massive full-length portrait of Frenchie in her prime. Warren didn't want to go anywhere else. But he had a family to think of now. If Wolfe cut up rough, what might become of Frenchie? Of Diamond and Aiden and Owen, his kids who he loved more than life itself? What if something happened to them, and it was *his* fault, because he hadn't moved quickly enough to save them, to spare them more conflict?

But then Warren started to hope. Everything was quiet, after all. On the strength of this, ever hopeful, he used the cash he'd saved up in Paris to buy a house, and hung Frenchie's fabulous portrait at the top of the stairs. With what remained, he bought a club called the Milano over in Wardour Street and the Butcher family called it theirs. Frenchie set to with great gusto, decorating the club interior with vivid reds and luscious golds. She was so proud when the opening night came, and there was dancing to a band, the drink flowed like water, everyone had a fabulous time. Then when all seemed to be going well, one dark rainy night someone put a lit rag through the letterbox of their house.

Warren was a bad sleeper – that was all that saved them. He was coming down the stairs to get his cigarettes and make a brew just before midnight when he saw flames erupting on the doormat. He ran down and stamped it out. Smoke billowed. He opened the front door and stepped out, heart thumping, staring around. The rain fell, hissing hard as a thousand snakes. But there was nobody to be seen. He tossed the destroyed mat out onto the path, still smouldering. The burned rag, too. Frenchie, having heard him opening the front door, was coming down to see that he was all right.

'*Chéri*, what . . .?' she asked anxiously.

Warren stepped back inside. His head was spinning. So here it was, at last. That bastard Wolfe was *never* going to let this go. The worst of it was, Warren knew that once again he was outgunned. Most of the coppers around the manor were already in the pay of the Wolfe mob. And Warren had lost touch with many of the boys who'd worked for him around the clubs, pubs and snooker halls he'd once run in London – before Gustav Wolfe had snatched it all away from him. The Wolfes had bigger numbers, but Warren had practically no-one to call on. His kin were up north, they hadn't been in touch for years. He'd never got on with his brother Victor, and his parents hadn't wanted to know either of them.

Now, *this.*

If he hadn't – by sheer chance – come downstairs, they might all have been dead by morning.

Frenchie was staring at him, pale and clutching at her throat in terror. 'Was it them, you think?' she said quietly.

Upstairs, their kids were sleeping. It chilled Warren to the bone, the thought of what could have happened.

Maybe Manchester *would* be good, Warren thought. Or – yes – even Birmingham.

But the Wolfe clan had tried to burn him out. Rage churned in his belly and clutched at his chest. They could have killed his kids. His wife. And now he was thinking of turning tail? Running away?

Just how far could you run before you got sick of it? Before you knew you had to stand your ground at last, and fight?

This far, thought Warren. *And no bloody further.*

He reached up, furious, and snatched down his coat, pulling it on.

'Where are you . . .?' Frenchie demanded, but he was already gone, out the door and away.

3

'You did what?' Frenchie said two hours later.

She'd been frantic, pacing the floor since Warren left, wondering what madness he would commit. Warren was hot-tempered at the best of times. Would he go, knock on the Wolfe door and call Gustav out? That would be crazy, but she wouldn't put it past him.

Now he was back – thank God! But what had he done?

'I put a lit rag through *his* letterbox,' said Warren. 'See how the fucker likes that.'

Frenchie couldn't believe it. *Stupid, stupid, stupid,* she thought. But she said nothing. In her mind, she was already gone. Manchester, yes. They'd try there. *Anywhere,* where there was no Wolfe mob waiting to snatch their livelihood away from them. But she was broken-hearted. In London, the Wolfes had smashed Warren's living. In Paris, the Wolfes had smashed them again. Now the Butchers had just one London club, their absolute pride and joy, the Milano, and she knew the Wolfes would take that too. She knew it. There was nothing for the Butchers to do now but flee. *Again.*

But before they could gather themselves, put the club on the market, a note – not a lit rag – was shoved through the letterbox. Frenchie watched as Warren opened the envelope and spread out the stiff sheet of paper inside. She read it, over his shoulder.

Tonight. Eight o'clock. Outside the Milano.

'Oh God,' said Frenchie, frozen with fear.

Warren scrunched the note and envelope up, stuffed them into his pocket.

'I'll be there all right. Mob-bloody-handed,' he said.

***

The Milano didn't open that night. Out in the street at the front of it, the clock struck eight and Warren and what boys he could muster were there, ready for a ruck. Then one by one, the Wolfe lot started to emerge from the shadows. Warren gulped as he saw them swelling in numbers; there were *hundreds* of them. The streetlights glittered off cudgels, knives, axes, bike chains. Then Gustav Wolfe stepped through the crowd, big as a barn door, his sandy hair swept straight back, his eyes black pinholes as he stared, half smiling, at Warren Butcher.

'You want to call this off then?' asked Gustav into the sudden silence.

'No,' said Warren, thinking of that burning rag on the doormat. This cunt thought *he* was a doormat, fit only to wipe his dirty Austrian feet on. Well, no more. 'I heard someone tried to set light to your arse,' said Warren. 'Shoved a lit rag through your letterbox. Is that right?'

Wolfe's smile froze on his face. 'You think you're funny, uh?'

Warren shrugged. What the fuck. His hand tightened on the axe he held. He'd sharpened it that morning, sitting at the kitchen table with Aiden running rings around him, Owen peacefully colouring with his crayons and his bits of paper, Diamond sitting gravely at the table, watching him.

'Enough talking,' said Warren, and let out a bellow, holding the axe high as he charged.

A roar went up from both sides and then Warren was in the thick of it, crashing into the opposition, pummelling his way in with the axe swinging wildly in his right hand, the brass knuckledusters on his left pounding faces, chests, arms. Bodies were falling, hitting the cobbles, and he was wading further into the Wolfes, falling over men groaning, their heads a mess of blood, slipping and sliding as the cobbles got drenched in it, treading on a hand and then realising it was detached from someone, and there was screaming and he was possessed, swinging the axe, wanting to reach Gustav Wolfe but unable to; everyone was clustering around Wolfe like he was their king and had to be kept safe.

Then there was an impact – a stunning, hideous blow that knocked him down, and he was crawling, half blinded, blood in his eyes and humming in his ears. He dragged himself all of three paces, and then was struck again.

This time, he fell and lay still.

4

They brought Warren Butcher home on a stretcher. What few of his supporters remained were blood-stained, battered, stumbling with exhaustion. They carried Warren into the kitchen and laid him out on the floor.

He was dead.

Frenchie saw it, straight away. His head had been caved in on the left side, baring brain and bone and blood. The life force was gone from him; he was nothing but a shell. She flung herself on his neck, crying, screaming with rage and pain and horror. Diamond grabbed Aiden and Owen and hustled them up the stairs, away from this carnage.

She sat upstairs with her brothers for a while, hearing voices down below, shouts, curses. Owen was trembling, leaning in against her and she had her arm around his shoulders and was talking to him in a low voice, soothing him as best she could. Aiden sat on her other side, saying nothing, but pale and taut as a bowstring.

Finally, she could stand it no longer. She had to know what was happening.

Telling her brothers to stay there, she left the bedroom and went down. She didn't want to go into the kitchen, but her mother was in there and so she knew she had to. She didn't want to see her dad again, stretched out dead and cold on the floor. She didn't think she could bear it. But her mother was there, suffering, so she had to suffer too.

Bracing herself, shivering with dread and fighting back tears, Diamond went into the kitchen. But there were no men there. There was no body. There was only Frenchie, sitting in the chair by the fire, hunched over, her hands to her face. She looked up as Diamond came in, her face smeared red where she had been clinging on to Warren. She held out a hand. Diamond rushed forward and took it, hugging her mother hard. She could smell her father's blood. She could feel Frenchie's tears, drenching her shoulder as Frenchie clung to her in desperation.

Frenchie sobbed. 'I knew it would happen. I told him. But he would never listen.'

Diamond didn't know what to say. There were no words of comfort she could give.

'I asked them if they saw him fall,' Frenchie gasped out. 'They said it was Gustav Wolfe, it was him who delivered the *coup de grâce* to my poor darling Warren. I hate that *cochon* so much!'

Diamond could feel the rage and sorrow seeping out of Frenchie and into her. The Wolfe mob. They'd been a torment to her family ever since she could remember. And now – this. Her dad was dead. What was going to become of them all, without his jovial, reckless, larger-than-life presence?

She hugged her mother while Frenchie sobbed again – wrenching, heartbreaking sobs of absolute despair.

'They have taken him to the morgue,' said Frenchie brokenly. 'My love, my beautiful man, they have taken him away from me. It's more than I can stand.'

Diamond held her mother tight. There was nothing else she could do. She hated the Wolfes. She hated them and she swore to herself that when she was grown she would have her revenge; she would harm them, in any way she could.

5

Diamond Butcher was just eleven years old when she first met her Uncle Victor at her father's funeral. She was standing, drenched to the skin, beside her mother and her two brothers at Warren Butcher's graveside. It was pissing down with rain, hammering her, the droplets so hard that she could barely hear what the vicar was saying.

Anyway, it didn't matter.

A numbness had engulfed her, ever since that awful night when they'd carried her father home. All that mattered was that Dad was gone. Gustav Wolfe had killed him. The Wolfe clan were their dreaded enemies. Thoughts of sweet vengeance haunted Diamond, day and night. There was a dead wife, she knew that, back in Austria. A son, she knew that too. And a daughter. More than that, she didn't know or even want to. All of them were evil, bad to the bone. She despised them.

'Ashes to ashes, dust to dust . . .' droned the vicar, rain dripping in cascades from his surpliced shoulders, splashing off the end of his beaky nose onto the open bible in his hands.

This last week had been a nightmare. The police – straight ones, or ones in the pay of Gustav Wolfe, who knew? – had come to call. Looking at them all like they were scum. Asking questions and not even caring about the answers.

Diamond clung on to her mother's hand at the graveside. She could feel Frenchie shuddering with tears, unable to comprehend what had happened. Now she was a widow. Aiden and Owen, on their mother's other side, were silent. Nine-year-old Aiden was holding back the tears, determined to be brave now he was the man of the family. Owen, who was just six, wore his usual expression of sweet bewilderment. How could they explain life, death, to him? He knew his colouring books and the kitchen table; that was all. Death and disaster, the horrors of the Wolfe clan, Warren Butcher's proud, brave and foolhardy fight for survival against insurmountable odds – all of that was beyond Owen.

Now the vicar had stopped speaking and was holding out a small rectangular wooden box to Frenchie. Diamond watched as her mother dipped her fingers into the muddy dirt it contained. She threw a handful of it down, onto the coffin. It landed with a thump that made Diamond's nerves jitter.

Dad's in that box.

Hatred and despair roiled in her stomach and she thought she would be sick. She'd been having terrible nightmares ever since the night of the gang fight; she'd been plagued by images of monstrous Gustav Wolfe, hammer in hand, charging at her dad, striking him to the ground. And now, without Dad, they were alone – unprotected.

What's going to become of us?

At last the ordeal was over. Frenchie was tugging her daughter and sons away from the grave. They would go back to the house – that at least was still theirs, for now – eat sandwiches, drink tea, and stare into a barren future.

'Come on. Let's go home,' said Frenchie, her voice hoarse with tears.

Then a man stepped up through the bucketing rainstorm, blocking their way. He was big – tall, broad, bull-necked, black-haired and – this was strange – he had a look of Dad about him.

'Frenchie?' he said as the crowds dispersed.

'Oh, it's . . .' Frenchie gulped, blinking. 'Victor? Isn't it?'

The man nodded. 'Sad day,' he said.

'We haven't seen you in a lot of years,' said Frenchie. Her voice was flat, Diamond noticed. Not welcoming. Not even warm. 'Children? This is your Uncle Victor. Your father's brother.'

'Let's get out of this fucking rain,' said Victor, taking Frenchie's arm. 'We got things to discuss, am I right?'

'I don't think so.'

She doesn't like him, thought Diamond.

'I do,' said Victor. 'Come on.'

6

'Fact is,' said Victor, who not three hours later was standing in front of the fire in the parlour, his hand on the mantel like he owned the place, 'you're in a bind, ain't that right?'

'I don't know what you mean,' said Frenchie.

'Yeah you do. Man of the house gone. Wolfe lot breathing down your necks. You're in trouble.'

All the mourners had departed after the wake and now an uneasy peace had descended on the house. The kids were grouped around the kitchen table. Owen was busy with his colouring-in; he was working on a picture of Mary Pickford, the 'world's sweetheart'. Aiden was watching Uncle Victor with wary eyes, Diamond was wondering what fresh hell this day could bring.

Diamond didn't like the look of Uncle Victor and she could see her mother didn't, either. Dad had been a big bruiser of a man but he had been humorous, jokey, warm and loving. People had looked up to him, turned to him for advice and direction. Victor was different. There was something cold and smug about him, like his own brother getting himself murdered was a good result, an opportunity, not a thing to be mourned over.

'Lucky for you I'm here,' said Victor.

Frenchie was staring at him like he'd just crawled out from under a stone.

'What does that mean?' she asked.

Diamond's eyes moved between the pair of them, her mother and her uncle.

'That accent. Always did like it,' he said. He was half smiling.

Frenchie's stare grew colder. 'Victor,' she said tiredly, 'it's been a long day.'

'Then I'll be brief. It's obvious, innit? I'll take over. Handle things. Christ knows, *you* can't.'

'I'd rather . . .' started Frenchie.

But Victor wasn't paying heed. He was looking at the kids, his niece and nephews, and his eyes were narrowed with irritation.

'Better get this lot off to bed, yeah?' he snapped.

Frenchie rose from her chair, holding out her hands to them. 'Yes. I had better do that,' she said stonily. 'Come along, children.'

***

From that day on, their lives changed forever. Hours later, the two boys were in their room, asleep, and Diamond was in hers, a tiny boxroom tucked up under the eaves. It was luxury, having her own room, when she could remember once having to share, top-and-tailing, with the boys when they'd been little, in France. But she was still awake, unable to close her eyes, unable to rest, when she heard Mum coming up the stairs. And there was another tread right behind hers, heavier, more deliberate.

Quietly Diamond slipped out of bed in the dark and went over to the door. She opened it, just a tiny crack, and peered out. Uncle Victor was there on the landing, with her mother. And her mother was crying.

'Enough of that,' she heard him say, and to her shock he pulled Mum toward him and kissed her, long and hard enough to bruise her. Frenchie was struggling to get free. Diamond could hear her own heart, beating hard. She was biting her lip in horror and confusion. She tasted blood.

'Now,' Victor said at last. 'Let's get on, yeah?'

He shoved Frenchie into the bedroom she had just a few nights ago shared with her husband. Then he paused on the threshold of the room, and looked back, along the landing. Diamond froze, sure that he could see her there. But then he walked on, into the bedroom – and closed the door behind him and his brother's widow.

7

1912

Now Uncle Victor ruled the roost. He'd taken control of everything after Warren's funeral and woe betide anyone who didn't fall into line when he said so. Straight away he'd assembled all the remaining Butcher Boys out in the yard and announced that he was in charge now, and if anyone had anything to say about that, they should speak up.

No-one spoke up.

'We're not the Butcher Boys any more,' he roared at them. 'I'm Victor Butcher and now we're the Victory Boys. All right?'

Then it was the turn of the hoisters – the shoplifters – to get their pep talk from the new boss. Mostly female, under Warren's rule they had been a small and amateurish force. Now, under Victor's direction they grew in numbers and began to terrorise the high-class shops around the West End. Day after day they set out in tightly organised groups, wearing specially made garments with concealed deep pockets sewn into every layer. Frenchie protested at her daughter's involvement, which Victor insisted upon.

'I don't want my girl ending up in jail,' she said.

But protesting against Victor's decisions was like spitting into the wind.

The girls would go into high-end stores and emerge onto the streets wearing five dresses beneath their coats, jewellery slung around their necks, every pocket stuffed full with goods – hosiery, leather purses, whatever expensive item they could lay their hands on.

Several times Diamond was caught inside a store and had to say that she was just taking an item to the light of the door so that she could see the colour better. Once she was chased down the street before she could catch up with her 'boosters', two heavy Victory Boys in a car, who took the goods off her and raced away with them. When stopped by the pursuing store detective and searched, there was not a thing on her to be found.

She hated it, but she had to do it. Victor said so. She got good at it, too.

There was something deeply intimidating about Victor, something quick-moving and frightening. One moment he'd seem calm, the next he could erupt into a terrifying rage. Diamond hated him. They all did. He seemed to delight in being cruel. He came into the kitchen, where Owen sat colouring in a newspaper drawing of the doomed *Titanic*. Frenchie, Diamond and Aiden had shivered when they'd seen the picture, but it meant nothing to Owen. It had been all over the papers that fifteen hundred souls had been lost when the massive and seemingly indestructible ship had struck an iceberg in the north Atlantic. Victor swiped the boy roughly around the head, seemingly playful but intending to hurt.

Whop!

'Trust a bruv of mine to have a fuckin' moron for a kid,' he said, laughing.

Time and again Diamond saw Frenchie bite her lip, swallow the anger she felt at him mocking her dead husband and being so cruel to her son.

'Victor's a bastard,' Aiden would whisper to Diamond. 'A fuckin' *bastard.*'

But Aiden was just a boy, young and weak, no match for a man like Victor. He took over, the dominant male, raking in all the monies from the hoisters, the snooker halls and the club, scaring the shit out of everyone around him. He had even fended off Gustav Wolfe, and that was no mean feat. By some miracle, when Victor arrived on the scene, the Wolfe nightmare receded. He didn't care about the Wolfe crew; he spat on them. Built up an army of thugs around him. The Victory Boys.

And every night, *every night*, Diamond saw him go into the bedroom with Frenchie. Her own room was right next door to the big master bedroom and she wished it wasn't because she could hear Frenchie's pitiful cries through the wall. She knew Victor was hurting her. Frenchie, once so proud and upright, visibly drooped under the strain of it all. Owen started to flinch away from Victor before he was halfway into the room, hiding out in the back yard even when it rained. Diamond often found her youngest brother outside in the khazi, shivering with fear.

As for Diamond herself, mostly she tried to keep out of Victor's way. She almost managed it, right up until her fourteenth birthday, when Moira – who had been cleaning Frenchie's house ever since she came over from Paris – baked a special cake and Diamond had to blow out fourteen candles. It was a happy occasion, one of very few since Dad died and Victor had come storming into all their lives, but for Diamond it was blighted because she was aware of Victor's speculative gaze on her throughout it all. Afterwards, while she was helping Moira with the washing-up in the scullery, with Moira's young son Michael out chopping kindling in the yard, she could hear Victor talking to Frenchie in the kitchen.

'Fourteen then,' he was saying.

'Yes. What of it?' Frenchie sounded guarded.

Diamond exchanged a look with Moira. Moira was her great friend, she'd been with thc family for years. She'd lost her husband a while back, and her son Michael, who was the same age as Diamond, was almost part of the family, just like she was.

'She's been good at the hoisting,' said Victor.

That was true. Even at such a young age, Diamond, as a Butcher family member, was now pretty much in charge of the rest of the girls.

'So?' asked Frenchie.

'She's old enough, I reckon.'

'For what?'

'You know for what. I don't carry no passengers. I thought I'd made that clear.'

'No, she's . . .'

'She's started her bleeds, I bet. Getting some tits on her. Nice-looking girl.'

Frenchie said nothing. In the scullery, Diamond and Moira listened, wide-eyed.

'She can help me out then,' Victor steamrollered on.

'She already does. She does the hoisting. Isn't that enough?'

'Nah, I reckon she could do the trick.'

'Victor, I don't think . . .'

'Who asked you to think? *I* do the thinking around here. And what I say goes – clear?'

No word from Frenchie.

'I *said* . . .' Victor's tone had dropped to a silky threat.

'Yes! All right,' said Frenchie.

Diamond froze. What the *hell* had she just been signed up for?

8

That night at the Milano in Wardour Street, Diamond started doing the badger trick. She stood nervously at the bar and chatted to a young gentleman. Victor had told her the drill, and you didn't disobey Victor. So she was smiling, flirting, encouraging the mark to buy her drinks and never quite finishing them, while Uncle Victor sat at a corner table watching the proceedings. She said – as Victor had told her to – that she would do a private dance for the young man in a room upstairs, if he liked.

Which, of course, he did.

Within the hour she was leading him up the stairs, bracing herself against self-disgust, fear and humiliation, dancing, removing her clothing bit by bit – and then Uncle Victor charged in and said, what the hell was going on? This was his daughter and this *cad* was dishonouring her. He should pay!

Diamond blanked her mind while Victor yelled and pounded the young man with his fists, then emptied his wallet, hustled him back down the stairs and threw him out of the club. She got dressed again. Then Victor came back up, smiling, saying what a good night's work, peeling off fivers, tossing her one.

'Good work, girl. Let's get home,' he said.

'I don't want to do this again,' said Diamond.

Victor stopped in his tracks. 'You what?'

Diamond repeated herself, her heart hammering with terror.

'Right,' said Victor, and moved like lightning, knocking her back on her arse. The blow caught her right in the eye. Then he yanked her up from the floor and struck again.

'We won't discuss this, ever again,' he told her, breathing alcohol fumes into her aching, battered face. 'You understand?'

Dazed, agonised, Diamond nodded.

'Good,' he said, and let her go.

***

Home didn't feel like home any more. The minute they were through the door, Victor, who'd been downing whiskies all night and was now the worse for drink, started. Victor was horrible sober, but he was a bloody sight worse when the drink was on him. He caught poor Owen just going up to bed and kicked his arse hard to hasten his flight up the stairs. Aiden, who was in the hall, burst out in protest: 'Hey!'

'What did you say?' snarled Victor, fists raised.

Aiden lowered his gaze and stared sullenly at the floor. 'Nothing.'

'Yeah, nothing. Nothing's what you are, you little son of a bitch. Where's your mother?'

Aiden nodded back toward the kitchen.

'Get yourself up to bed,' Victor said to Diamond, and with her head awash with pain she grabbed Aiden's arm and hustled him up the stairs before he could provoke Victor any further. Victor sober was dangerous, but semi-drunk he was fearsome and would pick a fight with the devil himself.

This was their life now. She was still obliged to do the hoisting. She was an expert at that now, her nerves diminishing.

Michael, Moira's boy, started helping out on the robbing, liaising between Diamond and the boosters who removed the stolen goods from the scene.

Michael talked about breaking away from the Victory Boys, having his own set-up. Much to Diamond's amusement, he took to standing about looking tough, cleaning his fingernails with a silver knife blade.

'That's what we'll be called,' he told her. 'The Silver Blades. You got the Black Hands, the Peaky Blinders, the Victory Boys, why not the Silver Blades?'

'Yeah. Why not?' said Diamond, smiling. 'You just keep on dreaming, Michael.'

She carried on playing the badger trick on unwary punters. Frenchie was getting sadder and sadder. Aiden was bristling under Uncle Victor's iron rule, Owen was always in a state of terror. Their life! And it was getting worse all the time.

9

1913

'Step back, Diamond *chérie*,' said Frenchie, grabbing her daughter's arm, hauling her back against the front of the ironmonger's, nearly tripping her over a tin bath and a pile of gas mantles and rugs. A steel watering can toppled and hastily Diamond caught it before it could hit the pavement. She put it back in place.

'What . . .?' she queried in exasperation.

They'd been out shopping, buying fruit and veg, jellied eels, new shoes for Aiden. They'd gone in the newsagent's with its gaudy shop window advertising Meccano sets, boiled sweets. They'd purchased a copy of *Woman's Weekly* for Owen – he loved to colour in the pictures. They'd passed Levine's, the kosher poulterers with the big colourful advertising signs up above it – for Colman's Mustard and Sainsbury's stores – and they were about to go into the baker's for a loaf when Frenchie's whole body stiffened and she clasped her daughter, pulled her back.

Step back?

Then Diamond saw. It was *them.* The Wolfe crew. They were coming swaggering down the street toward them, big coats flapping, arms held wide like gunfighters ready to draw their weapons. The boss Gustav was in the lead, a Trilby hat pulled low down over his eyes, his mouth a hard line under his massive handlebar moustache. The rest of the heavies were fanning out behind him. Diamond's eyes followed them while Frenchie kept her gaze averted.

'Don't look at them,' hissed Frenchie. Discreetly, she turned her head and spat on the pavement.

But Diamond couldn't stop herself. There was something both fascinating and terrifying about Gustav Wolfe and his mob. Self-confidence was oozing out of Gustav's pores as he strutted along, everyone stepping nervously out of his way. His gaze caught hers and held it for a long moment, but still she didn't look away.

Her dad's killer.

'He's German,' said Frenchie. 'The authorities ought to lock all the Germans away, they're causing trouble. They always do.'

'I heard he's Austrian,' said Diamond.

'It's the same thing.'

'Who is that one?' asked Diamond, indicating a younger man who walked beside Gustav.

'That's Toro, Gustav's son. Thomas really, but everyone says his mother called him Toro, her "little bull" so it stuck.'

Even the son looked arrogant, Diamond thought. Like a winner in a world of losers. He looked at her too, with a bold stare that she mulishly returned. He wasn't like his distinctly Austrian, pale and heavily moustachioed father. Everyone knew that Gustav's late wife had been Spanish, and it was the Spanish influence that was most evident in Toro. He was dark-skinned, dark-haired and somewhere, she guessed, in his mid to late twenties. How did he even dare *glance* at her, handsome bastard that he was? The *arsehole.* She hated him on sight.

'I said, don't look,' said Frenchie, and dragged her fifteen-year-old daughter into the shop, out of harm's way. Diamond glared at Toro Wolfe over her shoulder. And he *grinned.* 'Come on. We're going to be late. Victor's expecting us back.'

10

1914

Victor Butcher was feeling pretty pleased with himself. It was his opinion that his brother Warren had been a bloody fool, soft as shit, unable to see the opportunities that were all around him, focusing on clubs and a little hoisting when there were much bigger pickings to be had.

Victor had a sizeable organisation now with his Victory Boys. He had lots of petty dock thieves on the go, a big ring of pickpockets, a load of rigged boxing matches and a lot of racecourse intimidation. He particularly enjoyed a trip to Brighton races, sending his Victory Boys around with a bucket among the vendors, bookies, punters and grafters, telling them to throw in a half crown for 'services'. Anyone who was so foolish as to ask *what* bloody services was beaten to a pulp or cut, so most paid up and didn't argue.

So all was well and now here was Victor with his Sunday best suit on, his gold watch chain glinting in the sun. He was ambling along the street in a good mood because he had heard that Gustav Wolfe was seriously ill. *Terminally*, he'd heard. And that was good news. The best. He walked along, whistling, aware that he was very near the Wolfe family home, interested to see if anything was going on. And that's when he saw the girl.

He stopped and stared. She was stepping down off the running board of a dark blue Austin 7 Tourer motor car, wearing a navy-blue coat with a white fur collar, a blue cloche hat from which golden curls were artfully escaping, a lot of rouge on her face and her lips painted into a vermilion cupid's-bow. Her whole stance was confident, her head held high. She stepped down onto the pavement and went into the Wolfe residence, her driver staying behind the wheel of the car.

Victor stayed there, wondering when she'd come back out. He didn't have long to wait. Fifteen minutes later, when she was going back to the car, he stepped into her path. She looked at him with large surprised blue eyes. She was blinking back tears.

'Are you Gwendoline Wolfe?' he asked.

'Who wants to know?' she asked, very cool, looking him up and down. Physically, Victor was imposing. In his forties, he could almost be called handsome. His cheeks were florid from drink, but as he sucked the last of his cigarette and stamped it under his heel, Gwendoline looked at him and he could see a spark of interest in her face, despite the fact that she seemed upset. That was good. If Gustav was nearly out of it, maybe there was a merger in the offing. One that would benefit him and get this little honey into bed.

'I'm Victor Butcher,' he said.

'Oh. Yes, I think I've heard of you.' Gwendoline paused. 'Was there something you wanted?'

There certainly was. Victor stared at her and thought of Frenchie, wailing and sobbing while he had her, getting more than a bit frayed around the edges as she sank into her middle years, getting a bit fucking *tedious*, to tell the truth. But here was Gwendoline, so fresh and young.

'I wonder if I might take you to tea?' asked Victor. Or bed. Preferably bed.

She half smiled at that, showing white, even teeth. 'We haven't even been properly introduced,' she pointed out, flushing a little.

'Who needs that? I'm Victor, you're Gwendoline. Tea? What do you say?'

'Absolutely not,' she said, and climbed back into the car and was away.

***

Victor waited near the Wolfe place at the same time next day and for days afterwards. Every time she turned him down. Now here she was again, wearing black this time but climbing down out of the same car.

'Hello,' she said.

Her driver was staring straight ahead, deliberately not seeing what was going on.

'I just thought you might have reconsidered,' said Victor. 'Let me take you to tea at the Lyons corner house.'

'No,' said Gwendoline, and disappeared inside the Wolfe family home.

Next day, Victor was back. 'Tea?' he asked her, grinning. He felt happy as Larry. It was all over town that Gustav was dead, and that was great news.

'I am in mourning for my father,' she said sharply.

'I'm sorry to hear it,' he said, not sorry at all.

Gwendoline looked at him, long and hard.

'Perhaps tomorrow?' she said.

***

But tomorrow came and there was a change in the air. Crowds were surging everywhere and gathering in Downing Street and outside Buckingham Palace. Everyone was waving flags and singing the national anthem.

'What the hell's going on then?' Victor asked one of his Victory Boys, grabbing him as he ran cheering down the street along with many others.

'I'm off to the recruiting office,' the young man told him. 'Victor, I'm signing up.'

'Signing up?'

'Yes! We're at war. Asquith's just announced it. We're all off to the recruitment office.'

Then the youngster was gone, lost in the crowds. Victor gazed after him. War? Well, there would still be profits to be made. As for signing up? Fuck *that.*

11

11th November 1918

Richard Beaumont reckoned that he would still see her face, picture it clearly before him, even on his deathbed. *Diamond.* She of the slanting violet-blue eyes and thc gleaming cloud of hair, dark as a black fire, flickering with coppery flames when the sun caught it. And her face. Her body. Her skin, pale like ivory. Jesus, he could get hard just thinking about her.

On this day, this glorious day at eleven in the morning, the country went mad. Streetlights were uncovered, shop windows suddenly blazed with light, blackout blinds were ripped down, pubs opened and drinkers drank until there was no more beer to be had. Guns were fired. The King and Queen drove to Hyde Park, and Whitehall was packed with crowds cheering Prime Minister Lloyd George and the coalition cabinet.

Richard, a staff officer still in uniform, was mobbed by shrieking women as his car was driven through Knightsbridge. He watched it all with a weird sort of detachment. They'd said the war would be all over by Christmas of nineteen fourteen. Now, four years later, four years of carnage, of death and hell, here they all were, the remnants of a civilisation that had once been England, everyone screaming and cheering like maniacs.

Flags of every allied nation were flying all over the city. It was mayhem but it was wonderful. The war to end all wars was over. And then this vision called Diamond unexpectedly piled into the passenger seat beside him, smiling broadly, so beautiful, and what else could he do but kiss her?

He did that. There was a lot of kissing going on, that day.

***

By mid-afternoon, darkness had fallen but all over the city the revellers remained out on the streets, shouting, drinking, throwing street parties, none of them quite able to believe that it was done with at last, the Kaiser defeated. They had drunk wine – too much of it – and talked a little. Pearly Kings and Queens danced and Richard's head spun. Maybe she was a prostitute. He thought she could be, and he didn't care.

She coaxed Richard from the car, led him by the hand through the laughing, shouting crowds, and he followed, not knowing where she was leading him but more than willing to follow.

Up an alleyway – people pissing, a couple fucking in a doorway, a young lad being sick, all quick distasteful impressions which he ignored. After all that he'd seen, what did any of it matter? Then in through a door beside a brightly signed club entrance – the Milano. He closed it behind them, cutting off the noises outside. Up a flight of stairs and then there at the top another door. They were both laughing, panting, and he still couldn't quite believe it, because this girl could have her pick of anyone, and she was leading him into a flat.

It wasn't anything fancy. There was a sofa, a record player, a small dining table and two chairs under the window. Then she led him on, further, opening the door into a bedroom, kissing him again, passionately, deeply. Then she was slipping off her dress, a thin pink petticoat, and then standing there in her underwear, stockings and suspenders.

She walked over to the bed, sat down on it.

Richard threw off his coat and the rest of his clothes. A mood of huge euphoria overtook him. The war was over. And here was his reward for all those miserable months of campaigning, toiling through mud and sweat and blood and horror, here he was at last, and it was mad, but it was happening.

Naked, aroused, he went over to her, pushed her back, lay down. Unfastened her brassière and gazed upon luscious breasts.

'What's your name?' he whispered against her parted lips.

'Diamond,' she said.

Then the door crashed open and a huge man rushed in.

'What the fuck is all this?'

The man was massive and terrifying. Now he was bellowing that this was a disgrace, that his niece, always such a good girl, was being dishonoured.

'You're going to pay for this, sonny. I promise you that!'

The man hauled Richard off the bed. Diamond cowered back against the grease-stained red velvet headboard, clutching the sheets to her breasts.

The beating was short-lived, but brutal and efficient. Within minutes Richard lay on the floor, bruised and bloodied. The man demanded money and went to Richard's clothes, rifling through the pockets until he found a wallet. He emptied it, ordered Diamond to get dressed, and kicked Richard hard in the ribs while she struggled back into her clothes.

The man grabbed Diamond by the arm, and then they were gone, thundering back off down the stairs. Richard lay there on the dusty carpet, trying to breathe. He didn't know how long he stayed there for, but everything hurt. Finally there were more footsteps on the stairs and his batman stepped into the open doorway.

'There you . . .' The man's voice tailed away as he saw his superior officer lying there in the gloom, his head bleeding, naked as the day he was born. 'What the fuck, sir . . .?' he said, and dashed forward, grabbing Richard's coat and throwing it over him. He knelt at Richard's side. 'What happened?'

Richard told him.

As he spoke, his batman's face grew still and he nodded.

'It's the badger trick, sir,' he said at last. 'Oldest trick in the bloody book.'

Richard struggled to sit up. Oh, it hurt. That bastard had pasted him, good and proper. He sat there and thought *what?*

But his batman didn't elaborate further. Instead he put a shoulder under his officer's arm and hauled him to his feet.

'Come on, sir,' he said. 'Let's get you home.'

12

'Do you ever think you're too rough with them?' Diamond asked.

They were back at the Butcher family home and Diamond was still feeling disgusted with herself after the events of the day. But that was what she did now. Mostly these days she picked up young returned officers – she was always careful to target officers, they were the ones who'd have cash – inside the family club, with alluring tales of private dances upstairs for a five-guinea entrance fee. At that point, it was her job to get the mark drunk enough to lure him into a compromising position, and then Victor would burst in and demand compensation for her dishonour. Today – Victory Day – was the first time she had taken to the streets to snare a mark. She was far from proud of herself to have done it.

'Too rough? Nah. You're having a laugh, aintcha?' said Victor.

Diamond thought with regret of the officer she'd enticed up to the flat above the club. Handsome young chap. Long-limbed, lightly muscled. Not muscular enough to stand up to Victor. Nobody was. Aiden always said that if Uncle Victor fell on a concrete floor, he'd crack the bastard. She thought about the officer's honest and quite beautiful light blue eyes, his flopping fall of corn-blond hair, the angular hardness of his chest and stomach under her fingers. Thought about that moment when their skins had touched and they'd almost joined together. She thought – and she tried very hard not to think about this – about what he must have been through over there in those mud-soaked, rat-infested trenches. And what a rotten trick they'd just pulled on him.

'You didn't have to belt him as hard as all that,' said Diamond nervously, while Victor sat there counting out pound notes.

***

Victor blew out a puff of smoke from the cheroot clamped between his teeth and gave Diamond a glinting grin. The war had been good for him. He'd expanded his empire. Frenchie was still a tedious fact of life, but still he had the house, the snooker halls, the Bombardier pub – and the Milano. Bugger that place, he was in two minds about it. Warren's big dream! Warren's bloody white elephant, more like. He didn't think there was much more that could be done with it. He'd tried everything. They had a bar that was open until three, a cabaret with half-naked girls, one of the best bands from New Orleans, Diamond's little act upstairs, and *still* it wasn't paying. Maybe he'd sell it. Or burn the bastard down, cop for the insurance.

Over these last four years, he'd been fighting a war all of his own, right here on England's shores – the war to maximise all his profits, and the war to get into Gwendoline's underwear. She was at odds with her brother, she'd told him, who was her only remaining close relative. Toro Wolfe, who was now head of the Wolfe mob. Toro and Gwendoline didn't share the same parents and they didn't get on. Still, if Toro knew she was walking out with Victor, he wouldn't be pleased.

That appealed to Victor. Any chance to rile Toro was good with him. He hated the bastard and had tried to intimidate him. With Gustav gone, there was always the hope that a weaker man had taken over. Victor had shoved hard at Toro, a couple of times, invading Wolfe territory, terrorising people and businesses who paid the Wolfes for protection – and Toro had shoved back, very hard indeed.

Victor had tried everything to bed Gwendoline Wolfe, and finally he'd promised marriage. Some women you just had an itch for. And until it was scratched, it made you crazy. So he'd marry her, what the hell. After that, he'd see. He already had a cute little girl over in Chinatown to see to his needs. And there was still Frenchie. But right now? He *wanted* Gwendoline. And whatever he wanted, he got. He promised himself that tomorrow he'd have her. At last.

***

'That cunt deserved a belting. Teach the silly bastard some sense,' said Victor. He folded the money and went over to the safe, tucking it away inside.

'Still, I think . . .' started Diamond, troubled by the memory of that young officer. Mostly she tried not to think about the marks. Mostly, she succeeded. But not this time.

Ever since Dad died, they'd all been in Victor's thrall. Diamond herself had been pushed over in the back yard by him, skinning her knees on the cobbles. Shoved in the street so that she fell and broke her wrist. She'd been slapped. She'd been punched. She'd been sworn at and called a bitch, told she was stubborn as a mule and far too full of opinions for her own damned good – which she supposed might be true. He called her a gobby cow and told her it was all *her fault*, if she didn't keep flapping her lip at him then he wouldn't be angry, and she *made* him angry, so what else could she expect but a thumping?

Before she could even blink, Victor turned from the safe and came at her, his good mood evaporating like dawn mist. He slapped her open-handed around the head.

Her ears ringing with the force of the blow, she faltered back and he came at her again.

Whap!

A punch this time. Diamond fell over and lay, her head throbbing, staring stupidly at the floor. Then there were footsteps – Moira was coming in from the scullery, Michael at her heels. Reeling, Diamond felt their eyes on her and cringed, trying to get up, stumbling, crawling. Victor kicked her shoulder and she fell back again.

'What the hell . . .?' she heard Moira say.

'*You want some of the same?*' Victor roared. '*You want some of what I'm giving this little shit do you?*'

Diamond saw Moira step hastily back, a basket of dry washing under one arm.

'Then piss off out of it,' he said, and Moira vanished back outside into the yard. Michael didn't move. He stared at Victor. '*You want some too, do you?*' demanded Victor.

Michael didn't answer. Slowly, he turned and followed Moira outside.

Victor hauled Diamond back onto her feet. A beefy finger wagged in front of her nose. His grip on her arm was excruciating. 'You don't question what I say, you got that in your thick head, have you?'

Diamond swayed there dumbly, her head feeling swollen as a balloon, pain and humiliation ripping through her like a poison river.

'*Well, have you?*' he bellowed right in her ear.

'Yes. I've got it,' she said thickly, thinking that she was going to be sick, that she was going to faint.

'Good! That's good. Remember that. Or next time I won't be so fucking tolerant. All right?'

He didn't wait for a reply. He left the room. Diamond groped for a chair and slumped down into it.

More footsteps. Moira was back. And Michael was standing there, staring at Diamond's face. She turned her head away, embarrassed, shamed to her soul.

'That bastard,' said Michael.

'Shut up, Michael,' said Moira, looking nervously at the door Victor had gone through.

'What, you afraid of that big-mouthed cunt?' Michael fumed. 'Diamond? Listen. I've been getting some of my mates together.'

'Don't . . .' begged Moira.

'Nobody messes with the Silver Blades, not even Victor fucking Butcher. Tell you what, Diamond – talk to your hoisters. Tell them the Blades'll pay them more than Victor and look after them better. You know I don't lie. Will you do it?'

'Leave her, Michael, for the love of God. She's hurt,' said Moira.

'You know it makes sense,' said Michael.

'I'll fetch Frenchie,' said Moira.

13

When you drove up to Fontleigh, the house was enough to take your breath away. Richard Beaumont had always thought that, even when he'd been a small boy, even though he'd grown up in it. Now he was a man, home from the war, and he felt the same – awestruck, emotional; this was home and he had never thought he would see it again. But here he was. Right here.

Fontleigh was pure Gothic Revival, set out in the same style as the Houses of Parliament. It was golden glowing stone studded with cusped flattened Tudor arches, carved brick detailing, vast soaring barley-twist chimneys in the Elizabethan fashion; it was huge and it was lavish in the extreme. He'd always loved it and now he felt the house's warm ambiance fold around him like a hug. He needed home, right now. So many of his old pals had died – horribly – but he had survived and he could still scarcely believe his own luck; but, worse – he could scarcely bear the guilt he felt because of it.

He closed his eyes against the sun, which was sending hot dazzling shafts of light through the cedars of Lebanon that edged the sweep of the emerald-green lawns beside the drive. He'd been luckier than he had any right to be. Now, he had to go on. Find some way to justify his existence when he felt he didn't deserve to be still breathing, not when nearly all his friends had perished.

So here he was. Home again. The allies had won the fight and he'd celebrated and . . .

Oh, and then . . .

There she was, in his brain. *Diamond.* That cloudy dark hair. Those fabulous violet-blue eyes staring up at him, and her skin, so white, so soft to the touch, like silk over swans-down.

His eyes flicked open and he cringed at the memory of that huge bastard rushing in. George had explained the whole thing. Told him that probably the man who'd interrupted them had been Diamond's pimp and she was a prostitute. The badger trick had been worked a thousand times on unsuspecting men. There were people who made their entire living on such tricks, in and around the heaving, pest-ridden streets of Soho.

Forget her.

He would. As the car pulled up at the front of the house, he saw his mother standing there, and the line of servants. Everyone was smiling, ready to welcome him back, but he felt he had changed so much from the man who had left here four years ago. He'd been through the gates of hell and crawled out again. Alive. Somehow.

Diamond.

There she was again, gazing up at him. Beautiful. Her lips moist, waiting for his kisses.

Ah, forget her.

It had been the meanest of tricks, what she'd done to him. She was a whore and Diamond was probably not even her real name. And . . . he had Catherine, didn't he? Well, of course he did. Since childhood they had been together; they were of the same social circle, they were *meant.* He was engaged to sweet young Catherine, and they had promised that they would marry as soon as the war was over. Only . . . he wasn't sure how he felt about that, not any more. He'd seen so much, lived through it all and now he was different, and the life he'd known, the carefree life with his young fiancée, seemed like a world away. Another country.

He got out of the car, smiling although he didn't feel like smiling ever again, and he was instantly enfolded in his mother's embrace. This was reality, this was home. All the rest – the war, the whore who'd made such a fool of him – he was going to forget all that. He *had* to.

Then he realised with a sinking heart that the girl standing just inside the doorway, behind the lines of servants who had dutifully turned out to greet him, the one who stepped forward with her heartrendingly shy smile was her, Catherine. So blonde and pretty and . . . well, bland.

This was his life, the one he'd left and the one he now had to return to.

But could he?

Once, he'd been sure of everything – his place in the world, his direction, his future. Now, all that was shattered. He'd been to war. He'd met that entrancing minx Diamond – and the memory of her, whore though she undoubtedly was, refused to leave him alone. And it wasn't only her. It was *everything*. All that had once seemed safe and secure was now set loose, and he didn't know who he was or what he was doing, not any more.

14

Richard felt, since alighting from the car out on the big gravel drive, that he was sailing through a strange dark dream. Kissing his mother Lady Margaret on the cheek, who hugged him and whispered in his ear that his father would be waiting for him in the study. Then he was shaking the hands of the butler Benson and the rest of the staff, who were all beaming, all so ridiculously glad to see him.

And then he was confronted by Catherine Sibley, his lovely fiancée. He'd known her all his life. Her father Sir James Sibley was brother to the Lord Chancellor and the Sibleys' modest estate butted up against the much larger acreage of the Stockhaven estate. He'd known Catherine for so long and adored her; he'd played with her when they were children, along with her younger brother Teddy who was now a doctor and home from the front just like Richard, and his best friend in all the world.

The strangest thing of all was that he felt nothing whatsoever at the sight of Catherine's sweet and lovely face, streaked with tears of relief and gladness, nothing when he gazed into her soft grey eyes, nothing when she reached up on tiptoe and placed her trembling mouth on his and hugged him tight.

'Darling,' she whispered against his lips.

Somehow he responded. He could remember feeling love for her, he was sure of it. Before the war. He could remember laughing with her, and kissing her, and feeling young and free – but those feelings seemed to have abandoned him.

***

Now he was in his father's study and the Earl of Stockhaven was rising from behind the desk in the big book-lined room, so familiar, so warm, with big chintz couches dotted all around and each cosy corner lit by exquisite *cloisonné* lamps inlaid with carnelian, garnet, turquoise and lapis lazuli. The Earl's black Labrador Cherry was dozing in her basket. There was a cheery fire glowing in the big stone hearth. 'My boy! It's so good to see you back, safe and well.'

Richard didn't know how 'well' he was.

His father was coming toward him, hand outstretched, then, tossing his head at the formality, the Earl laughed and instead opened his arms, embracing his son.

Cherry stirred, looked at her master and his close proximity to Richard, and growled low in her throat. Both men stepped back and stared at the dog in surprise.

She doesn't recognise me, thought Richard.

'Cherry! Settle down there, girl,' said the Earl. 'It's only Richard.'

Cherry stayed half-upright, her eyes fixed on Richard, her hackles raised.

'Silly thing,' the Earl chided her. Then he turned back to his son with a warm smile. 'God, what a relief to have you home,' he said, his voice quivering with emotion. 'It's seemed endless, this blasted war.'

'Well – it has ended,' said Richard, pleased to see that Cherry had resettled in her basket. Even the bloody dog didn't know him. Had he really changed so much?

But he knew he had. Whenever he passed a mirror, he saw the evidence of the toll war had taken on him. The feathering of grey in his sideburns, that was new. And the weary shadows and lines under his eyes, the grim set of his mouth. He'd marched away to war with his troops singing victory songs, 'It's a Long Way to Tipperary', 'Pack up your Troubles in your Old Kit-Bag'. The women – his mother and his fiancée included – had waved the troops off at the station, en route to France, and so many – *so many* – had never returned. Or had come back crippled, ruined, their youth gone, their lives effectively over.

'Sit, sit.' The Earl ushered him into an armchair by the fire and went to the drinks cabinet and poured them both a brandy. He handed his son a glass and sat down in the other armchair and stared at him. He raised his glass. 'To homecomings,' he said.

'Yes. To that,' said Richard, and drank, the smooth expensive brandy burning a warm trail down his gullet.

This was like a dream, like the ones he'd had when he lay listening to the shelling in the trenches, wondering if the next explosion would come directly overhead and kill them all in their mud-spattered bunks. Through it all he'd held on somehow to a sweet dream of comfort, of home, of warmth and ease. Brandy and crackling fires. Christmas trees and the hall decked with holly. Now he was back at Fontleigh at last. It was real. And he couldn't take it in. Couldn't feel it.

'No wonder she doesn't know you,' said the Earl. 'Four years in that hell-hole. My boy, I thought . . . seriously there were times when I didn't think we would ever see you again. We've lost so many from the estate. Too many.'

Richard nodded. He didn't know what to say. He couldn't talk about the war. Couldn't even think about it, although it haunted his dreams, night after night.

'Was it terribly bloody?' asked the Earl after a moment.

'I prefer not to discuss it,' said Richard.

'Of course, yes of course. Crass of me.'

'No, it's just . . . I really can't.'

'I completely understand. When I was out at Rorke's Drift, I thought I was dead for sure. I still remember it, the terror I felt. When I got home, I just couldn't seem to . . . *connect* with home at all. I think it took me about a year to do that. To feel safe again.'

Richard nodded, relieved. His father, at least, understood. And that was good, because there were things he was going to have to tell him, things that would shock him no doubt, and unsettle him, and cause him grief, and Richard hated to do it. His father was the mildest, sweetest man, had been – mostly – kind to him, and indulgent, all his life. He wasn't looking forward to the conversations they were going to have to have. Not at all.

'We are having a small dinner party at the weekend. To celebrate your return,' said the Earl.

'That would be marvellous,' lied Richard, thinking that it would be hell.

For now, he would maintain the charade. But soon they would talk.

He had to light the fuse – then wait for the explosion.

15

'Darling? Did I tell you? I sent out the invitations,' said Gwendoline Wolfe to Victor.

At last, Victor lay naked in one of his many safe houses with the woman he had lusted after for so long. *Invitations?*

Victor blinked up at the ceiling. 'What? Already?'

'No reason to delay a moment longer. Everyone knows by now the way we are together. Don't they? I thought about bridesmaids. Perhaps that niece of yours, what's her name . . .? Never mind. She could be one of them.'

The Butchers didn't know a thing about Gwendoline yet. He hadn't told them. Gwendoline was his business. 'It seems soon.'

Gwendoline sat up sharply. 'You do intend to marry me, Victor?' She raised one delicate arm, indicating the bedroom, the disordered bed, their clothes in a muddled heap on the floor. 'We've done this, after all, and I'm sure you realise that I could very well be carrying your child by now. I've no wish to be disgraced.'

Victor watched her, this blonde Venus, with her tiny cone-like breasts, very high and full, and her long thin body. The dainty fluff of blonde hair between her legs, he loved that, it inflamed his passion. All through the days when her brother Toro had been off in France at the war, Victor had been busy trying to get her into bed. Lots of men had died over there, and Victor was just glad not to be numbered among them. No-one had ever dared give him a white feather. He'd greased a few palms, got out of it. No bloody way was Victor Butcher letting some Jerry use *him* for target practice.

At first – after months of chaste kissing in parks and gardens and anywhere they could snatch a private moment – Gwendoline would only allow him to touch her breasts, to lift her skirts and tickle her secret place with his fingers. Then when he'd been aching, nearly bursting with lust for her, she at last came to this safe house, stripped for him, let him see her naked for the very first time. Then he wanted her in bed, so badly, and she would sit on the edge of it, allow him to stroke her skin, and finally to take off his own clothes and lie with her. Then she would daintily, flinchingly, take his cock in her hand and give him relief, wiping her hands delicately afterwards while he sprawled out, triumphant. But it was never enough to just be touched by her, to look at her. He wanted more. Always more.

'I'm a virgin,' she told him over and over while he gasped and strained and wished to go still further. 'You know I am, Victor. I do want you, darling – desperately – but I am saving myself for marriage.'

He knew what he was doing was hazardous. That she was a Wolfe and he was a Butcher, and that the shit would fly when it all came out, which he supposed it might, well, it would, if the marriage ever came about. But the thrill of danger, of cocking a snook at that arsehole Toro Wolfe now that he was boss of the Wolfe mob, only made the sexual part of it all the more appealing.

Today – at last, for the very first time – she'd opened her legs for him, allowed him the sheer indescribable bliss of penetration. She cried afterwards, delicately, sweetly, and he hugged her and told her it was all right, they were going to be married after all. When he'd slipped her a length, Victor realised he'd committed himself to more than one course of action; he'd got what he so desired, that he'd been driven half crazy for, but he was also committed to the wedding, to the dreaded walk up the aisle a single man and back down it a married one.

It scared the shit out of him.

But Gwendoline had swung into action, arranging things, telling Toro the news, booking the church, sending the whole thing rolling along at a pace that made Victor wish he'd never started on this path at all. He could have had any number of whores, hostesses and dance hall girls. He'd done all that in his past – enjoyed them to the maximum degree, kissed them goodbye in the morning and had nothing to worry about. He probably had a few brats dotted around the town, but none had yet given him trouble. And he had his mistress, Lily Wong, over in Chinatown. But yes – maybe it was time – past time, really – that he was married. Give him a better status among the Victory Boys.

16

'Look at my portrait,' Frenchie said to Diamond, holding her arm and staring up at the massive painting which for years now had hung at the top of the stairs in the Butcher home. 'Wasn't I beautiful?'

'You were,' said Diamond. It was true. 'You still are.'

'Ah, *non*,' said Frenchie regretfully, stifling a cough. 'I'm tired, *chérie*. And this damp river air in London, it does me no good.'

Diamond had to stifle a smile at that. Frenchie complained every winter of the damp London air, but Paris was damp too, wasn't it? It had to be; the Seine ran through it. She knew that although Frenchie had spent years in London, her heart had never left France. She often, over the years, chattered away to her daughter in French, so that Diamond had quickly picked up the language. Aiden and even Owen could chatter away in it, too. Frenchie talked about Paris all the time, as if it was a magical, glittering place full of incredibly gifted people. Diamond thought her mother must be exaggerating – Frenchie was prone to do that – but still she found herself intrigued by the tales of scandals and love affairs and bitter enemies and everlasting friendships.

'I think Victor has another woman now,' said Frenchie.

Diamond looked sharply at her mother. They had never discussed the fact that Victor had muscled in on all their lives, filling Dad's place in Frenchie's bed on the night of Warren's burial. It seemed impossible to talk about it, so they never had.

'Does he?' said Diamond.

Frenchie nodded. 'I'm glad,' she said. 'It's been bad, you know. Very bad.'

Diamond felt tears prick her eyes. She didn't know what to say.

'But he has another, everyone says. He doesn't bother with me now. He tells me that I am old, and that his new love is young.'

That bastard. Diamond wanted to kill him. He'd used her mother just as he'd pleased, and now he was off elsewhere, ploughing a new field.

'Who is she? The new woman?' asked Diamond, staring up at the painting of Frenchie in her young glory, beautiful as a spring day.

'I don't know. And really? I don't care, just so long as his attention is elsewhere,' said Frenchie. She sighed, gazing up at the painting.

'Tell me about Paris again,' said Diamond. She wanted to take the sadness from her mother's face, to see her smile again. She could remember Frenchie's smiles, but it was a long time since she'd seen them.

'Oh, Paris! It's so beautiful. I had such a wonderful life there with your father.'

'What about when you were younger?'

Frenchie did almost smile at that.

'It was a great life. So much fun. So many friends.'

'Like . . .?' prompted Diamond. She already knew, she'd heard it all before, but telling tales of Paris always made Frenchie forget her woes.

'There were so many . . . one in particular though, Mimi Daniels. Haven't I mentioned her before? I stayed with her and my God! The fun we used to have in that little flat of hers on the Boulevard de Clichy. We argued sometimes, of course. But mostly we were good friends. If you are ever in Paris and needing a bed, *chérie*, go to Mimi. Say my name. She won't let you down.'

Diamond had heard about Mimi a thousand times and she never intended to meet her because she was not going to France. London was home – foggy, frosty, yes, damp old hole that it was. She knew life was far from perfect here, but every day when she stepped out onto the teeming streets of Soho with its steamy coffee houses and its even steamier nightclubs, she was glad to do so.

Now she had this thing with Michael to think about. He'd been serious in his offer of a merger with her hoisters – who answered to her, came to her with all their troubles – and his Silver Blades. But were they hers? No. Not really. They were Victor's because Victor's rule was absolute, and if he found out she was planning to lure the hoisters away to another gang, blood would flow.

She had spoken to some of the more sensible girls, swearing them to secrecy, sounding out the situation. Nobody liked Victor, so maybe a move was possible. Or maybe not. And what about Frenchie? Aiden? Owen? What about *her?* They all lived in this house with Victor; all of them could be tossed out into the street over this, if she decided to go ahead with it.

Diamond had voiced her concerns to Michael. To her it was an odd situation. Having grown up alongside him, she'd always thought of him as nothing more than a boy. But now Michael was a hard-eyed young man, fully grown. She was going to have to adapt to a new way of looking at him.

'We'll give you protection,' he told her. 'All of you. Get you out from under that bastard once and for all.'

But Diamond wasn't sure.

17

Frenchie was always first up in the mornings, singing old French songs and coughing. So it was she who found the invitation on the mat when she came downstairs. She took it to the kitchen table, read it, and then collapsed with a shriek of horror.

Mr T Wolfe requests the honour of your presence at
the marriage of
Miss Gwendoline Wolfe to Mr Victor Butcher
On Saturday, 24th April 1920
At 1 p.m. in the afternoon
St Anselm's Church, Chancery Lane
Reception to follow at The Ritz Hotel

Diamond, hurrying down the stairs at her mother's loud cry, came into the kitchen and found Frenchie on the floor. She ran for the smelling salts on the dresser and quickly waved them under her mother's nose. Frenchie flinched and her eyes flickered open. She struggled up, pushing the bottle away, and then sat there, blinking, swaying, staring at the card that was still in her hand.

'What is it?' asked Diamond, alarmed, recapping the salts.

Frenchie couldn't even speak. She handed Diamond the card, and Diamond read it.

Then she looked at her mother's bleached-white face.

'But . . . Victor? Getting married? No. This can't be right. This is lunacy. He'd have told us, wouldn't he? He wouldn't have just . . .' But then Diamond heard the words that were pouring out of her own mouth and thought *no.* Victor never told them a damned thing. Victor was like a king here, an absolute ruler. No-one questioned him. No-one dared. But Gwendoline Wolfe? One of the hated Wolfe clan? 'Not to her, of all people,' she finished weakly. 'Anybody else and I would have cheered to the rafters. But her! She's Gustav's daughter, isn't she?' Diamond could barely articulate her rage. Victor was taking up with a girl from that family, the one that had caused the Butchers such pain? When Gustav – that monster – had killed her dad?

Frenchie shrugged. 'Victor doesn't care that she's a Wolfe. Why should he? My darling husband's death allowed him to snatch our business away. He'd always been wanting to get his toe in the door with us, but Warren said he was no good, a drinker and too free with his fists. And I . . .' Frenchie's voice tailed away.

'You what, Mum?' asked Diamond.

'Nothing. Nothing!' Frenchie looked at the card, still caught in Diamond's trembling hand. 'Perhaps this could be a good thing. We might finally be free of him! When he sets up house with Gwendoline Wolfe, he won't want to stop here. Maybe he'll even do a deal with the Wolfe lot, with Toro, call a halt to all this fighting and fussing. That would be good. Because, *chérie*, I'm so tired of it all.'

Diamond wasn't tired of it. Ever since her eleventh year, when Dad had died and Victor had barged into their lives, her mind had been consumed with thoughts of revenge. She wanted the Wolfe clan dead, every single one of them. It had kept her going, fed her spirit, sustained her through all the rotten things she – all of them – had been through under Victor's iron rule.

She helped her mother to her feet and Frenchie sank into one of the kitchen chairs. Diamond sat down beside her, the card still in her hand.

'Someone must be having a joke with us,' said Diamond firmly. Surely not even Victor would wed a Wolfe. They were the Butchers' worst enemies. They were bastards.

'Where's Victor?' asked Frenchie.

Bloody good question, thought Diamond. She could hear Aiden stirring upstairs, and she'd glimpsed Owen, but Uncle Victor? So far as she knew, he hadn't come home last night.

***

Two weeks after the invitation arrived, Victor told Diamond that she would be one of his bride's attendants.

'I'm not going to be a bridesmaid,' she told Frenchie furiously. 'Not to a Wolfe.'

Frenchie's face creased with anxiety. 'But you have to! Darling, you must. It's traditional. We can't go against Victor. He'll get angry. *Chérie*, promise me you'll do it. I know it's awful, but it's one day, that's all. Swear to me you will.'

'Mum . . .' Diamond groaned.

She couldn't believe it. Couldn't believe that Gwendoline Wolfe would ask *her*, a Butcher, to trail after her up the aisle. But she knew that Frenchie would never stand the stress of her refusing. She knew too that Victor would punish every one of them if she did that.

So she had to be a bridesmaid. She attended the dress fittings at the high-end atelier in Bond Street, sitting sullenly in a corner, not taking part in the girlish chatter going on all around her. And the instant she could leave? She went.

18

Gustav Wolfe was long dead and rotting in his grave. But as happens in life, there is always some new bastard on the scene, waiting to take a person down a peg or two, no matter how well they seem to be doing. And the bastard waiting to scuttle the Butcher clan was the son of Warren's old enemy; Thomas – or as he was more widely known, 'Toro' – Wolfe.

'Like I'm scared of *that* bastard,' said eighteen-year-old Aiden as they sat around the kitchen table one morning. He shot a look at Victor, who was sitting in what had once been Warren's seat, at the head of the table. Frenchie, as was her usual practice, was seated down the other end, watching Owen pick over his porridge, bits of it sliding off his spoon and onto the table, and onto the open magazines that Owen called his 'books'. He carried them with him all over the house, colouring in the pictures, and was hugely excited every time Frenchie bought him a new edition to work on.

Diamond watched as Frenchie patiently mopped up Owen's mess while coughing delicately into her handkerchief. The London damp did seem to go straight to Frenchie's chest, every winter. Her frequent trips to Dad's grave didn't help, either. Each visit seemed to tear at Frenchie's health, making her sadder and weaker, it always seemed to Diamond.

'I don't know where Gustav Wolfe's grave is,' Frenchie said over and over. 'But if I did, I would shit on it.'

'None of us are scared of the Wolfe lot,' said Victor. He gazed around at the assembly. 'Right?'

Everyone nodded, even Owen, who didn't have a clue who or what Victor was talking about. Then Victor snatched up the last bit of toast just as Diamond was reaching for it.

Arsehole, she thought. And although she nodded agreeably, just like everyone else did, what Diamond was thinking as her Uncle Victor ate the last of the toast and she went hungry was that Toro Wolfe was very much to be scared of. She'd last seen him on that day before the war, in the street with Frenchie, but she'd heard all the tales. Toro was trying to buy the Butcher club, take over the bookies runners who worked for them, take over *everything*, just as his father Gustav had before him. And now those murdering arseholes the Wolfes were going to be their in-laws!

Diamond had considered Michael's offer, and turned it down. She couldn't accept it. The repercussions would be too severe for her family and for Michael's mother too. And anyway it would still be thieving, and she hated that, so what was the point of simply exchanging one man's rule for another?

Suddenly there was a hard knock on the front door.

Everyone around the table stiffened, except Owen, who carried on spooning up porridge and dropping gobbets of it on the polished table top.

'I'll go,' said Aiden, shoving his chair back and strutting out into the hall.

'Careful,' called Frenchie anxiously after him, catching at Diamond's arm in a spasm of nerves.

From where she sat Diamond could see down the hallway as her brother threw the front door open. Christ, anything could be on the other side of it. But *careful* wasn't in Aiden's vocabulary. She braced herself. You didn't know what the hell to expect these days. But Aiden flung open the front door and it wasn't the Bill, it wasn't one of Toro's lot brandishing a shotgun. It was just one of the Butcher runners, standing skinny and gasping there on the doorstep.

'What the fuck?' enquired Aiden.

'Club's gone,' said the boy, and that was when the family found out that Warren Butcher's pride and joy – the Milano over in Wardour Street – had been burned to the ground overnight.

19

When Victor and Aiden got to Wardour Street they found a scene of chaos. The whole road was obscured by a pall of thick choking grey smoke, fire engines still pulled up outside, firemen working around the area with hoses, damping down what remained of the flames.

They stood there and looked at the damage, Victor taking it all in silently, Aiden raging about what he wanted to do to Toro Wolfe. People were grouping around, staring, covering their faces to keep from choking on the smoke, taking an interest as people always do in the face of disaster.

One of the rozzers came over and said: 'You're the owner, yes?'

'I'm Victor Butcher,' said Victor, nodding.

'Not much left to save,' the copper remarked.

'Yeah. True enough.'

'Any idea how it could have started?'

'No. None.'

'I got an idea,' said Aiden. 'Fucking Toro Wolfe, that's my idea.'

The policeman stared at Aiden's red angry face. 'You got any proof of that, sir?'

'My nephew's upset,' said Victor smoothly.

The policeman nodded and ambled away to talk to the white-helmeted fire officer.

Aiden looked at the smouldering wreck of his dad's club the Milano and knew that this would break his mum's heart. Already, she wasn't strong. This would upset her beyond words. This old place, to her, meant Warren Butcher, the love of her life. And now it – like him – was gone.

20

Toro Wolfe was in bed with a woman at his Great Earl Street flat when the Bill came calling. Toro's late father Gustav had come over to England from Vienna over thirty years ago and married a Spanish señorita called Pilar. Then Pilar had died giving birth to Toro, and Gustav had married again – an Englishwoman this time, who already had a daughter called Gwendoline. The Englishwoman had died, but the daughter remained, fit and well, spoiled and capricious.

Toro was a very handsome man. His hair was black, his eyes a dark brooding brown. He had about him a whipcord toughness, a great physical presence, an alertness that made him a dangerous adversary. He was dark-skinned, almost swarthy, broad-shouldered and narrow-hipped, muscular, a man at the height of his powers, and he knew it. He had an inbuilt arrogance and poise that irritated men – and attracted women like bees to nectar.

The woman currently occupying his bed was a hostess at one of the Wolfe clubs. He didn't remember her name but she was sexually voracious and he'd enjoyed her twice last night and once this morning. Now she purred and curled against him, making kittenish noises, twining him up in the sheets, but the night was over.

His mind was turning over various deals, then meandering back to his sister Gwendoline, who was never anything but trouble. She meant it, the silly cow. She was actually going to marry Victor Butcher. He'd yelled about it, kicked the furniture, shouted from the rooftops, but his sister – well, she wasn't really his sister at all, was she? But he still felt responsible for the silly bitch. She was in love, she said, with Victor Butcher. And she was going to marry him. Toro was head of the family now and he took his duty of care seriously, even if she was a headstrong acid-tongued cow. He'd objected, said he wouldn't give her away. Nothing had worked. It was going to happen.

The knocking at the front door became a pounding. Toro irritably disentangled himself from the woman and went down the stairs and threw open the front door.

'What the fuck is it?' he asked.

The two policemen on the doorstep stepped back sharply. Each looked down at Toro's naked body, then quickly back up at his face. The older one of them said: 'Mr Thomas Wolfe?'

'Who wants him?'

'Are you Thomas Wolfe?'

'I am. And this is about . . .?'

'Put some clothes on please, sir.'

'You're the one banging at all hours of the night. I've just got out of bed to answer this damned door.'

Neither of the coppers thought fit to point out that it was eleven o'clock, hardly the break of day. And Toro didn't look very English. He looked like a Spaniard. Big as a barn door, packed with muscle and with his cock out, he made an impressive and rather frightening sight.

'We would like to ask you some questions, sir,' said the older copper. 'About a fire in Wardour Street.'

'What fire?'

'At Mr Victor Butcher's club the Milano. It burned to the ground last night.'

'Really. And what's that got to do with me?'

'If you could get dressed, sir, and accompany us to the station?'

'Who is it, Toro?' asked a luscious woman who appeared behind him, wrapped in a white sheet, her blonde hair dishevelled, her shoulders naked. Both coppers' eyes went out on stalks. She yawned and ran a languid hand through her hair, smiling at the younger one, who blushed crimson. 'What do they want?' she asked.

'Fire at the Butcher place,' said Toro. He turned back to the policemen. 'Is this going to take long?'

'Just routine enquiries, sir,' said the older one.

Toro said to his female companion: 'I'm off down the station with these two gentlemen. Answer some questions.' Then he gave the coppers a hard stare. 'Although they might like to wonder why I'd burn down my future brother-in-law's club.'

Disinterested, the girl turned away and went back up the stairs.

'If you'll excuse me, gents?' he said.

Toro closed the door in their faces and went to get dressed.

21

The dinner was fabulous, as dinner at Fontleigh always was; served in the big oak-lined candlelit dining room by smoothly discreet black-coated footmen, presided over by Richard's father the Earl and his mother Lady Margaret. Throughout it, Richard fielded questions about his military experiences, lying through his teeth most of the time. He felt anger growing in him, unreasonable anger he knew, but anger nevertheless. Did they think that war was a picnic? A glamorous excursion, an adventure?

All the things he'd seen. Things that haunted him. Men blown to smithereens, their guts hanging out, entangled in barbed wire and screaming in pain until someone had the good grace to shoot them and end their suffering. Mustard gas pouring over the trenches, blinding some, scorching the lungs of others. German tanks flattening them into the lethal Flanders mud. Horses thrashing, squealing in mortal agony, dying.

It was filling his mind again. He wished to Christ that they hadn't mentioned it. But they had. He'd returned home, alive, the hero. And they were curious. He'd written to Catherine and to his mother, they'd sent him food parcels. Chocolate and corned beef. Slabs of dense fruit cake. Now he looked down at the remains of dinner and felt faintly sick. Saw a curl of blood oozing from the remains of a pink steak, and felt his stomach start to heave.

'Richard?'

His mother's voice broke through the fog.

He snapped back to the present. Elegant and bejewelled, Lady Margaret was staring at him, her eyes concerned. She was on her feet. So was Catherine. So were the aunts.

'I'm sorry?' he said.

It was the Earl who spoke. 'The ladies are retiring,' he said with a smile. 'If you wish to . . .?'

Richard understood. Catherine was smiling, blushing. Now everyone expected the reunited young couple to go into the orangerie, away from the others. With a heavy heart he rose, leaving his father, Catherine's father Sir James and the other men to their brandy and cigars.

While his mother and the other ladies peeled off into the withdrawing room, he and Catherine went along the hallway and turned right, into the big wrought-iron orangerie with its tinkling fountain and its soaring grapevine that shielded the occupants during the heat of the day. There was wicker furniture set out on the black and white tiled floor, and tables set with glowing candles; it was a haven, intimate. A stage carefully set by his mother, he felt sure, for lovers. For him and his soon-to-be bride.

Catherine went and stood by the French doors that led out into the garden. It was dark outside; all she could see was her own reflection. Richard watched her, standing there. She was so pretty in her figure-skimming pale pink gown. The beading caught the candlelight so that she seemed to twinkle, fairylike. Her hair was done in the new ultra-modern style, 'shingled' they called it. He remembered her as she'd been before he left for France. Her ashy-blonde hair long and loose, her smile so young, so innocent and entrancing. They'd played together as tiny children, she and Richard. And Teddy her brother too, a year younger, he'd always been following the pair of them around, eager to be one of their little gang.

Catherine had changed too. Of course she had. The awful worry of the war, the concern for his safety and for her brother Teddy's must have weighed heavily upon her. Richard recalled her letters, expressing her love. He'd sent her postcards, when he was able to. Pretty little hand-embroidered things stitched by impoverished French women and intended for English wives and lovers. But now . . . try as he might, he couldn't seem to get the feeling back again. He'd loved Catherine chastely, sweetly, before the war, and had given her his late granny's ruby ring set in diamonds. They'd become engaged, and both their families had been full of rapture at this happy event.

Maybe survival of hell had made him selfish. It seemed to have burned away all the softness of his youth. Catherine might look at him and see the same old Richard. But he knew he wasn't. Somewhere deep in his heart, a catastrophic change had taken place.

'Darling . . .?' She was turning to him, stretching out her arms.

He moved forward, took her hands in his.

'It's so wonderful to have you back,' she said, her soft grey eyes shining.

'It's good to be back,' he said. It was. But also, troubling. Why should he have lived, when so many other, better men had died?

'We've so much to look forward to now,' she said happily. 'I was so afraid at times. I thought you might never come back. I thought you might be wounded. That something awful would happen. But . . . here you are.'

'Yes,' he said. Christ, what else could he say?

He couldn't think why he'd been spared. It seemed wrong that he should be here, home, safe, when so many brave souls – far, far braver than him – had perished in the mud and the blood and the gore.

'We have the wedding to plan,' said Catherine. She squeezed his hands. 'Isn't it wonderful?'

Oh God.

'Catherine . . .'

'What, darling?' she asked when he paused.

'Nothing.'

She came closer, slipping her arms around his neck, pouting prettily. 'Are you going to kiss me, Richard?'

He did. He felt nothing. Worse, when his lips touched Catherine's, *she* sprang into his mind. The girl in town who'd duped him. *Diamond.* He pulled back, away from her, his eyes averted.

'What's the matter?' she asked, her smile vanishing. 'Look – darling – I know this must be so strange for you. Coming back to normal life. I do understand, you know. I've no wish to rush you, but . . .'

'But you're going to,' said Richard. The words seemed to fall out of his mouth, unbidden.

She looked as shocked as if he'd slapped her.

Oh God. Here we go then.

'Catherine,' he said, taking her hands back in his. 'Dear Catherine. We've known each other for such a long time. We were childhood sweethearts, weren't we?'

'What are you saying?' Her voice was barely a croak now.

She was staring at his face. *She knows*, he thought. *I can't hide it. It's no good.*

'Darling Catherine, I can't marry you,' he said. 'I'm sorry but I can't.'

22

After the explosion came the fallout. Catherine reeled back at Richard's words and then she fled the orangerie and went to find her mother in the withdrawing room. He stood there, stock-still, listening to raised voices, shrieks. Then deeper voices joined in and he heard Catherine's father Sir James shout: 'What the hell?'

He felt deathly calm. He'd done it. He would only have made her miserable. Now, above all else, he needed to be free, to try and find his way back to normal life unhindered – if he could. Maybe he would travel. He knew his father wouldn't like that, that the Earl would be keen for him to stay at home now and resume his familiarising himself with running the estate efficiently. But the obedient boy of before was long gone.

Catherine's father was charging toward him like a maddened bull. Beyond the red-faced man advancing on him, Richard could see the open door to the withdrawing room and the women in there, huddling around Catherine while she yelled and half swooned in her mother's arms.

'I'll sue!' roared Sir James. 'You bastard, you won't let my daughter down. We'll sue for damages, for breach of promise! You haven't heard the last of this!'

The Earl was rushing up behind Sir James, catching hold of the arm that was raised, ready to land a blow on Richard.

Teddy was there too, Teddy who had seen it all just as Richard had and might have understood. Clearly he didn't. He was pulling at his father's arm and staring at Richard with disbelief. In the background, Richard could see footmen hovering, eyes bright with excitement at this unexpected fracas, squirrelling the scene away for later discussion downstairs.

Then Lady Margaret dashed out of the drawing room and came hustling into the orangerie.

'Edward, what's happening?' she asked the Earl.

'Your son,' said Sir James, rounding on her so that she shrank back, 'this *creature* has let my daughter down. Told her there'll be no wedding.'

Richard's mother stared at him. Then her eyes went to her son. 'Is this true?' she asked faintly.

'Of course it isn't true,' said the Earl. 'It's all been too much for Richard, getting home after all that he must have been through. It was thoughtless of me to insist on a dinner party so soon, I should have known better. When we have all had a chance to calm down . . .'

'I'm perfectly calm,' said Richard. 'And I am sorry for any hurt this may cause. But there will be no wedding.'

And he swept past them all, up the stairs and to his room. Then he closed the door on them, sank down on the bed, and wondered what the hell he'd just done.

23

Sir James didn't follow on with his promise to sue.

'That's because we are old friends,' the Earl told Richard. 'Much as this has hurt him and infuriated him, he wants to spare me public embarrassment. And to spare poor Catherine, too.'

Catherine had returned Granny's ruby and diamond ring, along with a note that told Richard exactly what she thought of him, which was very little. She called him a coward. A cheater. A cold-blooded monster. All of which he had pretty much expected. He didn't blame her.

'So what now?' the Earl asked him one day as they sat in the study at Fontleigh, the dog dozing at Richard's feet.

Richard didn't know what now. He could barely think straight; he felt shattered. Dutifully, over the weeks and months following his disastrous homecoming, he had been out and about around the estate with his father's land manager, examining the crops that had been gathered in, looking over the spring crops that were planted but would sit dully in the muddy fields until early the following year when they would burst into growth. He talked to the tenant farmers, showed his face in the village, apparently taking an interest but really? Feeling nothing.

Richard couldn't bear to think of the *now*. The now meant tomorrow, and the thing he'd been dreading for so long, the thing that there had been such huge preparations for – the service of remembrance; the laying of wreaths to honour the war dead at the newly erected stone memorial in the village centre.

What now?

'Who knows?' he said with a bitter little smile.

***

It was November, miserable, drizzly and sad, when the day finally dawned. The Earl's family attended at the church and then at the memorial itself. The local brass band played in the rain and then a single bugler sounded the Last Post while poppy wreaths were laid. There was a roll-call of the estate's glorious dead – farm labourers, thatchers, bodgers, charcoal burners, wheelwrights, who had all gone from the Earl's estate, twenty-six country men too young to know the meaning of fear, and who had all died, slaughtered for their innocence.

At his father's insistence, Richard attended in full dress uniform, although he hated it and wished it burned and gone and forgotten. He stood there and tried not to listen to the stifled sobs, the heartbroken wails from the loved ones of the lost. Two minutes of silence were observed as the onlookers grew damper, the wind starting to swirl around the memorial, the rain driving into their faces.

Then everyone proceeded to the village hall, which was decorated with the very last of the season's chrysanthemums in garish acid yellow, bronze and bright red. Trestle tables had been set up and tea and sandwiches and cakes were served to the shivering masses. Dutifully, Richard circulated while his mother and father did the same, shaking hands, talking gently, giving condolences. And to his horror as he moved among the crowds he came – shockingly – face to face with Catherine.

'Oh,' he said stupidly.

'Hello Richard,' she said, with more composure than he had ever given her credit for.

She was pretty as always; her hair a mass of ash-blonde tendrils, her eyes that same sweet soft grey. She was wearing a black wool coat and a matching cloche hat. She was deathly pale and despite the lavish thickness of her coat she looked frozen. 'Isn't this awful?' she said.

Of course, he and Catherine had always been on the same page. She always felt just as he did. Since childhood, they had simply, easily, understood one another. Recently, he had found himself missing the effortless familiarity of her, his old love. And seeing her today, looking so distressed, he felt a surge of warmth for her and a matching surge of guilt. He'd hurt her, badly. He hated himself for that.

'Yes, it's bloody awful,' he said in low tones so that only she could hear him. 'But we have to do it, don't we? And . . . how are you?'

Her eyes grew cold. 'As you can see, I am perfectly fine.'

'Yes. Of course.' And before he could embarrass himself any further he moved on along the line, praying that her father or Teddy wouldn't loom up in front of him next and cause a scene.

Her father didn't. Nor did Teddy, his dearest, oldest friend who he also missed, terribly. Teddy like him was a survivor of the dreadful war, he'd served with great honour as a medic in the trenches, seeing unimaginable pain and tragedy played out right in front of his eyes in a field hospital as he sawed off limbs and stitched up ruined faces, stuffed bowels back into bodies that would never, ever recover and would get sepsis, and die.

This day had brought it all back to him, so vividly. The horror. The death.

Now he was passing in front of Lady Mary, Catherine's mother. Christ, could this get any worse? She blanked him with a look of icy rage and contempt.

Finally, the whole thing was over and Richard breathed a sigh of relief when he could get home, strip off his hated uniform and put on his civvies. He thought again of Catherine, standing there in line today, looking so frail and lost.

Let it go, he told himself, aware that his head and his shoulders ached with tension. All that's in the past.

But what about the future?

When he dreamed that night, he didn't dream of Catherine, or the ghastly nightmare of the war.

He dreamed instead of Diamond.

24

Everything returns to normal in the end, or Richard supposed it might. For him, normality seemed to be a long time coming. Veering between town distractions and countryside duties, he did his best. On the estate, he threw himself into work, doing the rounds of the tenant farmers, some of whom were struggling. On Top Farm, Mrs Bryerson had two children and no husband and nothing to show for the loss of him but the awful telegram – which she had kept, of course – informing her of his death at Ypres.

'Do you think he suffered?' she asked Richard when he rode over there and she came to the door. Her two bleary-eyed and ill-washed children were clinging to her skirts.

'I'm sure he didn't,' Richard lied, having seen the many and gruesome ways that death could manifest itself over there in that mud-soaked hell. And yet here he was – him, the privileged one, the son of the landed gentry. A survivor. The guilt of it clutched at him again.

But Mrs Bryerson seemed to accept his words. Well, of course she did. It was a comfort, thinking of a single bullet-shot to the head, a tidy and almost instantaneous death. Better that than what had probably been the reality.

He went over to the next farm, Box Hill, and then the one after that, finding much the same tales of woe and also developing a creeping feeling that he, personally, had been judged and found wanting by this community.

Word about the broken engagement had spread fast in the country lanes and villages. Everyone knew he had jilted Catherine; and from what he could see, no-one thought much of him because of it. He couldn't help but notice that at most places he was greeted not with welcoming smiles but with cold stares. And he deserved that. He couldn't complain. Whenever he thought of Catherine, his mind flinched in horror at his own actions. He knew he had damaged his own reputation, which was bad – but he had also hurt her, and that was far, far worse.

He mounted up, shook out the reins of his ancient and placid dapple-grey hunter. Poor old thing, far too old to have been swept up in the war when all the younger and more useful horses had been requisitioned. And thank God for that. His father the Earl had shed real tears when the army had taken his beautiful black-pointed bay mare. He had never seen her again.

Once, all the farms on the estate had thrived. Now crops went ungathered or unsown, livestock were neglected, equipment sat unused and rusting out in the rain. Richard spoke to the land agent to get Mrs Bryerson and the others some much-needed assistance, and the man said he would try, sir, of course he would, but everywhere was the same now. Too many men missing after the war, too many women struggling to cope on their own.

'I know,' said Richard. 'But do your best.'

He rode on, feeling the weight of depression stealing over him again in the dank, dreary weather. The light was low and so were his spirits. Summer would come, as summer always did, but he hadn't the heart for it. He thought of the girl again – Diamond. Christ, that was another world, wasn't it? The London streets, where she plied her cheating 'trade'. She was a whore, he knew that, but somehow he still couldn't shake her from his mind.

25

Christmas 1919

Richard had been putting it off, but now he knew he had to get away. He had to go to town, to his club, just to try to reassemble what was left of his senses – if that was ever going to be possible, which he doubted very much. He didn't know himself any more. Sometimes he felt that he had lost his core, his essential self. He didn't know whether he was ever going to get that back. He was afraid that he was losing his mind. That the horror had been simply too much, that his father was right, that he really was a coward, a disgrace, beneath contempt. Maybe he was. Maybe in town he would be able to forget that, just for a while.

Time drifted. Then New Year was done and soon it would be spring. For Richard there was no cheer to be found in the warming of the seasons. In London he did too much gambling, far too much drinking; anything to distract him, to keep his mind away from the dark cold hours at night when he lay sleepless in bed and imagined he could hear the roar of the guns, the shouted orders and the screams of the dying, all over again. People said that during the war they'd been able to hear the guns firing in France on the south coast of England, and he didn't doubt it. He heard them now, when sleep did finally steal over him. In his dreams he heard the yells and the panic, people crying to God to help them. He tasted despair and smelled the mud and the blood of his doomed comrades.

He stayed on in town, didn't go home to Fontleigh. Couldn't face it. Couldn't face the worry in the eyes of his mother, or his father's obvious disappointment. No, he would stay here. Let time pass. Not even think about what came next. Just live, free and without anyone judging him. He spent a lot of time alone, because most of the friends he'd had before the war were dead. Yes, his closest friend Teddy, Catherine's brother, was a survivor like him, but Teddy wouldn't even look at him these days, far less speak. So he lost money at the tables, sometimes won on a nag or two. He drifted from one bar to the next with his old service revolver loaded and ready in his pocket because he was full of fear but trying to mask it. He got drunk and sang along in seedy bars to 'I'm Forever Blowing Bubbles' and 'Don't Dilly-Dally on the Way'. It was all false gaiety. He didn't think he would ever feel truly safe, or happy, again. And above all he tried – so hard, and so uselessly – to forget.

26

Diamond was now an old, old hand at the badger trick. She loathed it, but she was an expert at it. She was wracked with pity for the men she snared and full of disgust for herself, but Victor being Victor it was best never to object. Frenchie was right about that. Diamond's 'job' was to loiter at the bar – as she was doing now – in one of the new clubs Victor had bought, enticing wealthy-looking marks with alluring tales of private dances in the upstairs rooms – for a five-guinea fee.

She leaned on the bar, dressed up in her fanciest clothes, rouged and powdered, her violet-blue eyes outlined with kohl. She was watching everything going on around her, looking for a man who was young and wealthy. You could spot them from the good cut of their clothes, the expensive fabrics.

And there was one.

He had floppy blond hair and a thinnish look to him, like he could do with a good meal. He was standing at the other end of the bar, drinking down what looked like neat whisky at twelve noon, slapping his glass back onto the bar, nodding to the barman. *Fill her up.*

Victor was sitting across the room at a table in the shadows, watching. Diamond sent him a glance. *Get on with it*, he mouthed. She heaved in a breath, pasted a smile on her face, and approached the stranger at the other end of the bar.

'Buy me a drink?' she suggested, smiling.

He looked around at her. She thought that he had nice pale blue eyes, but there was some barely hidden pain in them. You saw a lot of men like that around town now. The survivors. They were the ones who jumped when someone opened a bottle of the cheap fizz they served in here, the stuff that they passed off as champagne. Poor dead-eyed bastards. But easy marks. She smiled broader, an invitation in her eyes. He just stared.

Finally he nodded. 'All right,' he said. 'Why not?'

27

Richard knew she didn't recognise him, but by God he recognised her. It was Diamond, the girl who'd snared him almost at the moment he'd landed back on British soil on 11th November, Victory Day. He'd been reeling about, full of an uneasy mixture of relief that he was still alive and self-hatred because of it.

She'd caught him out with the badger trick. Her lover or father or *some* damned thing had beaten him and his batman George – who was now his valet and waiting for his return at Fontleigh – had explained to him that he'd been duped, lured in by the girl in order that her accomplice could rob him.

Now, he watched her. She was gorgeous. Once seen, never forgotten.

The bitch.

She sipped her drink and smiled at him, made conversation. And all the time, she was inching closer, leaning in, stroking a hand down his arm, touching his hair, saying what a pretty colour it was.

'I do private dances, you know. Upstairs,' she said.

Once, she'd taken a whole half an hour to get the mark up the stairs and Victor had thumped not only the mark but her too.

'I can't be sitting about all bloody day waiting for you to do your job right,' he'd snapped at her, grabbing her hair so hard that he'd pulled out a chunk of it and left her bleeding. 'Don't be so fucking slow.'

'Oh. Do you?' Richard said, throwing back another whisky.

'I'm an excellent dancer,' said Diamond, leaning in. 'I can even take my clothes off for you. If you like.'

Richard stared at her face. She must have done this a thousand times. Of course she wouldn't recognise one man, out of so many. Yes, she was beautiful – he'd almost forgotten *how* beautiful. Now he marvelled again at the luscious brightness of her looks, the sheen of her black hair, the soft pallor of her skin – but for God's sake! How could any decent human being play a trick like this?

'How much then?' he asked.

'Five guineas,' said Diamond.

'All right,' said Richard.

28

Richard knew that he might, if he wasn't very careful, get beaten again, but right now he didn't much care about that. The release of sex was on his mind, and revenge on this girl who had humiliated him, crushed him, left him unsatisfied and yet somehow *fixed* upon her, daydreaming about her, wondering where she was and what she was doing.

Well, she was here. And what was she doing? The same damned horrible treacherous thing she'd always done. He must be going mad, dreaming about a whore like this.

'Money first,' said Diamond.

Of course, money first. Richard fished in his coat. He felt the cool reassuring weight of his service revolver as he did so and felt instantly better about this. He pulled out a brown leather wallet embossed with a gold *RB* on its corner. He extracted the money and handed it over.

Diamond tucked it into her skirt pocket. 'Right then. Up you come.'

Richard followed her up the stairs at the far side of the room as the band played on. Maybe this was the same place she'd led him to last time, he really couldn't remember. And it didn't matter.

Once in the room upstairs, Diamond started to disrobe, slipping off her jacket, her blouse, her skirt. When she stood there in stockings and chemise, he moved closer. Of all the disgusting tricks! Richard felt anger boil up in him, anger that she should do this, cheapen herself so badly, anger that she should take him for an idiot.

But . . . damn, she was exquisite! Standing there, you'd almost think that she really was reluctant. That she was a decent girl, worth more than this.

Richard approached her. 'You're so pretty,' he said, reaching out to touch her shoulder.

'Thank you, kind sir,' she said, smiling.

'So this dance . . .' he said, moving forward again, slipping his arms around her.

Diamond draped her arms around his neck. 'Yes, about that.'

'Go on then.' He pushed her back, away from him. 'But more clothes off first. Like Salome. The dance of the seven veils.'

He saw her eyes flicker, saw uncertainty there. But of course it was all fake. Pretty soon her pet ape would be coming up the stairs. She was safe enough. Or so she thought.

'All right,' she said, and seemed to brace herself before pulling the chemise over her head and letting it drift to the floor.

Her body was just as he remembered it. Perfect. Exquisite. She kept her eyes downcast, modestly, as if she was a virgin, unused to men.

'No dancing. I've changed my mind. On the bed.'

Diamond's eyes flicked up and he saw alarm in them.

'Ten pounds,' said Richard.

He knew it must be a fortune to a girl like her. Diamond went over to the bed and slipped under the covers. She seemed to shiver. This time Richard didn't disrobe. He followed her over to the bed, pushed the coverlet aside and stared down at her.

'You're beautiful,' he said, and sat down on the bed and kissed her.

The kiss changed into something deeper, harder. His hands were on her breasts, pinching her nipples. Then they roamed further and he looked into her eyes and saw panic there.

Yes, where is the pet ape? Shouldn't he be up here by now?

Fully aroused, he quickly unzipped and freed his manhood, forced her legs apart. Diamond gasped and shoved against him, trying to get him away from her. But he took no notice. He found the place he was looking for and pushed up, thrusting hard. She stiffened and gave a cry – still acting the virgin, he thought furiously – but he pushed and pushed again until the sensation of her hot wetness was too much and he came, convulsing.

There were heavy footsteps on the stairs now. Coming fast.

Richard pulled out of her and zipped up and was on his feet with the service revolver in his hand when the door burst open and Victor charged into the room.

When Victor saw the gun he stopped dead, raising his hands. 'Whoa,' he said. 'Steady now.'

Richard glanced at Diamond. She was cowering under the covers, her eyes wide with alarm. Then his eyes went back to Victor.

'Stand away from the door,' he said.

His hands still held high, Victor moved aside. Richard went past him, out of the door, down the stairs and away.

29

'He didn't get his knob inside you, did he?'

'Of course not,' said Diamond, embarrassed. 'Do you have to be so bloody crude?'

Victor pointed a menacing finger at her. 'Watch your mouth!'

He was counting up the day's takings in the parlour at home. Diamond felt sore and when she'd tidied herself up after the encounter with the blond man at the club she had found blood on her thighs. Her virginity was gone. She thought of the moment they'd joined together, her and the handsome young stranger, reliving that new and amazing feeling of his whole length sliding into her, hard as iron, slick as damp velvet. Two quick thrusts – and then it was over.

She felt herself flushing, growing hot at the memory. He *had* been inside her and although it had been a shock she'd wanted him to stay there. She'd felt the wetness from him, afterwards, snaking down her thighs. And the blood, of course. It was her own fault. She had misplayed her hand. She should have teased a bit longer, avoided that final act.

'He didn't get inside me,' she lied. She couldn't discuss this with *anyone* – and certainly not with Victor.

Victor had paused in his counting and was watching her speculatively through a cloud of cigar smoke. 'You're sure about that? Only. . .'

'Shut up, will you?' said Diamond, standing up, crossing to the door.

'All right then. If you say so,' said Victor, and carried on counting.

The young man's face swam in front of her vision. *RB*, she thought, remembering the gold embossing on his wallet. Ralph? Rolo?

Forget it, she told herself.

Aiden had just finished the milk run, collecting the monies for protection given by the Victory Boys from the snooker halls, clubs and bars all around the district.

Diamond didn't like the way Aiden was behaving these days, like a young tough; he'd loiter, hard-eyed, cleaning his fingernails with a knife, getting far too influenced by Michael. She didn't like that. She remembered, all too well, what had happened to her father and she had a dread of the same fate befalling Aiden.

'Good day's work,' he said, handing the cash over to Victor, who put it in the safe along with the takings from his trip to the club with Diamond. 'Everything OK?' Aiden squinted at her face. 'You look like you been hit with a brick.'

Diamond said nothing. She was watching Victor turning the dial on the safe.

Click, click, click.

'Bastard pulled a gun on me when we were doing him,' said Victor.

'Shit! What happened?' Instantly Aiden's eyes went back to Diamond. 'You all right, sis? You didn't get hurt?'

'I sorted it,' said Victor.

'Where's Mum then? Not up?' Aiden's eyes were anxious, still fixed on Diamond.

'She's taken to her bed,' said Diamond, who was worried. The Milano getting burned down had hit Frenchie very hard. She didn't seem to have gotten over it, even now. 'I'm taking her up some tea.'

Diamond brewed up in the scullery and then went upstairs, knocking at her mother's bedroom door. She went in, noting that the curtains were closed at the window. Frenchie's boudoir was an echo of her homeland, lush with cabbage-rose wallpaper, a big French daybed, a pair of gold velvet Victorian nursing chairs. Above the bed were strung ribboned nets that Frenchie had dyed herself with strong tea to exactly the right shade of *crème de café*. There were lavish gold-framed pictures on the walls, one of which – of Frenchie lit by limelight and perched on the edge of the stage at the Folies-Bergère – she claimed to have been painted by Degas, one of the great Impressionists, and gifted to her during her days in Montmartre.

'We had such hopes for it, our club, you know. I spent hours, designing the interior. The Milano! I can't believe it's gone,' came Frenchie's husky, tear-soaked voice from the bed.

Diamond set the teacup down on the bedside table and went over and drew back the curtains, admitting the daylight. She turned and there in the bed was her mother, one forearm thrown dramatically across her brow.

'Come along, let's get some of this good tea down you,' said Diamond, who was not one for dramatics at all; she was at heart a practical girl. She went to the bed, rearranged her mother's pillows so that she was sitting up, forced the cup into her hand. Frenchie wrinkled her nose but took a sip, then coughed. More and more, she was coughing. It worried Diamond. And she didn't find it quite so funny any more when Frenchie moaned on about the dampness rising up from the river. Maybe Frenchie was right. Maybe a break in some golden, toasty-warm place – Madeira perhaps, somewhere like that – would do Frenchie a power of good.

'The Milano! How am I to bear it?' she wailed.

'It's a building, Mum. Just bricks and mortar.'

'No! It's memories. It's your father.'

Warren had adored the Milano, it had been his baby. But now even that was gone, so what was the point of crying over it? Diamond watched her mother with fond exasperation. Frenchie was always one to over-egg a situation, to make big flamboyant gestures. She was very French. She expounded about how she felt, she pounded her chest, she demanded sympathy, gave in to mawkish sentimentality and made loud and frequent lamentations about the loss of her one true love. More and more, she seemed to find comfort in the past, winding her way down memory lane at the least provocation. That worried Diamond, too. Her mother was getting older.

'You see that painting of me? God, I was so young then. All the artists loved me.' Frenchie's eyes went from the Degas to her daughter. 'You're beautiful too, darling. More so than I ever was.'

'That's not true.'

'Oh – it is.' Frenchie put down her cup and put the cold fingertips of one hand under Diamond's chin. 'Look at you. Gorgeous. You all take after your father. Black hair and those strange violet-blue eyes, and you have that wonderful pale creamy skin.'

'Mum, come on. Time to get up, yes?'

Frenchie's lip curled. 'My life is a disaster! That *animal* Victor torments me, and now he's tying himself to that Wolfe creature!'

Diamond was getting sick of hearing this. *She'd* made the effort over the wedding, hadn't she? She'd gone to the interminable dress fittings, tolerated Gwendoline's pickiness, and she just wanted to get the damned thing over. Then they could kiss goodbye to Gwendoline and to Victor too, and *that* would make the whole damned thing worthwhile. They could cope alone, she and Frenchie and Aiden and Owen. Maybe she *would* join up with Michael's Silver Blades as he wanted her to. They could manage, she was sure of it. They would *have* to.

'And the final humiliation,' Frenchie howled. 'You have to trail after her up the aisle as a bridesmaid.'

It was traditional, of course. If the groom had a youngish female relative, then the poor cow had to be drafted in, stuffed into the most unflattering gown that could be found, and paraded around to the bride's complete satisfaction.

Diamond said nothing. She'd suffered through all the fittings of the hideous apricot-coloured dresses Gwendoline had selected for her attendants to wear. She'd sucked it all up, got through it, while Gwendoline Wolfe had queened it over her. Her aim was to keep her usual head-down attitude today, just get out the other side. It was what she was best at, enduring the seemingly unendurable.

'They killed your father, those bastards! And I bet it was them who torched Warren's beautiful club,' Frenchie finished with a flourish, when Diamond made no response.

Diamond had had years of hearing the whole family cursing the Wolfe clan, blaming them for every misfortune. But this time, with the fire at the Milano, she was puzzled. She'd love to lay it at the Wolfe door, but it didn't quite fit. 'Why would Toro Wolfe burn down our club when his sister is about to become a member of the family? It sounds crazy.'

Frenchie's eyes widened. 'Wash your mouth out! The man is a monster. His father before him was a monster too. He most likely has set out a marker with this attack. He's saying, make no mistake, we are still enemies, no matter what happens in church. And so we are. He intends to take over from Victor, to wrest the power from his hands. I'm sure of it. This is just the beginning of the war, *chérie*.'

'Maybe we'd be better off with Toro Wolfe than with Victor ruling the roost,' considered Diamond out loud. She hated Toro Wolfe, but at least she didn't have to *live* with him. On balance, she thought she hated Victor more.

'Don't say such things!' Frenchie shot a worried look at her closed bedroom door. 'What if he heard you?'

'Well, it's the truth,' said Diamond, thinking that whether he heard her or not, Victor would always be looking for an opportunity to lash out with his fists at her – at them all. She could be a fucking *saint*, and he'd still find some misdemeanour to accuse her of. So even if Toro Wolfe did take over the Victory Boys' holdings, would it really be any worse than what they already had?

Diamond didn't think so.

30

The sun was shining dimly through lowering clouds when the hunt assembled at the front of Fontleigh. Both the Earl and Richard were mounted in their hunting pink with black brown-topped boots and black velvet hunting caps, Richard upon his steady old dapple-grey hunter, the Earl on a skittish new white-starred bay. Stirrup-cups were offered, and cake, and then the hunt set off along the lanes.

There were around thirty hunters in attendance, and Richard felt a sharp pang of discomfort when he saw that Catherine was among them on a tall dun mare, riding side-saddle and looking very elegant in black riding skirt, tight bodice and neat veiled hat.

His father, of course, had acknowledged Catherine right from the off and had spoken to her. Later, he said to Richard: 'Look, be nice to the poor girl for God's sake, can't you? Speak to her, at least.'

Then they were off, clattering along the lanes and into woodland and fields, and there was no chance to talk. Richard was grateful for that, because what the hell could he say to her? He was sorry he'd broken her heart. Of course he was. But what had been the alternative, really? Breaking his own? Tying himself to a girl he was very fond of but could never, not in a million years, come to feel passion for, or love in the way she deserved?

'Duty is more important that feelings,' his mother was always saying. She'd been saying it to him since the cradle.

Maybe it was. But as the master gave the command to move off and search a covert for the fox and the hunt crashed full-pelt around him into thicker, deeper woods, all that was forgotten. Before half an hour was up the cry of the hounds had risen to an ear-shattering series of howling barks and the huntsman's horn was sounding. A shout went up.

'Tally-ho!'

They were galloping through clearings, brambles catching at them, the horses soaring over fallen trees, fences, gates, bracken flattening under their thundering hooves. The Earl was up at the front somewhere, giving chase. Richard saw Catherine away to his left, moving very fast, and then another fallen tree was in front of his grey hunter and on the approach he felt its powerful muscles bunch. Then to his shock Catherine's mount veered in front of his and she took the obstacle first, soaring over it. The dun's foreleg knocked against the oak and the mare stumbled, legs flailing. With a cry Catherine shot over the mare's neck and fell on the other side of the tree, her hand still gripping the mare's reins. The mare scrabbled upright, wrenched the reins out of Catherine's hand and galloped on.

Swearing, Richard realised that his hunter was going to clear the damned thing and land right on top of Catherine. He yanked on the reins but the beast was already in flight. He closed his eyes, anticipating a shriek of pain when half a ton of horse fell on her. His grey cleared the oak easily and swept on, three strides, four, then Richard pulled the big horse to a halt and leaped from the saddle, looking back frantically to see what mayhem had occurred.

'Catherine!'

She was lying there against the fallen oak, tucked in almost underneath the curve of it. As he ran to her she sat up, retrieving her hat from the ground.

'Good God, are you all right?' he asked in alarm.

'Oh for goodness' sake, I feel such a fool,' she snapped angrily. Then she looked up and realised that the man hurrying toward her was Richard. 'Oh! It's you.'

Suddenly he was on his knees beside her, not quite sure how he had got there. Everything had happened so quickly. Her dun mare had departed. The horns and the over-excited yapping of the hounds were sounding well away in the distance. The rest of the hunt had passed them by. Richard's grey hunter had cantered to a halt and was now eating the greenery, unconcerned.

'I thought I was going to hit you for sure,' said Richard.

'I thought you were too,' said Catherine, standing up, brushing irritably at her dirtied skirt. 'That's why I rolled in against the trunk. This is so embarrassing.'

He should have stayed in London. He'd found that girl, Diamond, and this time he'd played the trick, not her. So he'd had his revenge. It hadn't delighted him, but it was done – and maybe now he could move on, forget about her once and for all.

He shouldn't have come back here so soon, risked an encounter like this. He didn't know what to say to Catherine his old friend, the same girl who had played on the lawns of Fontleigh with him when they were small. He was at a loss with her. All their easy familiarity had vanished. Everything had gone wrong.

'There's no need for embarrassment,' he said. 'You fell off. I've fallen off a million times.'

'Yes, but why did it have to be . . .?' Her face screwed up and he saw a glint of angry tears in her grey eyes before she turned away from him. He knew what she had been about to say, of course he did. *Why did it have to be you?*

'Catherine,' he said.

'Yes, what?' She wouldn't look at him.

'We've been friends for so long. I think . . . well, wouldn't it be so much better, easier for both of us, if we could remain friends now?'

She turned, stared at him. Her shoulders slumped.

'Of course,' she said in a small voice. 'You're right. This is silly.'

'I've missed your friendship,' he said truthfully. He really had. Only now, speaking to her, did he realise how much.

She nodded. A tiny smile played around her mouth. She bent down, picked up her whip. 'I've missed it too. The rest of it . . . well, things changed, didn't they? The war and everything. I do understand that, you know. That you felt differently. That you couldn't go on with it.'

'Catherine, I'm sorry.' He felt choked, flooded by genuine regret. He knew that he *did* love Catherine, in a way – but it wasn't the *right* way. He loved her sweetness, her patience and tolerance, but he wasn't moved by her, inflamed to passion by the mere sight of her, and he felt he wanted that. After the privations of the war, he needed to feel that, to feel *alive* once again.

'It's all right, Richard,' she said.

Richard pricked up his ears. In the distance, a high-pitched Holloa sounded. They'd found the fox. He thought of it as he had never thought of it before, running for its life, terrified, fighting to stay alive. He'd done all of that, over in France in the war. To please his father, he'd been hunting all through the winter here in England. But suddenly he knew that he would never, in his entire life, ever hunt a single living thing again.

'Come on, let's get you up on old faithful,' he said, taking her hand. 'I'm going to walk you back to the house.'

31

24th April 1920

Gwendoline Wolfe was standing in her bedroom at the Wolfe family home and feeling both elated and sad. This was her big day, the biggest in the life of any girl, and none of her parents – not even Gustav, who wasn't her real father at all but who had taken on that role during her youth – were here to see it. But . . . maybe that was just as well, because she was marrying Victor Butcher, and the Butchers and the Wolfes had been enemies for so long that it was all lost in the mists of time. Even before the war, they'd been at each other's throats.

She was relying on Toro to give her away, and she was on edge over that. There was no love lost between her and her brother. Would he even show up? He'd gone out early yesterday and she hadn't seen him since. He'd been cursing and swearing about the upcoming wedding for months now, and she thought it was a distinct possibility that he would simply not come at all. He disapproved, absolutely. Had chewed the bloody carpet over it, moaned on and on to her until she thought she'd go mad.

But . . . she was in love with Victor, she was going to *marry* Victor, so to hell with Toro.

Now, one of her bridesmaids had told her something and she froze.

'*What?*' she snarled.

At the sharpness of her tone all the girls in the room – three of them, one very distant cousin and two friends, and where the *fuck* was the fourth, the Butcher girl? Her peach silk dress, identical to those already worn by her companion bridesmaids, was still hanging up on the back of the door. Diamond was late. And now they were saying . . . well, what *were* they saying, exactly?

'Didn't he tell you? It was a couple of weeks back. Toro had to go down the station. The police wanted to question him again about Victor Butcher's club burning down.'

'Again? You mean they've questioned him before about it?'

'Yes. They did.'

Gwendoline turned her searchlight blue gaze on the three younger women. Toro never told her *anything*. 'Where the hell is he? It's nearly eleven thirty. The wedding's at one!'

'Don't worry,' said Cecily, the oldest bridesmaid and a born peacemaker, patting Gwendoline's shoulder. 'He'll be here in time.'

'If he ruins this . . .' growled Gwendoline. If Toro didn't show up, she would be a laughing stock. She knew damned well that people were having bets on it. Would he be here? Or would he simply not bother?

'He'll be back,' said Cecily calmly. 'You look wonderful, you know. Fabulous.'

Gwendoline preened at that, appeased. She was every inch the supremely lovely bride. Turning back and forth in front of the cheval mirror, Gwendoline knew she looked like an angel – wispy, ethereal. She stood there pencil-slim in her figure-skimming dress of deep ivory chiffon moire, embroidered with silver thread and studded with pearls. The silver leaf girdle at her tiny waist had a trail of spring-green tulle that rippled to the ground. A simple wreath of orange blossoms adorned her head. Daffodils, grape hyacinths and Lenten roses were crowded among maidenhair fern for her bouquet. A yards-long train floated down from her shoulders, tumbling to the floor like a silken waterfall. There couldn't be a more beautiful bride.

'What, exactly, is Toro doing? Where is he?' she asked. She and her brother were not, had never been, the best of pals. Toro despised her, she knew that. That was fair enough. But all she asked of him was for this *one day* that he should turn up on time and do one simple thing. Now what the *fuck* was he up to?

'I heard there was trouble last night,' piped up Cassie, one of the younger attendants, pouting at herself as she applied rouge in the dressing table mirror. She couldn't see Cecily, behind her, giving urgent hand signals. *Shut up, Cassie.*

'Steady with that bloody rouge. You're twelve years old, not twenty,' said Cecily.

'They say whores rouge their nipples,' said one of the other bridesmaids.

'Shush!' said Gwendoline, indicating Cassie. She was too young to hear talk like that.

'Ever since the Butcher club burned down, Victor Butcher's been cutting into Toro's business affairs, playing tit for tat,' Cassie ploughed on, putting down the rouge pot and gurning at herself in the dressing table mirror.

Gwendoline paused in her perusal of her own shimmeringly lovely reflection. Her lamp-like blue eyes went to Cecily's. 'Really?'

'So I hear,' said Cecily. 'The Butchers blamed Toro for it.'

'They blame Toro for everything!' snapped Gwendoline.

Someone was knocking at the front door. There were voices down in the hall and then a quick tread came up the stairs. Suddenly Diamond Butcher opened the door. The peach dress fell onto the floor. She came in at a rush, stumbled and almost tripped over it. Then she righted herself. The assembled company glared at her.

'Sorry,' said Diamond. 'Am I late?' She didn't care if she was; she couldn't think *what* the hell she was doing here, pandering to a Wolfe woman when she hated all the Wolfe clan so much. She cursed Victor for dragging her into this.

'Yes,' said Gwendoline coldly.

'Oh.' Diamond disentangled the toe of her shoe, which had become caught in the peachy fabric on the floor. She pulled harder. There was a loud tearing sound.

'Oh for fuck's *sake!*' snarled Gwendoline.

'I'll sort it out,' said Cecily.

Then there were louder voices down in the hall.

'That's Toro,' sighed Gwendoline with relief. 'He's back.' He'd been saying for days that he'd be buggered if he'd give one of his own kin away to a bastard Butcher, literally boiling over with rage about it, and she had wondered, seriously, would he really just leave her standing? Simply not turn up? But here he was – at last! – and she could breathe again.

Diamond gathered up the dishevelled peach gown and found an empty stool to sit on. Now she was in the same building as the Wolfes and it gave her a fearful, queasy feeling. *The enemy*, her dad had called them. And he'd been so right. Gustav Wolfe must be turning in his grave at the thought of Warren Butcher's brother taking one of the Wolfe lot for a wife. Diamond was just glad that he wasn't going to be here today to see his own daughter obliged to walk behind this Wolfe bitch up the aisle.

'Give it here, I'll stitch it,' said the flustered one called Cecily.

Diamond gladly handed the gown over. She looked rotten in peach – it drained her skin of colour and turned it yellow like she had jaundice or some bloody thing. She had pointed this out during the endless fittings in the Bond Street atelier of Jeanne Lanvin in the run-up to the wedding, but her comments had been ignored. In fact, *none* of the bridesmaids looked good in peach, and Diamond thought that this suited Gwendoline Wolfe right down to the ground. *She* was the one who was going to shine today; she didn't want competition.

Gwendoline was eyeing up her reflection again, smiling at herself.

'Something blue,' she said suddenly. Then she turned, clicked her fingers, her eyes spearing Diamond. 'God, I nearly forgot. You!' A frown creased Gwendoline's brow and Diamond could see that her name had been consigned to the dustbin of history, that Gwendoline couldn't for a moment think what the hell it was. Then Gwendoline's face cleared. 'Yes you! Diamond, isn't it? The sapphire earrings, they're in my jewellery box in the front bedroom on the dressing table. Get them, will you?'

So she was going to be Gwendoline Wolfe's dogsbody for the day. Heaving a sigh, Diamond crossed to the door. Cecily looked up from the stool where she was making repairs to Diamond's gown. She rolled her eyes in sympathy. She was obviously used to Gwendoline's grand ways.

Diamond went out along the landing, passing other doors, heading for the front bedroom. She opened the door at the end of the landing and – yes – it looked like the right place.

The room was decked out in dark blues and golds, a running theme of parakeets and shrubbery in the wallpaper and fabrics all around the room, which gave it an exotic feel. There was a big bed, massive mahogany wardrobes, and a matching dressing table right in front of the window overlooking the street, with a big, beautiful tortoiseshell jewellery box placed squarely upon it.

Diamond went to the box, opened the lid and delved inside. There were gold necklaces, a rope of gorgeous pearls, a couple of ruby-studded rings and – yes, here they were – a pair of sapphire screw-on earrings. Diamond picked them up and the sunlight caught them, dazzling her with their beauty. She paused, staring at them, entranced.

'What the fuck are you doing in here?' snapped a deep male voice from behind her.

32

Diamond whirled around, startled to find a tall dark man standing in the open doorway. She dropped one of the earrings, quickly bent and scooped it back up again. Oh Christ – wasn't that Toro Wolfe? She could feel a hot blush sweeping up over her neck. It looked like she was *thieving* the things, didn't it? But she wasn't.

'Gwendoline asked me to fetch her earrings,' she said.

He was blocking her exit. Staring at her. Well, she'd only done what she'd been told to do. She had nothing to be ashamed of. Or nervous of, either. He was watching her, narrow-eyed. Then suddenly he said: 'You're one of the enemy, aintcha?'

'What? I . . .'

'One of the Butcher lot. You're the girl. Diamond. Queen of the hoisters, I heard. Oh – and very good at the badger trick too.'

'I'd better get these back to Gwendoline,' said Diamond, walking quickly toward the door.

He didn't stand aside. She stopped short, stared up at him. She'd only seen him close once before, years back, walking down the street with his father and a gang of men. She hadn't liked the look of him then and she didn't like the look of him now, either. He was too dark, too swarthy, his eyes too bold, his mouth mocking. He was wearing dark trousers and a grubby-looking white shirt with the sleeves rolled up to the elbows to show muscular forearms. His jacket was slung over his shoulder. He looked like he'd been out on the tiles all night, doing things he shouldn't. She thought of what the girls had said about the fire at the Butcher club. Implicating Toro. And maybe they'd been right. Maybe he *had* set the fire, wrecking the Milano, breaking her mother's heart in two. She felt that if she breathed in deeply, she would smell smoke on him, overlaying a deeper, masculine musk scent. Yes, of course he'd done it. Over the years, if anything bad happened to the Butchers, it was always *his* lot at the back of it.

'Will you let me pass please?' she asked coldly, feeling uneasy, aware that they were alone in a bedroom, and that their families were sworn enemies, and that nothing bad could be put past him, nothing at all.

'Did you take anything else out of that box?'

'No,' said Diamond. 'I bloody didn't.'

'I've only got your word for that. I've heard about you doing the West End stores over. What, you've decided to swap to jewels instead of clothes and furs now, have you?'

'Think what you want.' Diamond lifted her chin and glared at him with hatred. The brass neck of him, standing there blocking the door, accusing her of all sorts, when he'd done that, yes of *course* he had, burned down her father's treasured club the Milano, thrown her mother into fits of tears, into a decline that Diamond was fearful she would never recover from. 'Now get out of my bloody way, will you?'

She walked forward. Toro stood stock-still. He reached out and caught her wrist, grabbing the earrings from the palm of her hand.

'Let *go*,' said Diamond hotly, wincing. He was hurting her. He paused, still grasping her hand, turning it over. Her wrist was bruised; purple fading to yellow. Victor had grabbed it and slammed her against the wall, days ago.

'What's this then?' he asked.

Diamond snatched her hand away, hid it behind her skirts. She held out her other hand, palm up. 'Nothing. I fell a few days ago, that's all. Give me back the earrings, Gwendoline's waiting for them.'

Saying nothing, Toro dropped the sapphires onto Diamond's palm. Then with a stare of complete loathing Diamond barged past him and went back along the landing, aware that his eyes followed her all along the length of it.

33

It was the most beautiful wedding, but Frenchie Butcher didn't go to it. Diamond unwillingly trailed up the aisle of the church with the other bridesmaids behind a luminously pretty Gwendoline, on the arm of her 'brother', Toro.

As the vicar conducted the service, Diamond looked around at the assembled company. Her eyes wandered over Aiden and Owen, all spruced up for the occasion and seated on the groom's side. Aiden's face said it all. He hated this. Despised Victor. Loathed the Wolfe woman who was being foisted on their family. Despite the smallness of the Wolfe clan, the bride's side of the church was packed. Toro Wolfe had been decorated in the war, held the rank of Sergeant Major apparently, and he had friends and followers from his army days who were there in large numbers.

While Victor and Gwendoline recited their vows at the altar, Diamond took the opportunity to look over at Toro Wolfe. The dishevelled reprobate of this morning's encounter was gone, replaced by one that was smoothly groomed, beautifully turned out. As she looked at him, his head turned and their eyes met. Diamond looked away.

When the vicar got to the part about anyone speaking now or forever holding their peace, Diamond was certain he was going to shout out something to stop the wedding in its tracks. But he didn't. As the congregation sang 'Jerusalem' and the couple and their witnesses – Toro and Aiden, who was standing as best man – went into the vestry to sign the register, everyone seemed to be holding their breath. Toro and Victor – and Aiden – in the same room? It was a recipe for mayhem.

There had been too many clashes over the years, the hatred of the Wolfes for the Butchers – and vice versa – was too deeply established to be glossed over. They'd butted heads in business and in life. The Victory Boys thought Toro a mug for going to fight in the war. Toro and his gang loudly said to anyone who would listen that the Butchers were miserable stinking cowards, draft dodgers (which was true) who had let others die while they stayed home safe and warm.

But – surprisingly – the wedding party emerged intact and to Widor's Toccata the happy couple walked back down the aisle as man and wife. Cecily the chief bridesmaid was constantly – irritatingly – looking cow-eyed at Toro Wolfe and whispering at every opportunity to Diamond about how gorgeous he was, how brave, how absolutely *spiffing*.

'He made money out in Africa, pots of it,' Cecily hissed at her as they followed him and his sister down the aisle. 'Mining diamonds. And opals in Australia. He does trade all over the world, he's not just an East End thug like some of these others.'

While the couple meandered back down the aisle, Cecily said: 'Toro ships goods worldwide, you know. Carpets, cabinets, screens, anything that's in demand he supplies. He's very clever. And – of course – he's rich.'

'Cecily,' said Diamond as Cecily started on about Toro's delving into fashion, supplying feathers for flappers' headdresses and silks from the East, exotic perfumes from Grasse. 'Do shut the fuck up.'

'Well, that went surprisingly well,' said Toro to Diamond as they briefly stood side by side on the way back down the aisle. 'You're my relation now, I suppose. God help me. How's your mother? Couldn't be bothered to come?'

'She's ill,' said Diamond sharply. It was true. The nerve of him, talking to her about her mother after all he'd done. Frenchie had worked herself up into hysterics at the loss of the family club – and the thought of one of the Butchers tying himself to a Wolfe was beyond her. She'd had to go back to bed, coughing piteously and crying buckets.

'She'd better get used to the idea. Christ knows, *I've* had to.'

'I told you. She's ill.'

'Yeah and I'm a Dutchman.' As the crowds gathered in the church porch, blocking their progress, practically drowning the bride and groom with confetti, he flashed her a sideways grin. 'Nicked any good jewellery lately?'

'I'm not a thief,' said Diamond stonily.

'Well that's a lie. You're a thief from a *family* of thieves. Gwendoline must have taken leave of her bloody senses.'

'Victor has, certainly,' snapped back Diamond.

'Well at least we can agree on *that*,' he said, and then the bottleneck cleared and they followed the couple outside into the sunshine.

At the lych gate, the carriage waited, pulled by two pristine beribboned greys. Diamond quickly got some distance between her and Toro, taking her brother Owen's hand and leading him over to where the carriage horses stood patiently waiting, swishing their tails.

Aiden was eyeing up Toro and looking mean-eyed. Diamond hoped and prayed there wouldn't be any trouble. Aiden had always been feisty but now he was getting bolder by the day and she didn't think much of his chances if he decided to have a go at Toro.

'Look, Owen. Aren't they lovely?'

Owen was smoothing his hand down over the nearest horse's muzzle. 'Nice,' he smiled.

'Have a care, eh? He tends to bite,' said the coachman.

Like Toro Wolfe, thought Diamond angrily. The bollocks on that bastard, saying all that to her!

'What a fucking to-do, eh?' said Aiden, striding up to Diamond.

The head of the Butcher family, tied to a Wolfe. It didn't seem possible.

Now they just had the reception to get through, and then – thank God! – they could all bugger off back home.

34

After the cutting of the cake, the best man went missing and shouts and yells from outside the hall let them all know that Aiden Butcher had taken his grudge against Toro Wolfe outside.

'You burned down our fucking club. What was that, a message? Were you saying if Victor was screwing your sister then you were going to screw us, the Butchers? You rotten bastard. That was my dad's club, you *knew* it was special to us.'

Aiden was putting himself in Toro's face, barging his chest up against Toro's, glaring nose to nose with him.

'I don't have a clue what you're talking about,' said Toro.

'Fucking *liar*,' said Aiden.

'Oi! Oi!' It was Victor in his wedding finery, surging through the crowds, putting a hand on Aiden's chest and shoving him back. 'Not today. Come on.'

'He burned down our *club*. And worse. He *knows* what they've done to us, his lot. And look at the tosser standing there grinning.'

Toro was staring into Aiden's eyes with an insolence that was as big an insult as a slap across the face.

Diamond, falling out of the hall along with a crowd of avid onlookers, stared in horror but was barged sideways by Gwendoline, who very delicately raised a forearm to her brow and folded neatly to the ground in a ladylike faint.

Instantly all Gwendoline's three other bridesmaids clustered around her with shrieks of distress, fanning her, fussing over her, while Diamond kept her attention fixed on the far more alarming spectacle of her brother Aiden shaping up to that bastard Wolfe. It was her dearest wish that Aiden could be a big enough man to flatten Wolfe, right now. But she knew he wasn't.

'Back away, Aiden,' said Victor, who didn't seem too concerned that his new bride had collapsed at his feet as he stood there keeping Aiden from getting the pasting of his life.

Diamond glanced at the downed bride and her fussing acolytes and saw Gwendoline's eyelids flicker open.

She's faking, thought Diamond.

But all Gwendoline's fakery was failing to work. There was a shout and then the sunlight flashed on a blade. It swooped up and down, slicing Toro's cheek open in a scarlet shower. Blood spattered everyone around them, including Diamond. Aiden drew back, the dripping knife still in his hand, and Victor grabbed his arm in anger.

'What the *fuck* . . .' he shouted.

Toro calmly took out a handkerchief and held it to his cheek. On the ground, his sister was stirring theatrically.

'Fuck's sake, Gwendoline, get up, will you?' he said. 'It's your wedding day. Make the most of it. I'm fucking off, right now. This is a complete bloody farce.'

And he brushed through the ogling crowds and the snarling Butcher clan, nearly knocking Diamond over as he swept past. Then he paused.

'You've got blood on your face,' he said, and lifted the handkerchief and swiped it roughly down her cheek.

Diamond stepped quickly back, away from him. And then he was gone.

The bridesmaids were helping Gwendoline back to her feet. Diamond didn't bother. Aiden, trembling with impotent rage, tucked the blade in his pocket and went back inside. Victor remembered his bride – at last – and gave her his arm and took her off to get a restorative glass of champagne. The couple knocked past Diamond, following the rest of the group back indoors now the excitement was over. Owen squinted around in confusion and took Diamond's hand.

'Not to worry, Owen,' she told him brightly, although her voice trembled, just a bit. The feel of Toro Wolfe's rough touch on her cheek had seemed to burn. 'Just the boys, fighting as usual.'

It reassured him. She led him indoors, wondering if things were going to be the same, ever again. But then – she knew the answer to that, all too well.

35

Home had never been much of a refuge for Diamond, but after the wedding it was like a prison and she was stuck inside it with a bully for an uncle, a sickly mother – and a new aunt whose sole purpose in life seemed to be dominating her and making her life a misery.

Frenchie didn't get up again. It was as if this union of the Butchers and the Wolfes had drained the last of the fight out of her. She stayed in the big French bed in her room and said really, she couldn't be bothered. After the wedding ceremony and the shambles of the reception, Victor took his new bride off to Southend for three days, leaving Aiden in charge of Butcher affairs. Diamond heard him telling Aiden sharply not to go anywhere near Toro Wolfe.

'Why?' demanded Aiden. He was bitterly angry about the wedding, furious at the Wolfes marrying into the Butcher clan, but what could he say? Victor always slapped him down.

'Because he'll slit your throat if you do. He won't forget what you did. He's our fucking in-law now, so go bloody steady, will you?'

Then the honeymoon was over and Victor was back, Gwendoline with him, breezy and confident, casting avaricious eyes over the furnishings, the ornaments, everything – and to Diamond's horror they moved Frenchie and all her belongings out of the master bedroom and into one of the smaller bedrooms which was north-facing and perpetually cold. They then had the decorators in and took over the lavishly refurbished master bedroom as a married couple.

It had never occurred to Diamond, not even in her worst nightmares, that Victor would live with his new wife in the Butcher family home. But it was confirmed when Gwendoline started getting trunks full of her clothes and belongings brought over and carried up the stairs by Wolfe employees, who staggered under the weight of it all.

It was shocking, to even have Gwendoline – and the Wolfe boys – in the building. The thought of her, staying here, being here *all the time*, put Diamond's teeth on edge and sent Frenchie into an even more severe decline.

But Frenchie withdrawing from the world meant that Gwendoline could assert herself more freely in the household, and she took the opportunity to do that straight away, grabbing at the opportunity.

Owen, not really understanding any of it, went out with Diamond to the park. He wanted to get Gwendoline a posy, welcome her into their home, he said. He picked a few tiny spring violets and a bunch of vivid yellow celandines, and brought them back to the house, presenting them to Gwendoline.

'Lovely,' she said, looking like she'd stepped in something nasty. She took the small posy of flowers from Owen and left them out on the wooden draining board in the scullery, where Diamond found them hours later, wilting. Sighing, she trimmed their stems and put them in a vase of water and took them through to the kitchen table where Owen was sketching.

'If you put the red and the blue crayons together, you can get the exact shade for the violets,' she told him, and left him there, happily scrawling a masterpiece.

There were more shocks to come.

Moira had been with the Butcher household ever since Diamond could remember, ever since Frenchie and Warren had become wealthy enough to pay for help. Domestic duties had never been high on Frenchie's list of priorities, and she'd nearly expired with relief when Moira took that burden off her. But now . . .

'We don't need a cleaner, Diamond,' said Gwendoline briskly. 'You can do it, we can't afford all that fuss and bother, can we?'

With tears and hugs, Moira, who had been with them for so long, who was almost *family*, said goodbye.

Diamond got up the nerve to speak to Victor about it. But he waved her away.

'Christ, you women! It's only a bit of bloody dusting,' he said, not having a clue as to what cleaning a house of this size, a sprawling place set out over three floors, involved. 'Gwen's right, you can do it.'

'Everyone under this roof has to earn their keep, after all,' said Gwendoline, who had never yet lifted so much as a well-manicured finger around the place. Diamond was enraged to see during Victor's Friday count-up that the cash that was usually set aside for Moira was instead being pocketed by Gwendoline.

'But that's . . .' Diamond started to say.

Victor's head shot round. He was on his knees by the safe, his hands working.

Click, click, click.

The tumblers turned and the safe door opened.

'Did I ask for your opinion?' he growled at Diamond.

Gwendoline sent her a triumphant smile, folded the notes and tucked them into her pocket.

Diamond backed away.

Gwendoline had hired in a cook, so at least Diamond wasn't expected to do that too. Then within a month, the girl who did the laundry got tired of being shouted at and ordered around by the new mistress of the house and departed in tears.

'Putting a few bits and pieces through the mangle, it's nothing,' said Gwendoline. 'Diamond can do that.'

Victor agreed with Gwendoline. So now Diamond was cleaner and laundrymaid, and to add to it all, Victor took delight in her lowered status and bullied her all the more. At least Frenchie was now free of Victor's pawing – that was Gwendoline's job. Frenchie seemed to be really failing now. Diamond would awake every morning to a queasy stab of fear. She would wash and dress and then spend many anxious hours sitting by her mother's bedside, encouraging her to eat when she wouldn't, listening to her coughing, chatting to her about Paris, trying to lift Frenchie's mood.

'Tell me about Montmartre again,' she would say, and Frenchie's eyes would brighten and she would talk about the village in the north of Paris, set high on a hill above the Seine. For a while, she would forget her woes. Then she would start about the Wolfe clan again.

'They will haunt me to my grave, the Wolfes,' she said bitterly. 'They chased Warren out of London. Then in Paris we had the six clubs. We were *rich.* Then they chased us out of Paris too and then when we came here they followed, determined to finish us. They still persecute us, they burn down our lovely club and move their cursed woman into our very own house! Ah *chérie*, how can I bear it?'

Frenchie's aggravation would then set her coughing, and Diamond would dose her with honey and lemon, which seemed to do no good at all. Diamond's hatred of the Wolfes grew by the day. They were the cause of her mother's illness getting worse, there was no doubt about that. Maybe Gwendoline getting Victor down the aisle was all part of their plan to crush the Butchers once and for all.

When she wasn't fretting over Frenchie, Diamond was doing the hoisting up west, or the badger trick, or she was out in the back yard beating the heavy carpets or indoors dusting the ornaments, or in the scullery boiling up the household linen – and it was there that one day she paused, a lacy handkerchief embroidered with a flowery F in hand. There was a spatter of blood on it. Feeling weak all of a sudden, Diamond slumped down on the upside-down tin bath in the corner of the yard.

She looked at the handkerchief again.

Oh God.

Her eyes filled with tears, her throat closed. She knew what it meant.

'What the fuck's wrong with you then?' asked Victor, ambling out into the yard toward the khazi, unbuttoning his fly as he went.

Diamond quickly pocketed the handkerchief. She swallowed. 'Nothing.'

'Oi! Gwendoline said why haven't you done the front bedroom yet,' said Victor with relish. He loved seeing her forced to skivvy.

Diamond stood up and barged past him, back into the house. Once there, she put on her coat and left, heading for the doctor's.

36

She was halfway along the road when Michael sauntered over.

'Wish you'd taken me up on the offer?' he asked her.

Diamond's head was spinning. Frenchie was ill, her whole life was shit, and he wanted to talk *business*?

'I can't do this now,' she said, and went to hurry on.

'It still stands. You with the hoisters, me with the Blades, it'll work.'

'Not now, Michael.'

Then Victor came into view.

'What's this then?' he asked the pair of them. 'Cooking up secrets, is it?'

'Maybe,' said Michael.

'No,' said Diamond firmly. The last thing she wanted today was more trouble. She went to walk on. Victor caught her arm.

'I reckon we've kicked this pup's mother out of the house in the nick of time,' he said, smirking at Michael. 'Never did like the cut of him.'

'It's mutual,' said Michael, very cool, his eyes hard as granite.

'Yeah? I'm quaking in my bloody boots. You little *arsehole.*'

Saying that, Victor turned and walked away.

'One day,' said Michael consideringly, watching Victor go, 'I am going to slit that bastard open like a hog.'

'I have to go,' said Diamond, and hurried on.

37

'How long has she been like this?' asked the doctor.

He was a big tweed-suited man of middle years, and he'd come at her insistence. He was standing over her mother in the big bedroom. Having placed his stethoscope on Frenchie's chest and listened acutely to her heart and lungs, he looked at Diamond, who was watching nervously. She didn't like the look of any of this. Her mother was pale and sweaty. And she'd lost *so much* weight.

'She's been coughing for a long time. Two years perhaps,' she said. 'But it's got worse.'

'Fetch me hot water and a towel.'

When she returned, Frenchie's eyes were closed. The doctor handed Diamond a small brown bottle.

'She needs to rest. I'll give you this laudanum. She's to take three drops in water, twice a day.'

'All right.' He was washing his hands. 'What's wrong with her?' asked Diamond.

'Consumption,' he said briskly. 'Nothing to be done except to keep her comfortable, I'm afraid.'

The words were arrows, fired point-blank into Diamond's heart. When he was paid and gone, Diamond sat at Frenchie's bedside, staring down at her mother, once so vibrant and beautiful, now reduced to a small sweat-stained wreck. She was unable to cry, much as she wanted to. She stayed there for a long time, listening to Frenchie's tortured breathing. Then she rose and would have left, but Frenchie's thin hand grabbed hers and held on. Her eyes flickered open.

'Consumption, he said.' She moistened her lips with her tongue.

Diamond wished that Mum hadn't heard that. But she had. It was a death sentence, and not a nice one.

'He's given me medicine for you,' said Diamond, showing her the bottle.

Frenchie stared hard at it. 'Laudanum?'

'Yes.' Diamond went to the jug, fetched water, let three droplets of the stuff fall into a glass and added the water to it.

She helped Frenchie sit up and drink. Then Frenchie fell back on the pillows as if even this simple act had exhausted her. Diamond went to put the bottle in her pocket.

'No,' said Frenchie. 'Leave it on the bedside table with the water, so that if I need it, it's there.'

Diamond's eyes met her mother's. Words rose in her mind, words of warning. But this was *consumption.* If Frenchie wanted the laudanum, how could she say no? A terrible bone-deep sadness gripped her.

'It's all right, *chérie*,' said Frenchie softly. 'When I die I go to heaven and I shall be with your dear father.'

'Mum . . .' Now Diamond was crying. She couldn't hold back the tears.

'Shh,' said Frenchie, as if her daughter was the one to be soothed, not her. 'Now go. Let me sleep. I'll dream of Warren. And Paris . . .'

Diamond placed the small brown bottle on the table and left the room.

38

For Diamond, the day of Frenchie Butcher's funeral began with a fall. There had been a fair few falls, over the years. Little 'accidents', courtesy of Uncle Victor. Today, Diamond had been standing there at the top of the stairs, dreamily staring at the full-length portrait of her late mother, painted in Frenchie's heyday, when she had modelled in Paris for the artistic elite. Frenchie in all her glory at the height of the Belle Époque, Frenchie wearing a midnight-blue corseted gown with filmy chiffon shoulders and a plunging neckline, cobalt and purple feathers in her tumbling upswept glossy brown curls, her wide eyes teasing.

Now, on the day of Frenchie's funeral, her daughter stood there and admired it, shed a quiet tear over it, before turning, dressed in sober black, to descend the stairs and join the other mourners.

Then she fell.

Diamond went end over end and landed face-down on the hall carpet at the foot of the stairs. There was pain, several stunning impacts, an outrush of breath and then all at once she was lying there, staring at the Turkish carpet, wondering if she was *really* hurt. Gingerly, after a shocked moment or two, she started to sit up. Her shoulder was sore, and her back hurt, right between her shoulder blades. Otherwise, she was OK.

Diamond pulled herself to her feet. Straightened her dress. Glanced back at the stairs, back up at the portrait of her mother. Poor Mum, poor Frenchie. The laudanum had carried her off peacefully, before the consumption could tear its way through the last of her lungs, so that was a mercy. Now both Diamond's parents were gone and all she had left were her brothers. She felt tears fill her eyes and then blinked them back. No. She was *not* going to cry. Aching all over, she took a deep breath and crossed the hall and went into the front room, where all the mourners were assembled, awaiting the arrival of the hearse bearing her mother's coffin, ready for departure to St Anne's churchyard. Not two minutes after she did, Victor came into the room, closed the door behind him and shot her a gloating look.

'You all right, sis?' Aiden asked, spruced up in his Sunday best suit, concerned to see her looking so pale and shaken.

'I'm fine,' she said.

***

It was a long, long day. The service seemed endless. The rain poured, unstoppable, but still Diamond didn't cry. She knew the hand she'd had in Frenchie's death but she couldn't feel badly over it, not when Frenchie had been suffering so. She was gone now, all suffering over. And that was good.

Diamond stood at the sodden graveside with Aiden and Owen as the vicar wound it all up, throwing dirt on the coffin.

Back at the house, women had brought food and the drink flowed like water. Hour after hour, listening to platitudes, to 'she had a good life, didn't she?' Handing round sandwiches.

And smiling. Or trying to, while her sore, aching body protested every movement.

It had, after all, been a bad fall.

That evening, when Diamond could – at last – be alone in her room and then tiredly peel off her funeral clothes, she looked over her shoulder in the long cheval mirror and saw that between her shoulder blades the skin was starting to blacken with a massive bruise.

So – it hadn't been a fall. But then, she'd known that all along, really.

More of a *push.*

39

On the day after Mum's funeral, they were in the kitchen. Aiden was beside Diamond, Owen on the other side of the table. Gwendoline had gone out early. Breakfast had just been finished, Diamond had cleared the plates. Another damned day. Ahead, more hoisting, more badger tricks, more skivvying.

Then Victor leaned over and clouted Owen – who had been eating while staring at the paper open on the table beside him – around the head. Owen started to cry.

'Put that bloody paper away, thicko, and eat your breakfast like a normal person,' he'd said.

Diamond shoved her chair back, stood up and said it, almost consideringly: 'What a rotten piece of scum you really are.'

The expression of shock on Victor's face was almost comical.

Aiden shook his head sharply. *No, Diamond.*

Victor stared at her as if she'd suddenly grown two heads. 'You what?'

'You heard.'

'You cheeky cow.' Victor's chair scraped back and he came to his feet, towering, enraged, terrifying.

Aiden stood up too. 'Don't you lay a bloody finger on her,' he snapped out.

Victor levelled a finger at him. '*You* can shut the fuck up.' He charged without warning round the table and his fist collided with Aiden's cheek. Aiden reeled back. 'You both shut up or I'll knock your bloody heads together, the pair of you,' he roared. 'Christ knows what I've done to deserve you lot. I let you stay under my roof, I feed and clothe you, and what fucking thanks do I get? None, that's what.'

Aiden staggered but kept his feet.

'Let us stay? This is *our home*,' said Diamond. 'It isn't yours. You muscled your way in here after Dad died. You weren't asked. You just did it.'

'She's fucking right,' panted Aiden, clutching at his face.

'You *what*?' Now Victor was literally bellowing with rage.

Owen was cringing, crawling under the table to hide there, terrified by the shouting. Aiden, seeing Victor coming at him, ran into the scullery. Victor chased after him and Diamond followed, her blood singing with temper. The *bastard*! When she got there, Victor had Aiden over the sink and he was punching him. Aiden was half his size. Not thinking, not even intending to, Diamond picked up the flat iron from the top of the range and swung it at Victor's head.

The iron crunched against his temple and he keeled over sideways and lay on the floor, immobile, eyes shut.

Both Diamond and Aiden stood there and stared down at him in total shock.

'Oh Christ, I've killed him,' she moaned.

Aiden was mopping at his bleeding lip with his shirt cuff. He went down on his knees beside Victor. Blood was seeping out of a triangular wound on Victor's temple. Aiden put his face down close to Victor's.

'He's dead,' said Aiden, then Victor's brow came up and *smacked* into Aiden's. He fell back onto the scullery floor and

Victor came up too, dropping his full weight onto the smaller, younger man.

Diamond let out a panicky yell and struck again with the flat iron. Victor went down, and this time he stayed down.

'Christ Almighty,' said Aiden shakily.

'Is he dead now?' asked Diamond, barely daring to breathe.

Aiden moved over to Victor. This time, more carefully, he pressed his shaking fingers to Victor's throat. 'He's got a head like a fucking brick wall.' Aiden pressed harder. 'He's still breathing.'

'Oh God.' Diamond put down the flat iron with a shaking hand.

Victor had two big triangular cuts on his brow now; the blood had stained the lino.

There would be no going back from this.

'What the hell are we going to do?' she wailed.

She shouldn't have lost her temper like that. It was stupid. Self-destructive. But she was grief-stricken and then to see him laying into poor bloody Owen like that . . . she couldn't stand it, not for a moment longer. She could hear Owen crying still, out there in the kitchen. He was in his usual place of refuge, under the table where he felt safe. Poor bastard, he was terrified.

Aiden was staring down at his uncle with hate in his eyes. 'I saw him when we were young, you know,' said Aiden. 'Going into Mum's room with her. Forcing his way in.' He blinked, visibly upset. 'You got the slightest notion how I felt, knowing that Dad was gone and I was too young, too weak, to protect her from this bastard? I was just a kid.'

Despite her own fear and misery, Diamond's heart ached for him. For them all.

'You know what you should do?' he said.

Diamond shook her head. She felt sick and empty now that the rage had passed. Cleaned out and useless and staring into a bleak future. You *never* crossed Victor. Didn't she know that by now? When he came round, there'd be hell to pay.

'You should go,' said Aiden. 'I'll stay though. I'll look after Owen. Victor heard the rumours, you know. Some of his blokes have been talking.'

'What rumours?' asked Diamond.

'The ones about you maybe throwing in your lot with Michael and the Silver Blades. Taking all the hoisters with you.'

'I wasn't going to do that. I told Michael no.' That explained her 'fall' down the stairs, didn't it?

'Victor don't care about that. He'll be planning a pasting for you and Michael both. And *this* on top of *that*? He'll have it in for you ten times worse than he did before. You should go.'

'I can't! What about you? What about Owen?'

'Come on! Be serious. Owen's not right, you know he's not. Within a week he won't even notice you're not here.'

Though she hated the fact, she knew that Aiden was probably right. God, why had she done such a stupid thing? She'd crossed Victor – and that meant London wouldn't be safe for her, not any more. She thought bitterly of the Wolfe lot, who had caused all this, killed her dad and given Victor a toe-hold into the Butcher household. Damn them. *They* had brought this calamity down upon their heads.

'Diamond, you know it makes sense. You should do what Mum always said you should. Get out of it, once and for all.'

Diamond looked at her brother, wide-eyed. She knew he was right. That she had to leave.

'I'll go to Moira's,' she said.

'That won't be far enough,' said Aiden, shaking his head. 'You know damned well it won't.'

On leaden feet Diamond went through to the kitchen and got under the table with Owen, hugging him tight.

'Listen, Owen. I'm going away for a little while,' she told him. 'But Aiden is staying with you, he'll look after you. All right, lovey?'

He didn't understand. It was beyond him. But he was calmer now so she kissed his brow and left him there and went through to the parlour, Aiden following close behind her.

Click, click, click.

How often had she watched Victor open that safe and put money in, take money out? Too many to count. He'd never even bothered to conceal his actions because he believed her too scared of him ever to rebel.

Wrong, Victor.

She turned the dial just as he always had, six left, five right, three left – the safe swung open. Inside there were piles of money. Diamond grabbed a wedge of it and turned and looked at Aiden. She flung herself into his arms and hugged him tight. But he pushed her away and said: 'Hurry, Diamond. Just pack a few things. Quickly! And then go.'

40

Frenchie had already shown her the way. She had spent most of Diamond's adolescence regaling her with tales of Montmartre, of famous writers passing through, of the exotic friends she had made during her time there, of the artists she had posed for. She would stay with Moira for a while, sort out her passage, her tickets, all she needed to take with her. And then she would go.

Diamond planned and prepared.

'You sure you want to do this?' Michael asked her. 'The Blades will protect you if you stay. Get Aiden and Owen out of that rat hole and here to safety. We'll get set up, get the hoisters working, it'll be fine. You won't ever have to turn another trick.'

Diamond shook her head. 'No. I don't want to go on with the hoisting. It's best I go. But you'll keep an eye out for Aiden and Owen, won't you? Do that for me?'

Michael nodded. He'd do it.

She bought a train ticket, a boat ticket with a sleeping compartment, purchased a couple of new gowns then checked she had enough cash in the mound of money she had taken out of Victor's safe to pay for a hotel room for a few nights, in case things didn't go as planned. She posted a letter to Frenchie's oldest friend Madame Mimi Daniels, who lived in Paris in a flat opposite the Moulin Rouge. All the while she felt both excited beyond belief and frightened to death. She had never seen France, and now – at last – she was going to.

Then one day someone was banging at the front door. Moira peeped out of the window beside it and turned to Diamond. 'It's him!'

Diamond didn't even have to ask who. It was Victor of course. She had expected trouble and here it was, coming for her.

'What should I do?' asked Moira in a loud whisper.

'Don't answer it,' said Diamond. She bounded up the stairs two at a time, snatched up her bag, her money, her tickets – everything she had in the world. Then she went back down, and Victor was on the other side of the door howling: '*I know you got that bitch in there Moira McLean, you just open this bloody door and let me in!*'

Moira stared at her, wide-eyed. *Go*, she mouthed, and Diamond went down the hall, out through the scullery and into the back yard. She crossed to the gate and looked out into the alleyway beyond. One of the Victory Boys was down the end, heading away from her, talking to someone just round the corner.

Now or never.

Bracing herself, she nipped out of the gate and ran full-pelt in the other direction, until she reached the next road. Panting, expecting at any moment to feel Victor's heavy hand grabbing her coat and pulling her back, she slowed to a walk and then held up a hand to a passing hansom cab. The driver pulled his bay horse to a halt.

'Waterloo Station please,' she said, heart in mouth, and clambered inside.

PART TWO

41

The address her mother had given her for Mimi Daniels was in the Boulevard de Clichy on the Place Pigalle, on the border between the ninth and eighteenth arrondissements which spread out like a starfish from the central point of the Arc de Triomphe. Diamond alighted from the taxi, paid the driver in the French francs she'd purchased with pound notes from the post office back in London. The driver sped away.

The traffic was bad here – trams and smoke-chugging cars and teams of horses pulling carriages and wagons, all of them jostling for space. It was worse than Soho. Diamond lugged her suitcase onto a wide pavement, bumping into people and getting filthy looks. Everyone was coming and going at full speed. A shop selling tobacco, bonbons and magazines was right in front of her, and there was the door to Mimi Daniels' apartment, right beside it.

A petite blonde woman was sitting on a battered crocodile-skin suitcase right outside the little tabac shop, blocking the pavement and getting sworn at by passers-by. Every so often she would catch the eye of one or other of them and spit: '*Cochon!*'

Pig.

When she wasn't doing that, she was talking loudly and very fast to the shopkeeper, who was leaning out of his little kiosk at the front. The woman was waving her arms and the shopkeeper was waving his. Ignoring both, Diamond went to the door, selected the buzzer for flat 9A. Nothing happened. She rang the bell again, aware that the shopkeeper and the woman on the suitcase had both fallen silent and were now watching her as if she was some new and interesting addition to their own little debacle.

She rang again.

Nothing.

Diamond started to feel a twinge of panic. Had Mimi Daniels received her letter? Frenchie had always said, if you get stuck in Paris, you contact Mimi Daniels, 9A Boulevard de Clichy, and you won't go far wrong. Frenchie had always said that. Mimi Daniels was a dear old friend and a star in every way.

But what if the letter hadn't got here?

Aware that she now had an audience of two, she rang the bell again.

'Mam'selle?' said the woman perched on the suitcase.

Diamond rang the bell again.

'*Excusez-moi!* Mam'selle?' repeated the woman, louder.

Diamond turned, flustered, and looked at the woman. She was very elegant, dressed in luscious brown furs and a neat little hat that sat atop her dyed-blonde curls. At first glance, you would place her in her thirties, but on closer inspection Diamond realised that the woman was nearer to fifty. Her eyes were a startlingly bright blue, but there were crow's feet at their corners, and her vividly pink-lipsticked mouth, kissable though it undoubtedly was, had lines radiating out above it.

'Who are you knocking for?' the woman said in perfect, unaccented English. 'Are you trying 9A?' she asked, standing up.

Diamond eyed her steadily. The woman was *tiny*. Five feet nothing despite wearing toweringly high heels. 'Yes,' said Diamond. 'I'm looking for Mimi Daniels.'

The shopkeeper let out a loud honk of laughter.

The woman scowled at him. Then she turned to Diamond. 'And who are you?' she asked.

'I'm Diamond Butcher. Mimi is an old friend of my mother's.'

The woman said nothing. She was staring at Diamond's face.

'I wrote to Madame Daniels, telling her I was coming to stay,' Diamond went on desperately. 'And she's not in.'

'No, she's not,' said the shopkeeper. 'Because she's out here,' he said, then a customer entered his shop and he vanished into the interior, leaving Diamond staring at the tiny blonde woman, who stared right back her.

'I'm Frenchie's daughter. Are you . . .?' Diamond started.

'*Oui!* My God! You have a look of Frenchie about you,' said the woman. 'Just a bit. Around the lips. But your hair's different. And your eyes are not like hers at all. You say she's your mother?'

'She is.'

'And is she well?'

'She's . . . she's dead,' said Diamond, feeling tears start in her eyes. 'I wrote you a letter . . .'

Mimi's face froze. 'I didn't get any letter. Dead? Oh *chérie*, how tragic. My dear old friend . . .'

'And why are you out here . . .?'

'I've just been evicted,' said Mimi. Then she opened her arms wide. '*Ma pauvre petite!* Welcome to Paris, little one.'

42

It wasn't much of a welcome, all things considered. Diamond was trying to keep cheerful, but really! She'd landed here in this foreign country, ready to make a fresh start in life, thinking that she could count on her mother's old friend to help her settle in, to *house* her, in fact, and what did she find? Mimi didn't have a house. She didn't even have a roof over her head, not even a tiny flat in what Diamond was quickly coming to realise was a pretty dodgy area.

But then – she'd come from Soho, so she didn't think she was going to find it too shocking. Having summoned the shopkeeper back to his little front kiosk and conducted a quick conversation with him, Mimi slung her suitcase – and Diamond's – through the front door of the shop.

'For safekeeping,' she told Diamond, and then she was away, walking with tiny but very rapid steps around the other pedestrians, wafting clouds of lily of the valley perfume behind her. She dashed over the road. Horns started honking. She was slapping the hoods of cars, shouting out *Merde!* and waving a fist at a pair of big chestnut horses who whickered in alarm and backed up sharply, rearing up on their hind legs, bringing a volley of swear words from their coachman.

Diamond followed in Mimi's wake, trying to swallow her disappointment. She had expected to be fussed over, given tea, food, and to have her mother's friend gush with emotion over the sad loss of her mother. But there'd been none of that. Mimi didn't seem to be too concerned about her *own* predicament, much less Diamond's.

Up ahead was a curious-looking place, a complete oddity. There was a red windmill stuck up on the roof of what appeared to be a theatre, and now Mimi was shoving through the doors of it and into a shockingly lavish red-plush and gold interior. Mimi stomped across the foyer and through a set of doors and then through another – and then the music hit Diamond, hard as a steel ball fired from a catapult.

There was a long row of women up on the stage. They were wearing feathered headdresses, corsets and acres of frilled skirts and petticoats. The limelight beamed up at them, bleaching their faces to the whiteness of clowns. They were throwing their legs in the air while in the orchestra pit the conductor waved his arms and the violins and drums and trumpets went crazy.

Mimi stopped Diamond with a hand on her arm and they stood there between the rows of empty seats staring at the antics up on the stage. The girls whirled and skidded and did the splits and finally – when Diamond thought they must be flagging with exhaustion – they stopped, turned to the back of the stage. The music reached a hammering, triumphant crescendo and then they bent forward, tossed their skirts over their heads and let out a terrific '*WHOOP!*'

'Fuck me!' exclaimed Diamond in shock.

The dancers were still, stockings and garters revealed, a line of plump white thighs and – good God! – a line of naked arses revealed, too.

Mimi turned to Diamond with a grin. 'Shocking, no? It's the can-can. You ought to hear the gentlemen in the audience applaud when *that* happens.'

Diamond had heard of the can-can. Her mother had told her about it. She'd told her about the Moulin Rouge and said what a marvellous place it was. She hadn't told her the girls did *that.*

The girls straightened up, dropping their skirts back into place. They milled about the stage, all smiles, while down the front of the theatre a man stood up and applauded them, clapping loudly.

'*Magnifique!*' he shouted.

They curtsied and ran off. The orchestra started taking down music, packing away instruments.

'That's our cue,' said Mimi, and grabbing Diamond's arm she trotted down to where the man was standing, gathering up his jacket, picking up a big pad of paper and cramming pencils and charcoal into a worn tan leather case.

As they reached him, Diamond felt her heart literally stop in her chest. He was *stunning*. His colouring was so striking, almost luminous. He was red-haired and pale-skinned, his mouth a long straight uncompromising line, his eyes the cloudy slate-grey of an English winter sky. He was tall, broad-shouldered. He was as beautiful, she thought, amazed and transfixed, as any Botticelli angel.

'Fabien!' Mimi was hustling up to the man, tapping his arm, smiling flirtatiously. 'My darling, how are you?'

'Hello Mimi,' said the man, as lacking in enthusiasm as Mimi was full of it. He barely glanced at her, or at Diamond.

'Fabien, may I introduce to you my good friend?'

He had pad and case under his arm, ready to go, and he didn't like this interruption to his busy schedule, Diamond could see that. Overawed, she held out a hand.

'Hello,' she said. Her voice caught. She coughed and added: '*Bonjour.*'

'She'd make the most fabulous model for you, Fabien, don't you think? Look at that colouring!' Mimi gushed.

'I can't afford to pay another model,' said Fabien flatly, looking at Diamond's hand and pointedly not taking it. She dropped it to her side.

'We don't ask payment. Just a bed for a few nights, that's all.' Mimi's smile was incandescent. 'For the two of us, of course. I will be acting as my young friend's chaperone. I know what you artists are like!'

'And I know what women are like,' returned Fabien. 'They hustle their way in the door and then they're impossible to get rid of. I had all that with Madeleine. The answer's no.'

'But *look* at her, Fabien,' said Mimi. She grabbed Diamond's face and turned it, left then right. 'Look at that profile, isn't she superb? And that figure. My God, that *waist.* So tiny. What measurements do you have, darling?' she shot at Diamond.

Diamond told them. Her mother had always insisted she emphasise the neatness of her waist with a broad ribbon, tied very tight to accentuate it. And her breasts were ten inches more, like her hips. She reeled these facts off while Fabien stood there, looking unimpressed.

'Of course,' sniffed Mimi, 'I could always take her to Degas or Picasso, and they would steal a march on you, make her their muse – then you would be sorry but it would be too late.'

Now Fabien seemed to hesitate. He stared at Diamond's face. 'Degas wouldn't do her justice,' he said flatly. 'All he cares about is ballerinas. And that Cubist fool Picasso – what good would a girl like this be to him?'

'Of course! I agree! But you're leaving us with no choice, really. My poor Fabien, I know things have been difficult.

Things are changing so fast and I know you favour a more naturalistic style, which is fine, but this new breed do seem to be making their mark so I thought what you need is something *sensational.* And of course since that unfortunate business with Madeleine . . .'

Mimi let her voice tail away, let him take a moment to think what he might be losing. An exquisite model, and free! What could be better?

'It's all pearls before swine these days, in any case,' said Fabien, his mouth tightening in annoyance. 'Peasants don't understand genius. How could they?'

He was smoothing a hand over the reddish bristles on his chin and looking her over. *Such a beautiful chin*, thought Diamond. She felt overwhelmed. He was *so* good-looking, with that thick straight copper-red hair, which was so long that it was brushing his shoulders, and those brooding eyes that were such a captivatingly dark, thunderous grey, set very deep beneath a frowning brow. 'She'll work for a bed then? No money?'

'We are *both* part of the deal, that's non-negotiable,' said Mimi with a twinkling smile. 'I wouldn't trust her alone with you, you rogue.'

Diamond and the man stared at each other. She was tongue-tied by his beauty. She couldn't utter a word.

'What's your name?' he snapped out.

Mimi gave her a nudge. *Go on.*

'It's Diamond,' she said.

Mimi shot her an approving look. 'Diamond Dupree,' said Mimi, whipping an appropriately glamorous surname out of thin air. 'I tell you, you'd be doing yourself a favour if you'd only say yes, Fabien. This girl is going to be the toast of Paris, I promise you.'

He snorted. 'Kiki de Montparnasse has everyone calling her precisely that.'

'Diamond is more beautiful than Kiki could ever dream of being,' said Mimi.

Diamond kept her eyes down, aware that things were on a knife-edge. If he *didn't* accept Mimi's offer, what the hell were they going to do? She had a little money, but not enough to support her for any length of time. She would have to get a job. Skivvying again, no doubt about it. She thought she'd left all that behind, but clearly she hadn't. Her heart sank at the prospect.

'Where's she from then? She sounds English, like you. Is she? Why have I never seen her before?' he asked.

'She's from everywhere and nowhere,' said Mimi dreamily.

'Is she a whore?'

'Of course not!'

He was silent for a while. Then he said: 'She has a distinctive look, I'll grant you.'

'She does. Exquisite,' smiled Mimi. She arched a flirty brow at him. 'Bed, then? For the two of us? In the corner of your studio? We'll be no trouble. You won't regret it.'

'I'm starting to regret it already,' he said, sighing. He paused, then blew out his cheeks. 'All right then! Bed only. For a few nights, for the pair of you, and *she* sits for me. No money to change hands. And she sits eight hours a day if I require it and no bloody moaning about it either. All right?'

'Marvellous,' said Mimi.

43

Diamond was hot, tired and irritable. The choppy trip over on the steamer had made her feel sick. She felt she'd walked miles since this morning, when she had set off with such hope. Now, they were in Montmartre. Mum had told Diamond so much about this place, about the glamour and the beauty of it, this artists' quarter of Paris.

All she could see were hordes of people, people rushing everywhere, people sitting at sidewalk café tables smoking, drinking *café au lait* and eating macarons in rainbow colours. The sight of the cakes reminded her that she hadn't eaten since breakfast time, her stomach was growling. She was starving as well as exhausted.

Fabien stomped ahead of her and Mimi, so that they found it hard to keep up. Would the bastard never stop walking? But now they were in the Place du Calvaire and he was going to a doorway in a big block of grey-stoned and white-shuttered apartments. He inserted a key in a door, and at last they were hustling up a steep flight of stairs.

Finally they emerged into a big bright room that stank of oil paint. All around the edges of the room, canvases were stacked. Sunlight poured in from a bank of windows over to the right, where a pink chaise longue was positioned, a dirty grey blanket tossed across it. To the left there were easels and canvases, jars full of brushes, several messy-looking palettes, filthy rags and palette knives, stacks of dusty old books and periodicals, jars and tins of turps and varnish, a dust-covered old horned record player. All of it was flung out on chairs and trestle tables, which were set out here and there on the wide and seemingly unswept floorboards.

Across the room there was a small section, curtained off. Fabien went straight over to it and yanked the curtain back to reveal one double bed draped with a tangle of what was clearly unwashed linen.

'You can sleep here and I'll take the chaise,' he said to Mimi. 'Both of you, all right? And you can tidy up, Mimi, but never touch any of the canvases or I'll choke you and that's a promise.'

'I don't tidy. Or dust.'

'As you wish.'

'And no funny business,' sniffed Mimi. 'I want that understood, from the start.'

'What, with you? You're old enough to be my mother,' said Fabien cuttingly.

'I don't think you ever had a mother,' returned Mimi with a tight smile. 'I think they dug you straight out of the pits of hell.'

Diamond had dumped her suitcase inside the door and was now walking around, looking at the canvases. They looked like the work of a maniac, she thought. Hot swirls and slashes of colour and the same woman, painted over and over again in a variety of jumbled styles. She was golden-blonde, green-eyed. Glamorous.

'I see Madeleine's very much in evidence,' said Mimi.

Fabien didn't answer that. He put down his belongings and turned and looked at Diamond. Then his attention switched to the dusty and threadbare pink velvet chaise set out under the big bank of windows. 'I'll be comfortable enough on that. Look, there's laundry facilities downstairs, and a privy out the back. And now I have somewhere to be. I'll expect you to sit tomorrow, all right?'

Diamond nodded. He tossed Mimi two keys on a ring.

He was already crossing the room, getting ready to leave them to it.

Ignorant pig, thought Diamond. He might be the most exquisite man she had ever clapped eyes on, but manners cost nothing.

He slammed the door behind him and they heard him gallop off down the stairs.

'He is a bastard,' said Mimi. Then she smiled. 'But a legend in the making, of course. And we have a place to stay! Good, yes?'

'Yes,' said Diamond but she wasn't sure. Fabien might be handsome as an angel, but she didn't know what to make of him. And she had no idea what an artist's model actually had to do.

Mimi slapped her suitcase onto the crumpled bed, crossed the room quickly and said: 'Come and look, darling.'

Diamond followed her over to the windows.

'Look,' said Mimi. And there was Paris, flung out golden and heaving with life beneath them. Spring would be bursting into summer soon. They could see the Arc, away in the distance. And the big rose window of Notre Dame. And the Eiffel Tower, a steel finger pointing heavenwards. 'Beautiful, yes?'

'Yes,' said Diamond, and it was.

This was the thing that her mother had longed for all the time she had been in London. To return to Paris and see a view such as this. Diamond looked out on it and felt her eyes fill with tears. Frenchie had never made it home to this golden, glowing city. Aiden and Owen were back in London, far away. She missed Frenchie so much. She missed her brothers, felt her heart wrench in her chest when she thought of them back there alone, without her, coping with Gwendoline and Victor.

She looked at Mimi – her mother's old friend! But hadn't Frenchie once said something – no more than a hint – about a falling-out between them? She was sure she had.

'When my mother left Paris,' said Diamond, 'did you part on good terms, Mimi?'

'Of course we did!' Mimi's smile was radiantly sincere. 'I loved Frenchie and she loved me.' Then her smile vanished. 'It's so sad to think she's gone. That we will never meet again.' Mimi clasped Diamond's arm. 'But we will be friends too, yes? We will have fun together, you and I – yes?'

'Yes,' said Diamond, not entirely sure. Things seemed to move very fast around Mimi. Maybe *too* fast.

'Let's go and eat at Les Deux Magots,' said Mimi, brandishing the keys. 'I'm starving. Aren't you?'

'Yes,' said Diamond. She really was.

'You'll feel better after a croissant,' said Mimi. 'Now come on. Buck up! We have a bed, we also have a living if we're shrewd about it. Have you sat before?'

'Never.'

'It's easy. Now come on!'

44

'It means "the two figurines",' Mimi was telling Diamond when they were seated inside. Outside, it was raining, but in Les Deux Magots at 6 Place Saint-Germain-des-Prés there was a warm damp fug thick with Gitanes and the luscious scent of roasting coffee beans. A crowd of people were in, all chattering away nineteen to the dozen, drinking coffee and wine and eating pastries and reading the papers. 'There was a novelty shop on this site, years ago, and that's where they took the name from. Look, there's Hemingway. No *don't* stare.'

Hemingway was handsome, Diamond thought. And he looked alarmingly tough, with his thick dark hair and rugged features.

'Who is he?' she asked.

Mimi gave her a look of blank surprise. 'You're joking. He's *Ernest Hemingway.* He's a writer and trust me he is going to be *big*. He has this sharp, short style of writing, he calls it his iceberg theory. He's American.'

'Then why isn't he in America?'

'Prohibition, darling. Ernest likes to drink and the Yanks don't care for it right now.' Mimi smiled. 'I've seen Mark Twain in here too. And F. Scott Fitzgerald and that woman of his, Zelda. All the writers come in here. And the artists of course. All very new world, very avant-garde. Fabien doesn't paint that way, he's more of a traditionalist and perhaps that's partly his downfall, maybe he's just out of fashion.'

Diamond could see Fabien, over in a far corner. His eyes flickered over to her, then away. *Not interested*, the look said. Well, fuck him.

'Yes, you see him? He'll come round, don't fret. I've brought him Diamond Dupree, the toast of Paris.'

Suddenly Diamond felt very grateful to Mimi, who seemed to know this alien world so well, waving at people, blowing kisses. Mimi might be a bit over-active, but she was here at least, something solid to cling on to, and Diamond appreciated that.

'Are there any other artists in here?' asked Diamond. She didn't feel much like the toast of anything. She felt wrung out.

If she was going to be an artist's model, maybe there was someone altogether better than Fabien to model for? Someone *friendlier*? Granted, they would not have his impressive good looks, but they might be nicer.

'You see that chap over there with the blunt-looking face, the straight dark hair? That's Picasso. Now don't tell me you haven't heard of him.'

Diamond hadn't. She shook her head.

'Well, you will. Look, there's the designer woman, Chanel. *Très chic, non?*'

The woman was very long and thin, wearing ropes of pearls and one of the fashionable drop-waisted coats that were all the rage this year, a purple cloche hat pulled low over her short shingled hair.

The waiter came with their order. Diamond fell upon the pastries, starving. But when she next looked up, she saw that Mimi's exuberant mood had evaporated. The door had opened, admitting a sharp gust of damp cold air.

'*Merde*,' muttered Mimi as the man who'd entered came through the throng and stood right by their table.

He looked like a thug, Diamond thought. Scruffy, red-bearded, about forty years old, shabbily dressed with a tweed cap half covering his face. If you'd told her he was a tramp, she wouldn't have been surprised.

'Mimi,' he said roughly. 'I knew you'd be in here, among your artist cronies. When am I going to get my money?'

'Soon, Arnaud, all right?' Mimi huffed, waving a dismissive hand at him – but Diamond thought she looked nervous.

'Soon doesn't do me any good. What the fuck does that mean? You know, I ought to have chucked you out on your ear long before today,' he said. 'Too fucking soft-hearted, that's my trouble.'

'And now you have. Are you satisfied?'

'Not until I get my damned money I'm not. Three months' due you owe me, and I've had enough. Now I expect to get it.'

'And you will,' said Mimi more soothingly, her voice not quite steady. 'Soon, as I said. I have a new place to stay, and I'm earning, so be patient, all right?'

She was earning? Diamond heard that and found herself watching Mimi's face. Mimi had inveigled them into Fabien's place, but it was Diamond who would be doing the work as a life model – and she wasn't even being paid for it. Maybe Mimi had some other thing on the go, who knew?

'And who the fuck's this?' Arnaud asked, his eyes fastening on Diamond.

'This is my new discovery. She is going to be *big*.' Mimi gave a broad smile and announced: 'This is Diamond Dupree.'

'And who's earning then? Her? Because God knows you're too damned old to be an artist's model. You're starting to show your age, Mimi. Everything's slipping southwards. It's a shame, but it happens to us all, in the end.'

'I am not!' Mimi objected, and Diamond saw a flush of real irritation sweep up over Mimi's throat and face. Arnaud's comments had hurt, she could see that. 'Anyway, it's not me who's the sitter, it's Diamond. I am going to launch her on Paris and it won't know what's hit it. You think you've seen everything, you've seen Kiki de Montparnasse, but I'm telling you, *this* girl will leave the competition standing. *Look* at her.'

Diamond shrivelled in her seat as Arnaud's eyes crawled over her. Others at the neighbouring tables were turning, looking. A silence descended, all around them. She felt like a bug, pinned under a microscope. She wished then that she'd never come to this country, this foreign place, never swallowed the dream, the *illusion* that her mother had fed her. She wished she'd stayed in London and tried to make her own way there instead. But then – there was Victor, and he would want revenge for what she'd dared to do to him so that was out of the question. Much as she might miss Aiden and Owen, much as she might long to see them again, London was done for her – at least until things cooled down. Paris had always seemed so wonderful, a dream worth following, according to Frenchie. Now, she was not so sure.

'What, is she on the game too?' asked Arnaud.

Mimi glanced at Diamond and gave a merry – and forced – little laugh.

'On the *game*? I don't know what you mean,' said Mimi.

Diamond looked between the two of them. Good God – was *Mimi* on the game, a prostitute? But Frenchie had never mentioned that. No, surely she had slipped up on her French and misunderstood. That must be it.

'I'll give you until the end of the week,' said Arnaud to Mimi. 'Then I'm coming for my cash, and you'd better have it. Where are you staying?'

'That's none of your business,' said Mimi.

He reached down and grabbed her arm. Mimi let out a startled cry. Diamond shot to her feet, her eyes locked with Arnaud's.

'Let go of her,' she snapped. 'She said you'll get your bloody money and you will. So let go.'

Arnaud was grinning now. 'So the little kitten's got a bit of a bite,' he said. Men at some of the other tables were starting to get up, eyeing Arnaud. He released Mimi's arm with a contemptuous flick. 'Ah, don't bother. I'll find you. Don't worry about that.'

And he turned on his heel and left.

'Never have anything to do with that man,' said Mimi, rubbing her arm. She picked up her cup and sipped. Her hand, Diamond noted, was shaking. 'Now!' She pasted a smile back on her face. 'Come on. Drink your *café*, it's getting cold. And don't fret about Arnaud. He just can't help himself. He was born a bastard, and a bastard he will die.'

45

Diamond awoke next morning to two types of snoring. One, when she blinked open her eyes and saw daylight, was definitely Mimi, in the bed beside her, mouth open, emitting a dainty buzzing, like a miniature saw. The other was louder, obviously male, and coming from beyond the shelter of their little curtained alcove.

For a moment she imagined herself back in London, but then she remembered all that had happened yesterday. She was in Paris! She sat up, levered herself to her feet. Her suitcase was still beside the bed, yesterday's clothes draped over it. There were no wardrobes, where was she supposed to put her things?

There was a small sink over on Mimi's side of the bed, so Diamond edged around to it and turned on the tap. It emitted a gush of dirty-looking freezing cold water. Grimacing, she splashed her face with it, rinsing her mouth, shivering at the shock. Mimi dozed on and so, judging by the awful noise, did Fabien. Diamond went to her handbag – she'd slept with it under her pillow, for safety. She didn't know Fabien at all, and Mimi she only knew by her mother's recommendation.

She took out a brush and yanked it through her hair. Then she slipped on yesterday's dusty clothes and sat down on the bed and pulled out her purse. She counted her money and was relieved to find it was all still there. Hungry, she picked up Mimi's key, crossed quietly to the door and let herself out and down the stairs.

The sun was up. The light was somehow different to London, more golden than grey. Even the air smelled different, of cooked pastries and hot roasted coffee beans and the faint dank river scent of the Seine. People hurried by on broad pavements along cobbled streets, talking lower than Londoners, brief snatches of French drifting her way as she went to one of the pavement cafés and took a seat outside.

She sat there and thought of home, of sweet gentle Owen who would wonder where she was, and of Aiden. She'd had to leave them. She was worried most about Aiden, whose hair-trigger temper could so easily land him in trouble. Had Victor punished him for their outburst, made him pay? She hoped that Aiden had shown sense and kept out of Victor's way for a while, allowed him time to cool down.

'*Oui, mam'selle?*' The waiter was standing in front of her.

'*Un café s'il vous plaît,*' said Diamond. '*Et un croissant.*'

Diamond drank and ate while taking in the scene all around her. Then a shadow fell over her table.

'Oh, hello. It's the spitting kitten,' said Arnaud.

'Go away,' said Diamond. Her waiter passed close by and she raised a hand. '*L'addition, s'il vous plaît,*' she said quickly, and he brought the bill, put it on the table.

Diamond stood up, slapping francs down. She shoved past Arnaud, who was blocking her path. Close to, he smelled of tobacco and unwashed skin.

'What, so you won't even talk to me?' he said, grinning. 'I did good business with Mimi. Maybe I could do the same with you.'

What? Was this disgusting man offering to pimp for her?

'Mimi said not to speak to you,' snapped back Diamond. 'And I think she's a sound judge of character.'

'Yes, but the question is, are you? How well do you know Mimi?'

'Well enough.' Diamond was walking away, back to the flat, and he was following her.

'Not well enough, I'm afraid. That flat I let her stay in on the Place Pigalle, for God's sake. Such a little innocent you are. You remember I said that, mam'selle.'

Diamond stopped walking. 'I *said*, go away. Should I call for a gendarme?'

He shrugged, unconcerned. 'Call out the militia, if you like.'

Diamond reached the door up to the flat and fumbled with her key. She finally got it in the slot and dashed inside, slamming the door shut behind her. Gathering herself, aware that she was breathing much too hard, she trudged up the stairs, Arnaud's words still ringing in her ears.

46

Mimi went out at eleven o'clock next day.

'Shopping, darling,' she said. She flicked a look at Fabien, who was over by the window where the cold north light beamed in, working. He was dressed in a paint-spattered old smock and heavy rust-coloured cord trousers that matched his hair. He was adjusting his easel, setting out his paints and a freshly prepped canvas. 'You're going to be busy for a few hours, I'll go off and amuse myself, all right?'

Amuse yourself how? wondered Diamond. If she wasn't able to pay Arnaud, how could she go shopping? Mimi said she didn't have a franc to her name.

With Mimi gone and Fabien busy setting up for the day, Diamond strolled around the big room, taking the opportunity for the first time to properly look at the canvases propped against the walls.

The first thing she had to acknowledge was that there was no doubt about it: Fabien was gifted. There were charcoal sketches too, of children, of dogs, of old men, of bowls of fruit sketched so beautifully that you could almost taste them. This stuff definitely wasn't new wave, but it was exquisite. Mostly there were the canvases, some big, some *huge*, of this long-limbed golden girl with tumbling wheat-blonde curls, gooseberry-green eyes and bronze-toned skin. In some she was clothed, in others partly dressed, in others naked.

'Who is this?' Diamond tossed over her shoulder at him. 'This blonde girl, who is she?'

'Nobody you need concern yourself with,' he said sharply. 'Now. All right, I'm ready. There's a robe over there, put it on and we'll get started.'

The robe was a flimsy bit of red silk slung over a chair. Diamond went over, snatched it up, yanked it on over her dress.

'What are you doing?' asked Fabien.

Diamond stopped moving. 'You said put the robe on.'

He looked at her in exasperation. 'Well take your damned clothes off first.'

Diamond stood there, speechless.

'Well? Come on, hurry up.'

Diamond couldn't believe it. She thought of being forced to do the badger trick over and over again, promising but never delivering seduction to a deluded parade of men, slipping off items of clothing like Salome in front of John the Baptist. She thought she'd escaped all that. Now, what was going on? Was he playing games with her? Did he plan to assault her?

'I haven't sat for anyone before,' she said, feeling herself blushing, hating herself for it.

'Well there's a first time for everything.' He gave an impatient sigh. 'Go behind the fucking curtains there and get on with it, will you? We'll lose the light. What did Mimi say your name was? Diamond or something, wasn't it?'

Diamond felt temper build at the dismissiveness of his tone. 'I'm Diamond Dupree,' she said coldly.

'Ah yes.' He gave an ironic smile. 'And Mimi reckons you'll be the queen of Paris when my paintings go on sale. This is supposed to be the making of both of us, she reckons. And here you are, quivering with fright when you're supposed to be posing for a professional artist. It's hardly impressive.'

Diamond didn't say another word. She stalked over to the little alcove where she and Mimi had slept last night and swished the curtains around it closed. Angrily she tore off her clothes and put on the red robe. Instantly as the silk slid over her skin she felt cold. She drew back the curtain and stepped out. Fabien didn't even glance up, he was busy with the canvas. 'Sit down over there,' he said.

Diamond went over to the threadbare rose-pink chaise and sat down.

She waited.

Finally Fabien looked up. 'Take the bloody robe off for God's sake,' he snapped in exasperation.

Diamond took a breath. Then she shrugged off the robe and tossed it aside.

***

Fabien took up a fresh piece of charcoal and was ready to start work. As he did so, he looked over at the girl on the chaise longue and for the first time he actually *saw* her. A dark tumbling unfashionable mass of black hair. Big slanted eyes of the most extraordinary violet blue set under straight black brows. A broad pouting mouth. Skin pale as milk and the body of a fallen angel. Full pink-nippled breasts, a tiny waist, wide hips, beautifully proportioned and shapely legs. Diamond Dupree looked like something out of her time. She wasn't like the newly fashionable boyish flappers in their skinny drop-waisted dresses with their short shingled hair. She was like something from the turn of the century, la Belle Époque. She was lush. Full of erotic promise.

'Am I all right like this? At this angle?' she asked him.

Fabien had to clear his throat before he could reply. If Diamond was out of *her* time, maybe he was also out of his. He knew it was all Cubism and Pablo's stuff right now. Not his style at all. There was poor Munnings over the water in England, suffering from exactly the same problem. He – like Fabien – was a fabulous painter, but too old-school to satisfy the new post-war fashions in art.

'Perfect,' he said, and started to get this vision down on canvas before he gave in to the urge to behave in a most unprofessional manner. He'd made that mistake before, with Madeleine, and he wasn't going to do it again. He promised himself that. He put Nellie Melba on the record player, wound it up, dropped the needle in place. Then, he started work.

47

Sitting for Fabien was easy, although it was clear to Diamond that the rush of her move to France hadn't entirely agreed with her. She felt sluggish, and sometimes nauseous too. She missed Aiden very badly, and sweet Owen. But this was her life now and she had to accept it. As the weeks went by, Diamond passed through cringing embarrassment to mild self-consciousness and finally she reached the sunny uplands of feeling comfortable with her own body. Fabien painted her lying, sitting, standing up, smiling, frowning, sleeping, turning out canvas after canvas. Gradually it seemed to Diamond that the mystery golden girl with the green eyes was disappearing from the studio, new canvases of her own image being placed in front of them. Soon Fabien's studio was stacked with images of Diamond Dupree instead.

Day after day, he painted while she sat. And he slowly began to talk to her, to ask about her life, while he worked.

'So you're English,' he said, glancing from her to the canvas he was working on, then back at her. You never stopped looking, that was the trick to being a great artist, Fabien said. Paint the reality in front of you; never embellish. 'From where?'

'London,' she said.

'And what did you do, in London?' His eyes flickering to her, to the canvas, to her again, while the brush in his hand moved, deftly applying the paint.

'Nothing very much,' she shrugged. 'Let Me Call You Sweetheart' was being warbled out of the record player by a female singer, she didn't know who.

'Come on. Something, surely?'

'I was a hoister.'

'A what?'

'A hoister. We robbed shops. Are you shocked?'

Fabien half smiled at that and she thought again how beautiful he was, like a bronze angel.

'Not especially. We've all done things for money we wish we hadn't, I suppose. Tell me what else you did in London. Anything more shocking than that?'

'Much more,' said Diamond.

'Turn that shoulder just a little, yes? Right. So what then? What's this shocking thing you have to tell me?'

'I worked the badger trick with my uncle.'

Fabien paused, frowned at her. 'And what is that, exactly?'

'It's deceiving gullible men and taking money off them,' she said. She couldn't even say it without a sense of shame washing over her. But sitting for Fabien felt almost like the confessional with a priest. Anything could be said in here, and it was soothing to talk.

'So what you're telling me is that you were a whore?'

'No. Not that. Although it came close,' she admitted, thinking of the blond man, the mysterious *RB*, who'd foiled Victor and stolen her virginity away.

Fabien paused in his painting. 'You look sad when you say that.'

'It's not something I'm proud of.'

'You have family there then? This uncle you speak of?'

'Yes, I have family. Although I don't count him as part of it.'

'Brothers then? Parents? Sisters?'

'Two brothers.' Diamond felt her eyes fill with tears as she thought of them. Maybe she should have written to them. Taken the risk and kept in touch. But she'd felt nervous of alerting Victor to her whereabouts. She would go back, one day, and see them again. See Moira too, and Michael with his Silver Blades. She promised herself that. She blinked the tears away. 'And you? Do you have family in Paris?'

'God no. I'm from Arles down in the sunny south. Don't fidget. I miss it. Paris is dull and rainy.'

'So why come here?'

'To make my name.' He glared at her. 'I'm a fucking genius, in case you hadn't noticed. I need recognition. I need the art world and the whole world in general to acknowledge me. Fuck these Surrealists. *This*, what I do, is true art.'

God, he was arrogant! But he was also magnificent and in that split-second she felt something shift in her, a fluttering hunger that was like desire. Or maybe love. She'd felt it right from the first moment they'd met and she felt it again now, only stronger.

'Who is the blonde girl, the one with the green eyes?'

'That's Madeleine,' he said, and suddenly he was all business again, the shutters were down. 'Now shut the fuck up and sit still, will you?'

Diamond was remembering Arnaud's words to her outside the café. 'What's so special about the Place Pigalle?' she asked.

'Special? Nothing really. The Rouge is there of course, the place where Mimi introduced us, with the windmill. It's a red light district, do you know what that means?'

'I've lived in Soho. I'm not stupid.'

'That's yet to be proved,' he said.

Sometimes Diamond ached from sitting so long, but she didn't complain. It was obvious that Fabien was a genius and it was an honour to be a part of his life. Sometimes he forgot to eat altogether, but occasionally he remembered, and took her down to Les Deux Magots where they sat with legends like Picasso, Jean Cocteau, Cole Porter, all of them chatting, eating.

She was starting to love this new, uncharted life. Mimi was always flittering around in the background and always seemed to have plenty of money these days. Diamond was now pretty sure that Arnaud was telling the truth – Mimi *was* on the game, even if he wasn't her pimp any more. And would Frenchie really have been close friends with a whore?

Mostly it was just her and Fabien in the studio, and she watched him in unashamed fascination. The cold bluish north light in the studio sparked his auburn hair to flame-gold, his dark grey eyes were so intense as they roamed over her body. And she found that it was an erotic experience, being naked in his presence. Erotic for her, at any rate; *he* didn't seem affected at all.

***

While he painted and Diamond posed, Mimi went out about in the town. Sometimes, when Fabien could spare her – which wasn't often – Diamond went out too, shopping on the Rue de la Paix, looking in the boutiques at the dresses, staring in the windows of Cartier and seeing real diamonds twinkling under the lights, their rainbow hues shimmering back at her, out of her reach.

'Chanel's no good for you. That's not for Diamond,' Mimi told her.

'And how does Diamond dress, if Chanel's no good for her – not that she could afford it, anyway?' asked Diamond, amused.

'Like a queen,' said Mimi. 'Like she rules the city. Which she will. Soon.'

'What, after Fabien's exhibition?' Diamond had to laugh. Fabien's agent had secured a gallery near the Quai du Louvre to relaunch him upon Paris in the proper manner. The police had been over there checking security for the launch. Fabien had taken Diamond over there to see the place, and introduced her to a weird little detective inspector called Benoit and his handsome young sidekick, detective sergeant Golon.

'Yes, after that. *Then* everyone will know what's what.'

While they were shopping, Diamond couldn't fail to notice that Mimi's purse seemed to be bulging with notes.

'Have you paid him yet?' she asked.

'Who, darling?'

'Arnaud. Have you?' *And where did all this money come from, if you couldn't afford to pay Arnaud so he kicked you out?* Diamond was worried about this. Her own funds were dwindling, and that was a worry too. She told Fabien about it, and to her relief he agreed to start paying her now – not much, but enough to keep body and soul together.

Mimi blew out her cheeks but didn't answer. It was a 'no'.

'You really should,' said Diamond.

'Oh, for why?' Mimi was smiling. 'What a terribly law-abiding thing you are. So unlike your mother.'

Diamond frowned at her. 'I'm only saying that you should pay him because he looks like trouble, and you don't want that. And what do you mean about my mother? What are you saying?'

'Just that the Frenchie I knew had few quibbles about stretching the letter of the law.'

'Meaning?' demanded Diamond.

Mimi shrugged. 'Oh come, *chérie*, you can't be unaware . . .' Then her eyes widened. 'You don't know what Frenchie did for a living, before she met your father? Really?'

'She sat for artists.'

'Oh yes. Now and again, she did. But mostly I am afraid that your mother made a long and lucrative career on her back, before she met Warren. She worked in the brothels around Paris. Really it's as well that she got out of it when she did. God forbid she should have ended up in one of those gutter concerns with the slaughterhouse pimps and their brutal regimes. I've heard horror stories about those places, where the bell is rung every fifteen minutes and the girls are not permitted to even get off the bed between customers.'

Diamond's jaw dropped in horror. She hadn't known any of this. She hadn't known her own mother at all.

'Is that what you do now? Is that where your money comes from? From whoring?' she asked. A sudden realisation struck her. 'Mimi – is Arnaud your pimp? Is that it?'

But Mimi only tapped her nose and smiled.

Diamond let the subject go. She had just enough cash to trawl the boutiques hopefully and finger expensive straight drop-waisted dresses and to try on a few. But Mimi was right. They didn't suit her.

'You have an hour-glass figure,' said Mimi. 'You have breasts and hips. You'd look bulky in these things, they're no good. And cloche hats! Darling, they might suit me, but certainly not you.'

Diamond felt deflated. She was staggered by the news of Frenchie's past, wondering what was real and what was fake now when her own mother had lied to her all her life.

'What you don't want is anything by Chanel,' Mimi said. 'The "*garconne*" look is going to do you no favours. You want something with corsets. Something *structured*, to show off your curves, not hide them. What we need is an old-fashioned dressmaker, and I can find you one. She could have something suitable ready in time for your big night.'

'I can't afford a proper dressmaker,' objected Diamond.

'I'll pay. You can pay me back, later.'

They went to the dressmaker, a tiny wrinkled woman called Madame Delphine who lived in a high garret by the Seine, surrounded by bolts of fabric, a pile of adjustable dressmaker's dummies and a row of old dust-covered treadle sewing machines. She stalked around Diamond, frowned, sucked her teeth and said: 'Difficult.'

'Difficult or not, it's got to be done,' said Mimi.

'Not a fashionable figure,' remarked Madame.

'No. We realise that.'

'Colours?'

'Red. White. Or black. Maximum impact. I am thinking . . . theatrical. Spangles. Sequins.'

'Velvet?'

'Perfect.'

Madame Delphine applied her measuring tape to Diamond and started jotting down figures in a small notebook. Then she said: 'Give me a week and I'll have something for you.'

'*Merci*,' said Diamond.

Diamond followed Mimi out into the sunlit street, thinking that Madame Delphine hardly looked like she had the strength to stand up, much less produce a stunning gown for her to wear in time for Fabien's exhibition.

'She's a miracle worker,' Mimi told Diamond as they strolled off to find a café. 'You'll be amazed.'

There was a lot that amazed Diamond now. That revelation about Frenchie. She was still reeling with shock – her mother had never once even alluded to being a whore in the past. Well, of course not. Why on earth – *how* on earth – would a mother tell her daughter such a thing?

One thing she was certain of – Mimi was definitely still employed in the oldest profession in the world. Diamond often caught her out on street corners, chatting and flirting with different men – and these clothes of Diamond's from Madame Delphine's were going to cost a fortune, and how the hell could Mimi foot the bill for them, if she was not earning on a grand scale?

Sometimes, when Mimi had had a drink or two and spoke about the old days and about Frenchie Butcher, there was a strange edge of bitterness to her words, which made Diamond wonder. Had Mimi and Frenchie really been as 'close' as Mimi claimed they were?

48

A week later, they were back in Madame Delphine's tiny garret. Behind a curtain, Madame helped Diamond into a ferocious-looking corset, pulling the laces tight so that her small waist was accentuated. Then, gasping for breath, she slipped on a lush red velvet gown, very low at the black-lace-edged décolletage and puffed out on the sleeves. Madame fastened it, turning Diamond around before the mirror with her bony hands like claws on Diamond's shoulders.

'Needs a bit off there,' Madame noted, brushing her hands over Diamond dispassionately. 'A bit here, too. *Oui, c'est bien.*'

Madame swished back the curtain and let Diamond step out into the little room where she worked. Mimi rose to her feet and stared.

'How does it look?' asked Diamond. 'What do you think?'

'Hold your hair up.'

Diamond did.

'Earrings. And bracelets. Paste will do, it doesn't matter so long as it glitters. A lot of it,' said Mimi. 'And rouge on your lips to match the colour of the dress.'

Madame's wrinkled little wizened-apple face was split in a grin. 'Good, eh?' she said.

'*Marvelleuse, madame*,' said Mimi.

Diamond looked in the mirror. Suddenly she saw not herself but her mother there, saw how much she resembled her.

She felt emotional tears start in her eyes. Frenchie was gone forever. But she, Diamond, was still here. She shook her head in wonder. Would Fabien be so indifferent to her charms, if he saw her wearing this dress?

'*Magnifique*,' she said, and kissed Madame on both cheeks.

49

Fabien was painting Diamond, day in day out, but he was also ignoring her. Diamond had felt at first annoyed and then insulted by Fabien's physical indifference. He would finish another canvas, prop it against the wall, invite her to come and see.

'Your eyes are beautiful in this one,' he would say. Or: 'Look at the curve of your hip there. Exquisite.'

Diamond had never felt the urge to seduce a man before, but she felt it now. All that stuff she'd done while working the badger trick, that was all fake, unreal. *This* was the genuine thing, what she felt now. It tormented her, his coolness, when she was hot for him, ready for anything. She thought that she was beginning to understand true passion now, true love. She knew what had made her mother mad for her father. What had broken Frenchie's heart when he died. A heady recklessness was infecting her, making her bolder than she had ever been before.

Usually, during their breaks, she would walk around the studio with the red robe on, make tea, stretch her aching limbs. But now she decided that this called for action. She wanted him, arrogant bastard and merciless slave driver that he was. She was in love with him. And he *had* to be made to see that she was a woman, ripe for the taking, and not just an object he painted and refused to touch because of whatever had happened with that mad bitch Madeleine.

So she started leaving the robe off. Boldly she would saunter around the studio completely unclothed. Occasionally Mimi would come back and exclaim in surprise so that Diamond had to quickly snatch up the robe and put it back on.

'What are you playing at, little one?' Mimi would ask when they were alone. 'No, don't answer that. He's a handsome man and very virile by all accounts. Of course you're interested.'

'Yes – but he doesn't seem interested at all.'

'Oh, with a little gentle encouragement, I think he might be. He's being very restrained at the moment because of the trouble he had with *her*, but I tell you, there's a tiger lurking beneath that cool exterior.'

Diamond remembered her old life back in London, the day her Uncle Victor had married into the Wolfe clan; that young bridesmaid's louche remark about whores rouging their nipples. Discreetly, she started doing the same.

Mimi kept out of the studio now, most days. Diamond didn't know where she went or what she did, and really she didn't care. The whole focus of her attention was Fabien. Naked, rouged, her cloud of dark hair tumbling lushly down the curve of her back, she strolled around his studio, or stood at his side discussing the current painting, his arm a whisper away from the full globe of her breast. She could feel her nipples harden wantonly at such close proximity.

She was in love with him, desperate for him, why couldn't he see that? She kept her eyes on the painting and on his arm as it moved, lightly furred with bronze-coloured hair, the muscles lean and pronounced. She thought of his cock and wondered if there was bronze hair there too, a lush bed of it to cushion his manhood. The thought made her ache with desire. She was *obsessed.* And he *was* a genius. He made her look more beautiful, more other-worldly, than she had ever imagined she could. She would give herself to him, without a single solitary care.

But still – Fabien didn't take the hint.

50

Gwendoline was beginning to wonder if marriage to Victor had really been such a good idea. Before their wedding he had been such a gentleman, so considerate. But since marrying him she had discovered that he had these *rages.* He had been the perfect bridegroom, but now as a husband he just seemed so *angry* all the time.

Back in the early days there had been gifts – little trinkets and sweeties, hot house flowers, new dresses, cosy winter coats edged thickly with mink at the collar and cuffs, and she had thought *he's wonderful.* She'd hardly had a proper father, ever – or a brother, come to that; you couldn't count Toro as a brother – and it had been so nice, she thought, to have an older, more experienced and frankly rather *fearsome* man as her husband. It had been nice to have the head man of the Victory Boys.

Now, she was not so sure. When he stayed out late, or when he sometimes didn't come home at all for days, of course she would ask where he'd been. Victor never told her. But she heard from his female 'hoisters', who were always bitching about Diamond going missing and were very happy to see Gwendoline angry and disappointed, that he had a girl in Chinatown.

Gwendoline refused to believe it. And then *she* turned up one night in Victor's pub the Bombardier. She asked around and found out her name. It was Lily Wong, with her exotic Asian looks and her long bolt of silken black hair. Right in front of his *wife*, the woman flirted with Victor, told him that her honourable father was keen to meet with him so that they could discuss transportation of some valuable merchandise. Gwendoline had heard of the Triads, she wasn't a complete fool, and she wondered if Victor knew what he was getting into.

Infuriated by Lily Wong crawling all over Victor, she tackled him about it. And . . . *he hit her.*

She'd never been hit in her life before.

She had expected to be treated like a queen, and instead, increasingly, with Diamond gone and that surly creature Aiden and that idiot Owen hanging about the place, she found that she was very soon acting the skivvy.

Gwendoline didn't like the way things were going.

Every time she tackled Victor about *anything*, he responded with violence.

If she ran – and she was beginning to think of that – where would she go? Back to Toro, beg him for help? She couldn't stand the idea of that. Toro had never liked her: she would be humiliated.

So she was stuck – trapped.

51

When they picked up the dress, Diamond nearly fainted at the price. But she knew it would be worth it.

She passed the days before the exhibition in the studio, frequently nude, longing for Fabien, forever denied that pleasure because he saw her as something untouchable, like a statue that you might break if you weren't very careful with it. So she decided to be bolder still.

'This arm,' she said one day as she stood naked beside him in the studio. 'Is that right, do you think?' She pointed to the canvas. 'Here, is that correct?' And she took hold of his hand and ran it, very slowly, the whole length of her arm, from wrist to shoulder.

'Of course it's correct. It's perfect,' he said.

She heard him swallow, clear his throat.

'And this,' she said, indicating the left breast on the painting. She took his hand from her shoulder and placed it so that it cupped her breast. He seemed to become very still. 'Look, is that right? I think my breasts are a little fuller than that, don't you think? And my nipples are larger. And pinker. And . . .' She could hear his breathing accelerating. It gave her a heady feeling of power and happiness. He *wasn't* indifferent, after all. 'Here, just look. My hip. And here . . .' She moved his hand down, further. A slow, erotic journey that ended when it cupped her mound of Venus, that triangle of black hair that concealed untold pleasures. 'Fabien? What do you think?'

Fabien said nothing.

I've gone too far, she thought, suddenly anxious.

Then he put down his brush and turned toward her. His face was flushed. His hand moved up, over the indentation of her waist. It reached her tender, hard-nippled breast, caressed it. 'Diamond?' he said.

'Yes?' Her heart was racing. 'What is it, Fabien?'

'I want to fuck you,' he said, and then his mouth was on hers and it was wonderful, she'd won at last. 'I want to and I shouldn't.'

'Why not?' she gasped. God, he was going to back away. She couldn't bear it.

'Because this self-same thing happened with Madeleine, and it ruined everything. She was my muse, just as you are now, and I tired of her. It broke the spell. Things got . . . difficult.'

'They won't get difficult with me,' said Diamond. 'Fabien – I love you. I've worshipped you ever since we first met. You're a genius. You can do whatever you want with me. Anything.'

He was silent, his clothed body pressed tight against the front of her nakedness. She could feel his excitement, quivering all through his frame, could feel the hard jut of his arousal. She'd never experienced anything like this, never in her entire life. This was love.

'You want this,' she murmured against his mouth. 'And I want it too, so how can that be wrong?'

He gave in, right then. Lifted her up in his arms and took her over to the bed behind the curtain, lay her down on it and then very quickly shed his clothes.

'You're the most beautiful man I've ever seen,' she said when he was naked. He lay down beside her, stroked his hands over her body. He *was* beautiful. She caressed his chest, stroked her hands down over his hips, drank in the sight of his erect cock springing out lustily from its bed of red curls.

'I've wanted to do this ever since we first met,' he growled against her throat.

'Then why didn't you? I thought you didn't care for me.'

'I was just thinking it would be a bad idea, that's all.'

Diamond lay back. 'What if Mimi comes back?' she teased.

'Then she'll get a shock,' he grinned, uncaring now.

Triumphant, Diamond linked her arms around his neck.

'I'm sorry – this is going to be quick,' he said, and got between her legs and pushed home straight away, filling her just as she wanted to be filled.

It *was* quick. Too quick. He bucked and panted, thrusting very hard, very urgently, and pulled out of her and came while Diamond watched him in fascination. Her first real lover – she hoped her only one. Of course she had to watch him, to witness the weird mechanics of the male orgasm. The thing seemed to rule him for long seconds, his hand desperate, frantic; the spurting of his seed caused his face to crease up as if in anguish. Then Fabien flopped back beside her on the bed, covering his eyes with a fist.

'*Jesus*, that was good,' he moaned.

For her, it was not good but it was perfectly all right. She'd wanted him and this was what it was. Still, she was full of longing, aching with some unknown need. She cuddled up close to him, her hand tangling into the mat of golden hair on his well-muscled chest. He was so beautiful. If she'd had the slightest talent, *she* would have painted *him*.

'I'll be slower next time. It's just that I've been thinking about this – us – for too long. And you've been teasing me, haven't you? Walking around naked. Standing too close to me.'

It almost sounded like an accusation. Diamond propped herself up on one elbow and perused the entire length of his body. *So* gorgeous. She touched a hand to his penis, and unexpectedly it leaped, twitching like an eager animal, ready to start again.

'So soon?' she murmured, kissing his lips.

'I've been mad for you,' he whispered.

It was exactly what she wanted to hear.

'This time, I'll take charge,' she said, and pulled herself up and knelt over him.

She straddled him as he grew once again, then carefully she eased the tip of his cock inside her while he kneaded her very tender breasts with his hands. His grip was almost painful, such was his desperation. She moved down, trapping him, taking him fully inside her where she was wet, open, so ready for him. He groaned, straining upward. Then she raised herself up again, then down, then up, in a hypnotic rhythm. Pleasure seemed to build and build and build as she moved, then Fabien cried out and his grip on her breasts grew painful. He was pushing her off now and Diamond didn't resist. Instead, fascinated, she watched his nipples harden to points, watched his back arching as spasm after spasm of pure joy surged through him, watched while he let out a cry and then his member throbbed furiously in the final act of pleasure, arcing its creamy seed once again briskly onto the bedclothes. He moaned and then at last he was done, finished, still bucking like a stallion, giving his all.

Then – irritatingly – there was a light footfall on the stairs and 'Cooee!' said a voice.

Mimi was back.

Fabien looked up at Diamond and gave a tired grin – before today, she had never even seen him *smile*, not once. 'Time to get back to work,' he told her.

52

In peacetime, the Earl and Countess of Stockhaven held a summer ball every year at Fontleigh, just as the climbing roses were opening in brilliant scarlet profusion out on the front of the house. During the war, there had been no cause to celebrate the seasons; now, with hostilities behind them, it was marvellous to see the house come to life again. Lamps were lit all down the drive, huge bright floral displays were dotted all around the house, with the biggest and most vivid being reserved for the ballroom itself.

'It looks fantastic,' Richard commented to his mother, knowing that the praise would please her, pausing to give her a peck on the cheek as he passed through the hall.

'Do you think so?' asked Lady Margaret uncertainly. She thought her son looked pale. He had dreams, she knew he did. She'd heard the cries in the night. Heard him going down the stairs in the small hours, not able to go back to sleep or perhaps afraid to. But he was a man now, and she couldn't embarrass him by fussing. The war was over. Hopefully, soon, his nightmares would be too. 'It's not too much? All this?'

'Fantastic,' he repeated.

'Richard.'

'Yes, Mother?'

'I've asked the Sibleys to come. You do know that, don't you?'

Richard paused. He hadn't seen Sir James Sibley since he'd broken off his and Catherine's engagement. The memory still burned him like a brand, made him flinch. The Sibleys were good people, after all.

'They are our oldest friends,' Lady Margaret rushed on.

'I know that. Is Catherine coming too?'

Lady Margaret bit her lip and nodded.

Richard thought of the hunt and Catherine's fall.

'Catherine and I,' he said carefully, 'had a talk. We agreed to forget our differences. To be civilised with each other.'

And of course there it was; the instant flash of hope in his mother's eyes. 'Does this mean . . .?'

'No. It doesn't mean anything,' he said, smiling. 'All it means is that we've made our peace. That we are friends again.'

'Oh. Well, perhaps she has told her parents that?'

'Let's hope so. I'd hate there to be a scene at the ball tonight. Father loves this event, doesn't he?' The Earl was a very sociable man; he relished this type of gathering. Richard only endured them.

'The Sibleys have spoken to us since . . .' Margaret hesitated, waving her hand to demonstrate the shattering news of the broken engagement. 'Well, since *that.* Mary has been quite forgiving. And James, I think he's coming around, slowly. Although of course . . .'

'Yes. Of course.' Richard wondered what *he* would do, should a man treat a daughter of his so shabbily. Sir James Sibley would have been completely justified in knocking him to the ground; it was exactly what Richard himself would do.

'What about Teddy? Is he going to come?' he asked her.

'No. I'm sorry,' said Margaret.

Richard shrugged. He couldn't blame Teddy for holding a grudge. In his shoes, he would do the same. It hurt him, his old friend's ongoing rejection, but he knew that he deserved it.

'Where are you going, darling?' she asked.

'Out for a drive.' Richard was pulling on his goggles, gloves and his driving coat.

'Oh, that dratted thing,' tutted Margaret, referring to the brand-new Rolls Royce motor car that was sitting in a spare stable in the mews. 'I don't know how you can stand rattling around in that horrid machine.'

'It's the future, Mother,' he said, and kissed her soft cheek again and was away, out of the door, free.

'It's an abomination,' she corrected him – but he was already gone.

***

Although the ballroom was packed with people that night and the music was thrilling to hear as dancing couples circled around, *nothing* was the same. There were fewer people. Certainly, fewer young men. Most of those who'd gone from this area were dead in France. There was an air in the ballroom of enforced, almost hysterical gaiety. Someone had the piano player start rattling off a new dance craze. A few of the bright flirty young girls with their rouged cheeks and their too-short skirts started doing the steps, laughing and shoving each other.

But then the waltzes were resumed, the bright young things went for champagne and the sedater, older dancers took to the floor.

The Earl came up to Richard, glass in hand, face florid from the heat in the vast, tightly packed room. 'Catherine's over there,' he pointed out.

'Yes,' said Richard. 'I do know that.'

'Why not ask her to dance? Come on.' The Earl patted his son's shoulder. 'Your mother tells me that everyone has moved on from past events. That you and Catherine are being civil to one another. I'm very pleased to hear it, I have to say. So why not dance with the poor girl?'

Because I don't want anyone getting the wrong idea, Richard thought. *I don't want anyone – especially not you – thinking that things are back on again.* To his dismay, he realised that his father was hoping exactly that. That the whole rigmarole could so easily start again, if he wasn't extremely careful. He could hear the Earl's words . . .

Get engaged to her. She's a wonderful girl. You were upset, just back from the war and if you propose again, she'll understand and this time there'll be no confusion, things will go ahead as planned, and our oldest, dearest friends will become our in-laws, wouldn't that be wonderful?

To Richard, it wouldn't be wonderful at all. He was starting to relish being free, and . . . there she was again, in the back of his mind. That girl, Diamond. She was always there, like a low-level fever, the shocking black-haired whore who'd played the trick on him. Marry Catherine? No. He simply couldn't.

'Father, I'm sorry, I can't . . .'

The Earl looked in his son's face and his own hardened. 'For God's sake, *why?*' he demanded.

Lady Margaret was approaching, her face concerned. 'What is . . .?' she started.

'Ask your son. Ask him why he is being so *bloody* unreasonable,' said the Earl, and he turned his back on Richard and walked away.

Suddenly it was all too much. The crash and hammer of the music, the roar of chat and laughter. Richard felt as if he was being crushed in a vice. Lady Margaret took his arm, steadying him a little. He felt sweat break out on his brow. So hot in here.

'Come and dance with your mother,' she said, and led him out onto the floor as 'The Blue Danube' was played.

'Calm down,' she said after a few beats. 'Your father means no harm. It's something he's always dreamed of, you know it is. You and Catherine.' She smiled. 'I think his nanny over-indulged him when he was little, don't you? He has always been that way. If he thinks a thing should happen, he's always quite put out if it doesn't.'

'It's not going to,' said Richard, tight-lipped.

'Of course not. I do realise that. But you know, sometimes it's very hard to let things go.'

'I know.' Richard gave her a smile in return and spun her around to the three repeating beats of the beautiful Strauss waltz. The last note sounded and they stepped back from each other, good humour restored, clapping.

Then Richard saw Benson weaving through the crowds toward them as the drums announced the beginning of the 'Radetsky March'. Benson's face was set, grim. Richard felt a bolt of alarm pierce his chest as the butler came up to him and his mother.

'Your ladyship,' he said, sounding breathless.

Richard caught the man's arm to steady him. 'What is it?'

'It's the Earl,' said Benson. 'He's collapsed.'

53

Fabien Flaubert's exhibition was held in a gallery near the Quai du Louvre. Invitations had gone out to the great and good of Paris. Mimi said that they must arrive fashionably late, which they did. Mimi wore a soft spring yellow that offset her carefully tinted blonde hair, and Diamond was in the vivid red velvet creation that Madame Delphine the miracle worker had created.

When they entered the gallery, it was to find a crush of bodies already inside and the conversation at danger level, it was so loud. Waiters moved through the hordes, holding aloft trays of food and glasses of champagne. The whole room was cloaked in a fug of Gitanes. Fabien wasted no time in complaining about that to the gallery owner.

'It'll stain the canvases,' he said irritably. Then his eyes swept over Diamond. 'You look different.'

'Different how?' she asked. Her lover! She adored him. After all the misery of her younger life, now she had arrived, properly. She was in Paris. She was in love. She was – finally – happy.

'Dressier,' he said.

'Well since you've been staring at her naked arse for weeks on end, no wonder you're startled,' said Mimi, snatching a brimming glass off a passing waiter's tray.

But Fabien was already gone, moving across the room, mingling, doing his best to be sociable when in fact Diamond knew that he was anything but. He was an obsessive artist, his head too full of creativity to be bothered with small talk. He hated these affairs, but knew he had to show willing.

Mimi sipped her champagne then caught her breath. 'Ah! Here we go,' she said.

'What?' Diamond queried.

Mimi nodded, indicating with her eyes the woman who had just walked in the door: she was dressed in the new 'flapper' style, wearing a shimmering gold dress that fell down over her boyish body. She was tall, and her fashionable shingled hair was a deep corn-gold. Her eyes, which flashed across to where Mimi was standing, staring, were green as the flesh of a lime. Diamond saw Fabien standing there with her, and he looked angry.

That's the blonde in the canvases, realised Diamond. She felt a stab of something then that she had never experienced before – pure jealousy. *The ones Fabien had scattered all around his studio before I started sitting for him.*

'Someone I need to speak to,' said Mimi, and then she was off, joining a group of men, in the centre of which was a tall man with aristocratic features, with a very glamorous young man at his side and two snow-white dogs lounging at his feet.

When Mimi came back, Diamond said: 'Isn't that the woman in the canvases? The one Fabien used to paint?'

'Yes, that's her. That's Madeleine. And the paintings didn't sell. Not like *these* are selling. Look – you see all those red dots on them? This exhibition is going to be a great success and that is all down to you, his new muse. The poor boy was near to destitute before you came along and now at last he has a model who could be of some real use to him.'

'Why didn't they sell, the portraits of Madeleine?'

Mimi shrugged. 'Who knows?'

But Diamond could see a flicker of something like triumph in Mimi's eyes.

'It looks like her and Fabien are arguing,' said Diamond.

'Yes, I suppose it does.' Mimi didn't care. 'Oh! Look out, here she comes . . .'

Diamond watched as the tall blonde came surging across the room, through the crowds. Fabien was coming after her, snatching at Madeleine's arm. She shook him off and hurried on. People were turning, staring. Among the crowds, Diamond thought she saw a familiar face.

No.

Couldn't be.

Finally Madeleine arrived in front of Mimi and Diamond.

'So *you're* the replacement,' she snapped at Diamond.

'Darling, don't show yourself up like this,' advised Mimi.

The girl rounded on her. 'And you, you *bitch!* You set this up. This was all your idea, this is your revenge, isn't it?'

Diamond looked between the two women, who were glaring at each other.

'Madeleine, don't,' said Fabien, looking awkward.

'Don't what? Don't say how you betrayed me, *abandoned* me, and for what? For *this.* And this bitch put the word out around town. She breathed poison into the ears of all your buyers, searched out all her friends in high places and made sure they didn't purchase a single canvas of yours if I was in it. Say that's not true, you *cow.*'

Mimi shrugged, unconcerned. 'Fashions change and we have to change with them,' she said. 'Otherwise we just make ourselves look stupid. And pathetic.'

Madeleine's eyes fastened on Diamond, standing there silent. Then she whirled around and faced Fabien. 'Are you sleeping with her? Like you did with me?' she demanded.

'Maddy! For the love of God . . .' he groaned. Everyone was looking now. A hush had fallen. No-one wanted to miss a word of this.

'I am working with Fabien,' said Diamond icily. Her love life was *not* Madeleine's business.

'Oh, give it time. He'll give you that poor-artist routine, the tortured-genius nonsense and before you know it you'll be flat on your back with your legs open.'

'You shouldn't have come here tonight,' said Fabien sharply. 'You weren't invited. I don't know why they didn't stop you at the door. Look – just go.'

'You knew I'd turn up,' said Madeleine. But her eyes were fastened on Diamond. 'He'll tire of you, you know. Be warned. The minute you begin to look anything less than perfect, you'll be out the door and gone. They're users of people, these two. Sweet little Mimi, she'll barter you like a broken-down old nag, exploit you the way she does everyone she comes across. And when your looks go do you think he'll still want to be painting you? Of course not.'

Diamond stared at her. There was a grain of truth in there somewhere, she thought. Mimi *had* clearly made use of her to get revenge on this girl for some reason. She had used Diamond to get a roof over her head. Praised her to the skies with Fabien, so that he wanted to paint her. And by doing that she'd got her feet under the table too. Diamond thought of Arnaud, demanding his money. And Mimi seemed to have a lot of that, these days. But Diamond was willing to bet that Mimi *still* hadn't paid him.

'I'm just doing a job,' Diamond told Madeleine, although that was far from the truth. It hadn't been true, ever – not from the very first minute she had glimpsed Fabien there in the Moulin Rouge and been utterly captivated by him.

'I know nothing of what's gone before.' That at least was true.

'No. You don't. But *she* does.' So saying, Madeleine turned, very quick, and grabbed a handful of Mimi's hair and yanked it out by the roots.

Mimi shrieked.

Everyone stared, transfixed.

Mimi lunged out, smashing her fist into Madeleine's jaw. Madeleine reeled back, letting go of Mimi's hair. Madeleine staggered and tripped over a passing waitress who dropped a tray of glasses that crashed, shattering. Madeleine fell, sprawling onto the polished wooden floor amid spilled champagne and shards of glass.

'You haven't heard the last of this,' she howled, blood seeping down her chin, dripping down the front of the golden dress, staining it.

'For God's sake! Come on,' snapped Fabien, hauling her to her feet.

Madeleine lurched upright and stared at Diamond. 'You'll be sorry you ever met this cow, I promise you.'

'The woman's crazy,' said Mimi, gingerly patting her head. 'Is there blood? Did she draw blood? She's demented!'

'No, there's no blood.' Diamond was watching – *everyone* was watching – as Fabien dragged Madeleine back to the door and ejected her into the night. Diamond grabbed Mimi's arm. 'What was all that about? What's going on between the two of you?'

'Oh – nothing,' said Mimi.

'She said you'd been blackening her name around town.'

'So I did. So what?' Mimi was rubbing her head and wincing.

'Why would you do that?'

'All right, all right! She took a man off me, if you must know. We were deeply involved and then *she* came along all beautiful and – and *young*,' Mimi's mouth crumpled briefly. 'And suddenly he wanted nothing more to do with me. So I thought I'd fix her. And I did. And when *you* came along, you were like a gift from heaven. I could see a way to hurt her as she'd hurt me. I'd take away her lover, just like she had once taken away mine.'

'God Almighty. Mimi!'

Mimi drew herself up to her full tiny height. 'I'm not sorry I did it,' she huffed. 'Not at all. I'd do it again, in a heartbeat. I really would.'

Diamond didn't doubt it. The hubub of noise started up again in the room. Madeleine was gone. But Diamond's feeling of unease remained.

54

The exhibition – despite that scene created by Madeleine – was a success. All the canvases were sold. Mimi and Diamond fell out into the dark streets of Paris very late, giggling from excitement and too much champagne, and started walking back to Fabien's studio.

'I'll follow on,' he told them. 'Just clearing up. I won't be long.'

Diamond thought of Madeleine again as he said that, but Madeleine had left much earlier. He wasn't *lying*, was he? No. Of course not. But she felt that strange unknown surge of anxiety all over again. She'd never known jealousy, not with anyone. She'd never been in love before. Never even been involved with anyone. Until the blond *RB* had forced her during the badger trick, she'd been a virgin, untouched. This was all new to her, and – shockingly – it was painful.

'I promised you, didn't I?' Mimi said as they strolled arm in arm along the bank of the glittering Seine. Boats moved on the river, their bow-waves making ripples fan out, causing slapping sounds against the water's edge. 'The toast of Paris, didn't I say that? And it's coming true.'

Images of her would be hung on salon walls all over Paris and her fame as Fabien Flaubert's muse would spread. But instead of triumph, all Diamond felt right now was fear that she might lose his love. Madeleine was so beautiful.

And there was the disturbing fact that Fabien never, ever climaxed inside her when they made love. He was always careful to withdraw. *Always.* Some trauma around Madeleine had prompted this, she felt sure. Or maybe he did it . . . out of consideration for her – but somehow, she didn't think so.

'Oh!' Mimi stopped dead in her tracks as a shadowy figure moved out from under a light, blocking their path.

Diamond stopped walking, her heart rate picking up speed. As the figure moved closer still, she saw a glint of steel. He had a knife! Then she saw the outline of the face. The stubbly beard, the mean sunken eyes.

It was *Arnaud.*

He moved forward and they both stepped back automatically, into the darker shadows of an alleyway.

'Arnaud!' Mimi burst out, clutching a hand to her chest. 'What are you doing, scaring us witless like that!'

'I've come for my money,' he said.

'Oh, put that away, you always did have a taste for the dramatic,' said Mimi, and she laughed, but there was a tremor to it.

Arnaud came closer still. Diamond stared, transfixed. It wasn't a knife. What he had in his hand was a cut-throat razor, the kind men flick open and use to get a close shave. And having not paid him – as would have been the sensible thing to do – stupid Mimi was now provoking him.

'Mimi,' said Diamond. 'For goodness' sake, pay the man what you owe him.'

But she felt sure that Mimi wouldn't do it, not even when danger presented itself. She was getting to know Mimi very well now. Mimi loved to play games; taunting Madeleine, manipulating Diamond and now mocking Arnaud when he had a dangerous weapon in his none-too-steady hand.

'You should listen to your kitten,' said Arnaud, his words slurring. He was drunk! He was stepping in closer and laying the cold hard steel of the thing right across Mimi's throat. 'Pay up now, Mimi, or there'll be consequences. Bad ones.'

Mimi let out a sigh but it was more fright than exasperation. 'Oh very well.' She started rummaging in her tiny diamanté-encrusted evening bag.

Thank God, thought Diamond, feeling they'd escaped disaster by a whisker. She was furious with Mimi, stringing this out until the situation was desperate. Then she – hardly believing her own eyes – saw the pistol in Mimi's hand. By the faint light out on the main street she could see a glimmer of cream ivory chasing on the butt of it.

That's a toy, she thought, and time seemed to slow to a crawl.

But what if it isn't?

She was reaching for Mimi's wrist, trying to stop her from pointing the thing at Arnaud. Not believing what was happening, Diamond was thinking this was all a bad dream, a terrible nightmare, and she'd wake up at any minute. She snatched the gun from Mimi's hand. The thing bucked in her palm and fired.

Arnaud crumpled, the razor clattering onto the cobbles beside him.

'Oh my *God*,' said Diamond. She fell to her knees, half demented with panic, and clawed at Arnaud. 'Where is he hit? Did it hit him? Is there blood?'

Mimi was just standing there, saying nothing.

Diamond felt wetness under her hand as it rested on Arnaud's chest. She couldn't feel a heartbeat. Shuddering, she drew back and then she was aware that the gun – yes, it was as small and insubstantial as a child's toy, but utterly deadly – was in her hand. She'd killed him!

There was movement behind them. Someone was coming. Someone would call the police. She'd killed a man. She was a murderess. She had one hand on the gun, the other on the cobbles. Her fingers touched something metal and closed over it. Then she staggered to her feet and there was someone there, grabbing her arm, taking the gun off her.

'God's sake, what you up to now?' someone growled in her ear.

It ought to be Fabien, so that she could fall into his arms and tell him this wasn't her, it was all down to Mimi, it was Mimi's gun and entirely Mimi's fault. But it wasn't Fabien. It was a dark-haired man, swarthy, tall, muscular and *English.* The accent was unmistakeably London, and familiar. She thought she'd seen him inside, at the exhibition. Now she was starting to shake with reaction. It *had* been him. He was right here, her old enemy, the arch-enemy of all the Butcher family.

It wasn't Fabien.

It was that bastard Toro Wolfe.

55

'What the *hell* . . .' burst out Diamond.

'What the hell indeed. What've you got yourself into now?' He bent over Arnaud, who was not moving, not making a sound.

'What the fuck are you doing here?' she demanded, glimpsing the small scar on his cheek – the one that her brother Aiden had put there on Victor's wedding day.

'Oh very ladylike. As it happens I have business here.'

Diamond glared at him. 'Of course you do. Following me about.' Her voice shook. She was alarmed to feel that her whole body was trembling.

'You ought to be glad I did. Because I can sort this and you can't.'

Sort it?

'Disposing of a body's difficult. Grunt work.'

She felt dizzy. Like the whole world had gone crazy.

'Who is this?' asked Mimi faintly.

Ignoring her, Diamond ploughed on. 'Why would a Wolfe help a Butcher? Your whole damned family's been intent on killing off mine for as long as I can remember.'

'Just shut up and be fucking grateful, will you? Go home and forget this. Forget it ever happened. *Go.*'

That last word hit her like a whiplash and she flinched.

'Do you know this man?' said Mimi. She was fanning herself and Diamond could see that she was – for God's sake! – more than ready to flirt even now, when they were standing right here over the body of a man whose death *she* had just caused.

'No,' said Diamond. 'I don't know him and I've no wish to know him, either. Come on, Mimi.'

Towing Mimi along behind her, Diamond fled off along the street. The flower woman on the corner was packing up ready to go home; she'd do no more trade tonight. It was starting to rain and Diamond was shivering with shock. Behind them, did she hear a heavy splash? No. She told herself she'd imagined it. Her mind kept replaying the instant of Arnaud's death. Oh God – she'd killed him. Shot him dead. It was too awful to think about but she couldn't help it. When they got back to the studio, she hurried Mimi in and then locked the door securely – and even then, she didn't feel safe.

56

Fabien came back very late and the worse for drink, fumbling with the lock, stumbling up the stairs and then weaving his way across the studio knocking into things. Diamond and Mimi had fallen into bed and to her amazement and disgust Mimi went straight to sleep. Diamond couldn't sleep a wink. At gone two in the morning when Fabien finally came home, she was still awake, staring up at the cracks in the cobwebbed ceiling, feeling sick and wondering what on earth had happened to her life and why the *fuck* that lowlife bastard Toro Wolfe had to show up at the precise moment disaster struck.

Poor bloody Arnaud, dying like that. She could almost feel again the cold hardness of the gun in her hand as she snatched the deadly little thing off Mimi. The deafening *bang*. It had been so loud, so awful. Truly shocking.

I am a murderess.

Finally, somehow, she slept and fell into nightmares of bodies dripping water and crawling jelly-like and ruined out of the Seine, coming to eat her. When she snapped awake in the early morning, sweating, scrabbling at the covers, it was to find Mimi watching her.

'We don't have to talk about what happened,' Mimi whispered. 'It was lucky your friend arrived when he did.'

'He's not my friend.' Diamond sat up, dazed and disorientated. *And neither are you.*

'Don't snap, darling,' said Mimi, turning over with a luxurious yawn. 'I couldn't help Arnaud being a bastard. And *you* shot him, after all – not me.'

Diamond's head turned and she stared hard at Mimi. She knew Mimi now. All she wanted was to dine out on Diamond's fame. Use her to get revenge on Madeleine. Now she was saying Arnaud's death was on *her*, when she had only been trying to stop what was happening. She had been trying to *save* Arnaud from Mimi and had ended up killing him. She wished she could go back, relive last night, make it come out differently. She couldn't, but it had taught her something about her 'friend'. Mimi was entirely false and dangerous. She was the type of woman who would always scoop the prize, always find the shady seat beneath the parasol, always have champagne and chocolates laid out before her, the very best of everything, because she would charm and flirt and manipulate – but she would never, ever accept responsibility for anything. She would always shrug her problems off as someone else's.

'I'm getting up – it's nearly lunchtime,' said Diamond. She felt sick again and full of dread. Her stomach was churning.

Already she could hear Fabien stirring from the chaise on the raised platform under the windows. Should she tell him what had happened?

No.

She couldn't.

It was too hideous to be spoken of. It was awful but it was her secret. Hers and Mimi's. Oh – and this *really* made her want to vomit – it was Toro Wolfe's too.

***

When they went to lunch at Les Deux Magots, all the usual crowd were in, all the writers and poets, painters and designers. They were Fabien's crowd and now it seemed that they were *her* crowd too. When they entered the café and headed for their usual table, everyone stopped speaking. Then slowly a single waiter began to clap. Others joined in. Then every patron in the place was clapping too, and Hemingway was on his feet, grinning. Pablo Picasso came over and slapped Fabien on the back.

'Well done, you clever bastard!'

'What a coup!'

'To the artist and his muse! To Fabien and Mam'selle Diamond Dupree!'

She'd arrived, just as Mimi had predicted. Mimi was grinning like a Cheshire cat now, looking triumphant because *she* was the orchestrator of all this and was happy to bask in Diamond's reflected glory. Diamond was the talk of the town.

Yes, she'd arrived – just at the moment when the worst possible disaster had befallen her. She was going to be famous, but she was a killer. She could feel bile rising in her throat and wondered whether she ought to excuse herself and go to the lavatory right now.

Somehow she smiled and nodded while she was ushered to their usual table like she was royalty.

'Well done, *chérie*,' said Mimi, all smiles as she swiftly elbowed Diamond aside and grabbed the best seat for herself. 'And Diamond my darling? Easy on the puddings, yes? We don't want you putting on too much more weight, do we?'

57

A man found the body three days later, early in the morning. It was floating face-down in the river, the water bumping it repeatedly against a set of steps near the Pont des Arts.

Horrified, the man hurried to the nearest Préfecture de Police and raised the alarm. Before the hour was up, before a watery sun appeared, cowering in the grey drizzling sky, Detective Inspector François Benoit of the Sûreté's Brigade Criminelle arrived with his sergeant and together – with difficulty – they hauled the body out and up the steps.

Gendarmes arrived and waved away the onlookers who were starting to gather while Benoit and Detective Sergeant Golon cast their expert eyes over the body. It was a man in his forties, thinnish, grizzled, wearing cheap clothes. His eyes were opaque as they stared up at the lowering sky, seeing nothing. They found a small bullet hole, perfectly round, washed clean by the water, right over his heart.

Golon took notes. A cart was summoned by the gendarmes to remove the body to the morgue for further examination.

'A murder,' said Benoit, leaning on his Malacca cane and looking all around him as if the culprit could be found right there.

Benoit looked, the young and handsome Golon had always thought, like a dumpy oversized guinea pig, the hair on his head black, his beard white. A *piebald* guinea pig.

'*Oui*,' agreed Golon, tucking his notebook back into his pocket and thinking that he was in for a long day. Once Benoit got the bit between his teeth, it was round-the-clock work.

'Have these men search this street. Talk to that flower seller there at the end, you see her? Perhaps the murderer dumped the murder weapon somewhere nearby.' Then he looked at the river. If the gun – small bore, he thought – couldn't be found hereabouts, then perhaps the murderer had carried it away with him, dumped it further afield, or perhaps even kept it. Or . . . again, his eyes drifted to the rippling waters of the Seine. Where better to hide a weapon?

***

All that day, just as Golon had feared, Benoit irritably stalked the street beside the steps, his cane tip-tapping on the cobbles as he went back and forth. The cart arrived and the corpse was removed. Benoit walked up and down, noting the cafés, brasseries, galleries and boulangeries all along the length of the street, talking to the owners while Golon took notes. It was getting toward dusk when the searching of the whole street was complete; no gun.

'He could have dumped it anywhere,' said Golon, who was thinking longingly of home, food, his warm little wife and their warm little bed. Benoit, who was older, didn't have any of that to hurry home for. He was a bachelor, an introvert to his bones. He was irritatingly obsessive about his work. Trouble was, he expected everyone else to be the same.

'Yes, of course,' said Benoit, staring at the river.

'Don't you think so? Anywhere at all,' said Golon, tucking his notebook pointedly away.

'Say we were to investigate – what? – fifty yards in all directions from the point in the river where we estimate our victim went in?'

Golon stared at his boss. 'What – in boats? Dredging, you mean? That could take . . .'

'No, not boats. The navy have divers, yes?'

Golon looked at the river. It was *massive.* 'That's a huge undertaking, sir,' he pointed out. 'And expensive, surely.'

'Golon.' Benoit turned his dark eyes sadly onto his sidekick. 'A man has lost his life. And we – the Sûreté – are charged with finding the one responsible and bringing him to book. We must proceed and we must catch the culprit, you agree?'

'Yes. I agree. But . . .'

'No buts.'

'There is a but, I'm afraid. What good would it do, retrieving the weapon anyway? Even if we find it, what can we learn from it?'

'The place of purchase. Its origins. And so perhaps its owner. And our scientific colleagues are working on new things, too.'

'Like what?'

'They say that a criminal can be identified by the prints on his fingers.'

'Really?' Golon marvelled at that. It sounded ridiculous.

'Each individual has his – or her – unique fingerprint.'

Golon shook his head. 'But the water. Wouldn't that wash these "prints" off?'

'If the body was in the water for long enough, probably. And if the prints were only partial, it could be difficult.'

'The light is fading,' said Golon, wishing he worked with someone else. Only Benoit would think of such a mad scheme. Dredging. Diving. Fingerprints, for the love of God. He was so tired, his feet ached.

'Yes, so there is nothing to be done here now.'

Thank God! Golon heaved a sigh of relief. Home beckoned at last.

'So you must go back to the Préfecture de Police and contact the navy,' said Benoit. 'And I, meanwhile, have an appointment at the morgue.'

58

Incredibly, life went on. With Mimi out during the day, Fabien painted Diamond almost obsessively, slapping paint onto canvas after canvas, doing his most brilliant work, she thought. The paintings were stunning, and ever since the exhibition, people had been queuing up to buy them. Fabien Flaubert was a byword for excellence now, an artist that everyone clamoured for. Then, when the day's work was done, he would take her shopping, treat her to some small item from Cartier or Chopard.

'You deserve it,' he would say, kissing her. 'You've brought back my talent, and I feared I'd lost it.'

As time wore on, she no longer worried about any comeback from Toro Wolfe regarding Arnaud's death. She didn't see him again anywhere around town, and inch by inch she started to relax. But the stress of what had happened with Arnaud lingered, making her sometimes feel sick to her stomach, bloated, vile-headed. Everything felt tight on her, she'd have to see Madame Delphine and get her to make some alterations. Sometimes it was an effort to sit for the long hours Fabien required of her, and she had to take to her bed and hope that she could sleep a little, and not dream those awful dreams of dead bodies and deep water.

Then one day when she had been out with Mimi, she went back to the studio early. Fabien had said he would be out all day with his agent, meeting rich buyers, but he was here. Even before she got up to the top of the stairs, she could hear 'After You've Gone' burbling out of the record player. When she opened the studio door, there he was. Instantly, the happy smile fell from Diamond's lips.

He was with *Madeleine*.

'Oh!' she said, stopping dead in the doorway.

Fabien looked like a little boy with his hand caught in the sweetie jar. He and Madeleine sprang apart. Madeleine looked smug and flushed.

They'd been *kissing*.

Feeling cut to the quick, devastated, Diamond stood there and stared at the pair of them. But Fabien loved *her*! She was his inspiration, his muse! Wasn't she?

'What on earth is this?' she demanded. But she *knew* what it was.

Mimi came up the stairs and hustled into the doorway beside her, her eyes sweeping over Madeleine and Fabien in complete understanding. 'Well, this is very awkward,' she said.

'No, it isn't,' snapped Diamond. 'What this is, is *unacceptable.*' She glared at Madeleine. 'You! Get out, this instant.'

Madeleine looked at Fabien and he nodded. Then she strode across the room and shoved past Diamond, a look on her face that said it all. She was the cat that got the cream. Once, she'd lost Fabien – but now, without a doubt, she'd won him back.

Diamond looked at Fabien, standing there. Her lover! And he'd been here, cheating on her with that *bitch.* She was furious but she also wanted to cry. 'And what do you have to say about this? Anything?'

Fabien's eyes went to Mimi, then back to Diamond. He shrugged. 'We'll talk later,' he said, and without another word he too swept past her and off down the stairs.

To catch up with Madeleine, no doubt.

Diamond and Mimi stood there, and for a long moment neither of them spoke.

Then Mimi said: 'Well darling, I did warn you.'

Diamond stared at her. She couldn't take this in, this was a disaster, and now *what* was Mimi saying?

'Warn me of what?' she said, dry-mouthed, feeling like she might actually faint from the shock. She hurried over to the chaise – the chaise where she and Fabien had made love, over and over – and sat down quickly. Her head spun.

'I *told* you, darling,' said Mimi, coming over and standing in front of her. 'I did, you know I did. Fabien only likes what is perfect. The slightest flaw, and he's off. He loses interest. I did tell you.'

'*What?*' Diamond was staring up at Mimi, unable to understand.

'You know it's true.'

'What is true? I don't know what you mean. I don't understand.'

'You're gaining weight,' said Mimi softly, as if it pained her to say it, but Diamond caught the glint of a malicious sparkle in her eyes. 'All around your middle, you know it's true. I warned you about the pastries. *French* women don't indulge like that. They don't get fat.'

Diamond sat there, aghast. She *had* noticed that her clothes were fitting tighter and tighter – but she certainly wasn't eating more than usual. If anything, she was eating less. Feeling nauseous. Sore-breasted whenever Fabien gripped them too tightly. And – oh God in heaven! Her bleeds, which had always been patchy . . .

For God's sake!

Her bleeds!

When had she last had a period?

She counted up the days and thought *not since I arrived in France.*

'Oh my God, I think I'm in the family way,' she blurted out.

Mimi's eyes widened. 'It's Fabien's?'

Diamond sat there, her mind whirling. She had fallen in love with him and given herself to him, without taking any care at all. And now she was getting fat and he was turning his back on her. It broke her heart. She could feel a wail of despair building up in her, aching for release. He'd loved the *image* of her, not the reality with all its faults and foibles. He'd lusted after her – not *loved* her. He would start over with Madeleine, and she would be tossed aside like so much garbage.

But then she paused.

No. Wait a minute.

She wasn't a virgin with Fabien, was she? She remembered that last badger trick and the blond man *RB.* He had forced the conclusion she had spent years managing to avoid. He had entered her as an act of revenge, spilled his seed in her and now – as she added up the dates – she realised the truth of it.

She was going to have a baby.

And it was *not* Fabien's. There was no way it could be; the dates didn't add up – and anyway Fabien never even reached a climax inside her, did he? He was always rigorously careful not to.

It was *RB*'s, and she didn't have a clue who he was or where to find him. Not that finding him would do any good, anyway. He wouldn't want to know. She had tricked him once, successfully; but the second time their paths had crossed *he* had been in charge of events. He'd put his baby in her.

And now? She was in a mess.

59

Everyone at Fontleigh was in a state of shock. The Earl had been a big man, jovial, everyone's friend, with a keen appetite for life and all that it could offer. Without him, Fontleigh felt empty. The dogs sat in the study and whined, wondering what had become of their master. His wife shed bitter tears.

Having collapsed on the night of the ball, the Earl had fallen into a coma that lasted two days – and then the doctors shook their heads. 'His heart,' they said, and together Richard and his mother sat at the Earl's bedside as he gently slipped from this world into the next.

After his death, there came the horror of the funeral. The church service, the hordes of black-clad mourners. Everyone had loved the Earl. All the estate workers, all of the Earl's friends and distant relatives came to the service, and then the family gathered privately at Fontleigh to see the Earl interred in the family mausoleum.

Now there was reality to be faced. Sitting in the Earl's study – *his* study now – with the dogs still off their food and whining at his feet, Richard was confronted with the cold hard evidence of his father's lust for life. The bills for keeping racehorses – five of them – in training over in Berkshire. Massive. The upkeep on Fontleigh itself, which was staggering. Repairs to the Dower House and stables and outbuildings.

Fencing. Arboriculture work needing to be carried out. Staff to be paid. Cooks and gardeners and housemaids and footmen and the butler. And so many others, more almost than he could count. Food bills that were astonishingly lavish – the Earl had loved his salmon, his caviar, his fresh-caught trout from the gin-clear chalk streams of southern England, his foie gras imported from France, his Aberdeen Angus steaks from Scotland. And wine bills. The cellars were fully stocked with the most priceless, most fantastic vintages, enough to make the most knowledgeable and fastidious sommelier green with envy.

Richard was still reeling from grief and from the realisation that he had inherited not only an earldom but a massive pile of debt when the worst happened: official documents arrived from the Inland Revenue setting out the full extent of the death duties that were due to be paid.

A massive amount was owed, and he had no idea where he was going to find it.

In the Earl's desk he found a tiny velvet-lined box containing an exquisite pair of oblong emerald-cut diamond earrings – a present intended for his mother's fiftieth birthday in two months' time, he thought. He tucked them back into the drawer, disinterested. The jewels were clearly valuable, but not nearly valuable enough.

The estate was *hugely* in debt.

Now it was his and he really, really didn't want it – this giant, unwieldly burden on his shoulders. The family seat was two thousand acres all told, with parkland laid out by Capability Brown, brimming with woods, gardens, man-made lakes. There were ten farms, Stockhaven village, a Dower House and Fontleigh itself with its twenty bedrooms and its stunning glass cupola that dominated the vast entrance hall.

He felt the weight of it, crushing him. Every part of it had to be maintained for the generations to follow.

Didn't he have enough to contend with already? The dreams. The terrible, godawful *dreams* that plagued him night after night, of falling down in the trenches, squelching bodies under his feet, gas yellow and noxious over his head, choking him. Then the whistles sounding and the shouts of 'Up we go, lads!' and the next wave of victims would surge up over the top to be instantly shot to pieces, to fall in tangled heaps upon him, knocking him down, their blood flowing over him, drowning him.

'I will move into the Dower House,' said his mother at dinner one night. She was still wearing full mourning and picking at her food, her face ashen.

Richard stopped eating and stared at her. He'd consulted with the accountants and the bankers. He didn't point out that they might have to *sell* the Dower House, along with the five acres of gardens, grounds and paddocks attached to it, and even that wouldn't scratch the surface of their mountainous pile of debts.

Perhaps he could sell off some of the farms. He hated the idea, because once you sold off estate land, that was it: you never got it back. And the tenant farmers, the labourers, all those who lived and worked those lands, what would become of them?

Or maybe he could invest in trade of some description. The railways or something like that. His father had always sniffed at 'trade', but these were desperate times and Richard knew he couldn't afford to do the same.

'Why would you move to the Dower House?' he asked.

'Why?' Lady Margaret looked at her son in surprise. 'Because you are the Earl now. Because at this point you have to do your duty. You have to take a wife and ensure the line, and no wife would want their mother-in-law in the background, creating a fuss when she alters the soft furnishings or changes the curtains.'

Richard said nothing. He picked up his fork and resumed eating. Margaret nodded to Benson, who left the room.

'The thing is, Richard,' she said when the door had closed behind the butler, 'that your father tended to live with no thought for money. None at all. And so I am afraid that the estate may be somewhat in debt.'

Somewhat? Richard almost laughed out loud at that, it was such an understatement. He couldn't mention the tax bill to her; she'd have a fit and he was worried enough, without her adding to the burden.

'So a wife would be the answer. An American from a wealthy family, perhaps. That route seems very popular these days.'

'I'm not marrying an American, Mother,' said Richard, surprised that his mother was even aware of the uncertainty surrounding their finances. His father had handled the money; all his wife had ever had to do was see to their social life, which she had very competently done.

'Well then, some other nice girl from a family in good financial order, to inject a sizeable dowry into the estate. I was thinking . . .' Margaret hesitated . . . 'Darling, I know you may not want to hear this but I was thinking of Catherine.'

'Mother . . .'

'I know that you had your differences, but that's behind you now, isn't it? Her family are dear old friends and they are extremely wealthy. I'm aware that you two have become friends again. I know that Teddy is still angry about it all, but he'll come round, I'm sure he will. I hope – I really do – that you and Catherine could become close again, given time.'

'Mother, that's out of the question.'

Margaret tossed her napkin down onto the table and shoved back her chair as she came to her feet. 'I knew you would say that.'

'Then why ask it?' said Richard angrily.

Her eyes filled with tears. She turned and hurried from the room, leaving him sitting there, alone.

60

François Benoit's visit to the morgue had turned up nothing very surprising. The bullet had penetrated the heart, a clean shot, instant death. More interestingly, he now had the deceased's tobacco pouch, pipe and wallet. The wallet had a key and a scrap of paper tucked inside with a name and address on it. The leather of the wallet had, thankfully, protected the paper and the writing was not clear, but clear enough.

He kept this in here so that if he mislaid his wallet, some kind law-abiding citizen would hand it in to the police, thought Benoit.

So – the corpse on the slab was Arnaud Roussel. One evening, Benoit took a cab over to the address in the wallet. He tried the key in the door, and it opened.

Et voilà!

He went inside, moving through a small and very shabby apartment. His lip curled and his nose itched in disgust at the dust, the unwashed pots in the kitchen, the unmade bed with its dirty sheets, the general air of a low-rent flophouse. His own apartment was meticulously clean and tidy. He disliked disorder. He tap-tapped his way through to what seemed to be a seating area, but even in here there was rubbish piled everywhere, the rugs on the floor were stained, the sofa looked like a haven for moths and fleas, with dirty cushions and ingrained grease-stains on the antimacassars. Even the windows were filthy, with old pepper-plants lined up on the sills, the leaves brown and the forgotten fruits hanging like corpses. Clouds of fruit flies were clustered over the dirty curtains.

Picking his way delicately across the floor to a small dust-covered writing bureau, he pulled on his gloves and – with a wince of distaste – sat down on the chair there. He opened up the bureau and set to work on the papers stacked inside.

61

At the realisation of Diamond's pregnancy Mimi's attitude changed completely. She seemed to be *enraged* at Diamond for getting into this condition.

'What are we to do?' she would shout, wringing her hands and walking around the studio like a caged tiger when Fabien was out. Diamond, feeling sick and tired to death, would sit on the chaise and watch her. Yes, Fabien was out. If she cared to follow him, she knew where she would find him – over on the Rue de Mont-Cenis, near the Sacré-Coeur Basilica on the hill, where Madeleine kept a tiny rented flat.

But she felt too ill to bother. Too stung and heartbroken. Yes, she was a bold woman, a strong one – but her first and only love! She had believed in him, adored him, only to have him abandon her at the very first hurdle. Oh, he didn't tell her to go. He didn't have the guts for that. Gifted he might be, a great artist – but at heart he was a coward.

'You wouldn't consider . . .' Mimi paused. 'There is a woman who lives near Madame Delphine's, who solves problems like this one.'

'What?' Diamond stared at her.

'She could get rid of it,' said Mimi.

Diamond touched a hand to her belly. The thought of *that* made a spasm of disgust ripple through her. What? *Kill* her baby? Wash it out of her like it was nothing?

'No!' she said forcefully.

'All right, all right! I'm just thinking, that's all. Suggesting things. I know!' Mimi stopped in front of the chaise and stared in triumph down at Diamond. 'We must find you a patron. A new artist is out of the question, no artist will want to paint a woman in your condition. So we must get you a sponsor.'

'How?' asked Diamond. *We*, Mimi said. Diamond heard the word and felt her mouth twist in ironic amusement. Mimi had milked her like a cow, got a roof over her head here, basked in Diamond's reflected glory, and even when her prize cow was in calf, she was unwilling to let the poor thing go free.

'I have friends around town. People – gentlemen – who would be delighted to be your patron.'

'In this condition?' Diamond scoffed, cupping the growing curve of her belly.

'Well you can't sit for any more portraits. Not like that. No – you need someone *monied.* And the fact that you are *enceinte*? We'll keep that hidden. For now.'

'That will quickly become impossible,' Diamond pointed out.

'Yes, but by that time our patron will be besotted with you and maybe with a little sleight of hand we might even be able to convince him that the child you carry is his.'

Diamond stared at Mimi in disbelief. 'Where are you going to find such an imbecile?'

'All men are imbeciles when it comes to women,' said Mimi. 'And I told you. I will find one. And then you will see.'

62

It didn't take Mimi long to make her plans. She took Diamond back to Madame Delphine's dusty little hovel on the left bank and appraised her of the problem. Madame agreed that with skilful corsetry and some very clever cutting, Diamond's condition would be concealed for the requisite amount of time needed to bewitch someone and have him fall under her spell so that, pregnant or not, he would continue to support her. She set to work on three new gowns, cut very differently to the red velvet creation that had heralded Diamond's debut into the upper echelons of fashionable Paris.

'We need the first, the black one, by the weekend,' Mimi instructed, and Madame agreed that this would be the case.

A party was being held in a place, Mimi promised Diamond, where they entertained writers, artists, musicians. It was *the* place to be seen, to make witty conversation and be entertaining and entertained.

Not feeling very witty at all, Diamond was rigorously corseted and then dressed in the concealing and artfully spangled drop-waisted black gown, which billowed in all the right places to hide the – as yet mercifully small – fact of her pregnancy. Then Mimi added strings of pearls and elaborate earrings to the finished ensemble.

'To distract the eye from your lower half,' she explained. 'We want everyone looking at your beautiful eyes, your shoulders, your stupendous breasts – we *don't* want them eyeing up your belly.'

God Almighty, thought Diamond. Yes, the gown concealed a lot. But the corset was hellish, so tight that she could hardly bear to sit down. She felt sick. Bloated. The last thing she wanted was to attend a party.

She told Mimi exactly that.

'Now don't be silly, darling,' said Mimi sternly. 'Very soon Fabien is going to get so tired of you that he'll change the locks. He's already started making sketches of Madeleine again. You know he has. As soon as he switches to oils of her you'll be out! It won't be long before we get our marching orders, and what will become of us then?'

Diamond sagged at that. Mimi was telling the absolute truth for once. Madeleine had been back to the studio, gloating over reclaiming Fabien's affection. More and more Diamond was being shoved aside and soon – Mimi was right – they would both be booted out the door entirely. Her heart was broken in two. She barely cared what happened next, when she had lost the man she had believed to be the true love of her life. All her troubles had started in London. She cursed Victor, she cursed the badger trick, she cursed – most of all – that blond bastard *RB*.

'We have to get a patron lined up at the ready. It's essential,' said Mimi.

'We' again.

'What does having a patron involve, exactly?' asked Diamond.

'A patron will set you up with other artists, create a buzz of interest around you as a model – ready for when you get your figure back, you see. Of course he may take a small cut of your earnings, but that's to be expected. And you'll have time to deliver the child, take care of all that, while he will set things up for you when things get back to normal.'

Diamond heard all this and thought *she treats having a baby like it's an unfortunate illness.* But it wasn't. She was going to bear a child, and that filled her with all sorts of strange anxieties. For herself, she could cope with anything life threw at her. She was an old hand at doing that. Hardship at an early age had taught her toughness. But a baby! She put her hand to her stomach, feeling the faint flutter of new life there. Sometimes she felt happy and excited about the baby, at others swamped by fears for the child, *her* child. And she didn't like the way Mimi was so casually dismissing the boy or girl she carried.

'I owe it to your dear mother,' said Mimi, brushing away a sentimental and – Diamond knew – entirely false tear. 'I have to see you safely settled, particularly in your unfortunate condition. What would dear Frenchie say, if she knew I had mishandled this? She would never forgive me.'

So they had to find a patron. Though she might hate the idea, Diamond could see the sense of Mimi's plan.

And they hadn't much time left to do it.

***

Benoit's boss had said no to the navy diver. They could dredge, he said, but for a day or two only. These things cost money, did they think the stuff grew on trees?

Benoit and Golon set to and arranged for a small dredger, and they targeted the area where they believed the corpse could have entered the water.

The dredger arrived and scouted the bottom of the Seine. It enlivened the interest of the population, so police had to be on hand to shoo onlookers away. But no gun was found.

'So what now?' asked Golon.

'The papers I found in the murdered man's bureau suggested that he has an employer, the Marquis de Marquand. He collected rents for the Marquis on his city properties.'

'So that's our next port of call,' said Golon.

'Correct.'

63

When they arrived at the party venue, Diamond saw the gaudy sign over the club door as they stepped out of their motor-taxi and stopped short.

'What is it, darling?' asked Mimi, straightening her skirt. 'Pay the man, darling, there's a love.'

Diamond paid the driver, who roared off into the chaotic traffic. She looked again at the sign over the door.

'But this is . . .' she started, then found the words stuck in her throat. This was Cabaret de l'Enfer, one of the six clubs the Butcher family had once owned. It was macabrely decorated at the front. The entrance had the punters stepping through a giant's gaping mouth, lined with sharp-looking teeth – including two massive canines.

'Yes. Owned by Toro Wolfe, who I believe you know?' Mimi's eyes were sharp on Diamond's face. 'You seemed to, anyway, when we last met up with Arnaud.'

'Mimi! Keep your voice down.' It was horrible to remember that night. She didn't need reminding of it.

'Mr Wolfe owns six clubs around Paris. Cabaret l'Enfer, the Pompadour, the Miami Beach . . .'

'The Metropole, Ciro's and the Lopez,' finished Diamond.

'So you know.'

'His father Gustav stole the damned things off my parents, forced his way in and drove them out of town.'

Mimi shook her head, staring up at the sign over the entrance. 'What can I say? Time moves on. And I suppose your dear mother and father made their living quite nicely in London?'

'No. And even if they had – and they didn't – that wouldn't excuse what the Wolfes did to them.'

She couldn't tell Mimi or anyone about the horror of her father's death at the hands of Gustav Wolfe, or about the misery that had brought disaster down upon the Butcher family in the shape of Uncle Victor.

'Now come along, darling. It's starting to rain. No time for grudges! I've got such a wonderful surprise for you. I have found you *exactly* the right man this time. You won't have a moment's worry with him, and you are *precisely* what he wants and needs.'

They went inside, through the giant's gaping mouth. Diamond felt a shiver of apprehension as they did so. This was the last place she wanted to be. And what if Toro Wolfe was here? But as they handed their cloaks in to the hat-check girl, she told herself not to be stupid. Toro had six clubs over here in Paris, and business interests all over the world. What were the odds of him being here, tonight, at this one club?

As they moved into the main body of it she looked around the red-painted walls, lined with hellish scenes and stuffed lion heads, impalas and snakes. Among the other party-goers, Diamond recognised many of the writers and artists who assembled on a regular basis in Les Deux Magots. The guests were swaying along to a jazzy number. Drinks and food were set out on buffet tables, and the roar of conversation was close to deafening.

'Mimi! Sweetheart!'

A woman with enormous bosoms came shoving through the crowd. She had huge dark eyes and short coarse hair brushed severely back beneath a bright feathered headdress. She was fanning herself with a copy of today's paper. She grabbed Mimi and hugged her, then stepped back and looked at Diamond. Diamond expected at any minute to be grasped by the head and to have her teeth examined.

'She's exquisite!' exclaimed the woman.

'Didn't I tell you so? Diamond, this is Miss Stein, Gertrude Stein. And she has someone who is absolutely *dying* to meet you.'

The woman got hold of Diamond's arm and heaved her along. It was like being towed by a barge. She elbowed her way through the crowds with her prize and fetched up in front of a man who looked too tall for his own good, like he'd been pulled on a rack. He was sunken-chested, thin-cheeked, white-haired. He had pale watery-blue eyes. There was little of beauty about him, but he carried himself like a king. Two big pure-white Borzoi dogs, lusciously furred and with elegant tapering faces and soft black eyes sat at his feet, their broad jewel-spangled collars attached to his wrist by two long purple leather leads. She'd seen this man and these dogs before, she realised. They'd been at Fabien's exhibition.

'Monsieur le Marquis,' exclaimed Gertrude. 'Here she is, the beautiful creature everyone has been raving about, the one who's made Flaubert's name – Diamond Dupree!'

Diamond felt like she should probably curtsy. She didn't. The Marquis held out a long narrow hand.

'Mam'selle,' he said.

Diamond took his hand. The Marquis brought her hand to his lips and kissed the back of it.

'Charmed,' he said.

Diamond looked at him with interest: this was her first brush with aristocracy. She'd thought the French had killed off the lot of them during the revolution. Clearly, they hadn't. She reached down, smoothed a hand over the delicately tapered head of one of the dogs. Its tail slapped against the floor and its mouth opened in a friendly grin.

'This is Boris,' the Marquis told her. 'And this lovely creature here is Titania. I've heard so much about you, Diamond. But seeing you in the flesh . . . I am amazed. Humbled! My dear, you are so very pretty.'

'Thank you, monsieur.'

Mimi appeared alongside them. 'Isn't she though?' she barged into the conversation. 'Have you ever seen anything so gorgeous as this girl? Isn't she just exactly what you want?'

So this was the one Mimi had singled out to be Diamond's 'patron'. Well, fair enough. If that was all he ever intended to be, that was fine – because the thought of anything else with this elderly overstretched creature was not appealing. If Mimi thought she would be crawling into the Marquis's bed at any point, she was very much mistaken. She was only going along with this plan to secure a safe future for herself and so – of course – for her child.

'You have taken the whole of Paris by storm,' he was saying, leaning close so that she could hear him over the roar of music and voices.

'Hardly, monsieur,' she said, thinking of Fabien and feeling heartsore as she did so. God, she had loved him. Wanted him, so much. And now he was back with Madeleine. He would carry on painting, and all the canvases of Diamond he'd worked on in the studio would slowly be covered by images of Madeleine instead. It would be, in the end, as if Diamond had never been there.

'You are too modest,' said the Marquis.

'Isn't she though.' Mimi shot her a glance. *Come on. Wake up! Flatter him. Cajole him. We need him.*

Now he was talking about his place down in the Loire.

'Do you come up to Paris often, monsieur?' asked Diamond, shaking herself, smiling into his eyes.

'Rarely,' he said.

'So what brings you here at this time?'

'Just business,' he said. 'Staff matters to address, you know. One of my agents has taken off unannounced, and so I am here interviewing candidates to replace that bast— forgive me, mam'selle, my language. But I'm so angry with him! Arnaud Roussel has left me in the lurch. Caused me a great deal of inconvenience.'

Diamond felt her heart falter in her chest.

Arnaud?

She felt Mimi stiffen beside her but gathered herself and somehow sailed smoothly on. 'Then this misfortune has delivered some fortune too, monsieur. Had you not been called to town to sort out your business, we would not have had the opportunity to meet.'

The Marquis shot a pleased look at Mimi. 'You are right, madame, she is delightful.'

'I told you!' Mimi giggled.

Diamond felt sick. Mention of Arnaud brought that night back to her, all too vividly. She could feel a cold sweat breaking out all over her body. The corset was pinching her, making her struggle for breath.

'Excuse me . . .' she said, and turned on her heel and hurried off. But Mimi came after her.

'You're doing terribly well,' said Mimi, dragging her to a halt.

'You really think I'm going to get into bed with that man?' hissed Diamond. 'Just to keep us both in clover?'

'Oh!' Mimi looked at first surprised, then she started to smile. 'Oh dear, I see you have misunderstood.'

'What do you mean?'

'Monsieur le Marquis won't want you in his bed, *chérie*. Not now, not ever. Have you heard the term "beard" at all?'

Diamond hadn't. She shook her head.

'Well, sometimes, when a gentleman has certain leanings towards *other* gentlemen, he is aware that his tastes in that direction are frowned upon. Illegal, actually. And so what such a man needs is a beard – a woman who will act as his mistress, and if she is pregnant then of course so much the better because it would appear to the world at large that he has been paying her proper attention. Do you see what I mean, darling? In exchange for the cover you provide, Monsieur le Marquis is going to look after you – and of course after me, too, because I have done him this enormous favour of sourcing you and putting the two of you together. You will find the Marquis a very generous man, *chérie*. I can assure you of that.'

Diamond understood completely now. She *also* understood that Mimi would do very well out of this 'arrangement'. Mimi always did. She looked back through the crowds at the Marquis and he smiled over at her. 'I need a few minutes to think this over,' she said.

'Of course! But don't take too long. Off you go.'

Diamond turned and wove through the throng. She was heading for the exit, wanting to breathe in some fresh air, when she bumped into a solid male body, looked up, and said: 'Oh shitting *hell*.'

64

'God, it's the jewel thief again,' said a familiar voice.

She'd come up against Toro Wolfe, head-on. Six clubs, and he had to be in this one! The bastard always seemed to show up at precisely the wrong moment. She went to barge past him, but he stopped her with a hand on her arm. 'You look just about ready to fall down. It's hot in here.' He led her to a seat, sat her down, poured out wine and handed her a glass.

'Why do I have to keep coming across *you*?' complained Diamond.

'You are in my club,' he pointed out.

'Yes – that your family thieved off mine.'

'And now I'm selling it on. I hear that your family are wondering where you are,' he said.

'Are they? Well no doubt you'll tell them.'

'What's it worth not to?' He gave her a grin. 'Coming over here, changing your name, that indicates to me that you were perfectly happy to leave them behind. And now you're making overtures to rich men. Don't deny it, I saw you.'

'I wouldn't touch the Marquis with someone else's, much less my own,' snapped Diamond.

Toro laughed. 'That's the Londoner, right there, coming out at last.' He looked at her coolly. 'No, I don't think the Marquis will want to touch you, although it's hard to think of a man who wouldn't. So – you've abandoned your family. My sister is apparently very put out about it, by the way.'

Diamond's heart sank. He would do it – he'd tell that cow Gwendoline where she was. And then Victor would come after her, and she would have even more trouble than she had already.

'She'll find another skivvy,' said Diamond with a deliberately casual shrug. 'And if you tell her . . .'

'If I tell her what? Where you are? What you're getting up to?' His eyes were shrewd as they rested on her face. 'Why'd you run away?'

'No reason,' said Diamond.

'There must have been something.'

'There wasn't. It was a whim. My mother was French. I have always wanted to visit France. That's all.' She looked at him. She didn't want to ask him, of all people. But she couldn't help it. She *had* to. 'How is Aiden? And Owen?' she asked.

His eyes met hers. 'How the hell should I know? You were quick enough to leave them, now suddenly you're concerned? Gwendoline will have put them to work sweeping the scullery or something, you can bet on that. Why not tell someone where you're going, anyway? Why leave unannounced?'

'That's none of your business.' She hoped to God her brothers were OK. Her heart clenched with guilt whenever she thought of them. Her sweet beloved brothers – and she'd left them in the hands of Victor and Gwendoline. But she'd had to get out. There'd been no other option for her, none at all. It galled her beyond words that she didn't even dare write to them, her dear brothers, and that her life in London had become such a mess that she had been forced to go.

'What did you do with Arnaud?' she asked.

'Best you don't know,' he said, sipping the wine, his eyes on her face. 'What did you do with the razor?'

Diamond was jolted. 'The what?'

'The razor that Arnaud dropped and that you picked up and slipped into your bag. *That* razor.'

'I don't know what you mean.' She did, though. It was tucked in her stocking top right this minute. Rattled by what had happened with Arnaud, she now always carried it with her.

'Don't you?' Toro looked across the room. 'Fair enough. But I'd keep it close by, if I were you. The sort of company you're keeping calls for a weapon of some sort. Oh look – your new admirer is summoning you back to his side.'

'Bugger,' said Diamond, her eyes following Toro Wolfe's. The Marquis was there, grinning, flapping his arm at her. *Come back, Diamond*, he was mouthing. Irritated, she fastened her eyes on Toro. 'Burned any more clubs down recently, have you?'

'None. Not even the Milano. My best guess? Victor did that. For the insurance.'

'Ha!' Diamond swayed to her feet and for a moment she felt that she was actually going to fall. Sweat gathered along her hairline – it was so hot in here, so dark, so *crowded.* He steadied her with a hand on her arm. She snatched it away.

'Whose is it, anyway? The baby?'

She caught her breath. 'I'm not . . .'

'Yes, you bloody are.'

'I don't know his name,' she said after a beat.

'That's hardly a surprise. Take care, Diamond Butcher,' he said.

'*That's not my name*,' said Diamond in red-hot annoyance. He knew about the baby and he was passing judgement on her, saying she had loose morals, when she'd had no choice in anything that had happened to her back at home. *Victor* had been in charge of matters. She had been nothing but a pawn.

'Oh no. I forgot. It's Diamond Dupree.' His voice was harsh, cutting. 'You know – it suits you, your name. Hard like a diamond. And cold,' he said, and turned and walked away.

65

His words stung her. She wasn't cold. How could he say that? How *dare* he say that? She was only having to shift for herself, just like she'd had to do all her life. So she went back to the Marquis's side, and sparkled. Like a diamond, which she was. But bright and flirtatious – not cold in the least.

'When I have concluded all my dreary business, I shall go back down to the Loire Valley,' the Marquis was telling an admiring circle around him. At his feet, the two Borzoi dogs lounged, yawning. 'I miss the country so much whenever I am in town. And my friends, I am throwing a week-long house party there and you are all invited to come. Particularly you, my dear.' His pallid eyes skewered Diamond. 'And your dear little friend Mimi, who will be your chaperone.'

***

The weeks passed and her body changed. Her breasts grew fuller and there was a hard fluttering in her abdomen, a feeling that there truly was *something there*. A child. *Her* child. Time after time she clamped her hands to her belly and felt the movements with something like wonder. A baby to love, and nurture, to see grow to adulthood. She would adore it. As to the father, *RB*, that bastard who'd forced himself on her, well, to hell with him. She cared nothing about him, even though she knew he had acted not out of cruelty but out of a desire for revenge after Victor had beaten him.

Mimi was busy. Before the month was even halfway up they had another place to stay off the Place de Vendôme, one of the Marquis's very beautiful properties. And the Marquis was diligently kind to her, showering her with shopping trips and outings, gifting her with exquisite long pale furs and expensive jewels. He lavished money on her, had Madame Delphine furnish her with a suitably magnificent wardrobe of fabulous coats, dresses, skirts, whatever she required.

'You see?' Mimi crowed, 'It's all working out perfectly.'

Diamond could see that it certainly had, for Mimi. Hanging on her coat tails, Mimi attended every glamorous event in town, moved several notches higher up the social scale, picked up better and more monied clients.

And – yes – the Marquis was good to Diamond, kind and considerate in ways that put most men to shame. She grew to like him very much, and his lover Jean-Luc, and spent many happy times with the two of them, chatting, laughing, visiting the races at Deauville, attending lavish parties and the theatre and the opera.

'Darling,' the Marquis would say to her, time after time, 'I am so grateful to you. Whatever you need, just ask, all right? Anything! I mean it.'

When they'd left Fabien's far more modest abode, it had been without any fanfare at all. While Fabien was out buying paints, Diamond and Mimi gathered up their small cache of belongings and left, posting the keys back through the letterbox.

Unfortunately, they met Fabien out on the pavement, his arms full of fresh tubes of ochre and viridian and carmine, just coming back to his studio.

'*Merde*,' muttered Mimi.

'Oh!' Fabien stared at them, with their coats on and their baggage in their hands. He looked awkward. 'Oh – so you're going, are you?'

'Yes,' said Mimi. She gave a little smile. 'Before you kick us out, my friend.'

'I wouldn't do that,' he said.

Yes, you would, thought Diamond, feeling her heart break all over again.

'So you can get Madeleine back whenever you please,' she said. 'It must be so tiring for you, having to shuffle between here and her place. Now you won't have to bother.'

'Diamond . . .' he started.

'No.' Diamond held up a hand like a policeman halting traffic. She felt like crying, but she mustn't. She was determined to hang onto the tiny shred of dignity she had left. 'Don't, Fabien. Please don't.'

He nodded, his expression hangdog. Diamond wasn't fooled. By dinnertime tonight, he'd have his old muse back and he'd be happy. For a while, at least. Until he tired of her again, and started looking for fresh inspiration, a new model to fascinate him and sit for him and make the other artists slap him on the back and call him clever.

Poor Madeleine, thought Diamond. She might be heartsore, but at least she was out of it. Madeleine – the poor fool – was going to re-enter the ring for round two.

'Goodbye then, Fabien,' said Diamond, and turned on her heel and walked away.

That was it then – the end of her and Fabien. What she had stupidly, girlishly, taken to be her great lifelong love had been nothing but a brief and torrid affair. At first she had seen Fabien as a genius, an angel, a colossus; now she saw him for what he was – a vain man who would happily drift from one woman to another but who in fact put no woman, *nothing*, above his art.

Diamond had learned, to her cost, that all men, no matter how stunningly handsome they might be, were bastards, cowards, users. And that in this world, a woman had to fend for herself, take the knocks, do whatever was necessary to survive.

But she would not attend the party at the Marquis's grand château. Feeling sick a lot of the time, she thought it would be too much for her. She told Mimi so.

'Well for the love of God!' Mimi complained. She liked living in the Marquis's luxurious apartment, rent free. Diamond could see that Mimi was anticipating a life of ever greater ease and privilege as Diamond grew closer to him.

'I mean it, Mimi,' said Diamond. 'I'm not going.'

'Oh but my dear child . . .'

'Don't "child" me, Mimi.' Diamond's tone was firm. 'It's not going to happen.'

'Of course, you have such high principles,' sniffed Mimi. 'Which is a surprise, seeing as you arrived here pregnant with some unknown man's child. Perhaps there is more of your mother in you than I at first suspected.'

'Oh shut up, Mimi,' snarled Diamond.

'Your mother would be most displeased with—'

'And don't try that, either. My mother isn't here. I am. And I mean what I say.'

Mimi was silent. 'He'll be terribly put out. *Most* offended. The château is his pride and joy.'

Diamond was running out of patience. 'Then we will just have to find another patron. One that isn't quite so touchy.'

'Oh come on . . .'

'I mean it!' Diamond felt ill, swollen, ill-tempered and now Mimi was going on and on.

'If the Marquis objects to my absence so much, find another patron, Mimi. I'm sure you can do it.'

Soon Mimi was out about town, kissing cheeks and pressing her dainty hands into the hands of others who had money, position, power. Finally she came back to Diamond and said: 'All right, since you are determined to be difficult. I have found us another patron.'

'Go on then.' Increasingly, Diamond was feeling that her Paris dream was dead and that she might just as well go back to London. She felt sick with the baby, seriously unwell. She had arrived here so full of hope. But Fabien had ditched her. Everything had crumbled into dust. And how had this all blown up about the Marquis? She *liked* him. He wouldn't mind her staying away from the château, if she talked to him. Somehow, she'd painted herself into a corner, got into an argument that she wasn't even interested in.

'It's Toro Wolfe,' said Mimi. 'You remember him? I can't imagine that *he* would need you for a cover while he makes love to beautiful young men, can you? I think his motive is of a much more *direct* nature, where you are concerned.'

Diamond's jaw dropped. Then she clamped her mouth tight shut and said through gritted teeth: 'Mimi – I would rather *die*.'

'Be that as it may . . .'

'I mean it, Mimi.'

'Then I don't think we have any choice. Do you?'

'I'll come to the château,' sighed Diamond.

66

Richard came downstairs one morning after another awful wretched night to find his mother talking to someone in the hall, with Benson standing patiently by.

Lady Margaret had only recently moved out into the Dower House, but today here she was in the main hall of *his* house, talking to some other woman. They were laughing and chatting. As he reached the bottom of the stairs, he realised that the other woman was Catherine.

For God's sake!

As Margaret saw Richard there, she tucked an arm into Catherine's and turned to face him, a determined smile on her face.

'Catherine came to see me at the Dower House and I insisted while she was there that she should come and see you too, isn't that nice?' said his mother.

'Splendid,' said Richard through gritted teeth.

'Benson, will you see to some tea for the Earl in the drawing room please?' Margaret instructed the butler, who bowed and departed. Then she turned to her son. 'I shan't linger, darling, I've got a million things to do. Catherine, dear, stay and have a chat to Richard. I shall leave the pair of you now. Goodbye!'

Trapped, Richard escorted Catherine into the drawing room where the fire was lit and roaring.

'I think your mother is trying a spot of match-making,' said Catherine with a smile as she sat down.

'I know.'

'She means well.'

'I know that too. However . . .'

'Oh! Don't worry,' said Catherine. 'Friends we agreed and friends we will stay. All right?'

Richard nodded, relieved. The last thing he had ever wanted to do was hurt Catherine. She really was his oldest, dearest friend and he knew he would hate to lose her. He had missed her calm, quiet company, since they'd become estranged. Catherine always knew what to say, what to do, to make him feel better. They seemed to speak the same language, to fall easily into conversation, to each know how the other felt.

And now, as he looked at her, he could see that she had changed. Grown up. Her ashy-blonde hair was shingled in the new 'flapper' style beneath her neat little cloche hat. Her coat and dress were sky blue and fashionably short. Her crocodile-skin handbag and neat Mary-Jane shoes were in matching shades of tan. Three long ropes of pearls were revealed as she slipped her coat off and held her hands out to the fire.

Marriage? To Catherine?

No. He couldn't do that to her. He'd get bored and she'd be unhappy. What Catherine needed was someone who cared passionately about her, who *adored* her. And that wasn't him. He knew it would be the neatest of solutions to all his financial ills. That his mother would be ecstatic. And her parents too. Even Teddy might forgive him at last. But . . . he couldn't do it.

He *would* have done it, if the war hadn't happened and changed him so deeply.

But now? He couldn't.

'So!' She smiled at him, her warm grey eyes sparkling. 'Tell me what you've been up to, Richard. I suppose you've been off to that Brooklands place, racing your beastly cars?'

'You know me so well,' said Richard.

And that was the trouble. She did.

So many nice rich American girls are coming over here, his mother had told him. *If not Catherine, why not one of them?*

But no. He didn't want an American girl – and he didn't want Catherine, either.

Then *she* was there in his mind again. Irritating. Diamond, the whore. The one who'd tricked him, trapped him. The one whose image he could never seem to shake off.

But what use were daydreams of some lost – and definitely fallen – woman to him? No use at all. The estate was in debt *right now* and he needed to take action.

It broke his heart and he was glad his father wasn't here to see it, but he was going to have to sell off some of the land.

67

All in all, Victor was content with the way things were going. He had Lily Wong, who fucked his brains out on a regular basis and had introduced him to the marvels of cocaine and opium. He had his new Triad contacts, who were very agreeable gentlemen to do business with. Granted, he had Gwendoline, who had been a disappointment, always pecking at his head and wondering where he was when he was *out*, what was so difficult to understand about that?

There were other things to concern him. That little fucker Michael McLean and his Silver Blades, they were getting troublesome. Trying to nick his hoisters. Edging into his manor, trying to take over parts of it. And his nephew Aiden was a pain in the arse, kicking against his leadership, getting in his face, the little tosser. Something was going to have to be done about him. Annoying. Victor had found it necessary to cut a few, Blades and hoisters both, just to show them what was what. But still they kept on, so he went to Chinatown one evening.

It was very *civilised* there, he'd found. Of course the Triads would slice you up like a Sunday dinner if they thought you were of a mind to cross them, but he was in, he was in very sweet indeed with Lily Wong's father, and it was Mr Wong who met him one evening, elegant little Mr Wong who proudly tapped at a big tarpaulined object and said he had the thing that Victor had asked for, and it would be at a knock-down price of course, they would do a deal on the price of a couple of the pieces of their usual merchandise and the deal would be sweet.

'Let's see it then,' said Victor, and Mr Wong whipped off the tarpaulin to reveal the goods, the big round revolving cylinder with its blued barrel, the handle you turned to fire the massive and very impressive thing.

It was a Gatling gun.

***

Of course Gwendoline knew that if Victor caught her, she would be dead. She was painfully aware of her husband's tendency to violence, just like she was aware of what was going on between him and Lily Wong. Nevertheless, she followed him to Chinatown that night because it was all starting to worry her and she didn't like that, she liked to know what was going on.

She loitered in the shadows. Victor's men were all around, and the Chinese too, but she could be discreet when she had to be. She watched as Victor and a team of eight men loaded some big tarpaulin-covered something-or-other onto the back of a horse-drawn cart, watched as Lily Wong came out of her red-painted doorway and embraced Victor and led him inside when the cart had pulled away and was gone.

68

The Marquis's Parisian housekeeper was a dour woman, skinny as a rail, dressed in black and touting a bunch of keys that ought to have toppled her thin frame right over. Her dark suspicious eyes beheld the two men at the door – one of them tall and handsome and young, the other bent over a cane with a thick tuft of black hair on his head and a carefully trimmed white beard on his chubby chin. They both offered her their identification cards. She examined them as if they would bite.

'Inspector Benoit, Sergeant Golon,' she said, reading carefully. She handed the cards back. 'What can I do for you?'

'May we come in, madame? We wish to speak to the Marquis de Marquand on a serious matter.'

'What sort of matter?' she asked.

'That should stay between us and the Marquis.'

'Monsieur le Marquis isn't here in town at the moment.'

'Then where is he?' asked Golon.

'The Marquis would not wish me to give out that information.'

'But to the police, madame . . .?' Benoit encouraged.

'Is this a serious matter?'

'Very, madame.'

'Monsieur le Marquis will be back in town at the start of next week. You should call back then,' said the housekeeper, and started to close the door.

Golon stuck his foot in it.

'Remove your foot please,' said the housekeeper.

'Madame, this is a murder inquiry,' said Benoit.

The housekeeper visibly stiffened. She opened the door wider.

'What on earth could such a matter have to do with a man of the Marquis's standing?' she asked.

'That is what we are hoping to establish,' said Benoit. 'Madame, we can continue this conversation here, or we can ask you to accompany us to our offices where we can perhaps talk at greater length . . .?'

'Well, if it's as serious as you say . . .'

'It is, madame. It concerns a man in the Marquis's employ who has been brutally murdered.'

Her expression changed to one of horror. She stepped back from the door.

'Then of course you must come in, and I will give you details about the Marquis's whereabouts. Of course I will. I have no wish to appear uncooperative.'

'Of course not. Thank you, madame,' said Benoit, and they stepped inside.

69

'Look at her! Isn't she beautiful!' exclaimed the Marquis. 'She's been in my family for nearly a thousand years, isn't that remarkable?'

He was pointing ahead while they rattled along in the motor car, his uniformed driver at the wheel. After what seemed like a journey that would never end, finally they were here at the château. And Diamond, queasy though she felt after the long and none-too-comfortable drive, had to admit it: the château that towered in front of them in the bright late summer sky was simply stunning. The twin round turrets soared and glistened, the pale stonework glowed. The château was *huge*, truly a palace, tall and so imposing, squatting in its moat like a grand lady rising majestically from a bath.

The Borzois, who had been lounging at the feet of the Marquis up to this point, started stirring as the car was driven through the high, imposing gates. They sat up, and Titania whined. Boris's tail thumped the floor. They knew they were home.

'And it belongs to the Marquis,' said Mimi under her breath, nudging her hard in the ribs. 'And darling – I think the Marquis belongs to you.'

But Diamond knew the Marquis's true affections lay elsewhere. When the motorcade drew up in front of the château, the Marquis saw her safely down from the car – but then he went straight to the car behind theirs and helped Jean-Luc to step down.

All the servants turned out to greet the big line of cars and their excited occupants. Then the group was ushered inside to stand staring, entranced, open-mouthed, at huge high ceilings, massive lead-crystal chandeliers, a vast sweeping staircase that led up to their rooms.

Diamond was shown up to the second floor by one of the old retainers and into the interior of one of those big fairy-tale turrets. The room was perfectly circular, decorated in the grand *art nouveau* style with a huge ornate French bed, gilded chairs, gold-fabric-covered chaises, two matching and probably priceless chinoiserie vases, and vast mirrors. The walls were papered in the palest powdery blue and they shimmered like satin. Diamond went to the window and stared out at the moat, the fields beyond, the woods beyond that. In the far distance the sun beamed down on a small village.

'That is Monsieur le Marquis's village. It belongs to the château,' the retainer told her proudly. 'There are one hundred and fifty acres all told. A productive vineyard, too.'

She could see the vineyard with its neat lines of perfectly pruned vines some distance over to the left. She couldn't help feeling that she had come a very long way from the East End. Maybe this was somewhere she could actually live, her, plain little Diamond Butcher, who was now wearing a long white Arctic fox fur and an only slightly shorter string of freshwater pearls – both new gifts from the Marquis – and was now thankful for the loose drapery that was the current fashion, because it hid her pregnancy. For a while, anyway. She certainly couldn't fit into that rigidly sculpted red velvet gown any more. Little Madame Delphine had worked very hard to craft her a selection of gowns specifically to hide the bump of her belly. She was truly a miracle worker. But sooner or later the fact that Diamond was carrying a baby was going to be impossible to conceal – and it would then appear to the world at large that she was carrying the Marquis's baby, which would suit them both very well.

'Tell me what you want,' the Marquis said to her, over and over. 'And I will get it for you. Anything, darling. I mean it.'

It still hurt her, to think of Fabien. She had dreamed of a golden future with him; him painting her and having a family with her, the pair of them living an exquisite Bohemian life together, their children playing in a lovely cooling green glade by a stream, far away from the fog and noise and strife of the city. But all that had been nothing but a stupid, girlish dream. She had emerged from it bruised, bloodied, but unbowed.

At least, with the Marquis, she had friendship and support. He was so grateful to her for the cover she provided, which enabled him to conduct his affair with Jean-Luc in private; *he* wouldn't let her down.

On Monday, the men in the party went out shooting wild boar. On Tuesday, there was a dinner party in the evening followed by drinks and games. Then on Wednesday morning, she walked into the Marquis's study and found him there, with the dogs at his feet – and two strange men were with him, standing in front of the fire.

70

'*Chérie*,' said the Marquis, turning as she came in.

'Sorry! I thought you were alone,' Diamond said, not wishing to intrude.

'No. No! You can stay, *chérie*.' He held out a hand. She went to him, took it. 'This is Inspector Benoit of the *Sûreté*. And this is Sergeant Golon. I'm sorry, I've had a bit of a shock.'

Police! She'd heard about the fearsome reputation of the '*Sûreté*'. She felt herself stiffen and instantly into her mind came the night of Fabien's exhibition, Arnaud falling dead at her feet. She felt that guilt must be written all over her face.

'What is it then?' She forced herself to appear calm, cool. Perhaps they'd come about something else, something different. 'What's happened?'

'Gentlemen, this is my companion, Mam'selle Diamond Dupree.'

'Charmed,' murmured Benoit.

'A pleasure, mam'selle,' said Golon.

'Diamond, these gentlemen have given me sad news. They have told me that my Parisian agent Arnaud Roussel has died,' said the Marquis, leaning down to stroke an unsteady hand over Boris's silky coat. Then he looked up at her. 'It's awful. They fished the poor fellow out of the Seine. He'd been shot.'

'My God.' Diamond gulped and pressed a hand to her chest. Her heart was racketing away in there like a drum. Suddenly she felt hot, sweaty. 'That's terrible.'

'The worst thing is,' the Marquis went on, 'I was convinced the man had simply vanished, neglected his duties and gone off on some sort of pleasure trip. I said as much to you, didn't I, *chérie*? You remember?'

Diamond nodded. She didn't think she had spit enough in her mouth to utter a word right now.

'When in fact the very reverse was true,' said the Marquis. 'There I was cursing him, and he was lying dead in the city morgue.'

'You weren't to know, sir,' said Golon.

'Of course not,' said Benoit. 'But now you do, perhaps you would be so kind as to tell us what you do know of this man Arnaud Roussel? For instance, his family . . .?'

The Marquis shrugged and sighed. 'Please, will you sit down, gentlemen? Remiss of me, I'm sorry, I've been so shocked by what you've told me. May I offer you some coffee? Chocolate?'

Both officers refused refreshment, but sat down.

'*Chérie*, please sit,' the Marquis said to Diamond, and she took a seat. Both policemen watched her and she knew what they were thinking: a plain, skinny, rich and titled man and a much younger and attractive woman? It was a story as old as time itself.

'Poor Arnaud had no kin to speak of,' the Marquis began as Sergeant Golon pulled out a book and started taking notes. 'He was a bachelor and as far as I know he was estranged from his family. He never talked about them to any of my staff.'

'Or to you, Monsieur le Marquis?' asked Benoit.

'No. Well, we hardly had that sort of relationship. I employed him to do a job, he did it. We were not friends.' The Marquis heaved a heavy sigh. 'But how shocking, how truly awful, that he should end in such a way.'

Golon said: 'Your housekeeper in Paris said that he was something of a misfit. That he drank too much. Gambled too.'

'I really wouldn't know. All I can tell you is that he did the work I gave him very competently.'

'She said that he hung around the artists' quarter sometimes. Doing deals, she said. I had the feeling she didn't like him very much,' said Benoit.

The artists' quarter, thought Diamond. *Oh God.*

Arnaud had been 'hanging around' Montmartre – pestering Mimi for the money she owed him. She'd always brushed him off, shooed him away, but that 'pestering' had culminated in her pulling a gun on him on the night of the exhibition. And Diamond, intervening, trying to stop a catastrophe, had grabbed the gun and killed him.

She thought of the guillotine. That was what you got in France for murder. They chopped off your head like you were a chicken about to be roasted. The thought of that pin-sharp steel blade slicing through the flesh of her neck made her blood run cold.

Diamond stood up. 'I'm sorry,' she said. 'This is so upsetting. I think . . .'

The Marquis got to his feet and hurried to her side. Titania and Boris scrabbled up too, yawning, stretching. 'Darling, are you all right? This is all too much for you, I'm sure. Such a horrible thing to happen, and of course you don't want to hear it. Crass of me not to see it straight away. Go on, off you go, *chérie*. Take the dogs outside, get some air. Everything will be fine, I promise you. I'll join you just as soon as I can.'

Not even glancing at the two policemen, Diamond fled the room, the dogs at her heels. Only when she was outside did she feel able to breathe again. She was going to have to tell Mimi about this. And soon.

71

Later that same day, everyone went riding, even Mimi – but not Diamond. She was too rattled by that unexpected visit from the police and too fearful about the baby so she made an excuse. She sat in the library, Boris and Titania sprawled out at her feet. The dogs seemed to have adopted her, much like their master had. She worried about the police. That shrewd-eyed little Frenchman Benoit, the way he'd looked at her. Had he sensed her unease? On Thursday, another shooting party went out. Friday was a day of rest. Then on Saturday there was the farewell party, before all the Marquis's guests returned to Paris.

Feeling grateful to have got through the week, Diamond dressed in Madame Delphine's most elaborate creation, a dress that was a shimmering waterfall of pale beads, falling loose to just above the knee. It glinted and glittered as she moved. She clipped a white ostrich-feather headdress to her hair, which she tucked up to copy the current fashion that most of the women were wearing these days. She put on earrings to draw the eye away from her mid-section and up to her face. Put on red lipstick and rouge, looked at herself in the mirror, then went down to find everyone in the ballroom with its gilded walls and elaborately painted ceiling. The place was heaving, a band playing, waiters slipping through the crowds with nibbles and champagne.

She grabbed a glass from a passing tray and stood there, sipping her drink, watching the crowds moving around her, greeting a few familiar faces. There was Hemingway, who seemed to get himself invited to everything. And Cole Porter was at the piano, playing 'Alexander's Ragtime Band', with an adoring crowd of women gathered around him.

Diamond thought of her life in London, beating carpets in the yard and hoisting goods from shops and playing badger tricks on unsuspecting punters, and thought *well this is it. This is the high life – isn't it?*

But all she wanted to do was go back upstairs, take her tight shoes off her swollen feet, lie on the bed and be alone. The pregnancy was making her feel heavy, apart somehow from all this gaiety and laughter. She couldn't see Mimi, and she was glad of that but she knew she'd have to see her, talk to her about the police visit. Mimi's cheerful airy chatter was as irritating at times as that of a shrieking parrot. She went over to Cole and said hello, and Hemingway caught her arm and twirled her around in a dance step or two.

'Where's Mimi?' she asked him.

'No idea,' said Hemingway, drinking deeply from his glass and slapping the empty on a passing waiter's tray before grabbing himself and Diamond another.

'I think I'll go find her,' said Diamond, seizing on an excuse to absent herself from the crush and roar of the ballroom. She *had* to talk to Mimi.

Outside, staff glided around the cool corridors. Diamond made her way up to the first floor, to the room she knew to be Mimi's. She knocked on the door. There was no answer. She knocked again. Nothing. Tempted to just go to her own room and try to relax, she walked a few steps away; then the door to the suite creaked open and Mimi peeped around it, looking dishevelled.

'Oh! It's you,' she said, dragging a hand through her rumpled blonde curls, hiking her neckline back into place.

'What are you doing?' asked Diamond.

'Who is it?' called a young male voice from inside Mimi's suite.

'Nothing, darling, just Diamond.' Mimi turned back to Diamond with an impish grin. 'I shall be down in about half an hour,' she told her. 'I'm busy, as you can tell.'

'Mimi, come out here,' hissed Diamond.

'Oh really . . .'

'Is that a client?' she demanded.

'Oh for God's sake . . .'

It was. Diamond knew it. Mimi was turning tricks in the Marquis's own house.

'Come out here right now. And shut the door,' she ordered. A cramp hit her stomach and she winced. She'd been feeling unwell ever since the police visit. It was nerves. Or gas. Or something.

'Oh all right . . .' Mimi stepped out, pulling the door closed behind her, refastening buttons.

'The police were here,' Diamond told her. 'They were questioning the Marquis about Arnaud. Mimi, Arnaud worked for the Marquis.'

'I know that.'

'You *know*? Then why didn't you tell me?'

'It didn't seem to matter.'

'*Mimi!* This is the police, they're talking about a murder. They're trying to find out how Arnaud died.'

'Well we know about that, don't we, darling? You shot him.'

'The gun went off in my hand. It was *your* gun. And what the hell were you thinking? What the *fuck* were you doing, waving a gun around? Where did you get it in the first place?'

'Oh, I have friends who can lay their hands on most things,' said Mimi. 'Now if that's all, I have to get back to my dear Sebastian. He is *très bien au lit. Terribly* inventive. I could almost do him for free – but I won't.'

'How can you be so bloody flippant?' demanded Diamond. Another cramp hit her. Oh God, she would have to calm down. She would hurt the baby. But this *mess* of Mimi's creating seemed to be following her around like a bad smell.

'Darling, what can they find? Nothing. We're not telling, are we? Why would we? So just calm down. Go down to the ballroom, and have some fun. *I* intend to,' she said with a wink, and went back inside her suite.

Presently, Diamond heard Mimi giggle and then a man's laugh, louder, deeper.

Mimi was having fun.

Diamond? She was in pain.

***

She went down and loitered outside the ballroom for a while, wondering whether to go in or simply abandon the evening and retire to her suite. Periodically the doors of the great room opened and a roar of conversation emerged, along with a fug of cigarette smoke and the noise of the piano tinkling away in the background.

The baby was pressing on her bladder. She made her way to the *toilette* and emerged five minutes later into the dark, cool hallway, determined to plunge back into the mob and enjoy herself. She couldn't mope over the loss of Fabien or worry about the police investigation into Arnaud's death forever, but both those things seemed to haunt her.

Then a harder cramp hit her midriff and she caught her breath, doubling over. Then another. Clawing at the wall for support, she stumbled back into the *toilette* and slammed the door shut. She felt moisture running between her legs and groped with shaking fingers to see what it was.

Oh Christ – she was bleeding!

Giddy, she collapsed to the floor – and then cramp after cramp hit her. She lay there, unable even to stand and then after what felt like hours *it* happened.

The baby poured out of her.

72

Of course, the child – a little girl – was dead. Diamond's first feeling was one of utter, devastating loss. Eventually she all but crawled from the *toilette* and tidied herself up as best she could. Then, shaking, still bending double and clutching at the hard stone château walls with every step, she made her way upstairs, taking the servants' staircase. A maid or two passed her but they looked the other way. Well good. She had nothing to say to them, nothing to say to anyone.

Up in the safety of her room, she stripped off her clothes, bathed, put on her nightdress and wedged a towel between her legs. Would the bleeding stop soon? She had no idea, and she didn't want to ask anyone about it. Maybe she would simply bleed to death and join her poor dead baby. She lay on the bed and wept. She was painfully aware of how badly she had wanted this child, no matter how much of an inconvenience it might be to her. She had already thought of names for it. Had already pictured its sweet, smiling face. Jacqueline for a girl, Jonathon for a boy. Jacqueline, then. Somehow, she would have managed and her child – her daughter – would have been her most treasured possession. She would have fought like a tigress to keep her safe.

But that option was gone now.

In the wake of the hurt, the sorrow, the devastating loss and the pain of her cramping, agonised belly, came something worse – a crashing, roaring anger. *Men* had caused all this to happen to her. Men were the cause of all her problems. Her bullying uncle. That blond *RB*, raping her when she'd had no choice in the matter, none whatsoever. Fabien, using her and then tossing her aside. *Fucking* Toro Wolfe, robbing her family of their livelihood and then holding her presence in Paris and Arnaud's death over her head like thc sword of Damocles.

Bastards.

She lay there and it was hours before the pain subsided, the bleeding slowed to a trickle. More hours while darkness fell and she could still distantly hear the gaiety down below in the ballroom, the laughter. It was unearthly, coming from another world, one that did not involve her or her own private loss and fury.

Then – way past midnight, she guessed – there was a faint knock at the door.

'Diamond?' hissed Mimi's voice. Then she knocked again.

Groaning, Diamond hauled herself to the edge of the elaborately carved four-poster bed with its lavish blue and gold draperies. She sat there, literally drained, knowing she didn't have the strength to endure Mimi's chatter right now. She reached for the light, switched it on. The clock said a quarter past two in the morning.

Struggling to her feet, she went over to the door and unlocked it, swung it wide. Mimi took one long horrified look at Diamond and said: 'In the *toilette* downstairs, all the ladies are talking about it. Someone lost a baby. They could see it was . . . well, it was horrible. Afterbirth and everything. A little girl, they said. And then I thought – are you all right?'

'It was me,' said Diamond, and staggered drunkenly back over to the bed.

Mimi closed the door and followed as Diamond slumped back down with a groan of relief. Two more minutes on her feet and she would have passed out cold.

'Should we have a doctor called?' asked Mimi, flapping her arms, for once in her selfish life looking genuinely concerned for someone other than herself. 'You look like death, darling, you really do.'

Diamond shook her head. Another *man*, to poke and prod her about? No. To hell with that. 'I'll be fine by the morning, back in Paris by nightfall thank God. Don't fuss.'

'Shall I sit with you . . .?'

'No. I want to be alone.'

'All right then.' Mimi left.

Diamond lay there, nearly drifting off to sleep now that the pain was easing, and then there was another knock on the door. She snapped awake, angry, heartsore, ready to break Mimi's stupid head with the nearest blunt instrument she could lay her hands on.

'Go the fuck *away,* Mimi!' she called.

The door swung open. Mimi came in and to Diamond's horror she had the Marquis with her. He called out to a trailing manservant to summon the doctor, then closed the door behind them. They both came over to the bed.

'*Ma pauvre petite,*' he said, taking Diamond's hand in both of his. 'I had no idea. None. Are you in pain?'

Diamond shook her head and glared at Mimi, who shrugged. *What else could I do?*

'No,' said Diamond, and it was true. It was all over. There would be no bright chubby little baby for her to cuddle and love, to see toddle off to school, to see getting boyfriends, to see getting married, having children that would be her grandchildren, oh God, what did she have in her life? She had nothing. She had no-one. Suddenly she missed her mother so much, who would have seen her through this disaster, helped her come to terms with it.

Then she thought of Toro Wolfe's last words to her. That she was hard. Cutting. Yes, like a diamond. The rage had steadied now, and she was truly cold. Seeing things clearly, perhaps for the very first time. She would have to learn to be this way, the way the Wolfe person said she already was.

'Leave us, Mimi,' she said, a winter wind in her voice.

Mimi flinched. 'Well – if you're sure.'

The Marquis waved Mimi away from the bed and she left the room.

'What can I do for you, my darling?' the Marquis asked.

'Anything, you said. I could ask and you would get me anything I wanted.'

'And I meant it. Please, my dearest, ask for what you want. We're friends, aren't we?'

Yes. He was her friend. She actually *liked* him.

'The first thing is . . .' She hesitated.

He nodded. 'Go on.'

'Never ask me who the father was.' *Because I don't know.* The handsome blond stranger's face swam into her mind. *RB.* An unknown man to father an unborn child.

'I won't. I promise.'

'The second is this. I want you to set me up in business, when we get back to Paris.'

'I can do that,' he said, and smiled down at her. 'Easily.'

'I want a nightclub,' she said, thinking of Toro Wolfe. Thinking of the club with the giant's mouth at the doorway, the red interior with all those macabre stuffed animals on the walls. The Cabaret of Hell. Once, it had been a Butcher club. Now, to stop herself from sinking into despair, she could make it that again. Make it *hers.* 'I want Cabaret de l'Enfer.'

73

While the Marquis and his two dogs and all the other guests were transported by car back to the city, Diamond took the train up to Paris – she couldn't stand, in her still-delicate condition, another tortuous trip in that bone-shaking contraption. Within a week, she began to feel better and within a fortnight it was as if she had never been pregnant at all. The Marquis visited her daily at the apartment she shared with Mimi, sometimes even bringing the glamorous Jean-Luc with him. They fussed over her, kept her abreast of all the scandals that were happening while she was making her recovery.

It made life very easy, she noticed, having a title. People snapped to attention everywhere when the Marquis appeared, and Parisian estate agents nearly fell over themselves when he declared his interest in a particular property.

'But of course, M'sieur le Marquis,' they said, ushering him into the comfiest chairs, grinding fresh coffee beans, offering him the choicest little titbits to eat while they discussed the vulgar subject of money.

Mimi was intrigued. 'What are you getting up to?' she asked Diamond.

'Nothing very remarkable,' said Diamond, and then Toro Wolfe pitched up unexpectedly at their apartment.

'Will you excuse us please, Mimi?' asked Diamond.

'Don't I know you?' Mimi said with a coy smile at Toro.

'I don't think so,' he smiled back.

'Maybe I should *get* to know you,' said Mimi.

'Mimi!' said Diamond. 'Go, will you?'

With Mimi out of the way, Diamond said: 'Can I ask you a question?'

'You can.'

'The night of the exhibition. What did you do with the gun?'

'Not much.'

'What, exactly? Did you dump it somewhere?'

'Why are you asking? Better you don't know.'

'The police have been asking questions of the Marquis. Arnaud was his Parisian agent.' She hated lying about Arnaud and what had happened to him to the Marquis. The Marquis had been so good to her; such a firm friend. Keeping dark secrets from him made her feel awkward and disloyal.

Toro gave Diamond an arch look. 'And so you're getting jumpy? You want to know where the gun is.'

'Yes.'

He just shrugged.

'Tell me,' said Diamond through gritted teeth.

'Or what?'

Jesus! He was infuriating. *Hateful.*

'I heard you'd been ill,' he said.

'Ill? No. You must be misinformed,' she returned coldly.

'That you'd lost the baby. I'm sorry.'

'Sorry? There's no need for that.'

'All right.' He paused, eyeing her face. 'The Marquis has put an offer in on Cabaret de l'Enfer. You remember, I told you it was up for sale.'

'I do remember that, yes.'

'What is he then? Your sugar daddy? Are you a demi-mondaine these days? Or something else?'

'I've no idea what you mean.'

'He's bought it for you, I'm guessing.'

'Guess all you like,' Diamond invited.

His eyes narrowed. 'What is this? Revenge?'

'I beg your pardon?'

'Buying back one of the Butcher family clubs, is that it?'

'I'm not buying anything, Mr Wolfe. The Marquis might be, I really have no idea.'

Toro took a step forward, just close enough to be threatening. Diamond forced herself not to take a step back. 'You might be sorry,' he said.

'Sorry about what?'

'Have you heard of Le Milieu?'

'No. What is that?'

'The Corsican mob. They control a lot of concerns around Marseilles – and now Paris too.'

'What sort of concerns?'

'Prostitution. Drugs. Arms. Bookmaking. Money laundering.'

'And why should any of that bother me?'

'You don't want to cross swords with that lot.'

'I'm not planning on crossing swords with anyone.' She frowned at him. 'Is that why you're selling? Have you had trouble?'

'Not yet. But once you've been in a trench with mustard gas floating over the top, it tends to make you very well aware of which way the wind is blowing.'

'And you think it's blowing trouble your way, so you're getting out? But L'Enfer is one club. You have five others. Perhaps you'd give Monsieur le Marquis a handsome discount on a multiple sale?'

He stared at her for a long moment. 'You've changed somehow. I can't quite place it, but you have.'

It was true. She had. She'd lost a child. Had her heart broken by a vain, worthless man who everyone was now hailing a genius – thanks to her. Been cut adrift from her family. Got involved in a shooting because of stupid feckless Mimi. Bad things had happened, but she had survived. So what was the point of fearing trouble now? Thinking that Victor was going to come after her or that the police were somehow going to track her down, catch her, pen her in a cell awaiting Madame la Guillotine? Whatever happened, she would do as she had always done. She would *face* it.

'I wanted to warn you, that's all,' he said when she didn't speak.

'Duly noted,' said Diamond.

'I've heard around town that the Marquis likes pretty boys, not women.'

'Have you? I really couldn't comment.'

'So what you really are these days is an arse bandit's beard? Is that the truth of it?'

Diamond gave a thin smile and said nothing.

'There must be better ways to survive,' he pointed out.

Diamond gave him a blank look. 'Tell me – *are* you planning on selling off all of your clubs? All those places your family bullied and cheated off mine? Or is it really going to be only the one?'

'Just the one. For now. The Marquis has made a very generous offer. Full asking price.'

'Then you ought to accept.'

Toro let out a sigh, shook his head. 'Why don't you just go back to England?'

'What, and let that cow Gwendoline order me around in my own home? I don't think so.'

'You're heading into dangerous waters, and I think it's only fair to tell you so.'

'Why would you bother?'

'I'm fucked if I know.'

'Is that what you are really planning to do? Close up your business interests over here, and head back home with your tail between your legs, seen off by a few peasants from Corsica?'

He shrugged. 'Business is business, all over the world. You do know *something* about them then?'

She did. She'd seen them around town – stocky hard-eyed men moving in gangs, people stepping aside whenever they passed. Everyone had seen them, everyone knew of them. Protection rackets and extortion, counterfeiting, they did it all. It was best to keep out of their way, she knew that much.

'I'm selling one club. The others? I'll see.'

'And now, if that's all . . .?' said Diamond.

'Yes, it is,' he said.

'Good. Now,' she smiled sweetly, 'do fuck off.'

74

It was a bright summer's day when Richard saw all the Top Farm equipment, the seed drills, steam tractors, hoes, cultivators, pitchforks, *everything*, sold off. The dairy herd was next. Then even the magnificent pair of glossy black Shire horses with their white-feathered fetlocks, who had pulled the plough day after day in all weathers on Top Farm fields, were put up for sale at the town market. Mrs Bryerson, who had been struggling to keep her children fed and to run Top Farm since her husband's death, had finally given up and told Richard that she was going to stay with her sister in Glasgow and find work in service there.

Walking around the market, the local people were respectful of him but he still felt their coolness. After this, the sale, he supposed he would be even more the villain of the piece in their eyes. It didn't help his self-esteem to run into his old friend Teddy Sibley, who still seemed determined to snub him on his sister Catherine's behalf, outside the cattle stalls. This time he was determined he would speak, even if it meant further rejection.

'Teddy – hello,' he said, and held out a hand.

Teddy's broad good-natured face set in a grim expression and he didn't take Richard's hand to shake it. Embarrassed, Richard dropped his hand to his side. He didn't blame Teddy in the least. Teddy had always been the more constant of the two of them, the more reliable. Teddy was a deeply moral man. Richard knew that however he felt, he would never have changed direction as Richard himself had, never baulk at going through with a commitment he had already made, no matter what it cost him in personal pain.

'Look,' said Richard desperately. 'Say something for God's sake. Throw a punch at me if you like. God knows I deserve it.'

But it was worse than that. Coldly, Teddy merely stepped aside, and walked on.

***

It was horrible to think it, but for Richard Mrs Bryerson's departure was a blessing. It was as if fate was lending him a hand out of his financial troubles. He then received a call from the government offering a substantial amount for the purchase of a section of land for railway development. Top Farm proved to be on the required route, plus two others, Box Hill and Oak Farm. The Box Hill and Oak Farm tenants were reluctant to leave, but Richard took it upon himself to find the farmers and their families other holdings. So that was sorted out and the necessity of his marrying a rich American – or going cap in hand back to poor Catherine – had been avoided.

His mother, of course, was not happy. She cornered him in his study about it.

'Once you sell estate land you can never get it back again,' she sighed heavily. 'Your dear father would never have considered such a course of action.'

It was his dear father who'd landed them with the need to part with the land in the first place. Richard thought it, but didn't say it. Lady Margaret would be hurt, she would cry, she would sulk, and he couldn't stand any of that.

'It's progress, Mother,' said Richard. 'The railway will bring prosperity. People will be able to travel, to do business. Hotels are planned already for the stations. It's all for the good.'

'And what about that poor woman, sent off to Glasgow?'

'*Sent* off?' Richard echoed. 'I didn't send Mrs Bryerson anywhere. She couldn't manage Top Farm on her own, so she decided to go and stay with her sister.'

'Which was very convenient for you, you must admit it.'

'Well I do. It was.'

'Selling off estate land! Richard, the very idea . . .' she tutted.

'Needs must,' he said flatly, and rose from his desk. 'Now, if that is all . . .?'

'I still think that if you and Catherine . . .'

'I know what you think, Mother. Fortunately, the deal on the railway makes any such action unnecessary.'

'If you had married Catherine as planned, the *deal* would have been unnecessary and we could have kept Top Farm, Box Hill and Oak Farm too and all would have been well.'

Richard looked at his watch. 'Mother, if that's all . . .? I have rather a busy day.'

'Yes. I know. You want to be rid of me,' she said, and stood up and stormed out.

75

Aiden missed his sister, so much. He understood completely that she couldn't write to him and Owen, couldn't risk Victor finding out where she was, but the truth was that the heart had gone out of the house when she left.

Looking out for Owen with Victor and Gwendoline in the house was hard. They picked on Owen mercilessly and it was getting to the stage where Aiden was frightened of leaving his brother alone with the pair of them.

'Bring him over to Ma's place,' Michael offered. 'You too, Aid. Why not? Join the Blades. Leave those fuckers.'

Finding Owen trembling and in tears more than once, Aiden was starting to think it was the sensible thing to do – get Owen out of harm's way, avoid any more confrontations in the house.

So one day when he knew Victor was out and Gwen was down the shops, and Owen was sitting peacefully out in the back yard, he packed Owen's stuff up, all of his clothes and crayons and magazines, and was coming out of Owen's bedroom with Owen's belongings in his arms when to his shock he came face to face with Victor on the landing.

'What the fucking hell is this? Going somewhere, boy?' asked Victor.

'Just taking Owen over to Moira's,' said Aiden.

'For what? Boy belongs here, with his family.'

'Family?' Aiden snorted. 'Come on.'

'Come on *what*?'

Aiden's temper flared. Christ, he should have got out of this when Diamond did. Grabbed Owen and just gone.

'You know what!' Aiden surged forward, going to pass Victor. 'I'm getting Owen out of here.'

'No. You ain't. He stays. And so do you, where I can keep my damned eye on you.'

'Get out my way, Victor.'

Victor shoved him, hard. Aiden staggered back. 'Or what?'

'Or *this*,' roared Victor, and punched Aiden in the head. Unbalanced, agonised, Aiden dropped all Owen's belongings and stumbled, his hand going out to save himself but too late.

He fell, going end over end down the stairs. Lying blinking and stunned at the bottom, he saw Victor coming down toward him.

He ought to stand up.

He ought to run.

He couldn't.

76

Sometimes, Gwendoline could hear people in the house at night. Sometimes, she thought she must be going mad. Maybe Victor was drugging her with some of that stuff he took himself. She felt out of it sometimes, groggy, wondering if she could believe the evidence of her own ears.

But she definitely heard noises. People's voices, in the small hours. Footsteps downstairs. Victor hardly ever shared a bed with her now, and that was something to be grateful for, she supposed. Let Lily Wong have him, she no longer cared. A few beatings had made the scales fall from her eyes in a big way. She knew Victor for what he was now: a thug.

Sometimes she heard the cellar door opening. She knew the sound, she was *sure* that was what it was, but why would Victor be going down the cellar in the middle of the night? Who were the people she thought she could hear, murmuring voices, mostly female, then the *snap* of Victor's voice, so that they fell silent?

She didn't know.

She huddled beneath the blankets in her bed. She was afraid, and she was trapped.

There were arguments all the time between Victor and Aiden, shouting matches that terrified her. Aiden was a fool, to try and stand against Victor. And then one day when she got up and was preparing the breakfast, Aiden was simply not there any more.

'Where's Aiden today?' she asked Victor. Was he still in bed? Was he ill? Not that she cared much, but she was curious.

'Gone,' said Victor past a mouthful of tea.

'Gone where?'

'Fell down the stairs yesterday.'

'*What?*'

'Broke his stupid neck.'

Gwendoline's mouth was open in horror. 'My *God* . . .' she gasped out.

'Undertaker came. Funeral's on Friday.' Victor pushed back his chair. 'Is that the end of the bloody inquisition then? Is that *it*?'

Gwendoline didn't say another word.

She thought of Toro. Maybe she could get in touch with him. She knew he loathed her, that they had never been close or anywhere even near it, but he would help, wouldn't he? He would get her out of here. But when she went to the Wolfe house, he wasn't there and the man at the door said he was abroad, travelling.

There was no help to be had.

But she would tackle Victor about all these strange comings and goings, she *would*. When she felt braver. After all, she was still mistress of the house. She wanted to know what the *hell* was going on.

77

'Well – what do you think, my angel?'

The Marquis was watching Diamond anxiously as they strolled around the empty, cavernous club together. Boris and Titania were snuffling around the floor, exploring this new place, padding around silently like two white ghosts. The last time she'd been in here, she'd been carrying her baby. This time, that particular dream was dead and she was trying hard to make an effort to take an interest, to be appreciative, because she could see it meant a lot to him.

'It's fabulous,' she said, staring around.

She'd felt a shudder of misgiving as she stepped through the massive giant's mouth at the entrance, with its Cabaret de l'Enfer sign.

Well, maybe she would alter that. Make the place brighter, better. Strip out all the red, tear down those gruesome heads on the walls. Rewrite history, undo all the wrongs that had been done to the Butcher family, starting right here.

'Yes! You know, they used to have tiny waiters dressed as demons,' the Marquis told her with a smile. 'And they offered *attractions diaboliques*. Lots of evil goings-on. Only not really, of course. Slightly risqué, at best. But now everything will change. We will redecorate. And what acts will we offer our adoring public, hm?'

'Can-can dancers,' said Diamond. 'And acrobats from the east. A roundabout that emerges from the stage, with girls on. Topless of course. They'll complain that the twirling makes them dizzy no doubt. And there'll be food on offer, the very finest.'

Slowly, inch by inch, her spirits were lifting.

The Marquis had proved himself a friend. Wary of men, she had watched him with suspicion at first, but now she knew that she was perfectly safe with him, and secure. He wanted nothing more than her friendship, to bathe in their mutual glory as she strolled around town with him. All she had to do was cover for him, pose as his mistress while he pursued his dalliances with beautiful young men like Jean-Luc. Which was fine. She liked him enormously and she *loved* his dogs, sweet Boris and caring Titania. Whenever she felt overwhelmed by the ruins of her love affair with Fabien or – far worse – the baby, the sweet little girl she had craved for and lost, she would find a private corner and give in to the weak release of tears. Then Boris would sit whining at her feet, and Titania would lay her long elegant head in Diamond's lap in mute sympathy, gazing up at her with soft velvet eyes.

But what was there to do but carry on? Fabien was over, the baby was gone. So she made an effort, dressed up, painted her face, even though at times she felt she was dying inside. Time had passed while all the business of the property transaction was finalised. During that time, she lost the baby weight and now she was dressed, courtesy of dear old Madame Delphine, in a skilfully adapted version of the 'flapper' fashion, wearing a long drop-waisted lavender silk and chiffon dress and a toning purple marl coat with a luxurious apricot mink collar, topped off with a neat cloche hat with a frond of feathers tucked into the side. She'd still resisted the impulse to have her hair shortened to a shingle cut, but she wore her thick black tresses tucked back for the daytime in a neat bun; she looked stylish and expensive.

Inside, however, she still felt strangely dead. Like nothing was ever going to touch her, ever again. Still, she cooed over everything, admired the stage and the baby grand Steinway piano on it, touched a well-manicured finger to the keys and let out a delicious ripple of rich sound; saw the place come to life, reborn, as the decorators moved in and all the old fittings and fixtures were ripped out and replaced with new.

'When will opening night be?' she asked the Marquis.

'Whenever you require it, darling. Of course.'

'Next Saturday,' said Diamond. 'Will that give us time, do you think? To find staff and so on?'

'Most of the staff who worked for the previous owner are keen to stay on in their posts,' he said. 'There is a manager, of course, who will arrange everything.'

'They should all come in this week. I should meet them.'

'There is absolutely no need for that, darling. The manager will see to everything.'

'Still, I would like to familiarise myself with the running of the club.'

'Of course. If you wish.'

'It will give me an interest, now I no longer sit as an artist's model.'

'You'd never go back to that then?'

Diamond thought of Fabien and a shaft of pain ripped through her. 'No. Those days are done.'

'I'm glad to hear it, *chérie*. Because things have moved on, you know. I hear that Fabien Flaubert has wed Madeleine Rosa. Had you heard that?'

The pain hardened, turned leaden in her stomach. It had been *her* dream, and now Madeleine had robbed her of it. 'No. I hadn't heard.'

The Marquis shrugged. 'But you know the old saying. When a mistress becomes a wife, she creates a vacancy – and it's probably going to be filled. You know, he's a celebrated artist now. Everywhere he goes, he's fussed over and applauded.'

'He's a good painter,' said Diamond equably, but her heart hurt, literally *hurt*, every time she thought of Fabien.

There was movement at the door, men's voices, someone coming inside. The dogs raced over, tails wagging, eager to explore this new happening.

'Ah!' The Marquis smiled and rubbed his hands. 'And here's your surprise, *chérie*.'

Diamond moved down off the stage and watched as two men came into the main body of the club. They were carrying a cumbersome eight-foot-by-four-foot brown-paper-wrapped object.

'Gently now,' urged the Marquis, snatching up the dogs' leads and keeping them out of the workmen's way. The men carried the huge parcel onto the stage and placed it against the wall behind the piano.

Diamond watched as one of them took a knife out of his pocket and started cutting the paper wrapping away. A thick gold frame emerged, a dark background . . . it was a painting. Soon the red dress was revealed, and her own pale skin, skilfully recreated and enhanced by Fabien's clever brush strokes, and then there was her own face and her cascade of dark hair.

'I bought it on the night of Fabien's triumphant exhibition,' said the Marquis, coming over and giving her a quick hug. 'Darling, isn't it wonderful? I am going to hang it there at the back of the stage, where it will catch the light and be a magnificent centrepiece. What do you think?'

Diamond took a breath. She hated the thing. It reminded her of what she'd lost with Fabien. Of that heart-stopping, unforgettable and unrepeatable thrill of first love, when everything had been about him – the touch and the feel of him, the sight of the thin Parisian sun on his russet-gold hair, the musk and fresh hay scent of his skin. She had been *infatuated* with him, full of admiration for his skills, for his genius. She had drowned herself in his aura, made him into a star – and then he had discarded her like a worn-out rag, no longer fit for purpose.

'Lovely,' she said faintly.

'You like it? Don't you?' The Marquis looked anxious.

Diamond forced a smile onto her face. 'Of course I do. And it's so kind of you, to think of bringing it here. It's such a lovely surprise.'

'I am so pleased. I thought . . . I was afraid that it might be a reminder, something perhaps that you didn't want. But I am delighted to see that you like it just as much as I do. It will be a new beginning for this old place, won't it? And of course, there's to be fresh signage out at the front. We'll change the name.'

'To what?' Diamond asked. She hadn't considered that. 'Is there even time to get it done now?'

'Of course there is. The club will from this moment on be called Diamond's.'

78

'Darling, it's wonderful! Perfectly wonderful!'

It was opening night. Everyone was hugging and kissing Diamond and praising her to the skies. Hemingway was in at one of the best tables, and Picasso and his mistress. The place was packed to the rafters as the opening act – two Chinese men, wildly accomplished acrobats in shiny red suits – tossed a tiny Chinese woman dressed all in gold up in the air.

Everyone was delighted with the show. The applause was deafening in the packed confines of the club. The air was thick with the scent of expensive perfumes and hazed with grey from all the cigars and cigarettes being smoked by the smartly dressed clientele. Waiters hurried here and there among the tables, dispensing costly drinks and exquisite food.

Then there was a roll of the drums from the band and everyone gasped and applauded as the roundabout – which had cost a fortune and been an utter bastard to install – rose out of the stage, bearing its six white gold-bridled fairground horses on which were seated six beautiful girls dressed in multi-coloured harem pants, curly Turkish shoes, filmy yashmaks – and nothing else. Diamond had chosen each girl herself, going for those with the narrowest hips.

'It makes the breasts look bigger,' she told the Marquis.

All the girls complained, as she had predicted, that the twirling of the roundabout was too fast and made them giddy. She upped their wages, and their grievances were forgotten.

'It's spectacular,' said Hemingway, coming over and kissing her boozily on the cheek.

After the roundabout, there was a pause while the band played and the meals were brought out, then it was on with the cabaret, a cowboy called Tex McCloud who spun a lasso while singing 'For Me and My Gal', then a pair of comedy dancers, falling and leaping all over the stage, and a girl twinkling in a silver tassled dress danced to roars and shouts of approval. Then – at last – the finale. All the chorus girls came onstage, dancing and swinging their skirts; then the curtains closed.

***

Diamond was exhausted by the end of it. She was sitting there at her table beside the stage with the Borzois at her feet. Often now, the Marquis left them with her and she was frequently seen walking the streets of Montmartre, the two dogs moving ahead of her on their purple leads, elegance personified.

She heard movement at the front of the now deserted club. Probably just Claude the caretaker, tidying around, waiting to lock up. All the catering staff and the acts and the waiters had gone home, and the punters had headed home too, having eaten and drunk not wisely but too well. The Marquis and Jean-Luc had vanished into the night, arm in arm.

'Claude?' she called.

There was a man approaching her table out of the shadows. It wasn't Claude. This one was short and dark-haired

– broad across the shoulders, thick-legged, giving an impression of compact power. He was immaculately dressed. There were two women with him, and they stared at Diamond with hostile eyes as they came, one on either side of him. Diamond's attention was locked onto the man between them. His eyes were dark and very cold. His face was tanned; his mouth was smiling. She felt that she'd seen him before, but she couldn't think where.

Boris, who had been sprawled out on the floor beside his love Titania, sat up and emitted a low growl.

The man looked down at the dog. So did Diamond. She'd never heard Boris snarl at anyone before. She stroked his head, made soothing noises. He subsided but kept his eyes on the man.

'Diamond, *n'est-ce pas*?' said the stranger.

'Yes,' said Diamond, holding out a hand.

The man grasped it in his, brought it briefly to his lips. 'Mam'selle,' he greeted her.

'This is Monsieur Paoli,' said one of the women, a tall redhead wearing far too much make-up to cover her pitted skin, a fake beauty spot on her left cheek, her lips painted carmine red.

'Have we met?' Diamond asked the man.

'I assure you, mam'selle, you would remember me, if we had.'

Diamond frowned at his arrogance. 'For what reason would I remember you, m'sieur?'

'No-one ever forgets Angelo Paoli,' said the blonde huffily.

The man gave the blonde a look of faint irritation. 'Go, you two. *Allez!*'

The two women went off toward the bar and loitered there, glaring at Diamond. Monsieur Paoli sat down at Diamond's table, uninvited, and sprawled back in his chair, watching her with speculation in his eyes.

'They said you were a beauty,' he told her.

'Who?'

He shrugged. 'People. Around town. You know.'

'Yes?'

'They say you are the mistress of the Marquis.'

'Do they?'

'You are involved with him in some way, yes?'

'What is this about, m'sieur?'

'Nothing, mam'selle. Just idle chitchat, you know.' His smile was broad. Like an alligator, about to snap its jaws shut on its prey. She didn't like the look of him any more than Boris did. He made her feel uneasy.

'You know of us, then?' he said.

'Of who?'

'Us. Le Milieu Corse.'

Diamond sat back in her chair. Christ, this was one of the Corsicans. He was *mafia.*

She felt a cold hard thrill of fear shoot straight from her head to her toes as she remembered Toro Wolfe's warning. Her smile remained fixed in place, her composure outwardly unruffled. Inwardly, she shivered. She wondered where the hell Claude had got to.

'It's a pleasure to meet you,' she said, aware that her palms were suddenly damp.

'Likewise. Now – shall we get down to talk of business, mam'selle?' he said, leaning forward, placing both heavily ringed hands on the table.

'I was unaware that we had any business to discuss,' said Diamond, looking around, her eyes searching for Claude. He must have let Paoli and his two companions in and why, at this late hour, would he do that?

But she knew why. The Corsicans had a fearsome reputation. You wouldn't want to go against them, so it was prudent to just disappear – like Claude had obviously done. Like she wished *she* could do, instead of sitting here and waiting to hear what the hell this scum wanted from her.

'*Au contraire*, we do have business to discuss,' he said, shaking his head at her as if she was an errant child. 'We have important matters to thrash out between us.'

'Like what?' Diamond could feel her heart beating hard against her ribs. She could feel a worm of sweat trickling down her back.

'This place.' He waved a casual hand around. 'This club, mam'selle.'

'What about it?'

'I want it.'

Diamond narrowed her eyes and stared at his face. His own gaze didn't waver, not in the least.

'Well it's not for sale,' she said.

He was silent for a long, long moment.

'Mam'selle, you mistake my meaning,' he said very softly. 'I don't intend to *buy* the club. I intend to *take* it.'

79

Diamond's eyes were fixed to Paoli's face. His skin was bad, she noticed, like his red-haired companion's. Pocked with old scars. His eyes stared straight back at her, unwavering.

'You're not serious?' shot straight out of her mouth.

'Mam'selle, do I seem to you to be joking?' he asked, tilting his head to one side.

'Only this does sound like a joke,' she said. Yet another man, thinking he could push her around? The little arsehole had some front, you had to give him that.

'It isn't,' he said.

'Really.'

'Yes. Really.'

'This is intimidation,' said Diamond.

'Yes. Exactly.' He smiled, and there was a glint of gold in one of his incisors. 'Here is the deal, mam'selle. You pack up and you leave. And I take these premises over.'

'I don't respond to threats,' said Diamond. 'And anyway I don't own it.'

'Mam'selle. I am just laying out the facts. Whoever *does* own it will give it up. You will go, and I will take the club.'

Diamond thought of all the love they had lavished into this place, she and the Marquis, the sheer effort of will and the physical effort too. She had devoted herself to getting the place up and running to her satisfaction. She had poured so much into it. Now it was a success. And it was going to be taken off her? Just snatched away, like she didn't count?

'I'm going nowhere,' she said, not intending to say it, but *feeling* it, so forcefully, that there was simply no way to stop herself. 'And you'll find that the Marquis de Marquand doesn't bow down to threats.'

'What is that you say?' He couldn't believe it. She could see that.

'I *said*, forget that. I'm not going.'

He said nothing. He just stared at her face.

Then, very suddenly, he pushed his chair back. Despite herself, Diamond flinched.

He leaned down, quick as a striking cobra, putting his face up close to hers. Boris's deep-throated growl turned into a bark. He snapped forward, lunging for the Corsican's hand as a finger was thrust under Diamond's nose.

Titania sat up sharply too, barking. When the Corsican spoke, his voice was gruff with rage.

'You will regret this,' he hissed.

80

'What's going on here, Victor?' Gwendoline asked.

They were sitting at the breakfast table. She had never in her entire life felt so weary, so worn down, but she was a fighter, she wouldn't stand still and just endure what he was doing to her, day by day. She *couldn't.*

'What?' Victor barely looked up from his eggs.

Gwen had thought that with that surly little bastard Aiden dead and gone, things might improve in the Butcher household – but they hadn't.

The funeral had been a quiet affair, the church half empty. Even the wake had been subdued. She'd heard utterings about Aiden's 'fall', people were saying that Victor had pushed him, but that was none of her business. As for the idiot, Owen, he was to be found upstairs as usual, in his bedroom, keeping well out of Victor's way – and hers too. But neither Aiden nor Owen were her concern. *This* was.

'I know about that Chinese woman,' she said. 'I know you're carrying on with her, it's obvious.'

Victor's head rose from his plate and he stared at her as if surprised to see her there.

'What?' he repeated.

Gwendoline swallowed down a mouthful of tea because suddenly her throat was very dry. Then she said: 'And there are people in the house at night. I hear them when I'm in bed. People moving about, going down the cellar. It . . . it's not *right*, Victor.'

Victor finished his eggs. Slurped down some tea. Then he shoved his chair back from the table. 'Going out,' he said.

'Victor . . .'

His fist connected with the side of her head so hard that she snapped back in her chair and tumbled sideways, ending up on the floor. She looked up from where she lay, dazed, her head a riot of pain, her legs tangled in the chair, the cloth half pulled off the table. Cutlery clattered onto the linoleum. Victor pointed a finger at her.

'You keep out of my fucking business,' he bellowed.

Then he turned and was gone, out the front door, away.

Dully, Gwendoline pushed herself up against the table and slumped into a chair. She was so scared. So weary. So *trapped.*

81

Benoit, Golon thought, was like a dog with a bone. They had so much else to consider – when did they not? There were enough thieves and cut-throats on the streets of Paris to keep the whole department busy for a lifetime. But still he kept returning to the case of Arnaud Roussel.

'We never found the gun,' Benoit kept saying, over and over. 'That's crucial evidence.'

'We tried,' said Golon, who was sick of the entire subject. 'We asked for a diver and that was refused. We got the dredger. The dredging was done. It yielded nothing. We searched the streets. We searched all around. Nothing.'

'If we could find that gun . . .' muttered Benoit.

'Yes, that would be good. But we can't.'

'You filed your notes, the ones you took when we questioned the shopkeepers all along that stretch of the river?'

'All of them.'

'Get them out again. I want to go over them. What was there, along there? A charcuterie. A boulangerie. A café. A flower seller, out in the street. She was there late, didn't she say that? And a gallery. There was a party going on there, wasn't that the case, on the night of the murder? Lots of people coming and going. Did we get a complete list of the owners, and all those in attendance?'

'We did. But everything was closed up for the evening – apart from the gallery, and that flower seller, who was no help at all.'

'Get those notes out for me, will you? I want to look through them again.'

***

Next day, Golon was called into Benoit's office. Benoit had the notebook open and his face was alive with excitement. 'This man. This Marquis. The one we went chasing after down the Loire. He was there on the night of the murder.'

'Was he?'

'He was. But he never mentioned seeing Arnaud there that night, did he?'

'No. He didn't.'

'But perhaps he did.'

'Perhaps. On the other hand, perhaps he didn't.'

Benoit ignored this. 'Perhaps Arnaud was thieving from him, siphoning money off. Perhaps the Marquis – who has a collection of guns, we saw them at the château, you remember? – discovered his agent was cheating him, there were words exchanged, and he killed him?'

'On the night of a party? All those people about? Risky.'

'All that noise. A party! What a good cover for a killing.'

'Maybe.'

'Certainly maybe.' Benoit stood up suddenly, slapping the notebook closed. 'Golon! I want that château searched, top to bottom. We are looking for a .22 gun that's been recently fired. Maybe it's there.'

'Maybe it isn't.'

Benoit was staring into space. 'A *lady's* gun, though . . .'

This was a total waste of time. Golon knew it. Benoit was off on another of his wild-goose chases. He hated it when that happened. He respected Benoit, of course he did, and he liked him, he was his boss. Benoit had awesome flashes of sheer genius when he wasn't being a complete idiot. Everyone in the department knew it. Benoit could winkle out a solution to a case better than anyone else. But ask him to tie his own shoelaces? He'd be stumped.

'I'll get on it, boss,' said Golon with a sigh.

'You do that,' said Benoit, still staring off into the middle distance. 'There's a good lad.'

82

Days dragged by and everything was as normal. The club was full of happy punters, drinking, dancing. Diamond was centre stage, moving around the room, chatting, laughing, the two Borzois at her heels, the Marquis often in attendance; everything was fine and she hadn't bothered him with tales about that bolshy little Corsican. Why worry him over nothing at all? At first she'd been worried, yes: she'd taken to leaving the dogs with Claude the club caretaker overnight, and she continued to do that, for added security there.

He was just full of bullshit, like most men, thought Diamond. The Corsican had come in here, alarming her, but he was gone and no doubt he was now tormenting someone else. Well, thank God! She was enjoying having the club, entertaining the Marquis to lunch, meeting up with Mimi for a stroll with the dogs, hearing all the gossip, going shopping. All was well in her world, all her pains behind her.

She had put Fabien away in her mind, feeling older and wiser – and sadder, too. Did anyone ever forget their first love? She didn't think so. But that part of her life was over, and she was on to a new life now. Through the grapevine she heard that Toro Wolfe had taken himself off to Monte Carlo to visit the casino and then to spend some time at his place in Provence to enjoy the south's summer heat, which was a blessing because she couldn't stand the man.

And anyway who needed Monte Carlo and all its glamour? Right here in Paris, the sun shone, the nights were warm, the club paid, she was almost happy – when she could forget the baby she had lost, her daughter, her Jacqueline. And poor Arnaud's death was a niggle forever at the back of her brain, never completely gone. But Benoit's investigation was unlikely to turn up anything new now – wasn't it? She was trying her best to put that awful incident behind her, and mostly she was succeeding.

She was totally unprepared for the axe, when it suddenly fell.

83

One morning after taking breakfast with Mimi, Diamond walked over to the club and was surprised to see a little semi-circle of people standing outside it, blocking her view of the gaping giant's mouth with its two sharp canine teeth. Surprise turned to alarm when she saw a gendarme there too. She hurried forward and he stopped her with a hand on her arm.

'You are Mam'selle Diamond Dupree?' he asked, his bulbous eyes on her face.

'Yes. I am. What is this, officer . . .?' People were crowding around her. 'What's happening?'

Her eyes went to the giant's mouth. She glimpsed something there. 'What the hell . . .?' she said, and suddenly she was shoving through the crowd, hearing the gendarme still talking behind her, his voice rising as she moved away. Fear clenched hard at her stomach as she struggled through the throng.

'Get out of my bloody *way*, will you?' she snapped, elbowing the onlookers aside with a fiery blend of fury and fear. She couldn't believe what she was seeing, glimpsing through the shifting crowds. She *would not* believe it.

She began striking at the crowds, raining blows down on them, and people cringed back, thinking that a madwoman was in their midst.

Finally, the space around her cleared and she could see what was there. *Hanging* there. On each of the huge meat-tearing teeth on the giant's head there hung a limp, silky white form. On the right was Boris, his lead and jewelled collar gone. On the left, gentle Titania, her lead and collar also missing. They were hung there, each of the Marquis's beloved babies, by a rope around the neck. Straight away Diamond could see that they were dead.

'No. No!' she screamed, flinching away from the sight but then turning back to look again, unable to believe the evidence of her own eyes, unwilling to look but unable to look away, unable to spare herself when these poor creatures, who had been her companions, her friends, had been spared nothing.

The gendarme was there at her side again.

'Mam'selle,' he was saying. 'Are these dogs yours?'

Tears were flowing in rivers down her face. She gulped, gasping down a breath. Her chest felt tight. She felt panic and rage snatching her breath away. She looked again. Titania's eyes were half open but seeing nothing. Boris's were completely closed.

She thought of the Marquis, who would be crushed, utterly desolate, when he heard of this. She didn't know how she was going to tell him. She shook her head. Her eyes were still drawn back to the dogs, hanging there. And to the club door, which was ajar. 'They're not my dogs. I was minding them for a friend. Oh *God.* Is the caretaker here? He stays here at night. Claude. Claude L'Enfant.'

'I have been inside the club. The door was open when I arrived, alerted by one of these good people. There is no-one in there.'

So where the hell is Claude? The dogs had been in his care. And he was gone.

'Do you know who could have done this?' the gendarme was asking her.

Diamond nodded and swiped at the wetness on her cheeks. There wasn't a single doubt in her mind about who'd done it.

'The Corsican,' she snapped out. 'Angelo Paoli. He came in here and threatened me. He said he wanted this club and the owner, the Marquis de Marquand, was to hand it over. He said I would be sorry. And now *this.*'

The gendarme was writing in a small notebook. Again and again Diamond's eyes were pulled back to the beautiful dogs, hanging there, dead.

Oh God.

Diamond tasted bile in her mouth but swallowed it back.

'I want him called to account,' she said furiously to the gendarme. 'I want him thrown into jail. This is *monstrous*, what he's done. He can't get away with it. He *mustn't.*'

'We will look into this, mam'selle,' said the gendarme. 'Your full address, if you please?' Diamond gave it. 'You have a key to the club door?'

'I do.'

'Then please lock it. I will have the dogs removed and this matter will be fully investigated, I assure you.' He looked around at the crowd, which was growing denser by the minute as more and more people came to look. 'Now go, all of you. *Vite! Allez!*'

Slowly, some of them visibly dismayed, others unwilling to leave the site of all this excitement, the crowd started to disperse. Shuddering as she was forced to move between the two corpses of her beloved companions, Diamond went to the door and locked it. Then she walked away on unsteady legs, back to the apartment, knowing that the very first thing she would have to do was to tell the Marquis this terrible news.

84

When she told him later that same day, told the Marquis the awfulness of what had happened, told him how she had found his beautiful pets hanging there from the giant's mouth, dead, he was devastated. He *cried*, and she had never seen a grown man cry before.

'Oh my darlings. My sweet Titania. And my poor Boris,' he wailed.

'I'm so sorry,' said Diamond, hugging him, feeling bitter remorse. 'This is my fault. I shouldn't have left them there with that fool Claude.'

She gulped down a breath. She hadn't wanted to go back there in the afternoon, but she had. She'd forced herself to. The bodies of the two dogs had gone, but the place was still locked up. Claude was nowhere to be found and she guessed that the Corsican had frightened him off. She waited for the rest of the staff to turn up, but no-one did. So he'd done the same with them. Thrown a scare into them and now she had no caretaker, no staff to run the place, nothing. And Boris and Titania were dead and gone. That was the worst thing of all.

'A man came into the club,' she told the Marquis.

His tear-reddened eyes were fixed to her face. 'A man? What man?'

'A Corsican. A gangster.' Diamond took a breath. 'I ignored him. I'm so sorry. I think your poor babies died because of that.'

He was frowning at her now, not understanding. 'What do you mean?'

'He came into the club and he said that he was going to take it. Not buy it, nothing like that. He said he liked it and it was going to be his. I didn't take him seriously. I should have, but I didn't.'

'But that's . . . well he couldn't just walk in and *take* what's mine. You didn't report it to the police?'

'I did. Yes.' Although what the police could do about people like *that*, she couldn't begin to imagine. She knew gangsters of old, had grown up with them, and they lived by their own rules; they scorned the forces of the law. Laughed at them. Ran rings around them.

'But the police were there this morning. They saw . . .' He couldn't even finish the sentence.

'I told them he'd come in, making threats. I gave them his name. And I hope to God they find the bastard and lock him up.'

Even as she said it, she didn't think it likely. When it boiled right down to it, two dogs had been killed, not two people. The English were soft on animals; the French were, on the whole, not. The police would file the case under *not interested*, she thought, and they would forget it.

'I'm so sorry,' she said again to the Marquis.

He shook his head. 'Not your fault. These people are everywhere now. They think they can do exactly what they like, and when anyone crosses them . . .' His voice trailed away. '*Chérie*, perhaps you shouldn't have named this man to the police.'

'*What?*' Diamond couldn't believe what she was hearing. 'But I had to. After he did *that*? How could I just let it go?'

'I know, I know. But it might have been wiser not to.'

85

Sergeant Golon was busy with a group of *policiers* down in the Loire Valley, turning the Marquis's château over, much to the annoyance of his staff, in search of a .22 gun that they failed to find.

Meanwhile, Benoit was at the *Sûreté* national headquarters, sitting at his desk, churning over cases but going back, time and again, to the one that really intrigued him – the murder of Arnaud Roussel. He stopped for coffee mid-morning, promising himself a long lunch because his head was aching with all this unsolved rubbish going on. Then he returned to his desk, passing by two gendarmes in the lobby who were chatting over the latest happening on the streets.

'They were hanging there, dead as doornails, outside Cabaret de l'Enfer.'

'No!'

'It's true. Not that it's l'Enfer any more, the name's changed. It's owned by that fop Marquis now. The woman was there, you know the one he's always around town with, the model who sat for Fabien Flaubert?'

At the word 'Marquis' Benoit stopped walking. He turned back, confronting the two gendarmes. 'Who is this Marquis you're talking about? What's all this?'

They exchanged a glance. Then the younger of the two said: 'Sir, the Marquis de Marquand's two dogs were found hanging outside Cabaret de l'Enfer three days ago. They were dead.'

'That's terrible. He owns that club then?'

'He does, sir, *oui*. It sounds like a gangland thing, don't you think? Le Milieu are very active around that area. Maybe one of the gangs was trying to hustle in on the club trade, who knows?'

'And the woman . . .?' Benoit asked.

'She runs the show. They've changed the club name to Diamond's now. Everyone says she's the Marquis's mistress. She's famous. A great beauty. Diamond Dupree.'

It was the woman who'd sat in on his meeting with the Marquis at the château, the one with the black hair and the milk-white skin and those strange violet-blue eyes. Benoit was no lady's man, but even he hadn't been immune to her charms. Something was making his investigator's nose twitch. Two bad things happening – a man shot, two dogs hanged – and both times this glamour-girl was there, right on the spot.

He went back to his office and sat there at his desk, poring over Golon's notes. Lunchtime came and went, forgotten. Then Golon came in, puffing out his cheeks in exasperation.

'Well?' said Benoit, jumping to his feet.

'Let me at least get through the door.' Golon shucked off his overcoat and slumped down in a chair. He'd had a long tiring journey, not even a drink on the way, he was exhausted.

'Come on, Golon, what did you find down at that bloody place? Anything?' demanded Benoit.

'Nothing whatsoever.'

'Nothing?'

'It was always unlikely, we did agree that, didn't we? But we had to do it so do it we did. We searched the place, hoping that the Marquis had slipped the gun in amongst all his other weapons. But he hadn't. It isn't there. We searched the dungeons. We searched the attics. We searched the grounds. Sometimes, people do obvious things and that makes our job easier. This time, that wasn't the case. If the Marquis has ever had possession of that gun, he certainly has now dumped it miles away or hidden it away somewhere we will never find it.'

Benoit stared at his sergeant in annoyance. But Golon was a good officer; the best. If Golon said the place had been properly tossed, then it had.

'Have some men search his Paris place too,' he said.

'I will. Today.'

'Do you know about the dogs at Cabaret de l'Enfer?'

Golon looked blank.

Quickly, Benoit filled him in on the details.

'What a rotten thing to do,' said Golon, who – unlike Benoit – loved dogs.

'It's the sort of thing Le Milieu get up to, don't you think? They've been shoving out club owners all around that quarter, maybe they tried to shove this one out, too. Maybe this one resisted. And so his dogs died. Just a little warning. First the dogs, then you. You know what they're like.'

'Bastards.'

'*Oui*. But terribly efficient.'

86

Diamond went back to the club that night. Still there was nobody about. No Claude, opening up the doors under the giant's gaping mouth. Shuddering, she walked under the spot where Boris and Titania had died, glad that she had Arnaud's cut-throat razor tucked into her stocking top. She unlocked the door, turned on the lights. Would the staff come in this evening? She doubted it. The Corsican had killed the Marquis's pets, frightened all the workers away and now she supposed all that remained was for that bastard Paoli to get in touch with the Marquis and take possession of the title deed.

She looked around the club with sadness. *Her* club, named Diamond's for her. It felt tainted now, the atmosphere heavy with the stench of death. She went over to the big painting behind the stage, flicked on more lights so that her own image in the lavish low-cut red dress was highlighted there. That glamorous, unimaginably lovely Diamond looked ready to step straight out of the painting and onto the stage, to smile and charm and exude confidence and charisma.

Standing there looking up at herself, Diamond felt depression steal over her like a dark cloak. And then there was a noise behind her. Stealthy footsteps. She whirled around. It was *him*. The Corsican. Grinning from ear to ear.

Diamond took a step forward, anger washing through her in an unstoppable wave. 'You bastard!' she burst out.

'I warned you, mam'selle,' he said.

'I told you. I don't own the club. Monsieur le Marquis does.'

'I know.'

'So what the hell do you want now? To gloat I suppose? All right. You win. He'll get the title deeds signed over to you, if that's what you want. And I'll meet you back here when the Marquis has consulted his solicitor and got all the paperwork in order. Then you'll have the club. You bastard.'

And then, she thought, *I will slit your throat with Arnaud's razor. See if stealing the club off a sweet man like the Marquis, killing his pets, gets you anywhere when you're frying in hell.*

'That all sounds very agreeable,' he smiled.

Bastard.

Now there was more movement from the back of the club. Diamond glanced behind her, feeling a bolt of alarm shoot from her guts to her heart. Two men were moving, coming out through the red curtains behind the stage. She hadn't realised they were there. She looked back at the Corsican. He'd moved closer, too.

Oh Christ.

'You named me to the police,' he said. 'They called on me and that disturbed me. They asked me questions. I didn't like that.'

Diamond said nothing. She was wondering how quickly she could get the razor out. Not quickly enough, she thought. He was very close now, and she could sense his two thugs standing close behind her. She could feel their body heat. She was trapped.

'People cross me? They pay,' said the Corsican.

She was grabbed from behind. Struggling, she felt a pad of soft material clamp down over her nose and mouth. She couldn't breathe anything but a toxic chemical smell. She tried to scream but couldn't. Tried to kick out, but her limbs seemed suddenly heavy, useless.

She sank into darkness, and her last thought was *help me. Somebody help.*

But no-one came.

PART THREE

87

The first thing Diamond thought when she woke up was *oh Christ my head.* Her brain seemed to be swollen to double its normal size and it was trying to squeeze its way out of her skull. Her mouth tasted foul. Her nose stung. She sat up in semi-darkness, the movement causing a jackhammer to start bashing her between the eyes. Squinting, groaning, half blind with pain, she realised that she was about to be sick.

She was sitting on something – a hard mattress? – and she yanked herself to the edge of it, leaned over and vomited onto the floor. Wiping at her mouth, moaning, she hauled herself back and flopped onto a thin pillow. Her heart was banging against her ribs. She blinked with sore aching eyes and saw a room around her. A small room, no more than three metres by two. There was a tiny barred window above the head of the bed where she lay, casting a dim light inside the space. There was a chair, a small washstand with a rose-patterned jug and bowl and a cloth on it. A lit candle in a holder was beside the cloth. Nothing else, except . . . a girl.

The girl of about sixteen was standing at the end of the bed, dressed in a white cotton shift. She had long brown hair, a wide heart-shaped face and watchful heavy-lidded brown eyes. She was tall and very thin. She said: 'Feel better now?'

Diamond sat there, aware of sour sweat on her skin, feeling dizzy and almost dreamlike. Yes, that was it. This was a dream. Actually, more like a nightmare.

'That stuff's a fucker, isn't it? Chloroform. And he's a bit heavy-handed with it too,' said the girl. 'Takes a while for it to wear off.'

That was it: the last thing she remembered – someone slapping a pad of something noxious over her face. The Corsican standing there, grinning at her. Then, nothing. Grimly, she forced herself to try to get her bearings. Wherever this was, she was going to get out of here as soon as she felt strong enough to stand up, to actually try to walk. And then that Corsican bastard was going to be sorry.

'Where the hell is this?' she asked, casting a glance around this tiny cell-like room.

It smelled bad in here, stale – the bedding unwashed, the floor unswept, no sign of care having been taken with anything. The stench of her own vomit was adding to the general unpleasantness of it all. She could feel her stomach cramping again and swallowed hard, sweat prickling at her neck.

'It's home,' shrugged the girl.

Then there was a shout and Diamond stiffened in alarm. 'What's that?'

'Just one of the others,' said the girl.

'What others?'

'Mostly they behave but sometimes they don't. Some of them don't even get off the bed – the fifteen-minuters, I mean. One punter out, the next one in. Plenty of money made.'

Now she could hear someone crying.

Diamond watched the girl's face. She wasn't joking. And – oh Christ in heaven – Diamond had heard of this sort of thing from Mimi, hadn't she? Women – girls – tied to beds, restrained, while one man after another came in and took his pleasure. She wasn't sweating now. She was shivering.

She was in a whorehouse.

'Does the Corsican run this place?' she asked, dry-mouthed.

'Angelo runs most places.'

'And you. What do you do, here?'

'She does exactly what she's told,' said Angelo Paoli, stepping into the room behind the girl.

88

'*You*,' said Diamond.

'Yes, me.' He turned to the girl, indicated the mess on the carpet. 'Clear that up.'

The girl went to the washstand, poured water from the jug into the rose-patterned bowl. She dipped the cloth in it, then quickly mopped up the floor. That accomplished, she left the room, taking the jug and bowl and cloth with her.

The Corsican kicked the door closed behind her and turned back to Diamond.

You don't show a wild animal any fear.

Diamond remembered her mother saying that to her, more than once. Keep your spine straight. Be brave. Feeling sick, weak, anything but brave, she stared back steadily at Paoli.

'The Marquis will have raised the alarm,' she told him. Her voice trembled. She hated that. 'People will be looking for me. You've done a very foolish thing.'

He moved closer. Diamond could feel the reassuring cold weight of Arnaud's cut-throat razor still tucked into her stocking top. Of course they hadn't searched her. They were big, tough, strong men, the Corsican and the other two who had nabbed her, why would they fear a woman? If he so much as touched her, she was going to cut him, badly. She promised herself that.

'It was you, then, who killed the Marquis's dogs?' she queried. 'You'll pay for that.'

He gave a tight almost quizzical smile. 'Mam'selle,' he sighed, not answering her question. 'I will pay for nothing. On the contrary, it is you who will pay. You disrespect me? Me? You are nothing but a piece of flesh to me, mam'selle, and one that is going to raise me a good sum of money.'

Diamond felt her face drain of colour as she thought of that girl in the other room crying out. One of the fifteen-minuters? Unable – not permitted – to leave the bed in between one 'customer' and the next?

'The Marquis de Marquand will search for me,' she said, setting her jaw. 'The police will come. And then you will be sorry.'

'What a fool you are. I own most of the police in this town.'

'No, you are the—'

Diamond's voice was cut short as he surged toward the bed. He grabbed her by the hair and yanked her head back, leaning in to spit in her face. It was agony. Diamond winced but wouldn't give him the satisfaction of a scream. Her hand crept down, toward the razor. She'd do it. She'd cut him, right now.

'Listen,' he hissed. 'You bitch, you dare talk like that to me? Well I have a plan for you. I have a really good plan. And soon you will find out what it means to cross Le Milieu.'

He was going to beat her. Rape her. But she was going to get in first. She was going to kill him.

Then suddenly he drew back, releasing her hair. Her hand stilled on her thigh. He was breathing hard with temper. Her eyes held his, though: she didn't flinch away. He swore at her, a low ugly sound. Then he turned on his heel and left the room, slamming the door behind him.

89

'The woman's run off,' said Golon, hurrying into Benoit's office the day after Diamond's latest meeting with the Corsican.

'What?' Benoit looked up as Golon flung himself into a chair.

'The Marquis de Marquand is downstairs, saying he wants to speak to a senior investigating officer because his dear friend Diamond Dupree has disappeared. My arse!' Golon huffed in disgust. 'Bet you she's run off with a younger lover. I mean, look at the man. Wouldn't you?' Benoit pushed back his chair and stood up. 'Come on,' he said, and went out into the passageway and down the stairs to the lobby.

The Marquis was there, pacing the floor. When Benoit appeared, he dashed forward.

'I am very worried about my friend. I want to report her missing. I think she may be in trouble.'

'Please, sir, calm yourself,' said Benoit.

'I cannot! She was threatened by one of the Corsican bandits who you people let run riot in this city. My dogs were killed by them. And now she herself is gone. She didn't return to her apartment last night. And they've taken a valuable painting out of my club too, a painting of her by Flaubert.'

'What about her clothes, sir? Her belongings? Is there anything missing from the apartment?'

'Nothing. Only her.'

Benoit was getting more and more interested in this mistress of the Marquis's. Now, she'd vanished into thin air. Of course, an adult woman could come and go exactly as she pleased. But there was the small matter of the Corsican. And the dogs.

'Has she done this sort of thing before, sir?' asked Golon.

'Of course not,' said the Marquis.

Benoit laid a comforting hand on the Marquis's arm. 'Please don't distress yourself. We will find your friend.'

Or not, thought Golon. Maybe his theory was right and she had run off with someone younger and more attractive. Or maybe, having fallen foul of Le Milieu she'd be found dead somewhere, and that would be the end of that.

90

Most of the procedures on the motor-racing circuit at Brooklands were based – curiously – on horse-racing traditions. Cars assembled in the 'paddock', weighed by the 'Clerk of the Scales' for handicapping, cars were 'shod' with tyres, and drivers were told by the stewards to wear bright silks so that the spectators could more easily identify them – just like jockeys.

It was a grey rainy afternoon when all the cars lined up for the off. Up in the stands under umbrellas, the spectators were crowded together. They waved and stamped their encouragement to the drivers in their leather helmets and goggles. Catherine was up there in the members' enclosure, wanting to see her brother Teddy win the race. Richard was competing too, he was down on the starting line. He glanced across at Teddy, three cars away from him. Teddy was looking away, deliberately not meeting Richard's gaze. It hurt Richard, the loss of his friend. But he understood. If someone had jilted *his* sister then he would have been outraged too.

He revved his engine, and the roar of his and all the other cars as their drivers prepared for the off was deafening. This was what he loved. His passion for driving a motor car on the roads had quickly developed into a yen for racing, pushing the boundaries of speed and feeling the wind whipping like knives against his face as he sped around the track. There was danger to it, and that appealed to him too. Since the war, he'd felt a recklessness that had not been there before. Now he pushed himself, challenged others out on the track, just loving the speed, the excitement, the total focus it took to win.

Then the flag came down – and they were away. Count Zborowski in Chitty Bang Bang One surged ahead straight away, and Teddy was hot on his tail. Richard felt his car struggling for traction on the rain-slippery track, and steered into the skid skilfully, feeling the big car right itself again. He was going to overtake Teddy, he was determined on that. Then perhaps the obstinate bastard would acknowledge his existence. He shoved through the gears as they came flying up toward Byfleet Banking on the far side of the course, the speedometer showing eighty-five miles an hour. Again, he felt the loss of grip on the tyres. But he was gaining. Count Zborowski was way ahead, untouchable, but Teddy was there now and Richard was drawing level on the curve, inching in, then Teddy was steering out into Richard's path, trying to block his route through. Richard glanced across and saw Teddy, spattered with mud and rain, teeth clenched in determination.

Richard refused to give way, fall back. He put his foot down and the two cars bumped together, wheel to wheel. There was a hard metallic scraping and then Richard was pulling ahead, the road curving dangerously, and Teddy was heading nose-first into the side of the track. Richard shot past and was away – but glancing back he saw Teddy's Bugatti skidding sideways into the bank. It came to a juddering halt. He saw stewards running.

He bit his lip. The racer in him wanted to go on, but this was *Teddy*. He slapped on the brakes, pulled in as far off the track as he could get. Other cars were zooming past, edging around the crash site, racing on. Richard, shaking, shoved off his helmet and goggles and ran back.

'Teddy? Is he all right?' he yelled at the stewards, who were pulling Teddy out of the car, its front end crushed by the clash with Richard's motor, then mangled again by its nose-first impact with the bank.

'You bastard,' said Teddy loudly, and Richard grinned with relief as the stewards set Teddy on his feet. He was all right.

'I ought to knock your fucking head in,' said Teddy.

'Yes? Well I wish you'd done that sooner, rather than just cut me off. I would have preferred it,' said Richard.

'Right then!' Teddy came tearing toward him, fist raised. Then he looked at Richard, his oldest friend, standing there grinning at him and shaking like a shitting dog, clearly so glad to see that he was still alive and unhurt, and steeling himself for a walloping. 'You drove me off that bloody bend deliberately,' said Teddy.

'Yes. I did. But you noticed me though – didn't you?' said Richard.

'Oh for fuck's sake,' said Teddy in exasperation. 'You bastard! All right then. If Catherine can bloody well forgive you, you sod, then I suppose I can too.'

Richard held out his hand. 'Friends?' he asked, more in hope than expectation.

Teddy took Richard's hand and shook it. As the stewards looked on, bemused, both men started to laugh and then they stepped forward and hugged each other.

'Friends,' said Teddy. 'Of course we are, you old bugger.'

91

The Marquis was being a pest, always on at Golon and Benoit over this missing woman of his.

'I told you,' said Golon privately to Benoit. 'She's gone off with someone younger.'

'Don't show your ignorance,' said Benoit.

'Meaning?'

'She's a beard, Golon. Haven't you heard the term? The Marquis entertains young men and she covers for him, don't you realise?'

'You're serious?'

'It's obvious,' sighed Benoit.

'That's a criminal offence,' said Golon.

'So it is. But do we really want to try to drag one of the aristocracy through the courts? He has money to burn, that man. The best lawyers will get him off anything at all, up to and including child molestation, and it will cost the state a fortune, and us our jobs.'

'Clearly he values her highly,' said Golon, chastened.

'Of course he does. It's a mutually beneficial arrangement.'

'We've put word out.'

'And no sign?'

'None at all.'

Benoit sighed, rose from his chair and reached for his hat and coat. 'Then let's go back to the Marquis, see if we can get any more information that might help us track her down.'

***

The Marquis was at his Paris apartment; today Mimi was there with him. Of the two, Benoit thought that the Marquis was the more genuinely worried about this 'Diamond Dupree', although Mimi Daniels claimed Diamond to be her dear, dear friend.

'She came from England. She's the daughter of one of my oldest associates,' Mimi said tearfully, delicately touching a lace handkerchief to her eyes.

'So! Is that her full name?' asked Golon, taking notes.

'No,' said Mimi. 'Well her *real* name is Diamond Butcher. Her mother Frenchie was my old friend.'

'Possibly she's simply returned home, to England?'

'That is unlikely,' said the Marquis. 'She was unhappy there.'

'Why?' asked Benoit.

'She had an uncle who was unkind to her,' chirped Mimi. 'Victor Butcher.'

'I see.'

'You should be out there, looking for her,' fretted the Marquis.

'All the gendarmerie have her description. Everyone is searching, I assure you of that.'

***

When the police had departed, the Marquis shot a reproachful look at Mimi.

'Shame on you,' he said.

'Me? Why? What have I done?'

'She doesn't like to talk about her family back in London. There is a danger this uncle of hers could come after her. You know that.'

Mimi shrugged and smiled. 'Well, we all have our secrets to keep, don't we? Like your appetite for pretty young boys. But we'll keep quiet about that, shall we?'

92

They left Diamond alone all that night and next day. By the following morning the headache and the feeling of sickness had passed. She was starving, aware that she hadn't eaten for at least two days. She thought of the Marquis, who would be pulling his hair out by now, wondering what on earth could have happened to her. She thought of Mimi, who would probably be completely unconcerned and busy telling the Marquis that she was just out on the tiles, enjoying herself.

Bloody Mimi.

When the door opened abruptly she jumped, fearing the Corsican's return, but it was the brown-haired girl again, wearing the same white shift as before. She was carrying a small papier-mâché tray painted hyacinth blue and on it was a plate with a croissant and jam and a knife. There was a bowl of steaming-hot coffee beside it. She brought it over to the bed, placed it on the edge.

'Don't go getting any thoughts about the knife,' said the girl. 'It wouldn't cut shit, that thing.'

Diamond didn't reply to that. She had something a thousand times better than the butter knife on the tray, as that bastard Corsican would soon discover if he pushed his luck. She thought of pulling it out now, frightening the girl with it. But there was a big hulking slab of muscle standing in the doorway behind the girl. She'd never make it out of here, not past him.

Then the girl left the room and came back with a jug of clean water in the big rose-painted bowl, a cloth slung over her shoulder. She placed the jug and bowl on the washstand and the cloth beside it.

'You can get washed up, when you're ready,' she said. She looked at the untouched food and drink. 'I should eat, if I were you. Keep your strength up for what's ahead.'

'What *is* ahead?' asked Diamond, picking up the croissant and biting into its buttery flakes. It was fresh and tasted good, which she hadn't expected in a pest-hole like this. She took the knife and spread jam on the rest of it, then ate quickly, her eyes on the girl.

'For you? Not much, actually, until the word spreads.'

Diamond paused, swallowing, wiping her fingers. 'I don't know what you mean by that.'

'The word. You know. It gets around town. And further.' The girl stared at Diamond. 'Oh yes, I think we are talking a lot of money, all things considered.'

'Money for what?' Diamond picked up the dish of coffee and drank. It was good, hot and strong.

'For you, of course.'

Diamond choked on the coffee. Coughing, she put the dish back down on the tray. The girl came closer and patted her sharply on the back.

'Steady now,' she said. 'We don't want such valuable merchandise to choke on a croissant.'

Diamond glared up at her through watering eyes. She patted her chest, coughed again.

Merchandise?

'What the hell are you talking about?'

'He's put you out to the highest bidder. Angelo's very sharp, he works things out quickly. And he's worked out that you are best marketed as a virgin, untouched. Lots of upper crust overbred fools will pay a lot for that, you know. They all want to break a girl in, be the first. He's putting the word out on the street right now that he's got a beautiful virgin for sale, and he's got a painting of you, one he took from the club. You know the one? He's showing it to prospective buyers. They're swooning over the damned thing, it's very comical.'

It didn't strike Diamond as very funny. That bastard had stolen her portrait and brought it here to wherever this awful place, this whorehouse, was, and was using it as a tool to flog her like a very expensive piece of meat. As to the claim that she was a virgin? She'd passed that point a long time ago, when that damned posho *RB* had impregnated her. And since then? She had given herself, body and heart and soul, to Fabien. Much good had it done her.

'I have friends,' said Diamond sharply. 'Friends in high places. They won't allow this to happen. They'll be looking for me right now.'

'I wish you good luck with that,' said the girl, smirking.

'If you could get me out of here,' said Diamond. 'I would pay you.'

'Oh, don't waste your time,' said the girl, going to the door and opening it. There were no screams this morning. A distant babble of female voices, that was all. 'I'm Celestine, by the way. And you? You're to be sold. So you might as well get used to the idea.'

93

They kept Diamond confined to that little room – that *cell* – for days. She left it only to be taken to the lavatory by Celestine, with that great hulking brute always close at hand. She noted in passing that the big portrait of her that had once hung so proudly in the club was now propped up in some sort of reception space with another big bruiser of a man sitting beside it. She ate in her room, hearing laughter and screams by day and into the night, unable to sleep, unable to rest because she was in a state of perpetual fear.

Then one day – she'd lost count of *which* day – Celestine brought in rosewater and a clean white shift for Diamond to put on. Then the Corsican returned, all big cheesy smiles, bringing with him a man of middle years, red and fat in the face and hefty in the body, sporting a large sandy moustache, bulging blue eyes and a nose lavishly sprinkled with pimples.

Christ! He looks like Gustav Wolfe, thought Diamond with a shudder.

'Who is this?' she demanded.

'None of your business,' snapped the Corsican, then spoke in his own language to the man at his side, who was eyeing up Diamond like she was a pound of meat. The reply from the man was guttural. Was he German? Swiss?

The two men were conducting a conversation and Diamond couldn't understand a word of it. It started off amiably enough, then got louder and louder. She caught *francs*, mentioned in large amounts.

They were bartering over her. The German – she thought now that he must be German – approached the bed as if to touch her, and the Corsican snatched him back.

The money was going up.

Finally they seemed to reach an amount at which the German baulked. Voices were raised again. Then the German snatched open the door and was gone. Angelo followed. The door closed. Diamond was left sitting there.

***

More days passed, she had no idea how many. Perhaps she should have marked her cell wall, like a prisoner, so that she at least knew how much time was passing. But then Celestine came with another clean shift and the rosewater again, so she knew something was about to happen.

And it did.

This time Paoli brought in with him what was clearly an Arab. He was hook-nosed, dusky-skinned, clad in white robes. He had cruel eyes, that was what Diamond noticed most about him. She pictured him with a scimitar sword, slicing off heads in the desert. He was smoother than the German, though. Not openly aggressive. No shouting with this one.

'Stand up,' said the Corsican.

Diamond stood up.

'Turn around,' he said.

Diamond turned. If this Arab came too near, she was going to slit him open with the razor. She thought of shouting out that she was *not* a virgin to the Arab, telling him that he was being duped, but she didn't dare. Paoli would be angry – and that would be dangerous.

There was more conversation. Then the Arab left.

I'm never going to get out of here, thought Diamond, sinking down onto the bed.

94

Another day dawned, another long boring day of confinement. Late that evening, when Diamond was getting ready for sleep, having tucked the razor under her mattress, Celestine was back with another clean shift, and more rosewater.

'Who is it this time?' asked Diamond wearily.

'It's a Portuguese. Señor Lopez,' said Celestine.

'And tomorrow it'll be a Chinese, I suppose, and the day after that?'

Celestine shook her head.

'No, there won't be any more. This one's agreed top price and the money's already paid.'

'For my virginity,' said Diamond.

'That's right.'

'Don't you think this Lopez is going to notice that I'm *not* a virgin?'

Celestine let out a puff of air. 'You're joking! Men are stupid. They can't tell. You could be an old whore with ten kids and a fanny stretched to hell. They'd never know.'

This was concerning. *This* one wouldn't be just looking. But she still had the razor. She'd been guarding it carefully, concealing it while she slept, keeping it tucked into her stocking top during the day.

'Let's get you cleaned up for your big performance then,' said Celestine.

'It's certainly that,' said Diamond. 'I'm far from a virgin. All this is such a joke.'

'It's Angelo's revenge on you,' shrugged Celestine. 'He can't let you reporting him to the police go unpunished, or where would his reputation be? So he keeps you in here, selling you off to the highest bidder and saying what a delicate flower of a girl you are.'

'Which is a lie,' said Diamond, shrugging off the shift she was wearing.

Celestine looked at Diamond's naked body admiringly. 'The lie don't matter. Their *acceptance* of the lie is what counts.'

Finally, very late, she was ready – washed, perfumed. The 'buyer' was here. The door was opening. He came in very quietly, closed the door behind him and said: 'Diamond?'

Heart thundering, she was ready for this one. She grabbed the razor and was across the room in an instant, snapping it open, letting the blade rest lightly – dangerously – against his neck.

'Jesus! Don't kill me,' he said, speaking English – not Portuguese. And there was no accent.

'Who the . . .' Her voice tailed away as she peered in the half-dark at her 'buyer'.

'Diamond?'

It couldn't be.

It bloody *was.*

'Can you get that damned thing off my throat?' said Toro Wolfe.

Diamond lifted the razor away from the vein that throbbed in his neck. She snapped it closed.

'What the hell are you doing here? That fucking Corsican *bandit* told me that a Portuguese had made a bid for me, that he'd topped the German and the Arab.'

'That's true.'

'*What?*' She couldn't believe it. Their families had been sworn enemies for years, and now he was saying that . . .

'Oh. Right.' She looked at him with speculation. And unsnapped the razor. This was to be his final revenge, was it? To humiliate her, to actually defile the daughter of the hated Butcher family? Well – he could think again.

'Somehow I don't like the look on your face,' said Toro, his eyes dropping to the razor in her hand.

'Well then don't look at it. In fact, piss off. Your name's not Lopez. You're not Portuguese.'

'Lopez was my mother's maiden name. I'm half Spanish. I said Portuguese in case it rang any bells with anybody. Didn't they search you? Don't they *know* you've got that?'

Diamond scoffed. 'Of course they didn't. I'm a high-priced virgin, apparently. A delicate lily, white as snow and not very likely to cause anyone any damage.'

'They obviously don't know you very well.'

'They don't know me at *all*. And neither do you.'

'However . . .' Toro stepped back as Diamond advanced on him once again, the blade raised in a threatening manner. 'However, you're in safe hands. Listen. I heard the news around town that a perfect pure English virgin called Diamond was on offer. I put two and two together and made four. You cost me a lot of money and actually, you know what? You've seriously annoyed me, coming at me threatening all sorts. I've half a mind to collect what I paid for.'

'Oh – you have?' Diamond stared at him, eyes squinting with rage. The nerve of this bastard! 'Well do feel free to try,

Mr Wolfe. But when you're bleeding to death on this carpet, don't come complaining to me.'

There was a hard thump on the door and the Corsican shouted: 'Everything all right in there with you, sir?'

'Perfect,' yelled back Toro. Then he actually grinned at her, the cheeky son of a bitch. 'She's fucking exquisite.' So saying, he moved past her to the wooden headboard on the bed and smacked it hard – once, twice, three times – against the wall. 'You should scream,' he said in a whisper to Diamond. 'I imagine that's what high-priced virgins do when they're being deflowered.'

'Fuck off,' hissed Diamond, and he grabbed the hand holding the razor, squeezing hard.

Diamond yelped in pain and surprise.

The razor dropped to the floor and he snatched it up.

'Louder,' he advised, squeezing her hand harder still.

Furious, Diamond threw back her head and let out an ear-splitting scream.

'Better,' said Toro, and they heard the Corsican go off down the passage, laughing.

'I'll give that bastard something to laugh about,' said Diamond, rubbing her hand. '*And* you, Wolfe.'

'Perhaps later,' he said, pocketing the razor and pushing her toward the door. 'Right now, I think we've got other things to concern ourselves with. Like getting out of here.'

'What, now?' Diamond was still rubbing her hand. He'd *hurt* her, the sod.

'No next bloody Christmas. Yes of course now. Once deflowered, a virgin loses her market value. And she ends up getting used again and again, by anyone who'll pay a few francs for the privilege. That's what happens in this rabid hole, and I don't think you'd want to be subjected to *that.*'

God no. She wouldn't.

'So we have to get out of here, when they're least expecting us to do that. All right?'

He was going to help her! She had no idea why, but she wasn't about to look this particular gift horse in the mouth.

'All right,' she agreed.

'Good. Now come on. Time to make our move.' And he pulled a cosh from his pocket.

'Give me back the razor,' said Diamond.

He looked at her. 'No.'

'*Yes.* You've got that, I want something too. I'm not going out of this room without *something*.'

Toro Wolfe stared at her face. Slowly, he took the razor out of his pocket and handed it to her. 'Don't cut me by mistake,' he warned her.

'Don't *cosh* me by mistake,' returned Diamond, and she surged toward the door.

'Fuck's sake, get out of the bloody way,' he said, and she heard exasperation in his voice and a thin thread of laughter. 'This could get messy.'

'Well let's hope it does – for that short little *shit.*'

'Follow right behind me. Don't wander off.'

95

Once out of the room, Toro surged ahead.

They could hear the Corsican's loud braying laugh further along the passage; a woman's laughter too. If any one of them came out into the corridor now, him or Celestine or any of the other girls who worked in this hovel, the game would be up.

'What's going on?' asked the bruiser on the front desk as Toro Wolfe and Diamond crashed through at a run.

The man started to hurry around the desk, moving to stop their escape. Toro grabbed his head and slammed it down onto the desk top, very hard, three times, then whacked him with the cosh. The man collapsed to the floor, blood pouring down his face. Diamond felt a rush of air and a heavy footfall and then the Corsican came thundering along the passage and grabbed her.

She didn't even think about it; she spun on her heel and struck out with the razor, slicing a bloody trail down his cheek. He snapped his head back and she struck again as he raised a hand to protect himself. A portion of a finger spun off and hit the wall with a bloody *thwack!* Celestine had come out into the passageway and she started screaming as she saw her boss under attack. Diamond's third blow sliced his shirt open, digging a bright red track right through his skin.

He fell back, doubling over, wincing, clutching at his hand, cursing.

Diamond turned, following Toro out into the street. They ran, pushing through evening crowds out enjoying themselves, and finally, gasping, they stopped on the bank of the river. No-one was following. It was quieter here, peaceful. Diamond could hear the lap of the water and her own hurried breathing and she could smell fresh river air. It was *wonderful*. They both leaned on the railings and tried to slow their breathing down to a normal rate. It took a while.

'Put that thing away,' said Toro, seeing Diamond still had the blood-stained razor in her hand.

Diamond snapped it closed and tucked it into her stocking-top.

'We don't want the gendarmes asking questions,' said Toro. 'I warned you this would happen. We won't be welcome in Paris now. Your Corsican friend will have all his men out searching for both of us by tomorrow morning.'

He started to walk away, then when she remained standing there stock-still he caught hold of her arm, taking her with him.

'Where the hell *are* we?' complained Diamond.

He held up a hand as a cab approached. It stopped, and they piled on board, Toro telling the coachman to take them to the flat she shared with Mimi. Feeling shattered, Diamond was relieved to find the Marquis there too.

'But my dear girl, where have you *been?*' demanded Mimi, hugging her. 'Are you all right? What happened?'

'She hasn't got time for that,' said Toro. He turned to Diamond. 'Pack some clothes. Quickly.' Diamond went off to her room and started flinging items into an overnight bag. As she did so she could hear Toro Wolfe talking to the Marquis, telling him what had happened, telling him that the club was gone, the Corsican had it, and he should just leave it like that.

'Don't go back there,' Toro warned him. 'And don't talk to the police about it, or about any of this. Your little friend is lucky to have got out in one piece, now our only job is to make sure you both stay that way.'

Diamond emerged from her room with her bag. She grabbed her coat and her gloves.

'But where will you go?' demanded Mimi.

'She's going back to England,' said Toro.

Diamond's mouth dropped open. She stared at him. Thought of disputing it. But . . . the truth was, she did feel that she *wanted* to go back to England now. England was home, after all, and Paris hadn't been good for her. She'd suffered so much since she arrived here. She was beginning to see that she had fallen in love not so much with the exotic, gifted Fabien as with the whole *idea* of Paris itself. She'd absorbed the lifestyle, the Parisian glamour, the almost frantic gaiety after the terrible sombre years of the war. She'd dived head-first into its nightlife, into its air of sophistication and excess. But now . . . the madness had passed. Fabien had moved on and Diamond had fallen among dangerous people, and only been extracted by luck – and by her worst enemy, a Wolfe of all people. He was right. She had to get out.

There was no time for elaborate goodbyes. With a quick hug for Mimi and another for the Marquis, she followed Toro Wolfe down the stairs to where the horse-drawn cab was still waiting and he directed the coachman to the docks, where the steamers crossed the Channel.

'You don't think Paoli would follow, even to London?' she asked Toro as their carriage passed through the dark streets.

'Why would he? He'd come up against much tougher men than himself. Your uncle, for example.'

'I'm not going back to Victor's,' said Diamond, thinking of the misery she'd suffered at her uncle's hands.

'Gwendoline could always do with a dogsbody about the place I expect. And with your brother gone, I suppose she has need of one . . .'

Diamond's breath caught in her throat. She turned to him in the half-dark, clutched at his arm. 'What did you just say?'

She saw the glint of his eyes as his head turned toward her. 'Your brother . . .'

'What about him? Who? You mean Owen? What do you mean, gone?'

Toro was silent for a moment. Then he said: 'God Almighty. You didn't know?'

'Know *what?* Where is Owen? What's happened to him?'

Toro took a breath.

'For God's sake! *What?*' she demanded.

'I'm not talking about Owen. I'm talking about Aiden. He . . . died.'

'He . . .' Diamond couldn't draw breath. After all she'd been through, to hear *this*? It was too much. It couldn't be true.

But she could see that Wolfe was telling the truth. She could *feel* it.

She gulped hard, trying to take it in, trying and failing. 'But . . . *how?*' she wailed out at last.

'It was an accident, I heard. He slipped and fell down the cellar stairs. Broke his neck.'

96

It was a rough crossing. The steamer chugged its way almost blindly against the gale and Diamond was sick in body but also sick at heart as the salt spray pounded up over the bows of the ship and drenched her. After her ordeal at the hands of the Corsican, to suddenly be presented with news of her brother's death was too much to bear.

Thankfully, Toro Wolfe left her to her own devices while she stood swaying up on deck, clutching at the rail, thinking despairingly of Aiden her little and seemingly *indestructible* brother, while she vomited into the churning, uncaring sea.

He slipped and fell down the stairs. Broke his neck.

She had fallen downstairs on the day of Mum's funeral, having been shoved from behind by that bastard Victor.

Aiden had been walking up and down the cellar stairs ever since he was a child, sent down with the scuttle to fetch up the coal. Why should he now slip and fall?

And what about Owen! In her grief over Aiden, she hadn't thought about him. Anxiety filled her, cramping her stomach, making her sweat and shiver.

Should I have taken Owen with me when I left there?

The thought tormented her. But Owen couldn't cope with new places. The strangeness of Paris would have terrified him, and what about when the Corsican had come into all their lives, blighting them? How could poor simple Owen have coped, against scum like that?

He couldn't.

No. She'd had no choice but to leave, and leave alone. After attacking Victor, there was nothing for her to do but run.

Her brain whirled with it all. She knew she'd done the only thing possible when she'd left the family home, but to have this news was just too awful, too tragic.

By the time she got off the steamer in Southampton, she was limp with exhaustion, mentally drained, washed clean by the force of her grief.

She stood on the dockside with Toro Wolfe and he said:

'Where will you go now?'

But she had already decided that. It seemed like the storms of the night had purified her, cleansed her of everything but cold fury.

'My brother's dead. I want to find out what happened to him.'

'It was an accident. He fell downstairs. I told you.'

'There's things you don't know,' she said. Around them, stevedores unloaded freight. Women in furs strolled to waiting cars with their escorts, chauffeurs holding doors open for them. The laughter of the stevedores, the happy chatter of those pampered women, all offended her ears. She felt like she'd never laugh again.

'Like what?' asked Toro.

'On the day we buried my mother, *I* fell down the stairs.'

'So?'

'I was pushed from behind. And a couple of minutes later, Victor came down behind me.'

Toro stared at her face. 'He *what*?'

Diamond nodded.

'That's a coincidence, surely.'

'You think so? You don't know Victor.'

'Your partner in crime,' he sneered.

'What?'

'You did the badger trick with him, setting rich men up for a fall.'

Diamond's stare should have killed him on the spot.

'I was *fourteen* when I started doing that,' she pointed out. 'And the very first time, I told him I didn't want to do it. He blacked both my eyes. The second time I refused, he did that again. So I did it. And I did the hoisting too, because if I hadn't, he'd have beaten me for that, too.'

He was staring at her face. Then he stuffed his hands in his jacket pockets and let out a breath. He paced away from her, then back.

'So what now? You go back there and he starts on you all over again?'

Diamond shrugged. The truth of it, the truth that she could now admit to herself, was that life in Paris had really been Frenchie's dream – not hers.

Now she had come back to London as a full-grown woman. She'd been through so much. She'd loved and she'd suffered. She didn't feel so scared of Victor any more. Maybe that would change, if she confronted him face to face. Probably it would. The scars from her childhood ran deep. She thought again, painfully, of Aiden, her strong little bruiser of a brother. Dead in a box now, a pile of bones. She remembered lifting him up on her shoulders when he'd been small, recalled so vividly sweeping him up in her arms when he fell and was in tears; then chatting to him, laughing, consoling, wiping his tears away.

Aiden! She'd loved him so, so much. And now he was gone. She took a gulp of breath, blinking. Even though her heart was broken in two, she was *not* going to cry. Not in front of anybody, but *especially* not in front of Toro Wolfe.

'There've been a lot of changes in me since your sister's wedding to Victor,' she pointed out.

'Have there? Well my "sister" doesn't change. Like calls to like, sometimes. She always was a cruel little bitch. Maybe she sees that in Victor. You're not really going back there, to the family home? Knowing you'll be walking into trouble?'

Diamond gave a small, strained smile. 'God, I don't know. What about you, what are you going to do?'

'Find some new business. Get involved in that,' he said.

'Well – good luck with it.'

'You'd be wise to forget all about the Butchers now.'

'I know that,' she said.

But there was still Owen, wasn't there. Poor simple Owen, so sweet and so harmless, stuck there with those two – and now that Aiden was gone, Owen had no-one to protect him. But maybe Michael and Moira would be looking out for him. She hoped so – but she didn't really feel sure of that, or sure of *anything*. Not any more.

97

'He's back,' said Golon, coming into Benoit's tiny paper-stacked office.

'Who is back?' asked Benoit.

'The Marquis. Panic's over, apparently. The woman has returned.'

Benoit and Golon went along the passageway and down the stairs. The Marquis de Marquand looked up and smiled as they approached.

'She came back. Last night,' he said.

'Good,' said Benoit. 'And where had she been? Was she not concerned, leaving you to worry over her like that?'

'She was with friends,' said the Marquis. 'There was a mix-up, that's all. She left a message with someone to tell me, and they failed to deliver it. Gentlemen, I am so sorry to have wasted your time.'

'It's nothing, sir, please don't trouble yourself,' said Benoit. 'And she is staying with you now?'

Benoit saw something flitter across the Marquis's thin features. 'No, she is returning to England. She left last night. She has family there, you see. She misses them and so has decided to go back.'

'I see,' said Benoit.

'But thank you for all your good work,' said the Marquis.

'No trouble at all, sir,' said Golon.

The Marquis left. Benoit and Golon stood staring after him for several seconds.

'What do you think?' asked Benoit.

Golon shrugged. 'What did that woman Mimi Daniels say her real name was? Butcher?'

'She did.'

Benoit was thinking of the night of the exhibition, of Arnaud Roussel's untimely death, the Corsican mafia, and of the woman, Diamond Dupree. He'd been poking around in her background here in Paris. She'd been hanging around the artists' quarter of Montmartre and had once been seen in Les Deux Magots, that painter Flaubert had told him, arguing with the man who the regular clientele identified as Arnaud Roussel, who worked for the Marquis and had a lucrative little sideline pimping out Mimi Daniels and a few others, which the Marquis appeared to know nothing about.

'I have a friend who works out of Scotland Yard in London. I wonder if he has any information about this woman, where she's from, what she is really like?' said Benoit.

'You want me to enquire, sir?'

'Yes, I do. In fact I want you to go over there. Go to it, Golon. I'll get it cleared with upstairs, though they'll moan like fuck about the money. Meanwhile, I'm going to talk to the Marquis again. I think he's hiding something. And that woman too. Mimi Daniels.'

98

Diamond went to a humble row of terrace houses near Charing Cross and knocked at the door of one of them. The door was opened by Moira McLean. Moira's face was at first blank and then transformed into a joyous smile.

'Diamond!' she yelled and opened her arms.

Smiling, Diamond stepped forward into Moira's warm embrace.

'My God! Diamond! I don't believe it. Come in, come in!'

Diamond was ushered along a hallway and into a neat little kitchen. No surprises there – Moira had been a wonderful cleaner, of course she would keep an immaculate home.

'Take the weight off,' said Moira, pointing to a chair at the kitchen table. She bustled over to the sink, filled the kettle. 'Tea?'

'No. No, I'm fine.'

Moira put the kettle down and, all smiles, came and sat beside Diamond.

'I heard,' said Diamond. 'About Aiden.'

The smile dropped from Moira's face. 'Oh God. Yes. That was awful. So tragic. The poor boy.'

'Do you know how it happened?'

Moira shook her head. 'Well, they said . . . he fell down the cellar steps, didn't he?'

Or he was pushed.

'That's what I heard,' said Diamond.

'It's so sad,' said Moira. 'He was a great character, Aiden. Right little scrapper.'

And now he was dead.

'Diamond Butcher, back in the Smoke,' Moira went on, shaking her head in wonder. 'Can't believe it.'

'That's not my name any more.'

'Really? So what did you change it to? What – have you got married then?' Moira's eyes went to Diamond's empty ring finger, then back to her face.

'No. I started using "Dupree" instead.'

'Oh. Well.' Then Moira's eyes narrowed. 'Wait up! I've heard that name. Seen it in the papers. Haven't I?'

'Possibly.'

Moira slapped the table. 'Yes! I have. There was a piece about that French painter everyone's raving about. Flaubert. There was a picture of him, he's so good-looking! He did a series of paintings of a woman called Diamond Dupree and . . . but my God, that's not you, is it? It can't be.'

'Yes. It was me.'

Moira was delighted. 'You know, your dear mother, God rest her, used to sit as an artist's model.'

Only rarely. Diamond knew the truth now. Frenchie's *real* profession had been prostitution – like Mimi's. But she wasn't going to tell Moira that.

'What is he like, this Fabien? He looks like a god. He's so beautiful,' said Moira, sighing.

Diamond thought of telling her old friend that Fabien was an arsehole – a big-headed creature who would be even more insufferable after his rise to fame. Yes, he was married to Madeleine now, but would he be faithful? She doubted it. Fabien had all of Paris's women falling at his feet; there was no way he would confine himself to one, when he could have them all.

Poor Madeleine.

'Fabien's a bastard. Moira – about Aiden,' said Diamond. 'Did you see him before he died?'

Moira shook her head sadly. 'As you know, that rotten bitch Gwendoline sacked me.'

'She tried to get me to fill in for you. And she pocketed your wages for herself.'

'She never did! The cow!'

'How did you manage? After?'

Moira shrugged. 'I got another job skivvying, what else could I do? Had a few lean months at first, but soon settled into another job, which was lucky. I'm cleaning up at one of the Soho clubs now, and Michael's out working at this and that, so we get by.'

'So you didn't see Aiden at all . . .?'

'Before he died? No, I'm sorry. It's such a tragedy.'

The front door opened and a man entered and came along the hall to the kitchen, bringing with him a gust of cold wind from outside. When he saw Diamond there, he smiled – and suddenly she recognised him. It was Michael. When she'd last seen him he'd been little more than a skinny over-ambitious youngster likely to land himself in trouble. Now he had bulked up. His shoulders were heavy, his neck thick as a bull's, his arms beneath his coat bulging. He walked with the weighty assurance of a full-grown man. She looked at him now and saw him not as Mikey her childhood friend, but as Michael McLean, leader of the Silver Blades.

'Diamond! God, here's a surprise,' he said.

Diamond stood up. Michael held out his hand to her, but she embraced him warmly and held him by the shoulders and looked at him with real pleasure.

'You've grown up,' she marvelled.

'All the aunts and uncles still say that to me. Don't you start. It's embarrassing,' he grinned.

'He's handsome, isn't he?' asked Moira, her eyes shining with pride.

'He certainly is.'

'Shut up, the pair of you,' said Michael.

Smiling, Moira got up and put the kettle on to boil.

Michael sat down and Diamond did too. She was still staring at him, struggling to adjust to the change in him. To Diamond, Michael had always felt like a friend, almost another brother. It was so good to see him again.

'You see this one?' said Moira. 'She's been over in Paris, posing for that painter we were reading about. Fabien Flaubert,' she tossed over her shoulder at her son. 'She changed her name! Now she's Diamond Dupree, if you please.'

Michael looked at Diamond with a dead-eyed stare that could frighten children, she thought. The boy was gone, never to return. 'Really?'

She nodded. 'Yes, really. Michael, did you see Aiden before he had his accident?'

The smile fell from his face. 'I was sorry to hear about that,' he said. 'He was a good sort, Aiden. The best.'

'Did you? See him?'

Michael flicked a glance at his mother. 'Not very often. I'm sorry. I tried to keep tabs on him and Owen like I promised you. But it got hard, with Victor around.'

'I'm going to visit his grave today. Lay some flowers,' said Diamond, blinking back a tear.

'I'll come with you,' said Michael. 'That's not a thing you'd be wanting to do alone.'

'Thank you,' said Diamond. Then she thought again of Owen. Her other brother, her much more *vulnerable* one, she would have thought, but it was Aiden who had died. Aiden who had suffered an 'accident'. It had been Aiden who might one day have threatened Victor's supremacy as head of the Butcher clan. Who might – who perhaps had – dared to kick against his iron rule. And maybe paid the price for it.

She passed a weary hand over her face. 'I've got to sort all this out. Get my head straight. First I have to find somewhere to stay . . .'

'Stay here,' said Moira quickly. 'Of course you must stay here. You're more than welcome, any time.'

'That's kind of you.' She looked at Michael. 'Do you see much of the Victory Boys these days? Victor's crew?'

'Too bloody much. After you left, I took over a lot of Victor's hoisters. The Silver Blades own them now.'

'And Victor let you?'

'Don't think he could be arsed to stop us. Victor's into other things now, things that pay better.'

'Like what?'

'White slaving, I heard.'

'You what?'

'Serious.' Michael nodded. 'He ships poor bitches out through Chinatown. Got deals cooking with the Triads. Which means he's either very bold or just plain stupid. They're fanatics. Dangerous. They swear thirty-six oaths of allegiance to the organisation and pledge to accept death "by myriad swords" – I don't know what the fuck that means, but it don't sound good – if they betray their Triad brothers.'

Diamond couldn't take this in. Victor had always been cruel, a bully, a thug – but this was another level of low.

'Girls out, drugs in. I wouldn't touch any of them.' Michael grinned. 'Don't fancy being "chopped" with a cleaver or a melon knife just because a deal's gone wrong.'

'What about Gwendoline? His wife?' she asked.

Michael shrugged. 'Nobody sees her.'

'And Owen? Is he all right? Have you seen him?'

Michael looked at the floor. Moira came over to the table, poured hot water onto the tea leaves in the pot. Neither of them spoke.

Diamond looked from one to the other of them.

'Moira?' she said, but Moira wouldn't meet her eyes. She was busying herself with teaspoons and caddies and milk.

Diamond turned her attention to Michael. He was avoiding her gaze too.

'Christ, what's happened to Owen?' she burst out in sudden alarm, surging to her feet.

Moira caught her hand, held it. 'Look . . .' she said, shaking her head.

'What is it?' snapped Diamond.

'Diamond, you have to . . .' Moira started.

'I want to know what's going on. I need you to tell me.'

Moira looked at Diamond with bleak eyes.

'Say it. Whatever it is, just *say* it.'

Moira shook her head again, her face a mask of sadness.

'Victor's put him away, in the madhouse,' she said.

99

Someone was knocking at the front door of the Butcher household. Gwendoline rose from the kitchen table and her heart thumped with anxiety. Automatically her hand went to her mouth. Her two front teeth were missing. Victor had lost his temper a few days ago – she didn't remember which day, it was so hard now to remember which day was which – and he'd punched her, knocking her teeth out.

Since then, she'd lived in fear of visitors. Her teeth missing, that was such an obvious sign that she'd fallen or been hit, and she didn't want anybody starting to ask questions because then that might get back to Victor, and Victor would get angry all over again, she daren't answer the door.

But the person on the other side of it was persisting. Gwendoline, moaning with fear, stumbled into the hallway, her hand at her mouth. All right, she would answer it, but she had to be *careful.* She would keep her mouth hidden. That was what she would do. And it would be all right. She told herself that. It would be *fine.*

She opened the door.

It was Victor's Chinese whore, standing there looking so beautiful with her pale skin, exquisite eyes and her glossy black hair. She was expensively dressed in a bright turquoise coat with a white fur collar. Her lips were painted brilliant red. She saw Lily Wong's eyes taking her in, this wreck with her trembling hands clasped to her mouth. Lily stepped inside, not waiting to be asked, and swept past Gwendoline into the hallway and from there into the kitchen.

'Victor in?' she asked in a lisping accent.

'No,' said Gwendoline.

'You the wife, yes?'

Gwendoline, trailing after her, could only nod.

'You old news,' said Lily with a cold smile. 'You *yesterday's* news, lady. You gone. When Victor back?'

'Soon,' mumbled Gwendoline. She thought that maybe she ought to throw this dainty little thing out into the street, but she didn't think she was strong enough, not any more. She slumped down at the table.

'I wait,' said Lily, and sat down too, uninvited, and smiled.

100

Sometimes, things just fall in your lap and sometimes you have to dig like fuck to find them. While Golon did the digging over in old London town, Benoit sat in his office all nice and cosy. Having cleared away all the other files that demanded his attention, he read through the details of the Arnaud Roussel murder case again. Outside, it was raining. Post-luncheon, he was feeling almost weary, thinking that he would like to knock off earlier than usual today, go home, rest up. Maybe think it all through again. He was getting nowhere, doing this. And upstairs were getting tetchy about his lack of progress on other cases. Tomorrow he had an appointment to see the Marquis, and Mimi Daniels. Perhaps that would help. But he was close to dropping the whole thing, just letting it go.

Then the desk sergeant from downstairs came up and knocked on his door and opened it.

A small, shabby woman came trailing in after him.

'This is Madame Giroud,' he said. 'She has some information for you, she says. Regarding the Arnaud Roussel case, sir.'

Benoit rose politely and removed a pile of papers from a chair so that the woman could sit.

The desk sergeant departed, closing the door behind him. Benoit had received a lot of 'information' since the murder of Arnaud – and most of it had proved useless.

'What information do you have for me, madame?' he asked her.

'The night of the murder – such a terrible thing! – I was selling flowers on the corner of the street,' said Madame Giroud. 'On my usual pitch.'

Benoit nodded. He had noticed the flower seller, right from the off, when they had found Arnaud's body. Golon had spoken to her. She had given them nothing, then. She looked poor as a church mouse, he thought. Under-nourished, ill-washed. A little afraid of policemen.

'Because there was the party – the exhibition – going on at the gallery, I thought I'd stay late, maybe catch some more custom. I saw people coming out, people the worse for drink, all of them shouting and laughing. There were two women – one little blonde and a tall dark-haired one in a red dress, very glamorous. And a man. There was a sound. A noise like one of these motor cars makes.'

'Backfiring,' suggested Benoit. Scared the carriage horses to death, those things.

'Yes! Like that. The man fell . . . I'm sorry, it was hard to see. I thought he must be drunk. Before he fell there was shouting, like an argument. They were on the corner by the alley, so the light from the lamps was not clear. Maybe there was even another man there. It was dark, I couldn't be sure. They were all drunk, as I say. The others who'd come out before them hadn't been interested in my blooms so I gave it up. I was packing up my stall, ready to go home. It's been in the papers, hasn't it, that if anyone has any information they should come forward? Well, it's been troubling me. So here I am. I'm sorry, I don't suppose it's any help at all.'

Benoit was thinking. One very glamorous in a red dress, one tiny blonde. Mimi Daniels? He'd done some reading about the woman and she had a *very* colourful past. The other one though. Taller. Dark-haired. A bit of a mystery. He thought of that night club, the one with the giant's head at the entrance. The newly mirrored walls, the paste diamonds plastered everywhere inside it. He saw it again: the big Fabien Flaubert painting behind the stage. Diamond Dupree. Or Diamond Butcher. Or whatever the hell she chose to call herself these days.

He was going to have to get in touch with Golon over in London. Soon.

'I don't suppose this is much help,' said the woman sitting across the desk from him. 'I don't suppose . . . there isn't a reward, is there? For this information?'

'Madame, it is a huge help,' said Benoit. He felt almost feverish. A result, at last! He noted down his witness's name and address. 'Thank you so much for your assistance. Sadly there is little in police funds to allow for rewards. But here.' He handed her a few centimes. Her eyes lit up. 'Let me see you out.'

101

Both Diamond's parents had been buried at St Anne's churchyard off Dean Street, and it was to there that she went, with Michael in close attendance, stopping off at a florist on the way to get some chrysanthemums – yellow, because that had been Aiden's favourite colour – and some red roses for Frenchie her mother and Warren her dad, who she had lost far too soon and who she had never known as an adult.

Together they walked along the rows of gravestones until they reached those of Warren and Frenchie. Beside Warren's grave was another, only recently dug, with a wooden cross buried in the soil. *Aiden Butcher* had been scrawled out roughly on the cross piece.

'Oh my God,' said Diamond, and she knew then that somehow she had been hoping that there'd been some stupid misunderstanding and that Aiden was alive and not buried in this bleak, unlovely place.

The tears came then, floods of them, and she was unable to stop them. Michael went and fetched water-filled vases, took the flowers from her hands and filled them. He placed half the red roses on Frenchie's grave, the other half on Warren's, the yellow chrysanths on Aiden's. Then he stood back, allowing Diamond time to compose herself.

Aiden was dead. There was nothing she could do for him; he was already gone, beyond help. But *Owen* . . .

She thought of Victor lording it around Soho, and felt the familiar old fury rise up in her. She thought of not being here when her family needed her, not being there when Aiden died. Not being here when they carted poor gentle Owen off to some hell-hole where he would be among strangers. He would be frightened. *Terrified.* He wouldn't understand.

'You said they took Owen away to the madhouse,' she said at last, drying her eyes.

'Yes,' said Michael.

'Which one?'

'It was the Croydon one. Bad places, they are. Dangerous people, demented, put in with saner ones until the sane ones go mad too.' Michael looked at her face. 'Sorry. You don't want to hear that.'

Maybe she needed to. The thought of Owen, crammed in with all sorts, made her angry again, and anger was good. She needed to feel it, to kick against it, to fight back against Victor bloody Butcher and that evil cow his wife. They'd had it all their own way. Now, the tide was going to turn.

'Thanks for this – for coming here with me today, Michael,' she said.

He shrugged. 'It's nothing. Your dad was good to me when I was a kid, I've never forgotten that. So if you need help – anything – you've got it. Just say the word.'

'Come on,' she said, turning away from Aiden's grave. 'We've no time left today. The light's going.'

Dusk was settling over the cemetery, lengthening the shadows, turning the stone angels into lurking demons. She shivered.

'Tomorrow, we'll start again,' she said. 'We'll go and fetch Owen.'

102

Inspector Lockhart was not like Inspector Benoit, thought Golon when he entered New Scotland Yard, the London police headquarters on the Victoria Embankment. Lockhart was tall, Benoit was dumpy and squat. Lockhart had a friendly face, while if Benoit ever cracked a smile he could split his miserable mug wide open. But where they *were* the same was in their eyes. They both had eagle eyes, sharp as preying birds; fearsome.

'And how is my dear old friend Benoit?' asked Lockhart, ushering the young French detective into a chair, then going around the desk, seating himself.

'Inspector Benoit is in good health. He sends you his warmest regards. He says I am to talk to you about a person of interest, one Diamond Butcher.'

'Interest pertaining to what?' asked Lockhart.

'To a murder case we are in the process of investigating. A shooting. With a .22 handgun.'

'Tell me more.'

Golon did. He elaborated over the exhibition, the guests coming streaming out onto the night-time streets, and now he had more to add: he had been in touch with Paris this morning over the phone and Benoit had told him about the flower seller's statement.

'I have the Butcher woman's last known English address here,' said Golon. 'But of course, as a matter of courtesy I come to you first. I hope you feel you will be able to assist me?'

Lockhart nodded. 'Of course.' Lockhart and Benoit always operated on a 'you scratch my back and I'll scratch yours' basis. He glanced at his watch. Two o'clock, nearly. 'No time like the present, correct? We'll go now.'

103

The area wasn't the best, that was Golon's first impression of Soho. But then, roaming the back streets of Paris as he often had to do, he was used to a certain level of degradation. Here, the narrow terrace houses were packed in tightly together, the roads were hellishly busy with horses, carts, trams, cars, everything that made a noise and a stink. A pall of smoke from all the home fires cloaked the humid air as they arrived at the address of Diamond Butcher. But the woman who answered the door was not a tall dark angel in a red dress; this one was a very thin – almost emaciated – blonde, and her blue eyes, set deep above her sunken cheeks, had a haunted look about them.

'Madam,' Lockhart greeted her. He produced his card and Golon showed his too. 'Police.'

Instantly she looked alarmed. 'My husband isn't home,' she said, holding her hand in front of her mouth as she spoke.

They hadn't asked to speak to her husband. 'And your husband's name is . . .?' said Lockhart.

'Victor. Victor Butcher.' She glanced back over her shoulder as if Victor was going to come creeping up on her, unannounced. 'He isn't home,' she repeated.

'Perhaps you can help us? We are trying to find a Miss Diamond Butcher.'

The blue eyes sharpened. She gulped. Her hand still hovered over her mouth. 'Her? She left here ages ago. There was a rumour that she went to France, but who knows? Victor is her uncle.'

'Would he know where we can find her? You're quite sure she isn't here?'

'No. She's not. Victor won't know either.'

'We know that she's in England now, recently returned from France. Perhaps she will get in touch with him? And what is your name, madam?' asked Lockhart.

'I'm Mrs Victor Butcher. Gwendoline.'

'Your husband is at work?'

Golon was watching Lockhart with interest. Something was telling him that Lockhart knew very well what Victor Butcher's linc of business was.

'He owns properties. Runs clubs and pubs. He might be at the Bombardier.' She swallowed hard then went on. 'Sometimes he goes to Chinatown. In Limehouse.'

'Looks half frightened out of her wits,' Golon said when they had left the house and were hailing a cab.

'No wonder,' said Lockhart. 'I didn't put two and two together at first, but now I have. Victor Butcher's a twenty-stone brute and he has these two very interesting triangular scars, one on each side of his forehead. Rumour has it that this "Diamond" woman put the marks on him with a flat iron before running off, so there's not much love lost in that family. You have gangs in Paris, I suppose? Criminal gangs?'

'Of course. Every city has its share of scum.'

Lockhart smiled. He smiled a lot. Golon thought that it would be a lot easier, working with an amenable chap like Lockhart, rather than that stiff pedantic little article Benoit.

'They give themselves such pretty names, too,' said Lockhart as they boarded a cab and Lockhart asked for the Bombardier public house. 'The Silver Blades, they'd cut you as soon as look at you. The Black Hands, they mark their intended victims with black powder – a message they're about to be killed. Very professional they are about it too. The Forty Thieves, they're hoisters. All the West End shops live in fear of them. And I'm sad to say some of my officers do too. I'm even sadder to tell you that corruption from the gangs inevitably seeps into the police force. The gangs make big money, and who doesn't like a bigger pay packet? So some officers go to the bad. The Peaky Blinders, we don't see that much of them down here thank God, they're more for Birmingham and they blind people who cross them with razors sewn into their caps. And then there's the Victory Boys. That, my friend, is Victor Butcher's crew.'

Golon absorbed all this in silence as the hansom cab's scrawny-looking bay clip-clopped along the dirty cobbles, its driver sending it dodging around smoke-spewing cars, parked lorries, abandoned carts and meandering pedestrians.

'The Bombardier's a rough hole,' said Lockhart cheerily. He fished in his pocket, pulled out a set of thick brass knuckle-dusters and put them on his right hand. 'Always best to be prepared,' he said.

104

From the outside, the place looked grand. That was Diamond's very first thought when the carriage approached it up a long, straight driveway. On one of the big stone gates they had seen the sign, intricately painted: *Moorcroft Mental Institution.* And there was the house. Big lawns in front of its huge red-brick walls. A gardener, hard at work in one of the flowerbeds. Immaculate blood-red paintwork on the house's windows, doors and eaves.

The sight of it was not in the least disturbing. In fact, as Diamond and Michael alighted from their carriage, she found herself feeling a little less panicked. The night had felt very long and she had slept only a little, thinking of Owen, gentle Owen, confined in some hell-hole with maniacs threatening him. But as they went up the steps, Diamond found herself feeling reassured.

The two of them went into a reception area. It was clean. Tidy. Flowers on a table, magazines, a big double staircase and beside it, sitting at a desk, was a smiling woman in a blue nurse's uniform.

'Can I help you?' she asked.

'I've come to see my brother. Owen Butcher,' said Diamond, while Michael stood by.

'Owen . . .?'

'Butcher.'

'Do you have an appointment?'

'No. I don't.'

'Oh! Well, I'll fetch the doctor. If you would take a seat . . .?'

The nurse went over to a half-glassed door, the glass itself reinforced with a thick metal mesh. She took a key from a bunch at her waist, unlocked the door, went through, then locked it from the other side.

Diamond sat down. The care with which the nurse had just relocked that inner door had sent a shudder of misgiving through her. Michael sat down too. The heavy ticking of a grandfather clock beside the stairs droned on, puncturing the stillness of the reception area like darts hitting a board. Distantly, there were shouts. A barking, like a dog.

They waited.

Then suddenly the nurse appeared in the glass section of the door, and there was a white-coated man with her. The nurse unlocked the door and both of them stepped through. The man approached the seated pair. He was very tall, cadaverous. He looked about sixty, his hair thinning and grey. His teeth, when he smiled, were misshapen and yellow, but he had a professional, doctorly, almost *fatherly* air about him. Diamond and Michael stood up.

'I believe you're enquiring about a Mr Owen Butcher?' he asked. 'I am Doctor Mandleson.'

'I'm his sister,' said Diamond.

'Ah. Well his treatment is progressing very . . .'

'What treatment?' asked Diamond.

'We have various methods of improving mental capacity.'

'Owen's mental capacity can't be improved. Everyone who knows him knows that. The cord was around his neck when he was born and so he was starved of air to the brain. It can't be helped. He's a bit slow. He doesn't need any treatment.'

The doctor's cheery smile dimmed. 'Madam, I will be the judge of that. In my capacity as medical director, the decisions regarding treatment of patients are entirely my concern.'

'I want to see him,' said Diamond. 'Now.'

'That is, of course, your right,' said the doctor.

'Good.'

He stood there, hesitating.

'Now,' Diamond reiterated.

'I would advise . . .' the doctor began.

'*Now*,' said Diamond again, more loudly this time.

Michael stepped forward a pace. 'Did you hear what she said?' he growled.

'Yes. Yes! As you wish,' said the doctor. He nodded to the nurse, who unlocked the door to let them through into the main body of the building.

Once they were in, Diamond glanced back. The nurse was locking the half-glassed door from outside in the reception area. Diamond's eyes caught hers and the nurse gave her a blank, unblinking stare. Then Diamond turned and followed the doctor and Michael along the inner corridor.

105

Victor Butcher wasn't in the Bombardier and the barman wasn't about to tell the police where he *really* was at the present time, either – until Lockhart hauled the man over the counter and stuck his face in the spittoon on the floor and then repeated his question.

'Mr Victor Butcher. Where is he?'

The barman scrabbled up, wet in the face, gasping for air. Lockhart slapped his head down on the bar counter and held the knuckle dusters in his line of vision with the clear intention of beating the man about the head with them until he co-operated.

'Where?' demanded Lockhart.

'Chinatown. Lily's place,' he choked out.

Lockhart released him. He looked around at the silent, watching patrons. Then he smiled.

'Chinatown it is then,' he said cheerily. Trailing a deeply impressed Golon behind him, he left the pub and hailed another cab.

***

Lily's place was one of the many thriving whorehouses in Limehouse's Chinatown, set out right on the waterfront with lots of private rooms and a good supply of opium coming in weekly off the river to keep its clients happy during visits.

Victor Butcher was there with his mistress Lily, doing a bit of business that involved the Triads, arranging for cargo to be taken from Limehouse Docks down to Southampton and from there onward to Turkey and then on to Arabia, where top dollar could be relied on.

Business concluded, Lily was slipping into something more comfortable – a see-through fuschia-pink cheong-sam that suited her soft skin and waterfall of black hair to a nicety. Victor was half out of his trousers when the bouncer on the door announced they had company. The police.

Very bloody irritating.

Victor was fuming. Didn't he pay enough to be sure they didn't get bothered by the fucking rozzers? He pulled up his trousers again and went out to the front desk. A middle-aged bowler-hatted man stood there, along with a lanky younger one.

The older one tipped his hat politely to Victor.

'Mr Victor Butcher?' he asked.

'Who wants him?' snapped Victor.

Lockhart produced his identification; so did Golon.

'Police, sir. Are you Mr Victor Butcher?' asked Lockhart, an edge to his voice now.

'I am.'

'This is in relation to your niece, sir. One Diamond Butcher.'

'She ran away from home,' said Victor. 'Ain't seen her in over a year.'

'What is she like, sir? As a person?'

'As a *person*? She's a pain in the arse, that one. Disobedient. Lippy.'

'And do you know where she is now, sir?'

'I was glad to see the back of her, I know *that.* Why? What d'you want her for?'

'We are anxious to get in contact with her. We believe she may have information pertaining to a murder inquiry.'

'Fuck me. Really?'

'Really.'

'Well, I don't know where she is. You could try Moira McLean's house if you want,' he said, and gave them the address.

106

The noises were getting much louder. With every step they took, the volume of the cries and shouts increased. They passed steel doors with viewing traps set in every one, until at the fifth door the doctor stopped. He fished out a key from his pocket, inserted it into the lock, turned it. Pushed in.

Now there was an explosion of sound, making Diamond cringe back. The doctor gave a tilt of his head and went inside, indicating that she and Michael should follow. They did. Diamond walked forward when every fibre of her body was telling her to turn back. The din in here was inhuman, like the cries of souls in hell. And then she realised that they were standing on a raised walkway, without safety rails on either side, set eight feet above the floor of the vast room they were in.

Down on the floor of the huge room was a mass of people, all of them dressed in dirty-looking cream-coloured shifts. There must have been fifty thin heavily stained mattresses spread out on the floor below. The smell of unwashed bedding and filthy bodies rose around them on their raised platform like a stinking miasma.

Diamond couldn't believe what she was seeing. There was a man holding a huge doll, cradling it as tenderly as if it were a real live baby. Another was crouched on a bench at the side of the room, all skeletal arms and legs, huddling into himself as if to shut out the rest of it. A woman was pulling over and over again at her own hair, yanking clumps of it from her head. People moaned and screamed and rolled about on the soiled mattresses. Somewhere down there, someone was singing the 'St Louis Blues' in a cracked, dreamy voice.

Then, realising they were observed, some of the poor wretches stumbled over to the walkway and started clawing at it, staring up at the doctor and Diamond and Michael. Diamond stepped sharply back, then felt something touch her leg. She shrieked, glanced around. A tall man with crazy eyes was grinning up at her, trying to reach her, to touch her again.

'You all right?' asked Michael over the shouting and screaming.

Diamond nodded. Her eyes were searching the crowds, trying to find Owen. There were two bulky orderlies right down at the end of the room, lounging beside a steel door. Where the hell was Owen? She couldn't see him. Anxiety gnawed at her. Where *was* he? Her eyes were frantically searching the crowds.

Down at the other end of the room, a black-haired young man was sitting on a hard wooden bench, dressed in a cream shift just like all the other poor souls confined in here. He was gazing up at her.

Owen.

'There's Owen!' shouted Diamond, grabbing Michael's arm and pointing. 'Look! There!'

'I see him,' said Michael. 'Christ alive, what a place!'

Diamond turned to the doctor. People were grabbing at her feet. The big man with the doll was holding the ugly thing up to her, as if she were the Pope and he was asking for a blessing. If she were to slip off this walkway and fall down in there, what would happen? She stepped on someone's hand and they fell back. But others were coming. Squirming fingers touched her ankle and she shrank away, repulsed. Michael stamped on someone's fingers and they let out a howl. Owen was getting to his feet. He'd seen her.

'I'm taking him home with me. Today,' she told the doctor.

'Oh I cannot think that would be feasible, dear lady,' said the doctor.

Suddenly Diamond was ten feet tall and furious. *Her* brother, in this rat-hole! And this pompous *bastard*, talking down to her, like she was a helpless little woman without a brain.

'It's not only feasible, it's going to happen.' Her voice was icy.

'Oh madam, I really don't . . .'

Instead of reaching for the razor in her stocking-top, as she longed to do, and puncturing this over-inflated arsehole with it, Diamond reached into her bag and pulled out her purse. She pulled out a hundred pounds and saw the doctor's eyes widen. She thrust the notes at him.

'This is yours. And the instant you get my brother out of here and ready for me in reception, you will have another hundred. If you *don't*, there'll be trouble the like of which you will have never seen before.'

The doctor's eyes were fixed on the money in Diamond's hand. Greed and pomposity waged a war on his thin, febrile face.

'I'm taking Owen home without any fuss at all, or this gentleman here is calling in some friends of his to make sure of it. Trust me – you wouldn't like that option.'

The doctor looked at Michael, looming there.

'My dear young lady. . .' started the doctor, shaking his head.

Michael stepped forward and grabbed the front of his white coat, hoisting him into the air, glaring into his eyes.

'Don't piss me off,' he warned in a growl. Then he dropped the doctor back onto his feet.

The man hastily snatched the notes out of Diamond's hand and tucked them away inside his white coat. His hand was shaking. He indicated the door they'd entered through. 'All right! If you will follow me . . .?'

107

Diamond felt like she'd escaped from the depths of hell. The doctor vanished when they were out in the reception area again and she started to worry that perhaps she'd been cheated. She sat, twitching with impatience and anxiety with Michael at her side, the nurse behind the desk sending them occasional blank smiles.

'He's not coming,' she said more than once.

'He'd better,' said Michael as the minutes ticked by. But maybe he wasn't. Maybe instead this so-called 'doctor' had summoned the police and they were on their way here now, to throw out these unwelcome visitors.

Finally, just when Diamond felt that she couldn't take another single minute of this endless *waiting*, another door opened at the other side of the reception area. One of the bulky orderlies she'd seen in the dormitory came through, jangling a huge bunch of keys, and there, following him, was Owen. He was wearing clothes that looked as though they'd come off a beggar who was both shorter and thinner than himself. Which they probably had. When he saw Michael and Diamond there, his face split in a grin of disbelief and then he started to cry.

'Diamond, Diamond, Diamond!' he shouted, sobbing, and he ran across to her and enfolded her in a hug.

He stank, but Diamond didn't care. She held on to him tightly, cooing words of reassurance.

'It's all right. It's all right now, Owen, you're coming home with me.'

'Home?' he was staring at her face. He was frowning. 'Not home. Won't go.'

'To Moira's house,' she said quickly. She could see that the thought of going near Victor and his lady wife filled Owen with fear. Then she saw the doctor had come out and was standing by the desk. 'We'll stay with Moira and Michael, would you like that?'

'Yeah.' He snivelled, swiping at his eyes.

'Everything's going to be fine now, Owen. I promise.' Gently she broke free of him and went over to the doctor. Her eyes were hard and dark with fury as she stared into his face. 'You ought to be ashamed of yourself. But here. *Take* your bloody money.'

She thrust the promised hundred into his hand and then turned on her heel. 'Come on, Owen. Let's get out of this damned place.'

They walked to the gate and hailed a taxi and went back to Moira's. All the way there, Owen clutched onto Diamond's hand and wouldn't let go. His eyes were anxious, barely leaving hers, terrified that she'd somehow be snatched away from him, that he would lose her all over again.

This is Victor's legacy, she thought bitterly. *Owen thrown into a madhouse, Aiden dead.*

She was back now, and trying to set things right. But she couldn't deny it – the scars went deep. Victor did still frighten her.

Moira was overjoyed to see Owen – but horrified by the state he was in.

'My God, you're filthy, you poor boy, and where the hell did they find these rags?' she demanded.

'We'll shop for more clothes later. For now he can borrow some of Michael's, can't he?' asked Diamond.

'Of course he can. Michael – boil up some water out in the scullery and get the bath set up there.' She patted Owen's face. 'You'll feel better cleaned up. Then some nice hot food inside you.'

Clearly starting to feel a little less panicky, Owen trailed out after Michael while Moira and Diamond sat down at the kitchen table.

'How was it?' said Moira in hushed tones.

'Awful,' said Diamond. She was shaken, and she'd only spent minutes inside the place. What about all those other poor souls, condemned to live in such horrific squalor? 'People sleeping fifty to a room. No sanitation that I could see. Just . . . awful. Like a horrible nightmare.'

'But Owen's here now, with us.'

'Yeah.' Diamond's eyes went to Owen and Michael, through the open scullery door. Michael was laying out the tin bath in readiness, boiling up water, fetching towels. Every so often, he touched Owen's shoulder, reassured him. Owen's eyes strayed back to his sister's, and he smiled. Owen's smile was heartbreaking, as innocent and sweet as a child's. She'd missed it. She'd missed him. She missed Aiden, too. But although she had Owen back, Aiden was gone and it was far too late for goodbyes.

'What will you do now?' Moira asked, patting Diamond's hand, seeing her distress.

'Gather my thoughts,' said Diamond, gulping back a tear. She had been about to say 'pay a visit to Victor' but she knew she was not ready for that. And that maybe she never would be.

108

The same stick-thin housekeeper opened the door to Benoit at the Marquis's grand Parisian home, her face – at the sight of the detective – twisting into the same look of sour displeasure it had worn the last time he showed up.

She showed him into the sunlit drawing room where the Marquis was waiting. Mimi Daniels was there too. When Benoit came into the room, Mimi jumped to her feet, very nervy. Well, that was good. Nervy people said careless things.

'Monsieur le Marquis,' he greeted the man politely, bowing.

'Dear fellow, do come in,' said the Marquis. 'Sit down. May I offer you some refreshment?'

'No thank you, sir.'

The housekeeper departed. Benoit sat down and Mimi sat too. The Marquis stood by the fire. 'Now,' he said briskly. 'How can I help you?'

'Talk me through what happened on the night of Fabien Flaubert's exhibition,' said Benoit. 'Sir, you were there, weren't you?'

'I was at the exhibition. I bought a painting. Then I went home, alone.'

'And you, madame? After you left the gallery, what happened then?'

'What do you mean? Happened? Nothing happened. Diamond and I went home,' said Mimi.

Benoit gave her a cold stare. 'Madame, I have been looking you up on our files. Your past makes for very interesting reading, you know. And I am not at all surprised that you are nervous around the police. Prostitutes often are.'

Mimi seemed to shrink into her seat. 'That was years ago,' she choked out.

'Not so, madame. I have proof that your activities have continued, right up to the present day.'

The Marquis was looking at Mimi like he was seeing a whole new side to her. Benoit decided to push it. 'A new witness has come forward. She has identified three people and I believe that one of those is you, madame. The second is Diamond Dupree. And without a doubt the third is Arnaud Roussel.'

There was silence in the room.

Then Mimi said: 'Identified us as what? Diamond and I left the venue together, that much is true, but . . .'

'She has identified you at the point of a murder. You were present when Arnaud Roussel, the Marquis's agent, was killed. With a .22 gun. The witness saw you. She heard the shot. She saw Monsieur Roussel fall. I have to tell you that this is a very serious matter. To even be an accessory to such a crime is no small thing.'

'But we . . .' Mimi began.

'It is in your best interests to speak the truth now. If you don't, you risk further involvement and that could prove hazardous,' said Benoit, pressing his point home.

Mimi leaped to her feet and started pacing the floor. Then she burst out: 'I didn't do it. *She* did.'

'Mimi!' the Marquis said sharply.

She rounded on him. 'For God's sake! I'm not going to the guillotine to cover for *her*. You must be mad if you think that.'

'*She* did it?' Benoit repeated slowly. 'You mean this Diamond Dupree? Can we be clear on this?'

'No, no,' the Marquis was saying, shaking his head. 'Of course not . . .'

'Yes! It was her!' Mimi said. 'I'm telling you, she had the gun. Not me. It was *her* who killed Arnaud.'

A shocked silence descended. Then Benoit broke it by saying: 'I will need statements from you both.'

The Marquis was staring at Mimi, his pale eyes full of disgust. 'Shame on you, Mimi. You are a disgrace,' he said.

Mimi was breathing heavily, her eyes wide with fear and now brimming with tears. 'Look! She owned the gun. It was hers. She waved it at Arnaud, to frighten him off. He . . . oh Christ . . . he looked after me, you see.'

'He was your pimp. Your whoremaster,' said Benoit.

'That makes it sound so sordid!'

'Well – it is,' said Benoit.

'He took a cut of whatever I earned. Usually he was reasonable. But he was demanding rent money too, and threatening me, saying I'd short-changed him. He was drunk half the time and dangerous the other. He threatened me and she – *Diamond* – came to my defence and she shot him dead.'

Benoit stood up. He hadn't expected his business would be concluded so swiftly. 'If you will both accompany me to the station . . .?' he asked.

The Marquis was still standing there, his face blank with shock at the turn of events. Benoit could see that even if he'd known all this, he would never have given the game away. He could also see that Arnaud's little sideline as a pimp was news to him, too. The Marquis was a true nobleman. *He* would never have betrayed Diamond, the way Mimi Daniels just had.

109

Owen settled at Moira's after a few fretful days. There were a couple of nights when he awoke screaming and shouting at invisible enemies. A couple of days when he couldn't be still, when every noise, even the front doorbell ringing, would frighten him and he'd curl up in a corner, thinking he was about to be hauled away again. But time passed and he seemed to accept, finally, that he wasn't going to be snatched, that this wasn't just a pleasant hiatus in the middle of a living nightmare. He sat at Moira's kitchen table for much of the day, colouring in the new magazines that Diamond bought him, and she was pleased and relieved that he was getting back to normal.

'Happy little soul really, ain't he?' Moira asked her, smiling at Owen who was working away with his pencils, his tongue stuck between his teeth, his mind focused completely on his task.

'He didn't deserve what Victor did to him,' said Diamond.

'That's past,' said Moira, with an impatient click of the tongue. 'It's gone and you have to forget it now. Owen's safe here, and we're all like one happy family. You *will* forget it. Promise me.'

But Diamond couldn't. No more could she forget Aiden and what in her heart she *knew* had been done to him. Moira was gentler than she was. Moira would never concern herself with thoughts of sweet revenge when a wrong had been done to her. But Diamond would.

'Owen likes our Michael, don't he?' said Moira.

Owen did like Michael, very much. Michael was good with him. Although he could be frighteningly tough when it was called for, he could also be patient and kind, which counted for a lot.

'Owen must have been broken-hearted when that happened to Aiden,' said Diamond. 'I hate to think of him having to get through that all alone. And then to have *that* done to him.'

Moira sighed. 'Let it go, for the love of God, will you?'

But Diamond couldn't.

'He's safe now and he's happy. He don't have to put up with Victor or Lady Muck any more,' said Moira. 'Be glad about that and let the rest of it go, eh?'

Diamond knew that Moira was right. That to chew on all that had gone on would only bring her grief. She went over to the kitchen table and dropped a hand onto Owen's shoulder. He looked up, beaming, then returned to his colouring-in.

Diamond looked over his shoulder at the scene he was embellishing. Horses and carriages and smoke-spouting motor cars all bustling along the Mall. He was colouring a pair of beautiful grey horses in bright canary yellow.

'That's pretty, Owen,' she told him.

He carried on colouring.

Diamond's eyes drifted over the pages he had spread out. *Tatler* was a particular favourite of Owen's, showing lots of show business news and pictures of pretty women and occasionally veering into high society when the two happened to be linked in some way. Beside the Mall picture there was a shot of a stately old building constructed of pale Portland stone in St James's Street. It had a slate roof and a Palladian façade with beautiful French motifs.

She knew about that place. It was a gentlemen's club, the most exclusive in the land, counting aristocracy and even royalty among its members. Then Diamond's breath caught in her throat.

It couldn't be.

There, standing right by the club entrance, was the blond man who had forced himself on her – the father of her child. That was a face she could never forget.

It was *him – RB.*

'Let me see that, Owen, will you?' Heart racing, she pulled the picture toward her and stared hard at it. It *was* him. Dry-mouthed, she read the strapline underneath the photograph.

Such a dashing figure as he goes into his club, White's! Why it's Richard Beaumont, the Earl of Stockhaven!

110

'So you want me to have one of the boys loiter around there and see when he's going in and coming out?' asked Michael when Diamond approached him.

Diamond said: 'Yes.'

She'd been in shock for days after seeing that photo. Richard Beaumont, Earl of Stockhaven. She still brooded over it, what he'd done to her. Made her suffer so much when she had been nothing but an innocent party, forced to participate at Uncle Victor's whim. That upper-class bastard had impregnated her without a care. Forced her to endure the horrors of a bloody miscarriage, all alone. She'd lost her little girl. But now she was recovering her senses, and her churning over all those bad old memories was done. In its place was a cold hard rage. So he thought he could do a thing like that and get away with it, did he? He could bloody well think again.

'I'll have someone keep an eye out,' said Michael. 'You know him then, do you?'

Diamond could see that Michael thought it unlikely. The upper classes, in Michael's mind, didn't ever mix with the likes of him and her. But she *did* know him. To her cost. She wasn't about to explain the circumstances of her knowledge to Michael though, or to anyone else for that matter. It was too humiliating.

'Yes. I know him.'

'If that's what you want,' Michael shrugged. 'I'll see it's done.'

'Good. And when you're not doing that, I want you to do one other thing for me.'

'What is it?'

'Keep an eye on Victor. Tell me what he's up to these days.'

'No problem.'

***

Before very long Michael came back to Moira's with the information Diamond wanted.

'The Earl goes to White's on a Tuesday, for lunch,' he told Diamond. 'Goes in at eleven thirty and comes out at five. Then he goes to a townhouse in Belgravia – probably to sleep it off. I've seen him out around town twice with that music hall singer Beverley Barton.'

'And what about Victor?'

'Same old stuff. He runs clubs, hangs around the Bombardier, knocks heads together. Gets one of the new hostesses to run the badger trick with him these days, poor little cow. She can't be a day over twelve. Still married to the Wolfe woman. No sign yet of any kids. No sign of *her*, come to that. He drinks a fair bit and I've heard he visits the opium dens these days. Got a woman over Chinatown, I heard, and when his wife objected he knocked her teeth out. He's nasty enough when he's sober and not drugged up, fucking great bruiser that he is. You wouldn't like to come across him when he's had a skinful.'

'Just watch him. Take note of what he does on a regular basis. Don't get too close.'

III

On the following Tuesday, Diamond got up. She washed, sprayed herself with perfume then brushed out her hair until it shone like a dark mirror and styled it in loose, seductive waves. She applied rouge to her lips and cheeks and blacked up her eyes. Like a savage going into battle, she dressed as if preparing for war. She selected her most expensive French underwear, her best royal-blue lace-trimmed dress crafted by that genius Madame Delphine, her sky-blue chenille coat with its double-thickness sable collar and cuffs. Then she screwed on her sapphire-and-diamond earrings, a gift from the Marquis, slipped on black shoes, picked up her matching bag, and looked at the finished effect in the mirror.

Finally, she picked up the cut-throat razor and tucked it into her stocking top. There was no doubt in her mind that Richard Beaumont would turn nasty the minute she confronted him with what he'd done to her. And how he'd made her suffer. Well, fuck him. Whatever he flung at her, this time she was going to be *ready.*

She said goodbye to Owen and Moira and set off at eleven o'clock in a hansom cab with Michael, heading for St James's Street through roads packed with carriages and motor cars.

'I would love one of those things,' said Michael as horseless carriages surged past them, emitting hot stinking fumes and blasting their ears with the roar of engines and car horns.

'Can't imagine why,' said Diamond, who thought that horses were a much better, safer and cleaner mode of transport.

'It's the new world,' said Michael with a grin.

'I think I prefer the old one.'

They were at White's by eleven twenty. Michael paid off the driver and the carriage pulled away.

'You want me to wait with you?' asked Michael, looking dubiously up at the door of the club.

Diamond was about to answer when a black-pointed bay clattered up to the kerb pulling a hansom cab. To her shock, *he* got out, briskly paid the driver and then went off up the steps to the club.

'Bugger,' said Diamond, shocked.

'That's him!' Michael caught her arm. 'Hey! You *do* know women aren't allowed in there, don't you? It's a gentlemen's club. For men. Not women.'

She stood there, speechless. It *was* him. *RB.* She remembered him so clearly. Floppy blond hair, a tanned lean face, bright blue eyes. He'd barely changed at all. Whereas she – because of what he'd done to her – felt that she had changed beyond recognition. The liveried doorman greeted him with a smile and a tip of his hat. Without another word to Michael she charged up between the big black iron lanterns on either side of the steps, and up to the door.

The expressions on the faces of the two men standing there was almost comical. They couldn't believe their own eyes.

'Miss . . .' started the doorman.

But she directed her words straight to the Earl.

'Do you remember me?' she asked him.

From indignation at this sudden arrival of a female on this hallowed men-only doorstep, she saw his expression change to one of watchfulness. Then – slowly – to recognition.

'Christ!' he breathed out.

'You're not allowed in here, miss,' said the doorman, flustered. 'You can't come in.'

Diamond looked from Richard Beaumont to the doorman.

'Watch me,' she snapped, and surged past the pair of them and into the club.

112

'Here! Miss!' the doorman called after her, but she was already inside. She strode into the centre of the hall, looking around at a grand staircase, vast paintings, bowls of expensive flowers set out on tables. A grey-haired man with mutton-chop whiskers looked up from an armchair and threw down his newspaper in dismay. A *woman*, inside White's?

The man stood up and crossed the hall to an inner door and was gone. Diamond was starting to enjoy herself – until someone caught hold of her arm. She whirled around, expecting the doorman. But it was *him*, Richard Beaumont, and he looked not angry but amused.

'Good God, it is you. Isn't it? The woman who played the trick on me.'

Diamond couldn't see that it was anything to laugh about. She tugged away, but he held on grimly. 'Get your fucking hands off me,' she said.

'Sir, should I . . .?' asked the doorman, floundering.

'No, no. Let me have a moment, I'll sort this.' And so saying he dragged Diamond off to a door at the back of the hall and shoved through it. Only then did he release his grip on her.

Diamond stood rubbing her arm. She looked around. They were inside a library, lined floor-to-ceiling with books. There was a fire lit in a big sandstone hearth, costly rugs on the polished wood floor and many widely spaced deep comfy chairs. The place smelled sweetly, of lavender polish.

'Blimey, how the other half live,' she marvelled out loud, walking forward and going over to the fire. She held her hands out to the warmth.

Richard Beaumont followed her over to the hearth. He leaned a hand against the sandstone mantelpiece and looked at her. All this time, he'd thought about her. Wondered if any woman would ever come close – and doubted it. Now, she was standing here, right in front of him.

Diamond felt flustered, wrong-footed. She'd spent all this time storing up bile against him, but she had completely forgotten his physical impact. The gloss of his hair, the way he grinned with his head tilted, his eyes sparkling, as if he was really interested in what she had to say. Which of course he was not. And then, when his face was still, there was that sadness there, the same sadness she'd been aware of when they first met.

'I've looked for you, around town,' he said. 'Never saw you, though.'

'I spent some time in Paris. Working as an artist's model,' she said. 'Under the name of Diamond Dupree.'

'Paris? And did you like it there?'

Diamond shrugged. 'Some things were good. Some bad.' She stared at him. 'I lost a baby. That was the worst thing. But I suppose that some people would say it was just as well. Being as I was an unmarried woman.'

He was staring right back at her, the smile frozen on his face as her words sank in. 'I don't know what to say.'

Her eyes were fixed on his face. 'You might say sorry, for a start.'

'For what?' A flicker of exasperation showed in his eyes. Then the dawning of understanding. 'Wait! Now just hold on. You're not trying to tell me it was mine?'

Diamond looked him dead in the eye. 'Yes. I am.'

He was shaking his head. 'If you remember, it was *you* that played a trick on *me*, not the other way round.'

Diamond nodded. 'The badger trick,' she said softly, hating the memory.

'That's the one. When my batman dragged me out of that place after your uncle or your lover or whatever the hell he was . . .'

'He was – is – my uncle,' snapped Diamond.

'Well, when he beat me and robbed me and left me there, my batman explained to me what had been done. The badger trick, yes. I was fresh home from the front, from a living bloody nightmare and I just wanted . . . I don't know. Some softness, I suppose. Some relief from it all. And I got caught like that. I felt a fool. I'm not too proud to say that I wanted to get even.'

'So you thought you'd track me down?'

'I did. Yes.'

'And rape me.'

'Rape? Would you call it that? I wouldn't. You were playing that dirty trick on me again and if I hadn't been prepared for it I'd have been in for another beating, wouldn't I? All *I* was doing, if you don't mind my saying so, was getting my money's worth.'

Diamond's eyes flared. 'You *bastard.*'

'Really? How many hundreds of times did you rob men in that despicable way? Surely sooner or later you would expect *someone* to take full payment.'

Diamond turned and faced him.

'That baby was yours,' she spat out. '*You* made me pregnant. *You* made me suffer. And I was just a pawn in my uncle's games. He used me as bait, time and time again. It was never meant to end in me carrying a child. I was as much a victim as you were.'

Now there was not a shred of humour on his face as he looked at her. 'I didn't know that. How the hell was I supposed to know that?'

'You weren't. You didn't. But now you do. And I hope you feel ashamed of yourself.'

'Well of course I do,' Richard burst out. He walked away from her, then back. 'For God's sake, what kind of man do you take me for? I'm *horrified* that you were used like that.'

Diamond shrugged. 'I knew nothing else. I was put to work, first on the rob in the West End stores, then with the badger trick. I had to entice men so that he could thieve off them.'

He was silent, shaking his head. Finally he said: 'And you lost a child. *My* child?'

'Yes,' said Diamond.

'How do I know you're telling the truth? That the child wasn't fathered by someone else – another one of your "punters"?'

Diamond's face was stony. 'I was a virgin when you bedded me. The child was yours. I slept with no-one else for months afterwards. There is no way it could have been anyone else's.'

'Then I'm sorry. Desperately sorry, that you had to suffer through it all. Had I known . . .'

'But you didn't.'

'No.'

Diamond looked at him and then around her at the grandeur of their surroundings. This was his life, right here. Comfort. Luxury. Whereas she had known the rougher side of life, the streets of Soho, the cheapness of existence there. This place was a world away from that.

Exasperated, she shook her head. 'This was a mistake. I shouldn't have come here. I just wanted you to know, that's all. I was angry, thinking what you'd done to me, and I wanted to see if it hurt you too. I *wanted* it to hurt you too. And now there is really nothing more to be said,' said Diamond, and she went to the door and was gone before he could breathe another word.

***

'Is everything all right, sir?' asked the doorman when Diamond had gone off down the steps.

Richard had wandered out into the hall, half in shock at what she'd told him and wondering what to do about it. He couldn't believe what had just happened, but it was *her*, after all this time. He liked the way she was so natural, so unaffected around him, and so refreshingly frank – unlike his own family, unlike Catherine. They were all cautious around him, treading on eggshells. And just as they had before, her looks stunned him. Maybe his mind, which could all too easily play hellish tricks on him, dragging him into nightmares of blood and mud-soaked trenches, had steered him right, with Diamond. She was every bit as beautiful as he remembered. He wasn't going to let her vanish from his life – not when he'd found her again.

He made up his mind quickly. What she had told him was troubling – awful. But he wasn't prepared to lose her now. He fished money out of his pocket and pressed it into the doorman's hand. 'I want to know where she lives.' He peered out of the open door. Diamond was just getting into a cab with a man at her side. 'Take a cab. Follow her. Don't lose her. Come back and tell me where she's staying.'

113

Moira was busy pressing clothes in the scullery when Diamond came in. Owen was at the kitchen table, colouring. Michael could be heard out in the back yard, chopping kindling.

Diamond dropped a kiss onto her brother's head, patting his shoulder.

'We've had the police here,' said Moira.

Diamond grew still. 'What?'

'They were asking for you. For Diamond Butcher.'

'What did you say?'

'That I haven't seen you since you left to go to France, of course.'

'Thank you.'

'I don't grass people up. I thought you knew that. Now, this trip to White's. Michael told me all about it. Said you went in there with some nob or other.' Moira spat on the iron to test its heat. Then she started pressing a petticoat. 'Who was it you went to see then?'

Diamond sat down at the kitchen table. Michael breezed into the scullery, bringing with him a blast of autumn air. He dropped the kindling into the basket beside the stove and sent a grin Diamond's way.

'You should have seen her,' he said to Moira. 'Went in there like the wrath of God, she did. Gave them all a fit of the vapours.'

'Come on, Diamond,' said Moira. 'Who was it, this mystery man you were in such a rush to see?'

Diamond heaved a sigh. 'Nobody of any importance at all,' she said, realising that her head was aching, she felt exhausted, and she really, really wanted to crawl into bed and stop there. Her angry confrontation with Richard Beaumont had not given her the sense of satisfaction she had expected it to. It had drained her. It had felt like a pointless exercise. Moira had been absolutely right. What was the use of grudges? It was best to just let them go. And the police visit! What the hell was all that about? She thought of Arnaud, dead on a French street, and shivered.

'Did you go by Victor's place today?' she asked Michael.

'I did. He's been out and about around the clubs collecting monies. Did a couple of the old tricks too, he's using a poor scrawny little thing for that. Must be fucking terrified, poor little bint. Man's a bastard.'

'Are you going to be seeing this nob again then?' asked Moira.

'No. I shouldn't have bothered to see him at all. I won't be seeing him again,' said Diamond.

114

Diamond was woken early next morning by sounds coming from downstairs. Moira was a lark, always up early, so there were no surprises there, but this was knocking at the door. Not once, but five times. When the door was pounded upon for the sixth time, Diamond got up, washed, dressed, and went down. She went along the hallway and into the kitchen and stopped dead, staring.

Moira was in the centre of it all, looking around her in exasperation.

'Have you ever seen the bloody like!' Moira burst out in temper. 'What the fuck are we supposed to do with all this then?'

The whole kitchen looked like it was ablaze, that was Diamond's first thought. But what she was looking at was not fire but flowers. Everywhere there was bunch after bunch of exquisite, vivid crimson roses; they were spread out on every available surface.

'Oh Christ, here we go *again*,' complained Moira as the front door took another pounding.

Owen came hopping down the stairs and answered it. Presently he came into the kitchen clutching a huge bouquet. More red roses. He was grinning from ear to ear. 'Pretty,' he said, looking all around them in wonder. 'So *pretty.*'

'Yes, pretty, no bloody doubt it's *pretty*, Owen, but who the hell has this many vases to put the damned things in?' asked Moira. She squinted at Diamond. 'This is down to you, you know.'

'What?' Diamond's mouth dropped open. She was stunned by the sheer visual impact of it all. She had never, in her entire life, seen so many hot-house blooms assembled in one room.

'Look. There was a card with the first bunch and . . . oh *shit.*'

The door was being banged on again. Michael came down the stairs this time and went and answered it.

Moira handed Diamond the card. It said, simply: *Forgive me.*

'Diamond Dupree?' said the man on the doorstep, rendered nearly invisible by the massive bunch of red roses he was carrying.

Moira handed Diamond the envelope with the red deckle-edged card inside. Diamond took it, slid out the card, and read:

Would Miss Diamond Dupree please consent to taking dinner with RB at eight o'clock tonight?

Moira was craning over her shoulder.

How the hell had he found her here? What was he doing all this for? They had parted acrimoniously. She hadn't expected ever to see or hear from him again. But . . . dinner? For God's sake! She looked around again. All these bloody roses!

'Roses for romance,' said Michael, peering over her other shoulder at the card. 'He's got it bad, this one.'

'Shut up, Michael,' said Diamond. She stared at him accusingly. 'Did you tell him where I was living?'

'Nope.'

'Then how . . .?'

'Nothing to do with me.'

And then the front door was thumped again.

Michael went and opened it.

More roses.

'For fuck's *sake*!' yelled Moira.

115

Diamond decided that she would have dinner with Richard Beaumont. What did she have to lose?

'It's only dinner,' she said.

Moira was more cautious. 'It's never "only" dinner,' she pointed out.

But Diamond was, despite herself, intrigued. He must have followed her back here to Moira's. There was no other explanation. And that meant he was keen to continue their association, which puzzled her. She'd torn him off a strip, laid into him good and proper. And he'd deserved it, she told herself, although did she really in her heart believe that? Yes, he'd hurt her, caused her pain, but hadn't she said that they were both Victor's victims? She had, and it was true.

So by a quarter to eight that evening she was dressed in her best gold-coloured crêpe de Chine outfit, wrapped in one of the pale blonde furs the Marquis had bought her. She was rouged, perfumed, with her black hair swept up in a luscious pile and pinned with amber-jewelled grips. She sat waiting in the kitchen with Moira, who was patiently sewing while Diamond was wondering as the clock ticked toward the hour if anyone was even going to show up.

Then, promptly at eight, there was a knock at the door.

'Oh God,' said Diamond, nerves suddenly stabbing her with doubt.

Moira put aside her needlework. 'He's here then,' she said with a smile.

'Should I go?' Diamond was flooded with uncertainty.

'Go!' Moira stood up. 'Just go and enjoy it. Why not?'

Diamond had expected a flunky at the door, but when she opened it she found Richard standing there. He was elegantly dressed, his blond hair gleaming, his long angular face hopeful, his bright blue eyes full of humour.

'I didn't think you'd agree to come,' he said, his eyes sweeping appreciatively over her.

'Neither did I,' said Diamond truthfully.

There was a car at the kerb, the driver sitting motionless behind the wheel, the engine running.

Richard's eyes followed hers. 'Usually I drive it myself.'

'What? You drive a motor car?' In Diamond's mind these new-fangled monstrosities were dangerous beasts, and best left alone.

'I do. I race too, sometimes. I'll tell you all about it over dinner,' he said, gesturing for her to follow him to the car.

'Where are we going?' Diamond stepped out, pulling the door closed behind her.

'Claridge's in Mayfair,' he said, and took her arm. 'Lots of bright young things there these days. You'll fit right in.'

'All right,' said Diamond.

And the evening began, with her still wondering about that strange sadness she glimpsed in his eyes when he wasn't aware of being observed. The war had put it there, without a doubt. He was one of the 'lost' generation, she realised, living a self-indulgent and sybaritic existence as some sort of compensation for what they'd been through.

She was curious about him, this man who'd caused her such pain in all innocence. And the truth was, she was attracted to him, too. She didn't want to be, but she'd felt the pull of it, right from the very first moment they'd met.

116

Victor felt like he was on top of the world. He had the Gatling gun – and by Christ what a toy that was to play with! Just let bloody Michael McLean and his 'Blades' try anything now. He had a foot in the door of the Triads, and deals were firmly in place. Rifles and handguns were coming in now, and in return the very secret and special merchandise Victor dealt in was being shipped out, through Chinatown and onto the river and then onward to its exotic desert destination.

Soon, he was going to rule the world.

Money was flooding in. Lily Wong had given him a taste of the snow – that magical white powder – and he used that a lot. He was invincible! And she loved him.

'I love you, Victor,' she said to him, over and over.

He believed her. Chinese women were so much *better* than the English ones. They didn't moan and complain and drive you to drink and just *beg* for a thumping. Look at Gwen, for instance. Moany cow. Back in the day when they'd first met, he'd felt that he could have eaten her whole, he was so excited by her. Now, he *wished* he had, because she got on his bloody nerves so much with her whining. And she wasn't even pretty any more, now that she'd riled him up so much he'd knocked her teeth out.

One night he came home and she started again. He barely had a foot through the door and there she was, flapping the lip, accusing him of all sorts.

'What's going on down there, Victor? In the cellar? What's going on at night? I hear people coming and going at all hours, I hear the cellar door being opened, what's happening down there?'

Victor had had enough. He grabbed her arm. 'You want to know, do you?' he shouted.

Gwen shrank back.

'Come on then,' said Victor, and pulled her out of the kitchen and along the hall to the cellar door.

'Victor . . .' started Gwen, squirming against his grip. 'I didn't mean it. I just . . .'

'No, come on. You want to know, do you?'

There was a padlock on the cellar door.

When had he put that there?

It had never been there before. She hadn't noticed him putting it on. He released his grip on her and scrabbled in his trouser pocket and started to unlock the thing and Gwen ran, along the hall, trying to get to the front door before he could catch her.

She didn't make it. He dragged her back, unlocked the cellar door and now it was standing open. She could hear a ripple of voices, moaning like souls in anguish. She broke free and ran again. She was at the front door, scrabbling at the paintwork, when Victor caught her and hauled her back to the open cellar door.

'You want to know, that right?' he snarled.

'Victor!' she yelped.

He was hurting her. And the noises! She could feel cold air, pouring out from down there. She could smell something horrible. Now he was reaching in, switching on the light. She saw the steps, going down into the gloom below. She saw . . .

'Oh Christ!' she gasped out.

Victor was grinning. His eyes were alight with triumph.

'Yeah. Now you see, don't you? *Now* you know.'

And he shoved her inside, down the steps, down into the depths of this man-made hell.

117

'Well? How did it go?' Moira wanted to know, the minute Diamond got back. It was late – nearly midnight – but Moira had sat up for her like a fond mother, wrapped in a housecoat and cradling a mug of tea.

Diamond wasn't entirely sure. She sat down at the kitchen table with Moira, the whole room still a sea of scented red blooms, and wondered what had hit her. Richard – who she had been so determined to hate – had been sweet, gentle, entertaining. He'd chatted to her about Paris, which he claimed to love, and told her all about his new passion for motor car racing. Get him on the subject and he came to life. She had passed the evening in fascination, eating Beluga caviar off a small mother-of-pearl spoon, sipping vintage champagne, eating the finest foods she had ever tasted outside of Maxim's in Paris, and wondering what she was doing there with him.

She'd thought of revenge, for so long. She had scores to settle, and Richard was one of those scores. But now she was confronted by him, she found herself thinking *I like him. Good God, he's actually a very decent man.*

'Well? Was he nice?' demanded Moira.

'Better than nice,' admitted Diamond, shrugging off her coat.

'Really?' Moira's eyes sparkled. 'Tea?'

'No, I think I'll go on up. I'm tired.' And bewildered.

Moira grew thoughtful. She let out a sigh. 'You know, I always thought that perhaps you and Michael . . .?' She left the words hanging in the air between them.

'I know you did,' said Diamond. She loved Michael dearly. But not like *that*. 'We've always been best mates. But nothing else. Nothing more.'

'All right. Well, we'll talk tomorrow, yes? You get some sleep now.'

***

Diamond was startled from sleep late next morning by a heavy hand beating on the front door. Having drunk more champagne than was good for her, she rolled over in the bed and tried to ignore the voices down in the hall, seeking once again the peace of sleep. She didn't want to think. Yesterday evening had been a dream, quite wonderful, and she knew there would be no repeat of it. But she wasn't ready yet to face that reality.

The voices stopped. All fell quiet. Then there was Moira's light tread on the stairs. There was a tap on the bedroom door.

'Mm?' she murmured.

Moira opened the door and stepped in. 'There's been a delivery,' she said, yanking back the curtains to admit cold bright daylight.

Diamond groaned and pulled the blankets over her head.

'No, come on, it's something for you. From his lordship the Earl, the man said. Come on!'

Moira was tugging at the blankets.

Diamond emerged bleary-eyed. 'Oh all right. For fuck's sake! What is it?'

Moira was holding out a small square pink paper-wrapped box. Diamond took it. Moira, beaming, sat down on the side of the bed while Diamond peeled off the paper. The little box inside was encased in black leather. Diamond stared at it.

'Go on, go on!' urged Moira.

Diamond flipped open the lid and there, on a bed of black velvet, was a pair of earrings.

Moira caught her breath. 'My God,' she said weakly.

They were large emerald-cut clip-on diamond earrings. Each multi-faceted and exquisite stone was surrounded by a dozen smaller ones. Diamond held them up and stared at them. The light from the window caught them, sending up sparkling rainbow prisms.

'And there's a note,' said Moira, handing Diamond a thick glossy envelope.

With shaking fingers, Diamond turned the envelope over and saw two unicorns. It must be Richard's crest. She slipped open the seal and took out the note inside.

Diamonds for a diamond
Tomorrow? Eleven thirty a.m.?

She handed the note to Moira, who read it, biting her lip with excitement.

'You've got to tell me everything about him,' she said.

Diamond took one of the earrings out of the box and turned it over. The setting was expensive, hallmarked. 'I will,' she said, wondering what on earth she was getting into. She really wasn't sure about any of this – but she liked Richard. She loved his company. She hadn't expected him to ask to see her again and she was pleased that he had. Lunch this time, clearly. Less formal than dinner. Maybe he was ashamed of her. Maybe he was thinking that he'd keep her hidden away somewhere, out of sight of all his aristocratic pals.

Still – she did like him. She couldn't help it. She just did. And if he wanted to meet for lunch, fair enough. Lunch it would be.

118

Richard collected Diamond from Moira's house next day. To her surprise, instead of heading for a restaurant or hotel he drove his bone-rattling jalopy out of town and within an hour or so they were bumping and jostling up a long, sweeping driveway lined with thick dark rhododendrons.

'You're going to love this,' he shouted over the cacophony of the engine.

Love *what*? Diamond wondered. She was gritting her teeth against every single shaking heave of the car and wondering if she was going to be sick if this journey didn't end soon. Richard seemed as excited as a five-year-old. He'd chattered all the way about his Bugatti, about the races he'd been taking part in at Brooklands, the thrill of it, how much he adored it, while she just smiled and nodded and wished this trip would end.

Then the house suddenly came into view and Diamond's mouth dropped open in wonder. Autumn sunlight was twinkling on Fontleigh's vast soaring golden walls, kissing its clusters of barley-twist chimneypots. The trees crowding all around the house were dusted with bronze and a cool breeze was sending fallen leaves scudding across the huge lawns. She'd never seen *anything* so lovely.

'Isn't she a beaut?' Richard grinned.

Diamond could only nod. The car roared and spluttered its way up to the house and then he switched off the engine.

Stillness descended, the utter breathless quiet of the countryside. Richard jumped down, coming around the car to help Diamond. She saw the big black double doors at the top of the house steps swing open and there was a butler, black-clad, immaculate.

'Benson!' Richard took Diamond's hand and led her across, up the steps and into the house.

Benson bowed. 'M'Lord. We weren't expecting you.'

'Spur of the moment thing, Benson. This is Mam'selle Dupree, she is joining me for lunch, get cook to rustle something up, will you? And we'll take tea in the drawing room.'

'Certainly, sir.'

High above them in the hallway was a glass cupola around which were painted angels, cherubs and saints. Diamond nearly broke her neck staring up at it all. Then a girl darted forward and took her coat and hat. Richard sloughed off his own outdoor clothes, took Diamond's hand and led her into the drawing room. It was all sumptuous sky blue and gold, from the thick drapes to the shimmering wallpaper to the massive couches grouped around the – as yet unlit – fire.

'My God!' Diamond laughed. 'Richard! It's the most amazing place I've ever seen.'

'Yes. Beautiful, I know. Of course, I'm used to it. I was born here. But it startles everyone else. Do sit down.'

Diamond sank down onto one of the silk-covered couches. Bluebirds and bright-eyed golden finches frolicked all around her on the soft, glossy surface.

'I'm having a house party this weekend. Say you'll come,' said Richard, sitting down beside her.

'I . . .' Diamond ran out of words. The shocking reality of Fontleigh had rendered her speechless. She didn't know how she would cope with a party here. In France, she had been her own creation, assured of her welcome everywhere. But England was different, with its rigid class rules. What would his high-society friends think of her, a half-French, half-English low-born woman from the roughest streets in London? She felt a twinge of misgiving. What about his family?

'It will be very casual. Don't worry.'

'I don't know . . .'

There was a tap on the door and a maid entered, bringing a tea tray. She bobbed a curtsy, came over to the couch and placed the tray on a small and probably priceless table.

'Shall I pour, sir?' she asked.

'No, leave it, Maddy. We'll see to that.'

The maid left the room.

Richard turned to Diamond. 'Say you'll come. Please.'

'Richard . . .'

He hurriedly interrupted her. 'Look – I know we met in . . . well, shall we say somewhat strange circumstances?'

'We did. That's true.'

'But . . .' He paused, gazing at her intently. Slowly he reached out, took her hand in his. 'The fact is, I haven't been able to get you out of my mind ever since that day. Literally every time I close my eyes at night I see your face. I honestly believed that we would never meet again, that I would spend the rest of my wretched life wondering what could have been. But you came back to me. You were angry and hurt, and I was unhappy. Fate has thrown us back together, don't you believe that? I know I do. Our differences and the unfortunate way we first met don't matter to me. And I hope not to you, not any more. All I know is this: we mustn't waste this chance we've been given.'

Then he leaned forward and his mouth brushed against hers, very lightly. Before Diamond could even think of responding, he drew back, just a little, staring into her eyes. 'Did you like the earrings?'

'Yes. Of course I did. They're wonderful.' Her lips tingled and she found herself wishing that he hadn't drawn back quite so quickly.

'You're not wearing them,' he pointed out.

'They're too grand for daytime.'

'If you come at the weekend, will you wear them? In the evening? At dinner?'

Diamond's eyes teased his. '*If* I come? Perhaps I will.'

'What a minx you are.'

'Richard?'

'Hm?'

'Kiss me again, will you?'

119

After Fabien's treatment of her, Diamond had believed that she would never fall in love again. But she knew that was precisely what was happening to her now. After a great deal of kissing, the tea forgotten, they strolled in the grounds, down to the big ornamental lake, where Richard pulled her into the dark shadows of a cedar of Lebanon and kissed her again, over and over again, hungrily, their lips and tongues and teeth clashing, his hand straying to her breast, feeling through the thin silk of her dress and her underwear the way her nipple sprang to life at his touch.

'Darling,' he murmured against her throat, 'I am going to have to have you soon or I'll go mad.'

'Richard, behave yourself,' said Diamond, but she was smiling, dishevelled, and much to her own surprise, deeply aroused. Her mouth was sore from his kisses, her skin sensitised. Her heart soared. It was true: she was falling in love again. It was nothing short of a miracle.

When they got back to Moira's house, Richard kissed her goodbye and she promised that she would come to his weekend party at Fontleigh. Then she almost floated indoors to be met not by Moira but by Michael, who instantly demolished her happy mood.

'Victor's expanding again,' he said.

She almost, for a moment, had to wonder who the hell Victor was. She had come from a golden place with a fabulous man, and now it was like being plunged from sunshine into icy dark water as she recalled *exactly* who Victor was.

'What, buying places up?' she asked, going into the kitchen and sitting down at the table, wondering if she looked a mess. There couldn't be a trace of lipstick left on her mouth, and she felt feverish, over-excited.

'Not buying. Moving in and just shoving people out, people who pay protection to the Blades. Taking the piss. Beating them up.'

Diamond nodded. This was reality. Not Richard and Fontleigh. *This* was. Soho and badger tricks, hoisting and her hated Uncle Victor. How could she have forgotten that? She felt a giddy moment of complete and utter disconnection. This city, these people, these were her roots. But at the moment this place and even Michael and his mum felt strange to her, and her roots felt frayed.

'Is he still doing the badger trick?' she asked.

'Damned sure,' said Michael. His mouth twisted in disgust. 'Got little Gertie Madsell doing it, poor little cow. She's a fucking wreck with it all. Shakes like a leaf all the time. Of course that bitch mother of hers don't care, Victor pays her handsome.'

Diamond herself had been fourteen, when it had all begun. Gertie was only twelve. A curl of black anger unravelled in her gut as it all rushed through her mind. The harm that bastard had done to her. To Frenchie. To Aiden and Owen. This wasn't right. It wasn't fair.

She stood up. 'Every place he takes over by force, you should burn it,' she snapped out.

'Yeah.' Michael nodded sharply. 'And it'll be my fucking pleasure.'

120

'So darling – who is this person who has put such a spring in your step?' the Dowager Countess asked her son.

Lady Margaret was sitting in the very seat that Diamond had occupied just the day before and staring into Richard's eyes. She might have moved into the Dower House, but she had an army of spies in place in Fontleigh, not least among them Mildred the housemaid, who was 'walking out' with George, who had been Richard's batman during the war and who was his valet now. News had come from Mildred yesterday evening of Richard's glamorous visitor and of Richard whistling about the place this morning, looking happy.

Margaret didn't like the sound of this. Hopefully it would be just one of Richard's actresses or dancers, like that common Barton creature he met up with sometimes in town, a brief fling and not to be taken seriously. In her heart of hearts she was plotting all the time to get Richard back to the woman he *should* be with – sweet, biddable Catherine – had the war not swept him away and ruined all their plans. She was determined she would not give up on that. He *would* wed Catherine, one of these days. She would see to it. And Catherine, who understood him so well, would fill Fontleigh with new life – the grandchildren that Margaret would dote on. She had it all planned out. No other woman was going to interfere with it.

'What are you talking about, Mother?' asked Richard.

'There was a woman here yesterday, very pretty, dark-haired. I saw you with her, down by the lake.' Margaret hadn't seen a thing. But George had. George had chatted to Mildred, and Mildred had reported to her. 'Who was she?'

'Oh, her?' Instantly Margaret could see that Richard was on guard. 'Nobody, really. An artist's model, over from France.'

'And what is she doing here?'

'She's English. She's recently come home.'

'I mean *here*, Richard. At Fontleigh.'

'I invited her for lunch. She's a friend.'

And now you're skipping about the place like a spring lamb? She's more than just a friend.

'Actually she's coming back at the weekend, to join the house party.'

'Is she?'

'Yes.'

'Well then of course she will be made welcome,' said Lady Margaret.

'I'm pleased to hear it.'

'Where did the two of you meet?'

'In London. At the end of the war.'

'Oh! So she's not a *recent* acquaintance then.'

'No, Mother.' Richard smiled.

'Catherine's coming, isn't she? And dear Teddy.'

'I've invited them. There'll be quite a few other guests too. The railway people. The town mayor. You'll be hostess, won't you?'

'As always. I wish I didn't have to. I wish that you had a wife to do that, a companion. It's really time you did, you know, Richard. Someone . . .' Margaret pouted . . . 'Well, you know how I felt about that unfortunate business with dear Catherine. *Such* a sweet girl.'

'Yes. She is.' Richard stood up, glanced at his watch. 'And now, Mother, if you will excuse me . . .?'

121

On Saturday, the staff opened up the big blue tapestry-hung dining room ready for dinner that evening. The long oblong table in there could seat thirty. The candelabra were lit all down the centre of it, shooting gleaming sparks off highly polished cutlery and priceless Spode dishes. White roses, baby's breath and dark green ferns decorated all the spaces in between.

Richard, seated at the head of the table while his mother was seated at the far end, kept his eye on Diamond. The roar of conversation and laughter grew louder as the wine began to flow. She was down on the left, sitting between two of the engineers who had overseen the construction of the railway through Top Farm and on down to Winchester and beyond.

God, she is beautiful.

Then his eyes were drawn to Catherine, sitting almost opposite Diamond, and she smiled sweetly back at him. Beside Diamond, dear Catherine looked pale in her violet gown, almost bland with her grey eyes and her ashy-blonde hair. It wasn't fair to think that, but he did. Diamond was dressed in red, and it enhanced her ivory-white skin and looked fabulous against her coal-dark hair. She wasn't wearing his diamond earrings again, he noted, feeling a faint stab of annoyance at that. She'd promised, after all.

***

Diamond passed most of the dinner chatting happily to the two engineers as they explained the complexities of their job. They talked about the cost of laying railway tracks, about the tasks of wheel tapping and shunting, of what had to be done in case of emergency, the laying out of a series of explosives at the back of a stopped train to alert any oncoming drivers to the hazard it presented.

'And there's the language of bell tones,' said one.

'What's that?' she asked.

'Various bell tones are sent between the signal boxes to indicate certain things.'

'Like?' she prompted.

'A four and a one's an engine coming. And a three and a two is a goods train.' He tapped it out on the side of a dish. The elderly gentleman on Catherine Sibley's left looked across as Diamond laughed and smiled. He was in government, Richard had whispered to her earlier in the evening, and was Catherine's uncle Cedric, her father Sir James's brother. A very young girl who had been glued to his side ever since he arrived at Fontleigh touched his arm and whispered in his ear. *A mistress*, Diamond thought.

Diamond listened to the railway engineers and learned, interested. Then, looking around at the other dinner guests, she was shocked to see Toro Wolfe down at the other end of the table, seated on the right of the Dowager Countess, Richard's mother.

Throughout dinner the Dowager Countess had been shooting Diamond looks that should have killed her, which Diamond had cheerfully ignored. Richard's mother clearly didn't like the look of her at all, but she didn't matter; Richard did.

After dinner the ladies withdrew to the drawing room, and Diamond sat through a few awkward moments when it was made quite clear to her that she wasn't welcome. Only Catherine Sibley, the girl who'd once been engaged to Richard, spoke a word to her.

'I love your dress,' she said while all the other women ignored Diamond pointedly.

'Thank you,' said Diamond.

'I could never wear red, it would swamp me.'

'That lilac's perfect on you. So pretty. And you'd look lovely in pale blues and pinks too. Maybe even a mint green, that would be nice.'

'What do you think of Fontleigh? Isn't it beautiful?'

They chatted and all the while Diamond was aware that Catherine was being kind. She was surprised at that. Would *she* be so nice, if her heart had been broken, as Catherine's had? She knew she wouldn't.

'Fontleigh's lovely,' she agreed.

'Massive though, yes?' Catherine smiled. 'Have you got lost yet?'

'Several times.' Diamond found herself liking Catherine; she was so warm. But she also made Diamond feel guilty. Catherine should have been with Richard; *she* should have been given those diamond earrings – not her.

When they all joined the gentlemen the evening improved. Cards were played, and chess. Around eleven, she made her way out to the orangerie as arranged, and was annoyed to find Toro Wolfe halfway there, blocking her path. That same young girl who had been clinging on to Cedric Sibley all through dinner was there with him, crying and talking shrilly. When Diamond approached, she moved away and was gone.

'What are you doing here?' she asked him. 'Who's that girl?'

'I'm here for the same reason Pendleton and Smythe are here. And the girl? I don't know her, but she's upset. Which goes with being the mistress of an elderly gentleman, I imagine. She said she was going to throw herself in the lake.'

'Good God.'

'I don't suppose for a minute that she will.'

'Who are Pendleton and Smythe?'

'The two men you were chatting to at dinner. The railway engineers. Very clever chaps, those two. I told you I was diversifying. I funded part of the track construction and now the Earl's invited me to dine. What's your excuse? Missing the streets, are you?'

'Why should I?'

'Oh – because that's where you belong.'

'Oh yes? And what about you? Don't *you* belong there too, terrorising the public, and not flittering around the world?'

He grinned. 'I've got very little taste for terrorising. That was my father's main occupation, not mine. Personally? I couldn't see the point. It's a big world and there are plenty more rewarding deals to be struck.'

Diamond stared at him. There was something that had been eating away at her, for a long, long time. 'Were you there, then? On the night your father killed mine?'

Toro was very still all of a sudden. 'Is that what you heard?'

'It is. And it's true, yes?'

He was shaking his head. 'One day, when you're prepared to listen, maybe I'll tell you the *real* truth. Now tell me – what are *you* doing here?'

'I'm a friend of Richard's,' she said, frustrated by his evasion.

'Are you, by Christ?'

'Why shouldn't I be?'

'No reason. Only the Dowager Countess clearly hates you.'

'She doesn't know me yet.'

'She can see her son knows you pretty well.'

Diamond shrugged. *So?*

'And that pretty little thing in the violet dress – Catherine Sibley? – she smiles at you very kindly, but she can't be too delighted with you really, can she? Not when *she* was going to marry Richard before you came along?'

'If you don't mind . . .?'

Diamond hustled past him. In the orangerie, among the lush palms and beside the softly tinkling fountain under the grapevine, Richard was waiting for her. He held out his arms and she went into them and their lips met instantly. His tongue slid into her mouth and she welcomed it, kissed him deeply, felt like she was drowning in hot sensation. Finally, Richard drew back.

'You know, you're really annoying,' he said, half gasping, pushing her gown aside and biting her shoulder so that she shivered.

'Oh? In what way?'

'You're not wearing the earrings. You promised you would.'

He was kissing her throat. Diamond closed her eyes, smiling.

'Oh but I am,' she whispered.

He stared into her eyes. 'What?' Then he laughed. 'Where?'

Diamond shook her head, her eyes half closed, full of lazy promise. 'I would show you, but I don't know where your room is,' she murmured.

Richard told her.

'What time should I come?' Diamond asked.

Richard told her that, too.

'I'll be there,' she said.

122

Diamond was enraptured by Richard, adoring his silky blond hair, his rakish grin, his blue eyes that could sparkle with mischief or cloud sometimes with sadness.

So at the appointed time she crept along the silent hallways and knocked lightly at his door. Richard opened it and, laughing, he pulled her inside and quickly kissed her.

'You came,' he murmured against her mouth.

'Of course I came,' she whispered, heart racing. She kissed him back.

Richard took her hand and led her over to the bed, which was vast and softly lit by a pair of large cream-shaded lamps. 'Wait a minute. I want to know where those earrings are. Sit down.'

Obediently, Diamond sank onto the eau-de-nil silk coverlet and sat there, smiling.

'You minx,' he said, sitting down beside her, his hand going to her collarbone and then dipping down, over the rich pale slope of her décolletage. He kissed her shoulder, smiled into her eyes, kissed her mouth. His finger slid slowly down between her breasts.

'Are they here, then?' His hand moved to cup her left breast.

Diamond moaned, hot sensations stirring as his fingers found her nipple and tweaked it erect.

'No?' His eyes played with hers. His hand moved. 'What about here?'

Under her camisole, his long fingers closed over her right breast, squeezing lightly, rubbing, caressing.

'Richard . . .' she groaned, her hands clenching on the coverlet. She leaned back a little, her back arching as the delicious need for him grew and grew.

'No earrings.' His lips were at her neck now, placing tiny butterfly kisses from the base of her throat to her ear. 'Beautiful, beautiful breasts. Such big nipples! But no earrings,' he murmured, biting her earlobe quite hard. 'I want to see them,' he said hungrily.

'The earrings?' teased Diamond, feeling breathless.

'Your breasts. Show me . . .'

He helped her slip the red gown off over her head. Slipped off her petticoat and then the camisole. Then he sat there and stared at what he'd revealed.

'I've thought about this. *Dreamed* about it,' he said softly.

Richard leaned forward and kissed each hard nipple, very gently at first, teasing each one out with his tongue until Diamond thought she was going to lose her mind. Then he grew rougher, sucking each breast greedily into his mouth. As he did that, his hand moved, going lower, lower, until he was easing the tie on her drawers loose and shoving inside, going down, through the tiny triangle of pubic hair and further and further until . . .

'Oh!' he said.

He sat back. His eyes met Diamond's. 'Lift up,' he said, and Diamond, almost limp with desire, did just as he said.

Richard pushed down her drawers. Diamond kicked off her shoes. Wearing nothing now but stockings and suspenders, she lay back on the cool green coverlet and felt herself turn liquid with longing as his fingers delved down into her, sliding between her labia, where the diamond earrings glittered in the light from the lamps.

'Turkish belly dancers wear jewels in their navels, did you know that?' she said.

'And you wear jewels here,' he said, smiling, kissing her then staring again at the treasures she was wearing. 'Do they pinch?'

'They do. A little.'

'Do they hurt you?'

'Mmm. But it's a pleasure too.'

'God alive, you're driving me mad,' he said, half laughing.

'Show it then,' said Diamond, wanting him now.

Richard stood up. His eyes fixed on hers, he tossed off his shirt, his socks and shoes. Diamond watched as the long pale athletic musculature of his body was revealed. Finally he undid his trousers and underpants, shoved them down and stepped out of them. His cock was long and pale like the rest of him, jerking eagerly up from its bed of curling hair as he stared down at her.

'Hurry,' she moaned, spreading her legs.

Richard knelt between her white thighs. He slipped his fingers between her labia, feeling her wetness, her readiness, his eyes going back time and again to her black thatch of hair, to the glittering diamonds nestling there. Then, unable to wait a moment longer, he placed the tip of his penis in the place where it yearned to go, and pushed up inside her.

Diamond gasped and grabbed at his thighs, urging him in still further. Not wishing to squander this with haste, Richard started to move, very slowly, and then, when he couldn't help himself, he moved faster. Diamond lay back, enjoying his abandon, her arms thrown out above her head, and soon he was thrusting madly, furiously, and it couldn't last but he wanted it to, they both did but it was impossible.

Richard came with a shout of triumph, and stayed there, revelling in the feel of her against him. When he finally withdrew, he was full of remorse. He collapsed onto the bed beside her, his eyes anxious as they stared into hers.

'Darling, I didn't think. Selfish of me. I should have pulled out.'

'What?' asked Diamond lazily, her body still humming with desire.

'I didn't want to make you pregnant again. Make you suffer in any way. I know how awful that must have been for you. Losing the baby. In the heat of the moment I got carried away. . . darling, I'm sorry.'

'Don't be,' she said. If their coming together this time produced a baby, Diamond found that it was a wonderful idea, not a worry. Bad things had happened to her, but good things could, too. 'I'm not.'

Richard lay back. Then he turned his head and grinned at her. 'Then we can do it as much as we like?'

'Let me get my breath back first,' said Diamond, smiling into his eyes. She turned and curled in against his chest. *I love you* hovered on the tip of her tongue, but she bit it back. No. She'd scare him to death if she said that. She kissed his sweat-dampened chest.

Then *he* shocked *her*.

'I love you,' he said, folding her into his arms. He yawned, eyes closing. Then he murmured: 'You will marry me, won't you?'

What?

Very soon his breathing grew deeper, steadier. His arm across her body twitched in the first light grey layers of sleep. Carefully Diamond reached out and pulled the coverlet over to keep them both warm. Then she reached down and removed the diamond earrings. They *had* been pinching. She relaxed against him, closed her eyes, and slept.

***

Suddenly she was jolted from sleep by someone saying loudly in her ear: '*Gas! Gas! Down boys, everybody down!*'

Her eyes flickered open. The memory of where she was and of their lovemaking came back to her. In the lamplight she could see him, eyes closed, his face twisted in anguish.

'Richard . . .?'

'*Gas! Come on, boys!*'

He was shouting.

Diamond shook his shoulder. 'Richard! Wake up, you're dreaming.'

He was churning in the bed, writhing back and forth.

'*No! Look out! Look out, boys!*'

Diamond stared at him and felt chilled with horror. He thought he was in the trenches still. She sat up and shook his shoulder again, much harder.

'Richard!' she said loudly. 'Come on! Wake up! You're having a bad dream.'

His eyes flickered open. Diamond leaned over him and his hands grasped her upper arms, very hard.

'Richard, it's me. It's all right, darling, it's me. You're safe.' She knew she'd be bruised come the morning.

Slowly she could see sense coming back to him. He shook his head, swiped a hand over his brow. He was sweating. 'God, what . . .?' he murmured.

'You were dreaming,' she said.

'Yes. Right.' He sat up, rubbed his hands through his hair, leaving it sticking up in all directions. His eyes went to the clock. 'Darling, it's late. You ought to go back to your room. We don't want people to talk.'

'Yes. All right.' Feeling rejected, Diamond started scrabbling around for her clothes. When she was dressed, she scooped up the earrings from the bedside table. She glanced at the clock. It was two thirty in the morning.

'Goodnight then Richard,' she whispered, but he was lying back, his eyes closed. Already sinking back into sleep. She hoped not into that same nightmare.

She crept to the door and left.

123

'Who the devil is she? Do we know her family?' asked Margaret.

She'd corralled Richard next morning in the library and he'd told her the worst news in the world. She was *furious.* Horrified to the core.

'You are *what*?' she demanded.

'I'm going to marry her,' he said calmly.

Lady Margaret sat down with an undignified middle-aged thump. She stared at her son like he'd gone berserk. 'Don't be absurd,' she said.

Even on first sight, Lady Margaret had taken a dislike to Diamond. Seeing her arrive at Fontleigh, charming everyone around her, seeing Richard dancing attendance on her like some puppy fawning over its master, had all put Margaret's hackles up.

'And no, we don't know her family. Her background is poor,' he told his mother.

'It wouldn't surprise me if you said she'd come off the streets,' sniffed Margaret. Diamond Dupree was the type of woman she despised, one of those who emit a blast of sensuality that could knock any sane man flat.

And what about Catherine? she wondered.

She had thought everything was going so well in that department – she could see how Richard and Catherine had been growing closer again, renewing the childhood ties that had once bound them together. He had even admitted to her that he did miss Catherine, sometimes. So she had been confident that this whole affair would have a happy ending, the ending it *should* have had some time ago.

'It's a bad idea, Richard,' she said. 'A *terrible* idea.'

'Why?' Irritation was plain in his voice. Margaret eyed her son in exasperation. Of course, like most men, he didn't think clearly when he had a passion for a particular woman. He wasn't thinking clearly now. She was going to have to *make* him.

'Because I'm guessing she's from nothing and you are a man of great importance.'

'Why should that be an obstacle?'

'It just *is,* Richard. You talk a different language. You know different things. Everything is fine now, I'm sure, when romance is fresh and young. But as time passes you will realise that I'm right. She will embarrass you and you won't feel the same. You will wish you had chosen someone far more suitable.'

'What, like Catherine?'

The thing was, he still had a great fondness – yes, a love, he supposed – for Catherine. How could he not? Catherine was his old companion, his boyhood friend of many carefree summers, of course he *did* love her. He always had. But Diamond was his obsession, his passion. He couldn't let her go.

'Mother,' he said. 'I know you've been scheming to get us back together, but it won't work. I know Catherine suits you as a bride for me. Of course she does. You can make her do your bidding. But not Diamond. She has her own mind. It's Diamond I love. It's Diamond I shall have.'

'But she's *poor*, isn't she?' said Margaret desperately. 'For the good of the estate if for nothing else . . .'

'Look. I've sold land . . .'

'Yes, and your father . . .'

'I *know* he would never have done that. But needs must. I've sold things I didn't want to. Invested in commodities I never thought I'd even contemplate becoming involved in, and all to save the estate, to preserve it for generations to come. Isn't it better to cut off a limb rather than lose the whole body? So I have cleared our debts. The estate is sound for the foreseeable future. I don't *need* Catherine's family's money, or that from a rich American heiress. I don't need any of that. What I need is the woman I love.'

Margaret surged to her feet. 'That creature is not welcome at Fontleigh,' she snapped.

Now Richard turned on his mother, for the first time in his life.

'That *creature* may come here whenever she likes. That is not your decision to make, Mother. It is mine.'

124

When November came round again everyone laid wreaths, attended memorial ceremonies, thought back in agonised remembrance to the loss of a whole generation of young men who would have been the future but who were now firmly locked into the past. Diamond was back at Fontleigh within the month to attend a weekend lunch party with Richard. And she hadn't mentioned to anyone what he'd said to her on the night they'd shared a bed.

Will you marry me?

He'd been half asleep, it was probably just something said and then instantly forgotten. A lot of his friends were there at Fontleigh again for the weekend, among them that pale girl Catherine and her brother Teddy.

'This is Catherine, a dear old friend,' he said, standing Diamond in front of the girl, who was wearing another pastel gown, pale pink, very subdued. She had kind eyes, Diamond thought. But she already knew that Catherine was more than just a friend. One of the other women had told her that Catherine and Richard had once been engaged to be married.

'She does terrific charitable works,' said Richard, while Catherine blushed and told him not to go on.

'Yes, she's a saint, my sister,' chipped in Teddy, who was solid, muscular, with sandy hair and laughing hazel eyes.

'And this is Teddy, who is a doctor,' Richard told her. 'He's quite the charmer, so watch him. Also, he cheats on the race-track. Cuts people up all the time.'

'I'll bear that in mind,' said Diamond. She liked Teddy, right away. He seemed genuinely welcoming, whereas quite a few of Richard's 'friends' regarded her with hostility. Worst of all was his mother Margaret, whose gaze was gorgon-like in its intensity every time it swept over her.

It didn't take much to work out that she wasn't entirely welcome here, although she tried to be a good guest, chatting to everyone. If she became a fixture in Richard's life, they would just have to accept her – or lose him. He was openly affectionate to her in company, making his feelings very plain.

'You will, won't you?' he asked her one evening as they stood alone and close together in the orangerie.

'Will what?' she smiled.

'You will marry me? It's all I want.'

Diamond's smile faded. 'I thought you were half asleep when you said that. I thought you were dreaming.'

'I meant it.'

'Did you?'

'Of course I did. And you didn't answer.'

'Your mother would be horrified.'

'I know that.'

'She likes Catherine far better than me.'

'That's because she can push her around all over the place. She couldn't do that with you.'

'You were engaged to Catherine once, weren't you?'

'Yes. I was. Then I went through the war. And then *we* met . . . and there was no going back to that old life, not really. I just couldn't go through with it.'

'Your mother hasn't forgiven you for that yet.'

'I know. So, will you?'

She wanted to say yes. But this weekend had given her an uneasy feeling. They really were from different worlds. How would she fit into his? And what about the life she already had? What about Owen, what would be done about him? Would he stay with Moira, or move here to Fontleigh with her? But that would unsettle him. He liked the familiar, the things and places he was used to. Change frightened him. He'd had enough upheaval already.

'Say you will,' he said, pulling her into his arms. 'Or I'll go mad.'

'How could I tell the difference?' she teased, beaming up into his eyes. 'Give me a little time, will you? To think it over?'

'Of course,' he said, and kissed her.

125

'So how's life in the upper classes?' asked a male voice behind her.

She was standing out on the lawn playing an inexpert game of croquet with two of Richard's friends, an over-excitable and very well-bred young couple from Surrey. People were sitting in the warmth of the orangerie looking out at these mad youngsters playing games on the lawn. Inside, they were chatting, drinking tea or cocktails, and Diamond noticed that Richard was at one of the tables, Catherine on one side of him, Teddy on the other, and their heads were all bent together in concentration. Diamond felt a moment's unease. She felt *jealous.*

They speak the same language, she thought.

Lady Margaret was at one of the other tables, sending sour glances out toward Diamond while chatting to an older gentleman in a white Trilby – Sir James Sibley, Catherine's father. *Very* cosy.

Diamond half turned toward the man who'd spoken and there he was again – bloody Toro Wolfe.

'Life is very fine,' she said, and took a swipe at the ball, sending it careening off into the shrubbery.

'We're going in for some tea. It's too cold!' said the girl she was playing with, and she and her boyfriend put down their mallets and departed.

'You're holding the damned thing all wrong,' said Toro.

'Really,' said Diamond, not caring. Suddenly she felt out of her depth, that she shouldn't even be here. She loved Richard. She did. But . . .

'Yes. Look.' Toro placed a new ball in front of her, took her arm and to her surprise pulled her sharply around so that her back smacked up against his chest. 'Like this, you see?' His rough scarred cheek – scarred by Aiden, her brother – was nuzzling against her ear. It was curious, she thought, how that small scar didn't detract from his looks; it merely added to his dangerous piratical air. His hands slid hot and hard down her arms and folded over hers on the mallet. His whole body was pressed up against the back of hers. She could feel *everything.*

'Let go of me,' she hissed at him.

'Your feet are all wrong too,' he said, ignoring her. His boot nudged between her feet, pushing them apart. 'All right?'

Diamond swallowed. Heat was radiating off him.

'Now,' said Toro. 'Mallet on the ball. Square it up, you hit it side-on and it'll end up in the shrubbery with the other one. *Concentrate.*' He gave her a little shake. His breath tickled her ear and . . .

'*Christ!*' Diamond gasped.

He'd bitten her ear. *Hard.*

'Now. Straight. Look at the hoop. Focus your mind on it. That ball is going through that hoop. Yes?'

'Yes,' said Diamond faintly, hardly knowing what she was saying yes to.

'Now swing.'

His hands were still over hers. His whole body was moulded to her back. Something seemed to stir in her way down deep, something treacherous, something that she refused to even *think* of as an unexpected and unwanted shiver of desire. She swung the mallet. The ball travelled in a straight line and shot right through the hoop. Some people in the orangerie who were watching clapped and cheered. She saw Richard look up, look out. Saw him frown. And his mother, too.

'People are staring,' she said sharply. 'Let go.'

Toro released her and she turned around, almost stumbling. He was grinning.

'See? You can do it,' he said.

'I could have done it perfectly well without you pawing over me,' she said.

'No, you couldn't. How are you, Diamond?' Infuriatingly, he grinned. 'How are you dealing with Lady Margaret?'

Badly. 'Fine,' she said.

'Liar.' His eyes narrowed as he stared at her face. 'Still, if anyone can get past that cow it's going to be you. Don't you think he's a bit soft for you? A bit low-powered?'

'Richard,' said Diamond firmly, 'is kind and gentle. And sensitive.'

'As I said – soft. He's the sort of man who should never have had to go through a war. I wonder if he'll ever really get over it.'

Diamond thought of Richard's nightmares.

'So you're not interested in what's going on back in town then, while you're here swanning around among the aristocracy?' he asked.

'What *is* going on?'

'Things are ramping up. There's going to be a bloodbath very soon between your friend Michael McLean and the Victory Boys. Everyone can see it coming.'

Diamond frowned at that.

'Anyway – good luck,' he said, and turned and walked away.

Only then did Diamond realise that she was shaking.

126

She was hurrying back indoors, wanting only to be alone and out of the way of all these *people.* She was halfway across the entrance hall, passing the inlaid table with its thick visitor's book, walking beneath the fabulous glass cupola that beamed brilliant light down, when she was halted by a stern female voice.

'Diamond.'

She turned. There was Lady Margaret, standing at the door of the library. A maid was hovering beside the front door. Margaret gave her a chilling look and the girl scampered away. Then Lady Margaret pushed the library door open further, indicating that Diamond should enter.

Groaning inwardly, Diamond changed direction and went into the library. Margaret closed the door behind them.

'I wanted a brief word,' she said, walking over to a chair and sitting down.

'Oh? What about?'

'About my son. I have heard that he's proposed marriage to you.'

'Yes. He has.'

'Then I must urge you to do both yourself and him a favour, and refuse.'

Diamond stood there. They locked eyes.

'Why should I do that?' she asked.

'Because you're not right for him,' said Margaret.

'Shouldn't he be the judge of that?'

'No, I am the judge in this instance. I have heard how you met my son. You were in some seedy nightspot in Soho. On the day the war was over, you enticed my son into bed with you . . .'

Diamond froze, horrified. *How the hell does she know that?* Richard wouldn't have told her.

'Then you had one of your associates rob him and beat him.' Lady Margaret's eyes sparkled with hatred. 'Please don't bother to deny it.'

Diamond didn't. She was too astonished – and ashamed.

'So!' Lady Margaret went on. 'Is it money you want? I can pay you. We agree a sum, and you disappear from Richard's life before you wreck it.'

Diamond felt sick to her stomach, knowing that his mother was aware of her background. She couldn't say *it wasn't my fault.* She couldn't bring herself to defend her actions on that day, the very idea made her flinch like an oyster squirted with lemon juice.

'And what then?' she asked. 'You pair him off with Catherine, I suppose.'

'Catherine will be the perfect wife for him. She's patient. She's sweet-natured. And she's from his own class. She understands what is required of her. They have always been close. Her family live just over there,' she indicated the window, where gentle green hills rolled away into the purple distance. 'It's always been understood between our two families that one day they would wed. Do you realise, the very same doctor delivered them within a week of each other. I don't believe in things being "written in the stars" but I think in the case of Richard and Catherine, it probably was.'

'Richard and I are in love,' said Diamond. The words sounded hollow, even to her.

Lady Margaret half smiled and shrugged. 'Oh come now. A few passionate interludes don't add up to a love affair. You may be attracted to each other, I don't doubt that. But love? Love is something that grows, something that endures. Richard is a sensitive soul, you know. He was shattered by the war. He felt guilty because he survived when so many did not. He's lost his way and strayed into the path of you. He's fastened on you like a drowning man onto a life raft. If you had the slightest real care for him, you would step away and let him float back to shore, and sanity.'

Diamond absorbed this. 'He has nightmares. About the trenches. Did you know?'

'He's my son. Of course I know.'

'Would Catherine be able to cope with that?'

'Yes. She would.'

'How can you be so sure?'

'Because she loves him, deeply and truly. Because she always has.'

'You offered me money,' said Diamond.

'Yes. I did. How much do you want?'

Diamond's smile was icy. 'I can't be bought, Lady Margaret.'

Richard's mother got to her feet. She stepped up close to Diamond and glared into her eyes.

'What an audacious little mongrel you are,' she said coldly.

'Yes. I think you will find that's what Richard likes about me.'

'He'll come to hate you,' Margaret warned. 'I imagine it's exciting to occasionally trawl the gutter, but it will soon pall.'

'Perhaps I'll risk that.'

'You'd be wise not to.'

'As they say – don't they? – love is blind.'

'I won't offer again,' said Lady Margaret.

'Good. I am pleased to hear it. I've no wish to be insulted any more.'

'I would have thought you'd be used to it, a common little thing like you.'

Diamond smiled. Inside, her guts were churning. Outwardly, she was cool, composed.

'If that's all . . .?' she said.

'Yes. I think we've both said enough.'

127

When Diamond got back out into the entrance hall, Richard was just coming in from the orangerie. He looked anxious.

'Darling, are you all right? I came to find you.'

'I'm fine.'

He pulled her in close, kissed her cheek. Then his mother appeared in the doorway of the library. She went inside, closing the door on them.

'Has she been talking to you?' Richard looked grim.

'We talked.'

'And? I hope she hasn't upset you.'

'Richard – your mother hates me. I already knew that. Quite a few of your friends do, too.'

'I don't care about that,' he said.

But I do.

If they married, what kind of life would it be? Catherine would continue to hover ever-present in the background, a constant reminder of her close relationship with Richard and of Diamond's own shortcomings. Lady Margaret would be there too, and she would go on placing her acid barbs. Under so much pressure, would a marriage last? And why would she go ahead and accept him? To spite his mother, to prove her wrong? What was the point of *that*?

'Darling – I asked you to marry me. I meant it.'

'I know you did.'

'But you still haven't answered.'

'I know that too.' If he'd impregnated her again, it might have taken the decision out of her hands; but he hadn't. She didn't know whether to be sad or relieved about that.

'You need more time? I can give you that. How about until next weekend, we're all going to Brooklands. It's a big pre-Christmas occasion. Teddy and I have entered for the big race of the day. It's going to be such fun. I want you to come too.'

'All right,' said Diamond.

128

One of the Victory Boys brought the women in the cellar bread and water every day.

'Don't want to ruin the goods, do we?' Gwendoline heard Victor laughing on the top step one day.

The goods.

They were floating in their own filth down here. They had blankets, but they were frozen with the cold all the time, forced to huddle together for warmth. There was nowhere to sleep except for the hard concrete floor.

'Ship this lot out soon,' said Victor to his crew. 'Getting rank in here.'

Sometimes, faintly, Gwen heard movement upstairs. She heard the pealing laugh of Lily Wong, and Victor's deeper bass tones. She ate bread and drank water and wondered what was going to become of her. Her head itched, she thought she had fleas. At night, rats scurried around their feet, picking up crumbs.

Were they going to be taken abroad?

For what?

She didn't know. This was hell, but what worse fate could await her and all these other poor souls somewhere else? Some of the women were young and cried a lot. The older ones sat there dully, beyond desperation. Gwen spoke to a couple of them but was careful after one of the tougher ones tried to steal her blanket. She had to fight her off.

'They're going to sell us, I reckon,' one of the women told her.

'No! Don't be daft,' said Gwen.

But the woman's words rang true. Hadn't Victor always been saying about his valuable 'merchandise'? And this was it: these women, right here. Her included. Sooner or later they were going to be loaded up and shipped out.

129

'There's a problem,' said Lockhart to Golon one day in his office.

Golon sat down. 'Go on.'

'The people upstairs are telling me I must suspend enquiries into this woman for now.'

Golon eyed Lockhart with disbelief. '*What?* But we're close. You know that we . . .'

Lockhart held up a hand. Golon stopped speaking.

'My friend, listen. Above a certain level, it's not wise to chase these things down.'

'But we've done the groundwork. We know . . .'

'Whatever we know don't matter.'

'But *why*?'

'Why? Because she's taken up with the aristocracy and you don't mess with the likes of them. My bosses don't want the hassle of tackling a ruddy big fish like the Earl of Stockhaven. Don't worry yourself. It won't last forever. The nobs like their bit of rough but they rarely keep them around for long. When she's back in town, never fear, we'll nab her. Meanwhile, although we know damned well where she is and what she's doing – and who she's doing it with – our hands are tied.'

'*Merde*,' said Golon.

'Exactly,' said Lockhart.

'I'll phone Benoit. Let him know.'

'Yes. Do that.'

130

'They say Percy Lambert hit over one hundred and three miles per hour in nineteen thirteen. He'd promised his fiancée he would give up racing, but he crashed that day and died on the track. They say his ghost still walks about in full racing gear,' Catherine said, close by her ear. She was having to shout over the roar of the cars, to make herself heard.

'God, don't tell me things like that,' said Diamond. She really couldn't see the attraction of racing cars, but if Richard enjoyed it, what the hell.

'Don't fret. Safety's much improved now,' Catherine smiled.

The cars were all lined up at the start and it was raining lightly. From their vantage point in the stands, she could see the cars under the Shell banner at the start. Richard was in number nineteen, a sleek red Bugatti. Teddy was in the dark green number three. The drivers were revving their engines and people were dashing everywhere. She could see Richard clearly in his protective hat and goggles. She waved. He didn't wave back, he was busy, ready for the start. And then suddenly there was a loud burst of noise from the tannoy.

'And they're OFF,' boomed the voice.

The noise was deafening as the cars started to inch and then roar forward, everyone jostling for space on the grid. Suddenly they were all accelerating. Choking clouds of exhaust rose from the track. Diamond had decided that today she would give Richard her answer. Like Lambert's fiancée, she hoped that if her answer was yes, he would stop with all this racing business and concentrate instead on his duties on the estate.

If her answer was yes.

The truth was, she still had not decided yes or no. And she knew what that meant. She knew that despite her feelings for him, she was deeply unsure about matrimony. And being unsure, she'd be a fool to proceed.

'Oh Christ!'

The sound of an impact and the voice of a man nearby snapped her back to attention. Three of the cars had spun off near the stands, piling into each other like dominos as the serious business of getting to the front of the pack went on. Then the leaders were away again. Catherine was watching through binoculars as they roared off around the track. Richard had nudged up around the pile-up and was surging on until he made second, and Teddy was back in third. They shot off while, down below, the drivers started to emerge, mercifully unhurt, from the three mangled vehicles.

'*Clear the track, clear the track!*' screamed the tannoy.

Flatbed trucks fitted with cranes roared in and the debris was quickly removed. The drivers meandered to the side of the track. One threw his hat down in angry frustration. Another walked off and disappeared into the crowds.

There was barely time to clear the obstacles, but somehow it was done before the rest of the cars came zooming around the far bend and shot past the spectators full-pelt. A gagging smell of petrol rose to the stands. The rain was starting to come down more heavily, making the track glisten. Richard was nudging alongside the leading car, now fighting for first place. Teddy was close by, back in third.

I can't do it, thought Diamond.

She *couldn't* say yes to Richard. He would be devastated, but really she would be doing him a favour. Lady Margaret was right. She didn't love him *enough.* Not nearly enough to live the way he was used to, which for her would be like being trapped inside a gilded cage. Oh, she could say yes, just to prove everyone wrong. But they weren't wrong. She knew it, deep in her bones. *She* was.

So – the decision was made. Today, she would turn him down.

Having decided, she felt a little easier. Round and round the track the cars went but she paid them no attention now. Already she was thinking of getting back to London, seeing Owen, taking up the reins of her life, her *real* life, once again.

When the noise came, hellishly loud, she jumped so violently that she bumped against Catherine, nearly knocking her over.

'What the hell . . .?' Diamond said aloud, her heart in her mouth.

Something was happening far over on the other side of the track.

'Oh God, has there been another crash?' Diamond asked.

The race had stopped. None of the cars were moving. Catherine lowered the binoculars.

'It's too hard. The rain. I can't see . . .' she said.

Anxiety rustled through the crowds of spectators like bushfire through trees. There was quiet now – a long, ominous quiet. Then sirens started up. There was a fire engine racing around the track.

One of the men from down near the start was coming up into the stands.

He came up to Diamond and Catherine, whipping his cap off.

'Miss Dupree?'

Catherine took her hand. Diamond would never forget that. In this moment of extremity, Catherine tried to comfort her, *her*, who had caused her such misery.

'Yes?' Her voice was steady, but her body shook with nerves.

'There's been an accident,' the man said. 'You ought to come.'

'What? Is Richard all right? What happened?' She was babbling, but the man wasn't answering.

Diamond barely knew what happened next. Her mind seemed to have left her body. She was following the man and getting in one of the trucks. Catherine was there too, her face bleached of all colour.

Diamond wanted to ask the man if Richard was injured, but she couldn't form the words. The truck roared along, Diamond and Catherine were clinging to their seats, and soon – too soon – they were there. Teddy was standing out on the track and Diamond was alarmed to see that he'd taken off his helmet and goggles and was wiping at his eyes. Diamond walked over to him, Catherine following.

'He spun off on the bend. Smacked straight into the hoarding. It's . . .'

Teddy's voice trailed away. Diamond thought: *He's a doctor.* If Teddy was doing nothing for Richard, then there must be nothing that could be done. Teddy reached out a hand to her, squeezed her wrist.

'They've made it safe.'

'What . . .?' Her mouth was too dry. She couldn't speak. She swallowed, tried to compose herself, but she could feel hysteria building. 'Is he all right? They can get him out? Can't they?'

Teddy grabbed her arm. Stared into her eyes. 'Diamond! They can't get him out. Listen to me!' Teddy swiped again at his wet eyes. 'The steering wheel's crushed his chest. There's nothing we can do. Nothing at all.'

Diamond wanted to run away. She didn't want to see this. But she had to be brave now. This wasn't for *her*. This was for Richard.

She let Teddy lead her over to the mangled vehicle. Steam was coming off the back end of it, and she could smell smoke and the tang of hot metal. The front end of the car was gone, nothing left but twisted wreckage. Two men were standing grimly by with extinguishers at the ready should the fire restart. Richard was sitting in the driver's seat, his head thrown back. They'd taken off his helmet and goggles. He looked dazed and pale, his face wet with rain and sweat and smuts from what had clearly been a small fire. The steering wheel was bent out of shape and pressed hard up against his chest. There was a bloody mass there. Diamond averted her eyes from that, tried not to smell the blood or the fumes. She looked into Richard's beautiful blue eyes.

The rain was coming down harder now. Diamond ignored it. She stepped closer to the car. She couldn't even hold his hand, his arms were pinned, his legs too. He was broken. Dying. This was too awful. Another death, she couldn't bear it. She'd lost her dad, her mother, her baby, Aiden, and now *this*. How much more tragedy could she take? She felt her composure fraying, her grip on herself loosening. But she tried not to let her shock and anguish show on her face. She tried to smile. She barely knew if she succeeded; her features felt frozen.

Richard was trying to smile too. And wincing.

'You . . . haven't given me your answer yet,' he whispered. He blinked, swallowed. Winced again. A trickle of blood squirmed out of the side of his mouth.

'No, I haven't.' Diamond could hardly recognise her own voice. It sounded thin, strangled. 'Bad of me.'

'So . . .?' he rasped.

Back in the stands, she had decided the answer was no. But now she knew what she had to say. 'Yes, Richard. Of course I'll marry you.'

He closed his eyes. For a panicky moment she thought he'd gone. Then she *hoped* he had, to spare him another second of this. A deep shudder went through him. His eyes closed, then they flickered open again.

'Is Catherine here?' he asked faintly.

And there it was: the stark truth of it. He needed *Catherine* now – not her.

'Yes, my darling, she's here,' said Diamond.

She could do this one last thing for him. She could give him the woman he should have married, the one who was his dear childhood friend, the one who knew him the best, who understood him – and loved him better than she ever could.

She turned and beckoned to Catherine.

Red-eyed, weeping, Catherine approached.

'Stay with him,' Diamond said to her, and stepped away.

Catherine approached the mangled remains of the man she adored and forced a smile onto her face.

Moments later, Richard died.

It was Catherine who closed his eyes.

131

Diamond had no intention of staying for Richard's funeral. Coming back, dazed, almost stupefied, from the racetrack to Fontleigh, she went straight to her room while Teddy and Catherine went to break the news to his mother.

Once in her room, she closed the door and stripped off all her clothes in a madness of grief, hating the oily stink of them. And could she still smell Richard's blood? She was sure she could. She washed herself thoroughly, crying all the while, and dried herself, and applied talcum powder, and slipped into her peignoir, brushed out her hair, looked at the crazy-eyed woman in the mirror and thought *oh God, he's dead.*

And she had lied to him as he lay there dying. A howl of anguish escaped her and she clamped her hand over her mouth to stifle it. She went to the wardrobe and yanked out her case, throwing it onto the bed. She had to get away, out of here. Margaret wouldn't want to set eyes on her, nobody here would. Richard's dreams of marriage to her had been ludicrous, really. Everyone had seen that except him. For a while, she had got caught up in the fantasy too. But now, nothing was left. And she had to leave, quickly, to spare anyone the inconvenience and embarrassment of her presence. She stuffed the soiled clothes she had worn to the racetrack in the case, and piled her other dresses on top, not caring if she creased anything, ripped anything, what did it matter?

Then she stopped moving and the tears came again.

Oh God.

Poor Richard. So much to live for. He'd come all through that bloody war, survived it when so many others had not, and now his life had been snatched from him anyway.

What the hell was the *point* of it all?

There was a knock at the door. She wiped at her eyes and stiffened in alarm. *I can't speak to anyone.*

But whoever it was, they weren't going away. They knocked again.

Wiping furiously at her cheeks, Diamond went to the door. It was Catherine, standing there pale as a ghost. There was a smear of blood on the bodice of her dress.

'May I . . .?' she said, and stepped inside, closing the door behind her. Diamond saw Catherine's gaze take in the open suitcase, the garments thrown hastily inside.

'Oh – but you're not leaving, are you? Not yet . . .'

'Catherine . . .' Diamond didn't know what to say to her. She *had* to go. Then, to her shock, Catherine moved forward and enfolded her in a hug.

'It's awful,' said Catherine against her neck. 'I'm so sorry. It's too cruel, to have him snatched away like this. You poor thing. I know it's awkward here with Richard's mother. You must stay with us at Langstone until the funeral, I won't hear a word of argument about it.'

'How is she?' Diamond asked. Horrible though she thought Margaret was, still she felt wracked with pity for her. *She* had lost a child and now the Dowager Countess had too.

'She's shattered. Of course she is. But you know, she's very strong.'

'I was going to refuse him, you know,' said Diamond. 'I wasn't going to marry him. But when I knew he was . . . well, I just couldn't say it. Couldn't tell him.'

Catherine nodded.

'Right at the end,' Diamond went on, 'it was you he asked for, you he needed. Not me. If the crash hadn't happened, I would have told him to marry you. That you were the one for him, not me. Deep down I think he really knew that, anyway. I was just a diversion, freedom from all his troubles after the war. That was all. *You* were his true love.'

Catherine started to cry, great wrenching tears of unbearable loss. Diamond pulled her closer into her arms, held her shuddering body tight, smoothed her back, whispered soothing words to her. And as she did so, she realised that Catherine was not only Richard's friend; she was hers, too.

Still, she wanted to refuse Catherine's offer of accommodation. More than anything, she wanted to get back to London, to familiar things. The dream with Richard had become a nightmare and she just wanted to run. She had *intended* to anyway. But now – how could she refuse Catherine, who had been so generous, so sweet and considerate, when she had caused her nothing but pain?

Catherine was pulling away, her face blotched with tears. 'We'll be strong, yes?' she choked out. 'We can attend the funeral together. Poor Teddy's devastated. Diamond – I don't think I can do this on my own. Say you'll stay. Please.'

There was nothing for it.

'I'll stay,' said Diamond. 'Of course I will.'

132

Everyone turned out for the funeral, all the estate workers, all Richard's business and social contacts; no-one was spared. Diamond rode grimly in Teddy's Rolls Royce to the tiny Fontleigh village church where the service was held, all the while clutching on to Catherine's hand. She nearly turned and fled when she saw the packed church and at the head of it, standing still as stone, the Dowager Countess Lady Margaret, swathed in black, her face hidden beneath a thick veil.

When they brought in Richard's coffin, Diamond felt that she might collapse. Catherine, her face flooded with tears, clutched hard at her hand, lending her strength. The thing was beautiful and it was awful – gleaming dark mahogany with huge brass handles, draped in white lilies and bearing the Earl's coronet, carried by six strong young men, one of whom was – of course – Teddy.

It seemed to go on forever. The hymns. The eulogies. The blessings. And when finally it was over, Diamond found herself trailing after the others out of the church and into sunlight, which seemed obscene because Richard would never see the sun again.

People spoke to her, shook her hand. She neither heard nor saw them.

He's dead.

She would leave it a couple of days and then she would pack up and go, head back to London. She didn't belong here. Perhaps she never had. She was heading back to Teddy's Rolls. She hoped to God that Teddy wouldn't want to go to Fontleigh for the interment, but then she heard him say to someone else that yes, he was going there. She walked out among the crowds to the lych gate, feeling stifled, choked. There was a chill in the air, a faint suggestion of snow. People looked at her and they whispered.

That's the one. The painter's model, the tart that upset Margaret so much. And poor Catherine! That bitch, she ruined all their lives . . .

She looked back, but Catherine was still in the church porch, talking to the vicar, politely shaking his hand, exchanging a few words. Catherine was good at that. As Richard's wife, she would have excelled. It was bitter to acknowledge that, but Diamond did. Then she saw the tall figure of Margaret there. The thick veil hid her face, but Diamond knew she was staring at her, accusing her, *hating* her. She stepped out into the road and started walking. She had no idea where. She just walked.

'Hey! Wait.'

Fuck it.

It was Toro Wolfe, grabbing her arm, pulling her to a halt.

'Oh for God's *sake*!' she snapped angrily, wrenching herself free.

'Where are you going?'

'Anywhere. Nowhere. Away from here.' Diamond started walking again. Thick white flakes of snow were beginning to fall.

'Look.' He hauled her to a stop again. 'Let me drive you back over to Langstone Hall to collect your belongings.'

'And then what?'

'I'm going back to London, I can give you a lift if you want to get out of here . . .?'

God, she did. She really did.

'I shouldn't bloody be here,' said Diamond. 'I only stayed because Catherine asked me to. But I shouldn't have. I don't belong here.'

To her escalating rage, he smiled sourly at that.

'Well that's good. I thought you were clinging on, still trying to live the dream. Maybe even trying for Teddy now that Richard's out of it. The earldom's gone of course. That passes to one of Richard's distant cousins, that fat one standing over there, the lucky chap.'

'*What?*' What the fuck was he saying?

'You heard.'

'You utter *shit.*'

'Teddy wouldn't take much persuading. I've seen the way he looks at you, all doe-eyed. He doesn't have Lady Margaret for a mother. And his sweet sister Catherine won't cause you any bother. She likes you, the poor fool.'

Diamond's hand connected with Toro's face so hard that he rocked back on his heels. Actually *staggered.* Slowly he raised a hand to his cheek, and he smiled.

'Truth hurts, Diamond?' he said.

'That's not the truth.' Her teeth were gritted with fury.

'Yes, it is. And here's another truth. Richard was a wreck. Also, he was still in love with Catherine Sibley. You were a new fascination, nothing more than that. He should have made you his mistress instead of upsetting the whole bloody applecart by thinking about marrying you.'

Diamond stared at him. He was only telling her what she already knew, but it stung, just the same. The *bastard.* 'You finished?' she snapped.

'Yeah. I think I have.'

'Where's your bloody car?'

'Over there.'

'Then get in it. And fuck off, all right? *Just. Fuck. Off.* I'll get the train back, when I'm ready.'

Diamond turned and walked away, back to the church.

133

Returning to London after Langstone Hall, Diamond found the streets rammed with horse-drawn carriages, cars and trams. The rain was battering down upon the blackened pavements, soaking the pedestrians who hustled along, intent on getting into the dry. Thunder rolled in the distance as she stepped down from her cab. She paid the driver and walked up to the front door of the little terrace house and lifted the knocker.

She waited.

Presently Moira flung open the door, her hands covered in flour, her pinafore dusted with it. She stared at Diamond.

'Is it true then? What we heard?' she said. 'It was in all the papers, but I said to Michael it couldn't be right, it must be some *other* Richard Beaumont. He was so *young* . . .'

Diamond could only nod.

Moira crossed herself. 'God's sake! Come in, come in.'

***

Being taken into Moira's was like being enfolded in a warm embrace. She sat Diamond by the fire, gave her tea laced with brandy, hand-fed her tiny bits of the cake she'd just taken out of the oven. She took off Diamond's sodden shoes, and her damp stockings, and rubbed her icy feet dry. Then she sat down in the chair opposite and said: 'Tell me then.'

'I can't,' said Diamond, choked. The truth was – she hated the very thought, but it was true – Richard's death had bailed her out. Allowed her to escape. But escape to *what*?

Owen came in and put his arm around her, cuddled her. 'Sad?' he said, not understanding.

'Sad, yes,' said Diamond. 'Very, very sad.'

***

The next day dawned bright but very cold. Diamond stopped at the florist's and then went over to St Anne's churchyard to lay the flowers she'd bought on Dad's, Mum's and Aiden's graves. To her shock, she found her parents' headstones smashed to pieces, and Aiden's wooden cross broken in two.

Victor.

She walked back on the crowded pavements, hardly seeing or hearing anything that was happening around her, so deep was her rage. While she'd been gone, he'd done *that.*

The bastard.

When she got back to Moira's, she was still fizzing with anger, incandescent with it. 'Where's Michael?'

Owen was at the kitchen table, his favourite place, colouring in his magazines as usual.

'I'm here,' said Michael, coming in from the scullery.

'The gravestones have been smashed. And Aiden's cross, it's broken.'

'I told you. That's what he's like. He drinks and plays in the snow . . .'

'What does that mean?' asked Moira.

'Cocaine,' said Michael. 'Mum, you're such an innocent. He sniffs that stuff, then he's half off his head, and he was never too clued up to start with. Some say he's never been right, not since Diamond clocked him with that flat iron. He certainly don't look like no oil painting, the ugly bastard. He's bloody dangerous.'

'Look, I don't think . . .' chipped in Moira.

'He's got to be dealt with,' said Michael.

Diamond frowned, remembering what Toro Wolfe had told her about a bloodbath coming on the streets. Moira looked uncertain.

'What about his wife? The Wolfe girl, Gwendoline? Is she still with him?' asked Diamond.

'Nobody's seen her about for weeks. I'm guessing she's fucked off somewhere out of it. Wouldn't you? She thought she was getting a strong older man who could handle trouble, but it turned out he *was* trouble. I bet he beats the poor cow black and blue.'

'So what are you going to do?' she asked.

He looked at her. 'What do you think I should do?'

Diamond thought of her ruined girlhood. Her abused mother. Her bullied brothers. The misery that Victor had inflicted on them all.

'Finish him,' she said.

Michael's eyes held hers. Then, slowly, he nodded.

'I'll get the word out. Old Compton Street, eight o'clock. Get all the boys together, armed and ready. It's past time something was done.'

134

Twenty-three Silver Blades assembled in Old Compton Street that night. Sleet swept over them, nearly horizontal, relentless, as they stood there and awaited Victor's mob. Then the wind dropped, the sleet thinned and it turned to rain. Soon, thunder rolled and lightning flashed. The clock struck eight and no Victor.

The boys waited. Five past. *Ten* past. Then out of the gloom at the end of the street there appeared first one man and then another, each one bowler-hatted and in his best neatly pressed three-piece suit, watch chains hanging, shoes gleaming, more and more of them until there were thirty. Then more. And more still. Wariness coursed through the Blades. Finally, through a mob of over forty men, stepped Victor Butcher, dressed as neatly as all the rest but ugly as sin with two deep matching triangular scars on each side of his broad brow. He held a revolver almost casually in his hand.

He tipped his hat to Michael, standing at the front of the Blades.

'So why the meeting?' he bawled down the street as the two gangs confronted each other, not twenty yards apart.

'To tell you in plain English that it's over, Victor.'

Victor sniffed hard then swiped at his nose with one shovel-like hand. It came away bloody. 'What you call me?

Listen, you call me *Mr* Butcher, pipsqueak. Now run along home before you get hurt, the lot of you.'

There was a dead silence.

'Final warning,' said Victor.

Silence again. Then people pushed through behind Victor, wheeling something along with them. Two of the men yanked off a tarpaulin.

It was a Gatling gun.

A ripple of unease went through the Blades.

Then the shooting started and there was pandemonium as bodies fell onto cobbles drenched with blood.

***

Half an hour after the gangs met, there was knocking at Moira's door. Owen was in bed asleep but she and Diamond were sitting at the kitchen table, tense, waiting for Michael to come back with tales of how Victor had – finally – been overcome. Moira opened the door and nearly fainted with horror. Four of the Blades were standing there, bloodstained and limping. They were carrying Michael stretched out and bleeding on a door they'd picked up from a building site. They hustled him inside.

'We couldn't take him down the hospital, there'd be too many questions asked,' said Nev, one of Michael's closest lieutenants.

'In the kitchen. Hurry,' said Moira.

Diamond watched, horrified, as they lay the door on the table. There was a ragged chunk out of Michael's left ear. His belly was slashed, his white shirt stained crimson.

'We were outnumbered two to one,' said Nev, whose nose and mouth were bleeding. He paused and spat a tooth out, onto Moira's clean rag rug. 'They had this great bloody revolving thing, a Gatling. We couldn't stop 'em. It was a massacre. In the end we just had to turn tail and run like a bunch of fucking cowards.'

Diamond was about to go into the scullery, boil up water, look for clean rags. She felt gutted for Michael's pain and furious that once again Victor had come out on top. But Moira stopped her with a hand on her arm.

'This is your doing. *You* caused this, urging him on when you shouldn't have. He'd always jump through hoops for you, and now look where he's ended up. I said not to do this, and I was right.'

'Moira, I'm sorry, I thought . . .'

'You *didn't* bloody think, did you?' Moira burst out. 'You come back here and you cause nothing but bloody trouble! Get out of my sight, I can't bear to look at you.'

'Let me help . . .'

'No! You've done enough. Get out of it before I chuck you through that wall.'

135

Benoit didn't like sea travel. He tottered off the steamer in Southampton, steadying himself with his cane as he once again stood on dry land, feeling his guts still heaving after the trip. Golon was there, and his old friend Lockhart, who greeted him and hustled him into a waiting cab en route to the train station.

'So! Tell me where we are up to,' said Benoit.

'As I told you over the phone, there have been significant developments,' said Lockhart.

'Yes. Quite so. A tragedy,' Benoit nodded.

'But the death of the Earl puts a different complexion on things,' said Golon.

'So long as we keep his name out of it as much as is possible . . .' shrugged Benoit.

'Yes. Exactly that,' said Lockhart. 'We must proceed with extreme caution. Keep the mud-slinging to a bare minimum.'

'And your superiors agree?' asked Benoit.

'They do, or else I would never have coaxed you over the Channel. I know how much you hate boats.'

'It was worth the discomfort,' sighed Benoit. 'So now, to London.'

'Yes, my friend. And then . . .'

'Then we can go ahead and charge her for the murder of Arnaud Roussel,' said Golon.

136

When Diamond came downstairs next morning after a long sleepless night, she found Michael asleep on the sofa in the parlour, his wounds dressed, Moira dozing in a chair at his side. She crept past them to the kitchen, put on the kettle to boil. Then she sat down at the table and wondered what next. Before very long the kettle was whistling and Diamond made the tea and put it on the table. Moira came out of the parlour and the two women looked at each other.

'I'll go,' said Diamond, 'if you want me to. You're right. This was my fault. I didn't understand what they'd be up against and I shouldn't have encouraged Michael like I did. I saw the graves desecrated and I just . . . Moira, I'm sorry.'

Moira, yawning and turning her neck from side to side gingerly, slumped down in a chair.

'He's all right,' she said. 'That's the main thing.'

'You want me to go?'

Moira heaved a sigh. 'No. Of course not. I was speaking in anger. The state of him! I was frightened half to death. But it was better than it looked. I stitched him up and cleaned the wounds, and he's sleeping now. He'll be all right.'

'They were outnumbered.'

'Two to one, he said.'

'Diamond?' It was Michael, calling her from the parlour. His voice was faint, but clear.

'God alive, *rest*, will you?' snapped Moira back at him.

They went through and stared down at him.

'What is it?' asked Diamond.

'We tried. We really did. But we had to retreat. Couldn't do anything else.'

'Don't worry. Just get better, that's all you have to do,' Diamond told him.

'A couple of inches deeper and that belly wound would have gutted you like a cod,' said Moira furiously.

Michael tried to smile. 'Sorry, Ma.'

'Never do that again to me, frighten me that way, you little arsehole.'

'Can't guarantee it.'

'You better bloody had, or I'll kill you myself, with my own bare hands. Can you eat?'

'Yeah. I think so. A bit.'

Moira went off into the kitchen to prepare food. Diamond remained there, looking down at Michael.

'We need more men,' said Michael in hushed tones, so Moira couldn't hear. 'We can't do it otherwise. I didn't realise he'd grown that strong. All our coppers have switched sides, he's paid them more. They just looked the other bloody way.'

'Shut up, Michael. Now's not the time. Moira's right. You rest up, get back to normal, that's all you have to do.'

'It was fucking humiliating.'

'He who fights and runs away, lives to fight another day. There *will* be another day. Just not yet. When that day comes, you'll be ready and Victor Butcher will get his just deserts. All right?'

'*No.* It's not all right. Not all right *at all.*' Michael stared up at her fiercely as he spoke. 'You know who we need for this. Get him, Diamond. Toro Wolfe will help the Silver Blades because he hates Victor as much as we do. We can carve up the streets between us. And there's the matter of his sister . . .'

'He doesn't care about her.'

'Doesn't he?'

'I won't ask him,' said Diamond.

'Then Victor's going to wipe us out. And all that's been done to you, to Aiden and Owen and all the rest of it, he gets away with it. Your *mother*, Diamond. Mum told me what he did to her. And *you*. You were a child. Taught to whore and steal, am I right?'

'Michael – you can't trust the Wolfes. You must know that. They burned down my dad's club. And more. They're *scum*. So no. I won't ask him.'

'You owe it to Aiden's memory.'

'Don't give me that!'

'I have to. To make you listen. We met up, Aiden and me. He was going to join up with the Blades.'

Diamond stared at him. 'I didn't know that.'

'No. You didn't. Victor must have got wind of it because a few days later, Aiden was dead. So for Christ's sake *get* him, Diamond. This has gone on long enough. Offer Wolfe a slice of Soho, a slice of *anything*, but get him onside.' Michael slumped back, but his eyes were full of fire as they stared into hers. 'Listen, Diamond. You take over now.'

'*What?* Michael . . .'

'You were queen of the Forty Thieves, weren't you? The boss of the hoisters. Well for now you can be boss of the Silver Blades, and do what has to be done. I've told the boys. It's up to you, now.'

'Michael, I can't . . .'

'Do it,' he said, closing his eyes tiredly. 'For Christ's sake! Get Wolfe. Take charge. Just fucking *do* it.'

137

Of course, he wouldn't be home. He wouldn't even be in *England*, probably. He was a traveller these days, living the high life, flitting around France, Africa, Australia, wherever the fancy took him, wherever new and exciting businesses would be found. Diamond delayed all day but in the early evening she gave in and went over to the Wolfe house, thinking back to the time she had come here to be a bridesmaid and Toro Wolfe had called her a jewel thief. She felt like she'd aged a hundred years since then.

After a couple of taps at the knocker, she turned around, thinking *that's that then.*

She was halfway out the gate when the door opened.

Diamond stopped dead in her tracks.

'What the hell do you want?' he said.

Diamond turned back. Toro Wolfe stood there, staring at her.

'To talk,' she said.

He stared a moment longer. Then he stepped back, holding the door wide. Against her better judgement, feeling shaky and unsure all of a sudden, Diamond walked back up the path, and went inside.

***

'I wouldn't be here at all, but Michael wasn't in a fit state to come himself,' she said when they were in the parlour.

'I know about that,' he said. 'Had a run-in with Victor's boys and came off worst, I heard.' He struck a match on the grate and lit a cigar, peering at her through the smoke as he exhaled.

'You heard right.' Diamond swallowed.

She felt nervous, being here, closeted with him in this stiflingly small, warm room. The Wolfes were bad, they were animals, they would hurt you if they could. Hadn't Frenchie always said so? Some things you never, ever forgot. She remembered when she'd been just fifteen, seeing Toro pass by in the street with his father Gustav; there'd been something very frightening about him then, that hard physicality he had, that bullish confidence. She also remembered her childish urge to be revenged on the Wolfe clan; something she had never yet been able to achieve.

'What about your sister?' she asked. 'I've heard she's not been seen recently. Is that right?'

'Gwen? As you well know, we're not properly related and God knows there was never any love lost between us. I've heard what you heard. Nothing more nor less. I haven't seen her.'

Diamond sat down. 'Look, Michael needs your help,' she said quickly, before the words could choke her.

'Then where is he?' asked Toro.

'I told you. He couldn't come. He's laid up. Injured. He asked me to come here or else, believe me, I wouldn't have bothered.'

'What sort of help would he be needing?'

'More men. You have men, or at least you always used to. We need them.'

'We?'

'Michael.'

'But you want Victor sorted too, am I right?'

'Of course I do. I hate the man.'

'Say I was to help out. What's in it for me?'

Michael had already thought of this: he'd primed Diamond just this morning.

'A half share of any of the clubs on the manor if we get Victor dispossessed. Full ownership of the Bricklayer's Arms, that's been with the Blades for years, but it's yours, signed over to you in its entirety, if you help out now.'

Toro paused, puffed out a plume of smoke.

'That's Michael, not you. What are *you* willing to give me, if I pull Michael's arse out of the fire?'

Diamond thought of the emerald-cut diamond earrings Richard have given her. And the furs, gifted to her by the sweet Marquis.

'I have jewels. Furs.'

'That,' said Toro, tossing the remains of his cigar into the fireplace, 'isn't what I mean. And you bloody well know it.'

'I know nothing of the sort,' said Diamond. The room felt hot, stifling.

'Yes, you do. And you know that it's been building up between us for some time, this thing. You felt it in Paris, and you damned sure felt it when I was teaching you to hold a croquet mallet at Fontleigh. So – Diamond Butcher – what are *you* going to give me, in return for this favour?'

Diamond stood up. Temper turned her cheeks pink. 'I'm not going to tell you again. You *don't* call me that. My name is Diamond Dupree.'

'All right then. But I want something as a down payment. A kiss, at least. To start with.'

Diamond stared at him. 'This was a stupid idea.'

'That's it. Run and hide.' His voice was mocking.

'It's perfectly clear that what you are suggesting is . . .' Diamond paused, groped for the right words . . . 'Is *disgusting.* And you think, you *kid* yourself, that I've no alternative? Well, I have alternatives. I have *plenty.* So *fuck* you, Toro Wolfe.'

'All right,' he shrugged, and turned away.

Damn it, damn it . . .

Diamond hurried across the room before she could change her mind, stepped around him, slid her arms around his neck and kissed him. She had intended a brief peck on the lips, but Toro's arms fastened around her like a steel clamp. She couldn't move to pull away, much as she tried. His mouth ravaged hers, his tongue sliding over her teeth, his lips caressing. Heat shot through her like a sheet of flame.

Finally, she got her hands against his chest and *yanked* her head back. 'Stop it,' she ordered.

'No,' said Toro, and kissed her again. She'd never felt anything like it. The touch of his lips on hers was consuming. She was sinking, drowning in sensuality. When he drew back – at last – she nearly fell.

'See? Not so bad,' he said, smiling.

Diamond twitched away from him. What the *hell* was she doing? This was Toro Wolfe. One of *them* – the enemy. What was she *thinking?*

'I'm going,' she snapped, bewildered, wrong-footed.

She tore along the hallway and out, slamming the front door behind her.

Fuming, she stood outside and hailed a cab. That *bastard.* But then she thought: *alternatives*? She didn't have a single one. But she would find a way to get Michael the help he needed without going cap in hand back to Toro Wolfe. She *must.* She swore to herself that she was never, ever going to cross the threshold of the Wolfe residence again.

When she got back to Moira's house, the front door was standing open. She came up the path and stared at it. No sign of Moira. Moira worked obsessively, doing her chores with a fervour that had always struck Diamond as fanatical. She'd be out white-leading the front step or sweeping the pathway at all hours. Then Diamond looked more closely.

Shit!

The lock was broken.

She hurried into the hall. 'Moira? Michael?' she called anxiously.

The table had been pulled over and was half blocking the hall. Moira's prized maidenhair fern was out of its pot on the floor, dirt spilled all over the tiles, its elaborately glazed pot smashed. Nervously Diamond stepped over the mess. She hurried into the kitchen and there was Moira, sprawled on the lino, her head in her hands. Diamond fell to her knees beside her.

'Moira! What's happened?' Diamond demanded. 'The door . . .'

'It was Victor's men,' said Moira, in tears.

'What did they do?' Diamond looked through to the parlour. No Michael. Owen's colouring books were spread out on the kitchen table and she felt a jolt of real alarm now. No Owen, either.

'Where's Owen? Where's Michael?' she asked Moira.

Moira was sobbing.

'Moira?' Diamond grabbed her shoulders and shook her. 'Moira, where are they?'

'I tried to stop them but they just laughed at me. There was nothing I could do. Victor took them,' said Moira brokenly. 'He took my boy. And Owen. He took them both!'

138

'Back so soon?' said Toro a half-hour later, when he opened his front door and found Diamond standing there. He crossed his arms and stared at her, leaning on the door frame, very relaxed.

'Victor's taken Michael. And my brother. Owen,' said Diamond, her voice shaking. 'I think he'll kill them.'

Toro stepped back, the smile slipping from his face. 'Come in,' he said, and Diamond hurried past him, her mind whirling with horrible scenarios.

She could picture it all. Owen and Michael, tied up, tortured. Cruelty came naturally to Victor, she knew that, she'd lived with it herself for long enough. He would relish it. Smacking Michael down for all to see, showing himself to be the big man, the boss. And Owen? He had always hated poor Owen, derided him for being a fool, not being kind as he deserved but deliberately setting out to frighten him. Owen would be truly terrified and lost. Diamond couldn't stand to think of it.

'We have to do something,' she said, pacing around. 'All right? Anything. I agree to anything you like. Only for the love of God *do* something.' She could hardly draw breath, she felt so panicked.

Only an hour since, she'd felt fully confident of finding a solution to all this. Now, she couldn't even get her scurrying thoughts to group into any sort of order at all, and her legs shook underneath her as she thought of what horrors Victor could be unleashing upon her friend and her poor little brother.

'Stay here,' said Toro, and he went out into the hall and pulled his coat on.

'What are you . . .?' asked Diamond, trailing after him, the words catching in her throat. 'No! I'm not waiting about here wondering what the hell's going on. I'm coming with you.'

139

That night, a group of Wolfe men and some from the Silver Blades went and checked out Victor's warehouse down by the Albert Docks. They torched it and all the goods Victor had stashed there. Another gang went to Victor's pub the Bombardier, emptied it of regulars and then blew it up with black powder. Yet another crew got to his snooker halls and burned them out. Others were in action too, following Toro's orders, and the police in Toro's pay joined in.

Finally, Toro and Diamond arrived at the Butcher family home. They had a mob of thirty men behind them, all armed. As they marched up to Victor's front door, the street was eerily silent. The locals didn't want to show their faces, not tonight. Everyone knew there was trouble abroad. A fine rain was falling, making the cobbles gleam under the lamplights. The sky was black as soot.

Toro walked up and pounded on the door.

The house was in darkness.

'Do you really think he's in there?' asked Diamond. 'He could have taken them anywhere, couldn't he? Anywhere at all.'

Having got no answer at the door, Toro stepped back and applied his boot to the lock. He struck it three times, and on the third impact it juddered open, showing the hall in darkness and the stairs beyond. The place, once so familiar, looked frightening now to Diamond. As Toro's torch flicked on, the bright beam of it lit the stairs. At the top, there was no painting of Frenchie. That was gone. Diamond thought of falling down those same stairs – being *pushed* down them – on the day of Mum's funeral. Her blood froze at the memory.

Where was Victor?

Her flesh seemed to crawl as they moved inside, Toro edging her back behind him. He had a pistol in one hand now, the torch in the other. He pushed open the door to the front room, swung the torch's beam inside. Nobody. They moved along, the others following behind them, some of the men flicking on more torches and going up the stairs to search. Toro opened the door into the kitchen. He moved into the scullery, Diamond trailing behind him, her heart thumping in her chest. Then out into the yard. Toro kicked open the door to the privy, looked out the back gate.

Nothing.

Then Diamond had a thought. 'What about the cellar?' she said.

140

Toro and Diamond moved back inside. Men were coming back down the stairs, shaking their heads. Nobody up there.

'We've been up in the loft, all over the place. Nothing,' said one of them.

Diamond followed Toro as he moved along the passageway and came to the cellar door. The house felt like it hadn't had a fire lit inside it for weeks: she could see the breath pluming out in front of her face like smoke. She reached out to the cellar door, anxious, wanting to get down there, to finish this torture. She thought of Owen. Of Michael, injured. Thought of Aiden, tumbling down the cellar steps to his death.

Toro pushed her sharply back.

'Don't fucking do that,' he hissed, and lifted the padlock on the cellar door. He stood back and shattered it with one single, deafening shot.

Instantly, as the door juddered open, they could feel cold air flooding out from below, could sense the drop in temperature that came with being below ground level. And there was something more. They could smell unwashed bodies, excrement. They could hear something scurrying about, too. Mice or rats, probably. Toro flicked on the light at the top of the stairs and there was a murmuring, a series of small shrieks. He stepped in and descended a few steps. Diamond moved in behind him, clutching at his shoulder.

'What . . .?' she started, staring along the torch's beam as it swept down over the cellar floor. There was movement and she flinched. God, what the hell . . .? She could see a large square brown shape propped against a wall. Her mother's painting. It *had* to be. Fucking Gwendoline must have consigned it to this dusty hole, hating to see Victor's last woman hanging above what she now considered to be 'her' staircase.

Victor wasn't down here. But . . .

'Christ Almighty,' breathed Toro.

The torches swept over women – they were huddling together, blankets wrapped around them. Pale dirty fear-filled faces were turned to look up at these intruders.

And there, in the midst of them all, her blonde hair matted, her cheeks gaunt from hunger, was Gwendoline, Toro's sister – and Victor Butcher's wife.

141

The police in Toro's pay brought a wagon and took the women to hospital so that they would be cared for. Gwendoline remained behind, blanket-wrapped in the parlour, sipping hot tea that Diamond had made. Gwendoline's eyes were anxious and always going to the back door, as if Victor might suddenly appear there and throw her back down into hell. Her two front teeth were missing and she kept holding a hand to her mouth, trying to cover up the gap.

'He put us in there. We've been in there for weeks,' she said, shivering, holding her thin hands out to the fire that Toro had lit in the grate.

Diamond stared at her aunt's face. Gwendoline was so changed that it didn't seem possible that this was the same arrogant creature she had once known.

'What happened?' she asked. 'With you and Victor . . .?'

What would a wife have to do, to merit such treatment? she wondered. Oh, she knew Gwendoline had been a bitch. Certainly she was no saint. But *this* . . .

'We argued. He kept taking this stuff. The white powder. And drinking. He'd come home and beat me. Then I found out about him keeping women down there, moving them around.' Gwendoline's eyes filled with tears. 'He's a white slaver! How could *any* woman stand for that? I objected, and . . . and he put me down there with them.' Now

Gwendoline was howling with rage and pain. 'He said he was sorry he'd ever set eyes on me and he'd get more out of me if he shipped me out of the country and sold me on. Like he was doing to all these others. But I was his *wife*! How could he do that?'

Toro was saying nothing. He was walking around the kitchen and his face was stony as he listened.

'Where would he be, right now? Do you know?' he said at last.

Gwendoline shrugged tiredly and mopped at her eyes. She looked like a frail, exhausted child. Diamond couldn't wrest her eyes from Gwendoline's bare feet. They were skeletal, and black with dirt.

'At the Bombardier?' she said, trying to compose herself. Her eyes rose to Toro. 'You were right. I should never have married him. He's a monster.'

Diamond could see that being proved right gave Toro no satisfaction at all. He shook his head. 'He's not at the Bombardier. We blew it to kingdom come.'

'Good.' Gwendoline's face twisted with bitterness. 'That's the least he deserves.'

'Where, then?' Toro persisted.

Gwendoline thought for long moments. Then her gaze sharpened and her poor battered mouth turned down in a grimace of distaste.

'He's got a whore he goes to. Lily Wong. They're in this dirty business together. She runs an opium den in Limehouse. In Chinatown.'

142

Chinatown had been set up at the turn of the century to service the needs of the many Chinese sailors who came in and out of the London docks. A huge number of Chinese who had made homes and set up businesses there – laundries and restaurants and stores stocked with herbal remedies and exotic fruits and vegetables – were making good money as a result.

Toro and Diamond, along with ten good Wolfe men, went to the place Gwendoline had told them about and Toro banged smartly on the red-painted door. Fierce-looking golden foo dogs guarded it, one on each side. Up above, a *bagua* mirror had been placed to deflect evil. Big red lanterns swung high over their heads.

A fat Chinese came to the door and unleashed a torrent of his mother tongue at them. Toro shoved him and he came back at Toro with a machete. Toro grabbed a big brass plate off a table and whacked the Chinese around the head once, twice. The machete fell from the man's hand and Toro's men piled in. They grabbed the doorman and started pounding him with fists and chair legs. Soon he was on the floor and they were kicking him. Leaving that behind them, Toro and Diamond went on, flicking aside curtains, opening doors into dimly lit rooms.

A youngish woman dressed in nothing but a transparent turquoise-blue robe, leaped from a bed and shouted at them furiously. Smoke billowed from an oil diffuser, tickling their noses with faint hints of scorched lavender and rosemary, but there was another odour, stronger. The room was soaked in the sweet scent of opium. Behind the woman, a filmy screen of fabric was billowing in a breeze.

Toro shoved past the woman and out through the curtain. There was a door leading out into a yard there, and he could see Victor's bulky form charging ahead, past a vast ornamental pond. Koi carp glided back and forth in the waters, nudging the lily pads. Victor was going for the gate. Toro ran after him, catching him just as he reached it, kicking him hard behind the knee to stop his escape.

'Get him!' yelled Diamond. He wouldn't get away, she swore it. All the misery he'd inflicted on her family burned in her brain. He *had* to pay for it.

But Victor turned, knife in hand, and slashed at Toro. Toro fell back, out of the way of the blade, and Victor was gone.

'No! We have to catch him,' she raged.

'We will,' said Toro. 'Come on.'

143

Diamond followed in Toro's footsteps, out through the gate Victor had gone through and onto the dockside. Toro was running fast ahead and it was hard to see. The river slapped up against the wharf but the blood thundering through her body was louder than the water. Here on this very wharf was where Gwendoline would have ended up, thrown aboard a ship with all those others, destined for hell. Cranes were ghostly black fingers poking up against a lighter sky. The stench of river weed filled her nostrils.

The huge bulk of a warehouse was on her left and she saw the dark outline of Toro turn and vanish inside it. She fell through a door and knocked straight into the back of him.

'Where is he?' she panted. 'Where'd he go?'

Toro shook his head in the gloom, raised a finger to his lips. He flicked on the torch and down the long cone of light she could see a vast empty space. Pigeons fluttered high above their heads, disturbed by their entrance. Water dripped monotonously down around them and everywhere there were rusty gleaming-wet stanchions set into a dingy concrete floor.

'Oh Christ,' she gasped out, her eyes fastening on a seated form.

It was a man. As they stood there, staring, his head turned and Diamond saw the man's face.

144

'Michael!' Diamond burst out.

It was him. His face was bloody and bruised, and he was sitting there tied to a chair. She started forward.

'Careful,' said Toro, catching her arm, and he aimed the torch's beam all around.

The beam caught a man, standing mere feet away from them. He was massive, scarred, grinning. Diamond felt the blood freeze in her veins and a shriek escaped her. It was Victor – and he was holding a gun, pointed straight at her.

'My little niece,' he said, swiping at his nose, sniffing. 'Back in the country, yes? The very same one who joined up with *this* little son of a bitch.' He indicated Michael, tethered there, with a tilt of his head. 'Took most of my hoisters away, didn't you, you little shit? Just have to keep trying my patience, don't you? Can't help yourself.'

Toro stepped forward, in front of Diamond. 'You don't want to do anything hasty, Victor,' he said.

'What, like shoot the fucking lot of you?' he laughed. 'Why not? You're all a pain in my backside and I think now's the time to set things straight.'

Diamond grabbed at Toro's arm in terror. 'Victor – don't,' she said desperately.

Michael was struggling against the ropes that bound him, but he couldn't get loose. He was too weak.

'Let's talk this over,' said Toro. 'You and me, Victor. We'll strike a deal. You name it, we'll do it.'

'Nah,' Victor shook his head. 'No deals. Not a single one. This has all gone on too long, I've been too *tolerant*, you see, and now the game's up. Time for a reckoning.'

Victor raised the gun.

145

Toro stood there, immobile. Diamond shut her eyes, knowing that this was it. They were all three of them going to die here, at Victor's hands.

The shot when it came was deafening in the echoing confines of the warehouse. There was a shout of pain. Above them, birds fluttered, disturbed.

But she was still standing. So was Toro. She was huddled in against him, holding onto him like a rock in a stormy sea. Had he shot Michael first, was Victor dragging this out, enjoying himself?

She opened her eyes. *Forced* herself to look.

A huge rush of air escaped her. Michael was still sitting there – alive.

But Victor?

His hand was empty. No gun. There was blood dripping from his fingers and his ugly face was contorted with agony. She could see the weapon down on the floor. Victor started to bend, to pick it back up.

'Stop there,' said a sharp, accented voice.

Out of the shadows, one Oriental man appeared. Then another, and another. Then more. They were all armed. One stepped in front of the rest, a small elegantly dressed man. He looked at Victor, at Michael, at Diamond and Toro. Then his eyes moved back to Victor.

'You have disappointed me, Mr Butcher,' he said flatly.

'Mr Wong . . .' started Victor.

The Chinese man held up his hand, stopping the flow of words.

'The shipment, Mr Butcher. You made a deal to supply merchandise, and you failed to do so.'

'That wasn't my fault,' said Victor, wincing, sweating, clutching at his damaged hand. 'Christ! My fingers . . .'

'You made a deal,' said Wong, a snap of cold steel in his voice. 'You let me down.'

'No, I . . .'

'You have made me lose face. My superiors are angry with me. Because of *your* failure.'

'Wait! I . . .'

Again, Mr Wong held up his hand. Victor stopped speaking. Wong looked at Michael, tied there. At Toro. At Diamond.

Oh Christ, she thought. These were Triad.

'You three? You can go,' said Mr Wong.

Toro moved, going to Michael, untying his bonds. She looked at Victor, surrounded by the Triad members, wounded – finished.

Toro helped Michael to his feet.

'Come on,' he said to her, and they moved away, out of the warehouse and onto the dockside, leaving her uncle there with the Triad gang.

146

When they were safely outside, Diamond said: 'Where's Owen, Michael?'

'Christ,' said Michael with a grimacing smile. 'I thought we were never getting out of there.'

'Owen, Michael?' Diamond persisted.

Then they all froze. Back in the warehouse, someone screamed – a long, hellish cry of agony.

Michael gave a grim smile. 'Didn't I say it, Diamond? About death by a thousand cuts.'

'We'd better keep going,' said Toro. 'In case they change their bloody mind.'

Another shriek. Frantic, hideous. Toro slung an arm under Michael's and heaved him along the dockside, Diamond following close by, shuddering, wishing she could stop up her ears.

Suddenly the noises ceased. They could hear a chain, clanking. Diamond grabbed Toro's torch and aimed it upward. There was a creaking high overhead, something being hoisted up to swing softly in the wind. A patter of raindrops hit the walkway.

No. Not raindrops. *Blood.*

There was something being suspended from a loading chain up there, something hanging out over the walkway.

It was Victor.

He was swaying to and fro, tied by the neck. Tatters of the blue shirt she'd last seen him wearing remained on his blood-red torso. But what hung there scarcely looked like a man at all – more like a butchered hunk of meat you'd find in an abattoir. She had to look away.

'Come on. Let's get out of here,' said Toro.

147

Moira was almost delirious with relief and pleasure when they got back to her place and she could see her son was alive. She greeted him with hugs and kisses, scolding him for making her so worried, hustled him into the parlour, fed him, gave him tea and brandy while Toro went back out in the street to talk to the men standing guard there and Diamond sat at the kitchen table and tried to take in the horrors of the evening. Fear for Owen crushed her.

'Where could Victor have taken him?' Diamond was wondering out loud, over and over.

She was clutching at her aching head, thinking of the Chinese, the docks. Michael had been a turf rival to Victor, and the women Victor had moved out like cattle, both had a value to him; Owen did not. The thought frightened her. Victor could have killed him on a whim, tipped him in the river and forgotten about him.

Moira came and sat down beside Diamond and took her hand. Diamond felt her eyes fill with tears. Her poor little brother. She looked down at Owen's scribbles, his crayons still laid out on the table, pieces of the *Tatler* magazine with society beauties smiling up from the page at her. She wondered if she would ever see him again. How could they ask Victor now where Owen was, how could they demand he deliver the poor thing back to her? Victor was dead.

'So you've made your peace with the Wolfe lot,' said Moira, nodding toward the front door.

'What?' Diamond's head was full of Owen. It took her a moment to snap back to the present, to what Moira was saying. 'No,' she said. 'Of course I haven't.'

'And Victor?' Moira asked. 'That bastard?'

'He's dead. It was horrible, Moira. The Triads finished him.'

Moira didn't seem overly concerned about that. 'Good bloody riddance,' she snorted. Then she paused and went on: 'That bloke . . .'

'Who?'

'Toro Wolfe.'

'What about him?'

Moira let out a huff of breath and stared wide-eyed at her friend.

'*What?*' asked Diamond.

'They do say there's none so blind as those who will not see,' she said. 'And that's you, Diamond, isn't it? Right there.'

Diamond stared at her blankly.

Moira tilted her head, her expression exasperated. 'Look! You told me you had a knife to Toro Wolfe's throat that night when you were in the Corsican's whore house.'

'What . . .? Well, I did. Well not a knife. A razor.'

'And you say you hate him? You say that his father killed yours, and that the Wolfe clan are a pack of filthy dogs, fit only to have their throats slit? Well, didn't you say that?' Moira demanded. 'Haven't you *always* said it?'

'Yes, but . . .'

'Then why didn't you do it, right then? What stopped you? You thought he was coming into that place to rape you, that he'd paid money to the Corsican for the privilege. So *why didn't you kill him when you had the chance?*'

Diamond was completely wrong-footed. 'I . . . I don't know.'

'Never mind running after painters and the ruddy aristocracy – and just look how that ended! You know, I think it's all to do with your dad dying when you were so young. You keep mistaking sex for love, don't you? I've always thought it. But what about a man who talks exactly the same language as you, who understands where you're from and who you are, and who would have you in his bed in an instant if he thought you'd only say yes.'

'I don't know what you mean,' said Diamond.

But she did. Oh Christ. It was hitting her now, but still she couldn't accept it. *Toro Wolfe?* The man who called her a jewel thief, the one who always seemed to show up *exactly* at the wrong moment? No. It couldn't be him. But something about what Moira was saying was ringing a bell at the back of her brain. She'd lost her dad so soon – too soon. Could that really be why she had got into love affairs with completely unsuitable men? Fabien was an egotist, concerned only with his art. Richard had been weak, battered by the war, blowing this way and that; a lost soul.

And Toro?

He was bloody full of himself, she'd always thought that. But there was no weakness to be found in him. He didn't seem to be afraid of anything in the whole damned world. The war had tempered him like fine steel and now he was hard; you wouldn't want to get in a fight with him, that was for sure. She thought of his body pressed against hers when she'd been playing croquet on Fontleigh's lawns. She'd felt it then, that deep shudder of animal desire. She knew she had. And when he'd kissed her, it had been something different to all that she had known before.

Moira threw her hands up in the air. 'Oh all right. I'll drop the subject, but just think about what I've said, will you? Oh God, Diamond.' She drew in a tired, shaky breath. 'Poor Owen, he wouldn't hurt a soul, he's good as gold, and to have this happen . . .' She ran a hand over Owen's scribbles on the *Tatler* pages, brightly drawn in yellows and reds.

Diamond was biting her lip, deep in thought. They'd searched the Butcher home, and they hadn't found him. They'd only found the women, mired in filth, and got them out of there. But there was one other place they *hadn't* searched, wasn't there? Just one, beyond the place where the women had been contained.

She stood up and ran out along the hall to find Toro, leaving Moira staring after her.

148

As they stood bathed in moonlight looking up at the dark front of the Butcher place, Diamond felt like time had stood still. That she was still a young girl, forced into working the badger trick, forced to organise the 'Forty Thieves', her hoisters, around the posh shops, forced into a life of crime and misery by Victor. This place was *so* familiar.

She would insert her key in the lock, and push open the front door, and go inside, and there they would be, all the warm, welcoming, beloved ghosts from her past. Frenchie and Warren and Owen and Aiden too. All alive and well.

No. Not any more.

Only Owen remained of all her family. If she was wrong, if he wasn't in the place she suspected, she didn't know where else to look for him. And Victor would never be able to tell them, either. The lock was shattered on the door, broken earlier by Toro. She pushed it open, very carefully, and stepped inside. Toro's men had checked the attic. They had checked the cellar. They had checked the privy in the back yard. Every corner had been looked at. But perhaps they had missed this one small hiding place?

'You really think he's going to be here? We tossed the whole place,' said Toro, following her in.

As a young girl, she had known every nook and cranny of this place. There was literally *nowhere else* for them to look.

She knew that, deep down. But she couldn't accept it. Not answering, turning on the lights, Diamond went along the hall. She didn't *have* to light the way, not really. She could have done this blindfold, she knew the house so well. She went into the parlour where once Frenchie had held court. The lace curtains at the windows let in cool white shafts of moonlight. The room was empty. She went into the kitchen, then into the scullery, then she retraced her steps to the hall and looked long and hard at the cellar door while Toro stood aside, waiting.

She walked over to the door with its shattered padlock.

If nothing else, she was going to get Frenchie's portrait out of there. Ignoring the scuttling sounds of vermin coming from below, ignoring the stench of the place, she switched on the light at the top of the stairs.

'We looked down there. When we took all the women out. You know we did,' said Toro.

Diamond started down the stairs.

149

It was disgusting. The women had been kept in here in appalling conditions, unwashed, no sanitary provisions, nothing but bread and water to keep them from starvation. Diamond had to hold her breath, keep a hand over her nose and mouth, but she couldn't keep the stench out of her nostrils, much as she tried. She looked all around the cellar walls; nothing. There was the big oblong still propped up over on the far wall – Frenchie's portrait, it had to be. The police had come down here, helped the women climb the stairs and get out. But no-one had thought to move the portrait.

Diamond went over to it straight away. 'Can we . . .?' she said, and Toro grabbed hold of the big thing and shoved it over, inch by inch. It was heavy and moved slowly, but he pushed it over a couple of feet.

'There,' said Diamond, indicating what he'd uncovered.

It was the small door, barely more than two feet wide and two feet high, that led into the coal hole. Out in the back yard, there was the coal chute, where the men came and put the coal down into it.

The tiny little door with its wooden handle was in place. Here was where they came with the scuttle as kids and filled it with coal, lugging it back upstairs to fuel the fire.

Toro was kneeling, tugging at the handle, pulling the small door out and away from the hole. Diamond held her breath.

She couldn't look. If Owen wasn't in there, then where the hell would he be? He would *never* be found. The secret of his whereabouts would have died with Victor. And alone, unprotected, Owen would surely die too.

'Is he . . .?' she gasped out. 'Oh Christ, he's not there, is he?'

'Get down here,' said Toro, and Diamond got down on her hands and knees and peered inside the coal hole.

Toro shone the torch in there. Staring back at them, his face streaked with tears and blackened with coal, was Owen.

150

When they got back to Moira's and Toro left them at the door, Diamond felt giddy with relief. All would be well now. Victor was gone, Michael was safe, Owen was rescued. But then, when she hurried along the hall and into the kitchen with her brother at her side she came to a dead halt.

There were three men sitting at Moira's kitchen table. Moira was there, standing, dispensing tea to them. When Diamond entered she put the teapot down on the table and hurried to Owen.

'Poor boy, look at the mess you're in! Come on, let's get you upstairs and clean.' She looked at Diamond. 'These gentlemen are from the police,' she said, and Diamond saw the wariness in her eyes. Police calls were never good news. Were they here for Michael? 'They want to talk to you,' she said.

As Moira hurried Owen from the room, the three men rose to their feet and looked at Diamond. A tall gangly young man, an even taller thick-set man of middle years and a short pudgy man with black hair, a white beard and a Malacca cane. Two of them, she knew straight away. Her heart was suddenly in her mouth.

'Mam'selle Diamond Butcher?' asked the short one in a thick French accent.

'Yes. That's me,' said Diamond, feeling shaky, feeling that she had avoided this for so long and now here it was.

She knew what they were going to say. She knew what she had done. She felt that ever since her encounter with two of these men down in the Loire Valley at the Marquis's château, this scene had been waiting to unfold itself. It was almost a relief, to have it happen at last.

'Miss Butcher,' said the thick-set middle-aged one, picking up his bowler hat from the table. 'I am Chief Inspector Lockhart of the Yard. This is Detective Inspector Benoit of the French police and this is Sergeant Golon.'

They nodded. Diamond nodded back.

'I wonder if you'll be so kind as to accompany us to the station?' said Lockhart. 'We have questions to ask.'

'Regarding a murder, mam'selle,' said Golon.

'The murder of Monsieur Arnaud Roussel,' said Benoit.

Now the truth would be out, it would be a colossal weight off her shoulders. At last, she would lay down her burden of guilt and be free of it.

'Yes,' she said. 'Of course.'

151

They questioned her at the station and she told them all about the night of the exhibition in the gallery near the Quai du Louvre, leaving nothing out except the presence of Toro Wolfe right there at the scene. She didn't know why she did that. Well, maybe she did. After all, he had helped her, time and again. Moira was right about that. She didn't know why, but he had. So there was no way that she wished to implicate him in this.

Finally – it seemed like hours later, hours when she had sat talking, sipping water, a uniformed officer standing guard behind her, the three men seated on the other side of the table, the youngest one taking careful notes, the older two watching her face – the tale was done. Lockhart left the room to get her statement written up. It would all be all right, she was sure of that. The crux of the matter was that Mimi had pulled the gun from her bag, and Diamond had tried to avert a disaster, save Arnaud, by snatching the gun off her. But then – the gun had gone off, and Arnaud had died.

'I tried to stop her,' said Diamond, over and over.

'*Oui, mam'selle,*' Benoit said.

'I really did.'

'Of course,' said Golon.

Then Lockhart came back with the statement. She read it, signed it.

'The unfortunate thing is,' said Benoit, when she was sure that this was all done with, 'it was you who pulled the gun, not her, according to Mimi Daniels. Arnaud was your – shall we say – protector? It sounds nicer than the word most would use. He was pestering you for money you owed him. And you shot him, fully intending to do so. What did you do with the gun, mam'selle?'

152

Diamond looked at the three of them, now seated again across the desk and staring back at her.

Her throat was very, very dry. She blinked.

'*What?*' she said hoarsely.

'We have questioned Mimi Daniels. And she says . . .'

'But she's lying!' Diamond burst out.

'She insists she is telling the truth. And what became of the gun, mam'selle?' asked Benoit.

'The gun?' Diamond's heart was racketing in her chest. This wasn't going the way she had expected – not at all. She could feel sweat gathering around her hairline. She felt hot and chilled, all at once. 'I've no idea what happened to the gun.'

'You were shocked by what you had done, *non*?' Golon said. 'You threw it down and maybe it fell in the river? We searched but it could not be found.'

'I've no idea where the gun went. I told you. It was Mimi's gun. I snatched it off Mimi because she was threatening Arnaud with it, and it went off.'

Toro Wolfe had pocketed the gun. She wasn't going to tell them that.

'Sadly that doesn't match with her version of events.'

'But it's the truth!'

'You have a chequered history, Miss Butcher,' said Lockhart. 'Dubious in the extreme, I would say. You are a woman of ill repute. Not a woman of sound character, not even a woman of slightly loose morals like Miss Daniels. You have involvement with thugs and criminals – robber gangs like the Victory Boys right here in London. The boss of the Victory Boys is your uncle and according to his associates you stole money from him, assaulted him. And the Silver Blades. You're in tight with Michael McLean and your "hoisters" have told us that you were going to transfer your – and their – allegiance from Victor Butcher's mob to the Silver Blades. You've even been staying with the mother of their leader. Do you deny it?'

'Wait! No . . .'

'Queen of the hoisters, don't they call you? Boss of the Forty Thieves? And playing lucrative whore's tricks on poor unsuspecting men. Well, Miss Butcher, some of those men are eager to come forward and tell their story to aid the prosecution. It could go badly for you, I'm afraid. Your background is not good – whereas Mimi Daniels, apart from being a harmless high-society whore, has a much better name.'

'I wasn't given a choice over any of it,' Diamond protested. 'My uncle forced me.'

'I'm perfectly willing to believe that your uncle is a very bad man indeed, Miss Butcher,' said Lockhart. 'If only he could be contacted to give a better account of your character, that would be good. But he's not to be found, anywhere.'

Of course not. Victor was dead at the hands of the Triads. Yet another thing she couldn't tell them.

'Furthermore,' concluded Lockhart, 'I am willing to believe that you are a very wicked woman.'

'Wait . . .' Diamond couldn't believe it. Victor and his vile tricks had done for her. Lockhart was right. It did look bad.

'I advise you to get yourself a lawyer, Miss Butcher. A damned good one. Diamond Butcher,' said Lockhart, rising to his feet, 'I am arresting you on suspicion of the murder of Monsieur Arnaud Roussel. Anything you say . . .'

'No!' Diamond objected as he droned on.

Lockhart finished what he was saying and nodded to the uniformed officer standing at her back.

'Lock her up,' he said.

'It's a pity,' said Golon when the officer and Diamond were gone from the room. 'Such a stunning woman.'

'Don't be soft-hearted, Golon,' said Benoit. Frowning, he turned to Lockhart. 'Of course she'll be tried in France?'

But Lockhart shook his head. 'I've spoken with the Chief Constable. She's to be tried here, he says, to protect her rights as an English citizen.'

'Well, that is a discussion we must have,' said Benoit, displeased. 'The ideal would be to have her extradited to France to stand trial, since the crime occurred on French soil.' This was *his* coup, not Lockhart's, catching the woman at last.

'The Chief Constable was most insistent,' said Lockhart. 'He has orders.'

'From who? God Almighty?' sniffed Benoit.

'Such a shame,' said Golon, shaking his head. Cut or hanged, he hated the idea.

'Yes,' agreed Lockhart. 'It's regrettable. But my friends, I promise you this – she's going to swing.'

153

The lawyer came – paid for by Michael – and visited her in Holloway. He listened to what Diamond had to say and shook his head. He was a big fat man, bald and scruffy with sad bulging blue eyes.

'The trouble is,' he said, 'your connections. I am afraid that for a long time the law has been eager to slap down the criminal gangs of London. You are directly connected to the Victory Boys, a despicable mob and one that the judiciary are keen to make an example of. They will be delighted to have cornered you on this – or on any other charge. The murder of Arnaud Roussel in Paris is a gift to them.'

'But I didn't do it,' said Diamond. 'It was an accident.'

She'd been in custody for weeks. Bail – which would have been paid, again, by Michael – had been refused. Holloway Prison was her new home. She was penned in a cell, alone, awaiting trial. She wondered if this nightmare would ever end.

Michael and Moira had come to see her, just twice. She had asked them if they'd seen Toro, but he was away, they said. Out of the country, by all accounts. Keeping out of the way of all this shit that was flying about the place, she guessed. On his first visit, Michael told her not to worry, he would sort the lawyer, he would see to everything, he would get her *out* of here.

But she didn't believe it. And the lawyer – Phelps, his name was – seemed equally dubious about her prospects.

'The gun went off in my hand when I snatched it off Mimi, to stop her from doing something stupid. It wasn't *my* gun, it was hers,' she told Phelps, over and over.

He shrugged. 'At least we've dodged extradition. Christ alone knows how, but we have. You'll be tried here, at the Old Bailey.'

Diamond looked around at the gloomy room they sat in. This was where visitors were received. A female warder stood impassively nearby, watching, listening.

'It's going to go against me, isn't it?' she said.

'This Mimi Daniels is coming over as star witness for the prosecution in the Crown versus Diamond Butcher. It's not looking good. If we can get together a reasonable defence, have someone vouch for your character – *not* Michael Mc Lean, perhaps his mother? – and do some digging into this Daniels woman, see what dirt we can uncover . . . there's always hope.'

'Catherine Sibley and her brother will vouch for me.'

'That's good,' said Phelps.

'Where's Toro?' she asked Michael again, when he came to see her. Suddenly, she felt desperate to see Toro.

'I dunno. Ain't seen him. Travelling, last I heard. Like I told you.'

She was on her own.

154

The wheels of justice ground extremely slowly, Diamond found. Day after day she sat in her cell in Holloway, ate the rubbish food, shivered in the cold, listened to the sounds of despair all around her and wondered when the hell all this would be over.

Then the first day of the trial arrived at last. Moira brought her in a decent dress to wear, and hugged her, and said it would all be all right. Then she was led out blinking into bright daylight and pushed into the back of a dark van and driven down Liverpool Road to the Angel, past Spitalfields market and from there to the Central Criminal Court, the Old Bailey.

Michael and Moira were there in the public gallery. No Toro. Christ, didn't he even *care* what was happening to her, the bastard? He'd chased her all over the place but now it was clear he didn't give a fuck.

The press were in. Big criminal gangs were always a draw. Rowdily the reporters and photographers perched in the gallery like a load of carrion crows, exclaiming over this and that until the judge threatened to throw them out.

The trial began. It wound on for days and she stood in the dock and told the truth of it, time after time. She'd snatched the gun from Mimi's hand and it had gone off. *Mimi* had intended Arnaud Roussel harm – not her.

Lockhart was seated across the court, watching her stonily. So too was that odd little chap Inspector Benoit and his sidekick Golon. All three of them gave their statements to the court, batted away Phelps's questions, then were given an easy ride by the prosecution.

Diamond's gloom lifted a little when first Catherine and then Teddy took the stand. They spoke eloquently of her, and Catherine – touchingly, moving Diamond almost to tears – told of how she had brought life and hope back to their dear friend Richard Beaumont when he had been in deep despair after the war.

Then, after days of deliberations and statements, the prosecution barrister called Mimi Daniels into the witness box. Diamond was shocked by her appearance. Mimi looked ten years older. She hadn't attended to her hair and it looked like grey straw, instead of its usual carefully tinted blonde. She wore no rouge, no colour on her lips and so she looked drained. From nowhere, she had also cleverly produced a disability. She was leaning heavily on a stick and had to be helped up into the witness box, smiling sweetly at those who assisted her, wincing delicately as if with pain. Instantly Diamond could see the jury contrasting this tiny, frail old hobbling thing, so sedately dressed, so sweet in her expression of injured innocence, with the robust upright young woman standing opposite her in the courtroom.

The prosecution proceeded to question Mimi politely, and Mimi shed heart-wrenching tears at the accusation that the gun had been hers, that she had waved it in Arnaud's face and threatened him.

'How could I? Me? I really couldn't do a thing like that.' Then Mimi's tear-filled eyes rose and she glared at Diamond. She dabbed at her eyes with a handkerchief. 'I took in Miss

Butcher in remembrance of her dear mother, who was a friend of mine. And I soon learned to regret my generous action! There's bad blood in that family but I was unaware of it up to that point. How was I to know that she would do such a terrible thing?'

Mimi didn't mention Toro's presence on the night of Arnaud's death.

Then it was Phelps's turn. He dragged up everything about Mimi's past, her immoral earnings, and finished with a thunderous: 'And Arnaud Roussel was nothing to do with Miss Butcher, but everything to do with *you*, Miss Daniels. He was your *pimp*. And you defied him. Refused to pay him. He came after you. Miss Butcher wished to protect you from him, which was foolish of her but in no way malicious. And the gun was *yours*.'

'No,' said Mimi weakly, looking around the courtroom with appealing blue eyes. She started to sob brokenly. Diamond watched her and thought that Mimi was a much, much better actress than she could ever hope to be. 'She did it. *She* had the gun. I felt so sorry for the poor girl. Dragged up like she was, with Frenchie for a mother – a terrible hardened prostitute . . .'

'Madam, *you* are the hardened prostitute here,' snapped Phelps.

'Objection!' yelled the prosecution.

'Overruled,' said the judge. He looked at his watch. 'We will break now for recess. And then I will sum up.'

155

Diamond was taken back down to the cells and given food that she couldn't eat. She felt too sick to face it. She was alone and shivering with fear. She was going to hang, she knew it. Nothing could save her.

Maybe she would get the famous Tom Pierrepoint, an expert in the hangman's trade. It was said he could snap your neck in a second; there was no suffering. Or if she was unlucky – and why wouldn't she be, after all this, a murder trial, and Mimi's betrayal? – then she would get an unskilled hangman who would leave her dangling half-dead, choking by slow degrees.

She thought of Toro, who'd abandoned her to her fate. Where was he? Didn't he care about her at all?

She knew the answer to that. Of course he didn't. He just didn't want any of her mud sticking to *him*, that was all. He was keeping clear.

When she got to heaven, would her baby be waiting for her? Her family? And poor sweet Richard?

She didn't cry.

She had no tears left.

156

The judge came back after lunch, summed up the case and the jury were sent away to deliberate. When they returned – too quickly, Diamond thought – the judge asked the jury for their verdict.

'Guilty,' said the foreman.

A ripple went through the courtroom. Moira shouted 'No!' and the press surged out of the room, heading for the telephones to call in their stories. Everyone was riveted by this tale of the 'Black Beauty of Death', as they were calling her. Mimi sat opposite Diamond, eyes downcast. Was she stifling a smile? Diamond thought she was.

Guilty.

Diamond felt the world spin around her as it sank in. She watched, mesmerised, as a court official approached the judge and carefully laid a square of black cloth on top of his grey wig.

It was official.

She was going to die.

157

Michael came to visit with Phelps, to tell her there was an appeal process under way and that she wasn't to worry; all this would be sorted out.

'Yes,' she said numbly, but she didn't believe it.

When Phelps had left, Diamond said: 'Michael? I want Moira to look after Owen.'

'She's looking after him now, and soon you'll be back with him,' he said firmly.

'You know what I mean. You know perfectly well. When I am gone, Moira's to look after him.'

Michael stared at her face; then his eyes dropped. 'There are things being done, Diamond. I promise you. You can't give up hope.'

Diamond gave a thin smile. 'Hope's a torment,' she said. 'Why build yourself up to be knocked down again?'

'Diamond . . .'

'Hush, Michael. Leave me alone now, will you?'

Michael had no arguments left.

158

The Right Honourable Cedric Sibley didn't like being woken early. As Lord High Chancellor of Great Britain he expected his subordinates to manage matters until a decent hour of the day. But his butler had dragged him from his bed and his assistant was now in the study with him, talking about the Crown versus Diamond Butcher and other matters, things he really didn't want to hear about.

Things, frankly, that he would rather forget.

Like that unfortunate liaison with a girl young enough to be his granddaughter. It had been, he could admit to himself now, nothing more than a foolish old man's last throw of the dice, that fling. But the girl had been unstable and had drugged herself to death in his town house. He had avoided a scandal by only the narrowest of margins. He could still break out in a cold sweat, just thinking about it.

Now here it was again, coming back to haunt him.

'Sir, you have to do something. Right now,' said his assistant urgently. Not only his boss's position but his own very comfortable job was on the line. The shit would fly and a lot of it was going to stick – to both of them.

Cedric Sibley had quashed the French extradition request for the cursed woman, which had caused the most godawful stink – but he'd smoothed it all over and prayed that would be the finish of it. But now he knew he was going to have to quash this, too. Or it would cost him, and it would cost him far too dear. It had all been laid out for him, what he stood to lose. His standing in the community. The respect of his peers. His family. His marriage. It was far too much.

He hated to do it, but he had to. He signed the papers put in front of him and hoped that was the last of it.

Then he went back to bed, where his wife slept on, all unknowing.

159

Diamond sat in her cell and listened to the sounds going on all around her. Somewhere in the big stark echoing chill of Holloway Prison, a woman was wailing. Another was shouting and banging on the bars of her cell. Diamond made no sound. She watched a finger of daylight send a column of gold onto the cell wall and thought *this can't be happening.*

But it was.

It was five o'clock in the morning, and today was the day. The hangman was waiting for her because she had been convicted of murder. Phelps's appeal hadn't worked.

She looked down at the drab, scratchy prison garb she wore. Usually for her it was silks, laces, long pale furs and exquisite jewels. Diamonds, mostly, because she was a product of her own invention and she had learned exactly how to market her wares. It was usually diamonds, set in gold or silver, twinkling in warm candlelight while she sipped vintage champagne. Diamonds like the Marquis had given her. Like Richard had given her. *Poor darling Richard.*

Then the cell door opened. Her hands fell to her lap.

It was the female warder, grim-faced as usual. It was always the same one. She was bringing Diamond's breakfast.

'Not long now,' she said, setting the tray down beside her.

Not long until she hanged.

Well – it was better than the guillotine, wasn't it? She'd been saved extradition, at least. Somehow.

A sliver of panic was suddenly lodged in Diamond's gut, making it clench. She looked at the dish of porridge as the warder withdrew. She knew she wouldn't eat it. She couldn't.

Today, she was going to die.

This couldn't be happening, not to her.

The present was terrifying, and the past was gone. No good thinking back, not now. Back to all her adventures. To hoisting from the West End shops and doing the badger trick with Victor. To Fabien Flaubert and to poor doomed Richard Beaumont. And the man who was forever on the fringes of her life, her enemy Toro Wolfe. There were questions about him that would never be answered now. She was Diamond Butcher, the oldest and only girl in a family of London thieves – but she had been reborn as Diamond Dupree, the toast of Paris and the beloved of the English aristocracy. And she had to stand tall; not show her fear.

Promptly at six, the door opened and there were two female warders standing there, along with a priest.

At last.

It was time.

160

On trembling legs Diamond walked along corridors, a warder on each side of her, the priest trailing behind. A door opened, they passed through. Then another. All around there was the echoing clang of metal gates, the distant wails and shouts of women penned up in this hellish place.

Soon, she would be out of it.

She wondered if Frenchie would be waiting for her in heaven. And Warren, her dear dad. And Aiden! Wouldn't it be wonderful if they were there, waiting with open arms for her to join them?

Now, through another door. She was walking down a set of stone steps, the warders holding her arms as she descended. She looked ahead and the breath stopped in her throat.

The hangman was standing there up ahead, very neat in his suit and tie, waiting for her up on the platform. The noose hung there waiting too. Behind her, the priest started reciting the Lord's Prayer.

She hesitated there, feeling the strength go out of her legs as panic took over. But the warders' grip on her arms was firm and they led her on, across the room and up the steps to the platform where the hangman stood ready.

He placed the noose around her neck. Asked – very politely – if she wanted the blindfold.

She didn't. She shook her head. The hangman's hand was ready on the lever that would open the trap door. She thought of Frenchie, and Warren, and Aiden as the priest droned on. She closed her eyes, thought of heaven, of her family, waiting for her.

The noose scratched her neck.

She braced herself. Too late for tears now. Too late for *anything.*

161

'Hold on! Hold on, will you?'

It was a man's voice. Diamond's eyes opened.

A man was running toward the platform, barging past the warders, nearly knocking over the priest. He was waving a piece of paper in his hand.

'Stop! *Stop*, for God's sake!' he shouted.

'What is it?' asked the hangman.

'A full pardon from the Lord High Chancellor! Get her down,' the man ordered.

Dazed, Diamond was led back down off the platform, across the room, up the steps, and then she was taken back to her cell.

Next day, she was released from Holloway.

Michael, Moira and Owen met her at the gate.

162

Two days after the 'Black Beauty of Death' was released from prison and all charges against her dropped, Diamond washed, dressed in her Sunday best, clipped Richard's emerald-cut diamonds onto her ears and then breakfasted with Moira and Owen.

'Your friend called. The posh French one,' said Moira as they ate toast and drank tea. 'He's going to come back later. I told him you were still asleep.'

Having come out of prison, Diamond had for the past day or so felt that she could sleep forever. She hadn't even heard a knock at the door. The luxury of a real soft warm bed to sleep in was so marvellous it almost made her cry, but she was too tired, too wrung out emotionally, to even do that.

'The Marquis? He's come over?'

'Very grand he was. But nice. Had a lovely young man with him.'

Jean-Luc.

'He said he'd call back at six.'

She had plenty of time, then. As soon as breakfast was over she kissed Owen goodbye and left him there at the table, happy with his colouring books. Several gentlemen of the press were loitering hopefully out on the pavement. They shouted questions at her. Wasn't she glad to be out of jail? Was she really innocent? Was she going to sue for wrongful arrest? She ignored them, hailed a cab and went across town and pitched up at the door, not believing he'd be there, wondering what the hell she would say to him if he was.

He was in.

Toro Wolfe opened the door wide and without waiting to be invited Diamond stepped inside.

They stood there in the hallway. For a moment, there was nothing but silence. Then Diamond said: 'Where the hell have you been?'

'Oh – here and there. Busy. You know.'

'And how is Gwendoline?'

He shrugged. 'Fine, so far as I know. Travelling in Devon, visiting her mother's relatives I believe. No doubt trying to forget all about Victor Butcher and what happened when she was tied to him. How are you?'

Diamond thought about that. 'I feel like I'm shell-shocked,' she said at last.

'You'll feel better in a few days. It's been tough, I know.'

'How do you know? You didn't even try to visit, did you?'

'No. I didn't. Who did you rob *these* from, jewel thief?' Half smiling, he raised a hand to her ear, touching one of the diamond earrings.

'Richard gave them to me.'

'Did he? He should have given them to Catherine.'

'I know that,' said Diamond.

'And anyway,' he said, stepping in closer to her. His hand came up again and he pulled off first one earring, then the other. 'It's impossible to improve on perfection. *He* should have known *that.*'

Toro dropped the earrings into her hand. Diamond put them in her coat pocket.

'Toro?' she said.

'Hmm?' He was standing so close to her, so very close.

'Can you tell me now?'

'Tell you what?'

'What did you do?'

163

'Do?' Toro stared into her eyes.

'Yes. You did something. I *know* you did something.'

He shrugged. 'Nothing much. Just applied pressure here and there. Mostly to Cedric Sibley, Catherine's uncle. I suppose you know he's Lord High Chancellor.'

Diamond thought of that dinner party at Fontleigh, the old gentleman seated across from her, Catherine on one side of him, a very young over-excited girl on the other.

'No,' she said. 'I didn't know that.'

'Catherine's a great friend to you and Teddy adores you, you probably do realise that. They begged Sir James to intervene, to plead your case with his brother, to put forward an argument against extradition, but Cedric wasn't playing. And if he wasn't going to play on *that*, then there was every chance you were done for. But fortunately . . .'

Diamond was listening intently. 'Fortunately *what*?'

'Fortunately Cedric has a taste for inappropriately youthful girls. Like the one who was with him that weekend at Fontleigh, the very highly strung creature who was going to throw herself in the lake. Which she didn't. Although she did kill herself later, in Cedric Sibley's London home. Which I heard about from the people I'd placed around him, and made use of.'

'Oh.' It was all starting to make sense now.

'So I applied pressure, and Cedric realised he had far too much to lose if he didn't halt both your extradition and your execution. He's a stubborn old bastard, though, and for a while it was looking unlikely that he'd co-operate.'

'So you weren't sure it would work.'

'No. But it did.'

'Christ Almighty.' Diamond sagged against the wall, closed her eyes. Then she opened them, looked at him, standing there so full of himself, exuding confidence as he always did. Handsome son of a *bitch*. 'Tell me – what did you do with Mimi's gun?' she asked him.

Toro's eyes held hers for a long, long moment. Then he reached into his waistcoat pocket.

'You mean *this* gun?' he said – and pulled out a .22 pearl-handled lady's gun – *Mimi's* gun.

Diamond looked at it, then at him. 'You bastard,' she said, shaking her head almost in admiration. 'What are you going to do with it now?'

'This little thing's going back to Paris,' he told her. 'It's going to be secreted among Mimi Daniels' belongings. And that odd little chap Benoit is going to get a tip-off. Let's see her wangle her way out of *that* with a few tears and a limp.'

Diamond had lived in such fear for so long, and now she could feel it draining away from her, leaving her washed out but somehow clean. 'That cow Mimi,' she sighed. 'She turned on me, didn't she? After all she said about being my mother's friend.'

'And you believed that?'

'Why wouldn't I? She *was*, after all.'

'No, she wasn't,' said Toro, repocketing the deadly little weapon. 'She was never your mother's friend. In fact – Mimi Daniels *hated* Frenchie Butcher.'

164

'That's not true,' said Diamond. 'That *can't* be true.'

'My father knew all about it. He told me, years ago. Your dad dropped Mimi like a hot potato when he met Frenchie. She never forgave her for it. Even if she did pretend to be her "friend", she never was. And when you pitched up in Paris, you were in the line of fire – even though you didn't realise it. Mimi used you time after time – to get lodgings, to barge her way into the best places. And when the accident with Arnaud happened, you were the perfect patsy. Frenchie's daughter! What could be sweeter than finally having her revenge on Frenchie's own child. To see you strung up for something *she* was responsible for.'

Diamond stared at him, thunderstruck. 'That's rubbish,' she said, but she was thinking of Mimi's catty pleasure in seeing Madeleine's distress on the night of the exhibition – because Madeleine had once crossed her, and she wanted revenge.

'Is it? I don't think so.'

'I shouldn't believe a word that comes out of your mouth,' said Diamond. This was a mistake. She turned, heading for the door. Toro caught her arm.

'Why? Because I'm a Wolfe? Because I'm the enemy?'

'*Yes!*' Diamond spun back and shouted in his face. 'Your father killed mine. Sometimes I almost forget that. And I shouldn't.'

'No. He didn't.'

'Let go of me.'

'Listen to me, will you? I was there on the night of the fight, I saw it all. You think my father did for yours? I'm telling you, he didn't.'

Diamond wrenched herself free of his grip and was going to the door again when he said: 'Diamond! For Christ's sake. It wasn't my dad who did it. It was *Victor.*'

165

It was as if time froze at that point. She turned back to him and it all steamrollered onto her, all the years of loathing for him and his kind. They'd robbed her family. Intimidated them. Chased them out of London then Paris then London again. *Persecuted* them. And now he was saying . . .?

Fury gripped her.

'You fucking *liar*,' she burst out. 'The Butcher Boys told us what they'd seen. Gustav did it.'

'No,' said Toro firmly. 'I'm not lying. My dad didn't strike the killing blow. Victor paid the Butcher crew to tell your family that. But I was *there*. I *saw* what happened. I saw Victor come up behind Warren and hit him with a hammer.'

She was very still, staring at his face. Handsome bastard. *Too* handsome. So appealing and yet at the same time a *Wolfe*. Yes – the enemy. And now he was saying that *Victor* had been the one to land the killing blow?

It was fresh in her mind again, the memory of that night. The men carrying her dad, her beloved father Warren Butcher, into Frenchie's kitchen, then Frenchie falling upon Dad's neck, sobbing, hysterical, the heart wrenched out of her. Dad's blood staining the floor, her clothes, her hands.

Ah, the horror of it . . .

She was shaking her head, over and over. 'No! Gustav Wolfe killed my dad.'

'He didn't. He was a cold man and he was a bastard, that much is true, but he didn't do that.'

'He had someone put a lit rag through our door,' she remembered. Frenchie had been terrified. Later, much later, she had told her daughter about it.

'No, he bloody didn't. It can't be proved now, but it must have been Victor, wanting to ramp up the aggro between the Butchers and the Wolfes. And it worked. Didn't it?'

Diamond was shaking her head. 'No! Victor was Dad's brother! Why the hell would anyone do such a thing to their brother?'

'That's easy to explain. Warren had a gang established, he was a big name on the streets. Victor wasn't. Before he grabbed what Warren had worked for, he was strictly small-time and low-life. He was jealous of all that Warren had and he wanted it for himself.'

Diamond couldn't take it in. She *refused* to. And yet . . . somehow, what he was saying was making perfect sense.

'They brought Dad back to us and he was . . .' She swallowed. She felt sick, remembering. But now she was remembering something else, something that could prove the lie. She stared at Toro with hard eyes and said: 'All right! You say that's true, do you? So tell me, what side was he struck on?'

Toro stared into her eyes. She waited, her heart in her mouth. This was like flipping a coin, wasn't it? Too easy. He would just guess, and hope he'd get the side correct. That was all. None of this could be true.

'The left,' said Toro.

Diamond fled.

166

Diamond walked the streets, barely thinking of where she was going, scarcely noticing the people moving around her. A couple of them stared at her face, someone shouted something at her, recognising her from the papers. She didn't care. She walked on until she was too tired to walk any further. She found herself at St Anne's churchyard, staring down once again at the smashed gravestones. Staring at them but not seeing them.

The left.

Toro hadn't hesitated. Hadn't sounded unsure.

He'd just guessed correctly, then.

Or he was there and he really did see it, said a treacherous voice in her brain. *Not a guess at all, in that case. A fact.*

Was it really so hard to believe that Victor had taken the opportunity of the confrontation between the two gangs to move in, to take his chance, to kill Warren, grab what had belonged to his brother and take it for his own?

She thought of standing at her bedroom door as a child of eleven, terrified, bewildered, her father dead and her mother being herded into the bedroom along the hall by Uncle Victor. The memory was painful. *Too* painful.

Dusk was falling. She walked back to the main road, hailed a cab and went home to Moira's place.

167

When she got there, the Marquis was there with Jean-Luc, filling Moira's humble home with loud theatrical exclamations and the scent of very expensive perfume.

'Darling! Oh my darling, you poor thing!' fussed the Marquis as Diamond came into Moira's front room, which was *never* used, as a rule, but kept strictly for best.

Diamond had wandered off to the Wolfe place, forgetting all that Moira had said, that the Marquis was coming back at six. It was gone that now.

The Marquis hugged her tight. Jean-Luc too. Moira brought her a cup of tea, clearly a little intimidated by these very grand visitors, and Diamond sat down on the couch beside the Marquis and somehow made conversation.

'And how are you, sweetheart?' the Marquis asked her, clasping her hand in his.

'I'm well,' she said.

She knew she didn't look it.

'That *cow* Mimi,' sniffed the Marquis. 'Well it won't do her any good, all that she's done to you. She won't get a single invitation anywhere now. I'll see to that. To Parisian society, Mimi Daniels is *dead.*'

Diamond thought that acceptance in Paris's high society was going to be the very least of Mimi's troubles, once Toro got that gun back in her possession and alerted the French police.

'How is Toro?' asked Jean-Luc.

'Yes, have you seen him?' asked the Marquis.

'No,' said Diamond. She couldn't talk about Toro, not now – probably not ever.

The left.

Had he just guessed it? *Had* he?

And *did* Frenchie take Dad off Mimi, back in the day?

But Frenchie wasn't here to ask.

Somehow she stayed there with Moira and the Marquis and Jean-Luc, chatting, laughing, while her brain spun in circles.

'You'll come over to Paris again and see us?' asked the Marquis as he was leaving.

'I'm not sure the French authorities would make me very welcome.' Phelps had advised her not to go back there, after the trial.

'Then we will come to you,' said Jean-Luc. 'In the summer.'

'That would be lovely.' She would introduce the Marquis to Catherine and Teddy, take him to Langstone, have all her friends together.

As the Marquis and Jean-Luc were leaving, the Marquis drew her to one side.

'So – are you still at odds with that gorgeous man Toro Wolfe?' he asked.

Diamond couldn't answer.

'He moved heaven and earth to get you out of there, you do know that, don't you? While we all ran around like headless chickens, he was working behind the scenes to free you. Darling, the very fact that you are standing here at liberty is down to Toro. He's your friend.' The Marquis sent a loving glance to Jean-Luc, standing there talking to Moira. 'It's no small thing, to have such a friend, you know.'

'There's nothing like that between us,' said Diamond.

'No? So tell me, darling – would you *like* there to be?' The Marquis winked and patted her cheek. Then he was gone.

168

Diamond went back to the Wolfe house but he wasn't there. She finally found him at the biggest of the Wolfe clubs, propping up the bar, a bottle of whisky and an empty glass beside him. As she watched, he unstoppered the whisky bottle and refilled the glass and sluiced it down in one. Slapped the empty glass just a bit unsteadily back onto the bar.

'Are you *drunk*?' she asked as she stood behind him.

Toro looked back over his shoulder at her. Took a long, long look. 'I thought you were gone,' he said.

'Gone?' Diamond pulled up a bar stool and hoisted herself up onto it.

He nodded.

'I think you're drunk,' she said. She had never once seen him even slightly out of control. This was a novelty.

'I'm not drunk,' he said. 'I'm trying to head that way, though.' He poured more whisky. Stared at her, long and hard. Drank the whisky. Then he pointed a finger at her. 'Do you know what it was like? Do you?'

'What *what* was like?' she asked. She hitched a finger at the barman. 'Another glass, please.'

The barman brought her a glass. Diamond poured herself a hit of the whisky. Sipped it. It was very strong. Christ, how was he even standing up?

'You,' said Toro. 'Throwing yourself at that French fop Flaubert. And then at poor bloody Richard. Getting yourself pregnant . . .'

'That wasn't my fault.'

'Yes, all right, I see that. I do. But then the court case. It's nearly driven me crazy. That old bastard Sibley was resisting. You know something else? At one point I thought he was going to call my bluff and go ahead and just let you hang. Right up to the last minute, I thought that. And then after all that, I had to tell you about Victor and what he did. Not my father, God rot him, but *your own bloody uncle.*'

She sipped the whisky again. 'I've thought about what you said about Victor killing my dad on the night of the big fight.'

His eyes were fixed on her face. He was a tough man, a hard man, but in that instant Diamond saw something there, something vulnerable. Something that could be hurt.

'And?' he asked.

'And I believe you.'

Toro was still staring at her. 'What . . .? You do?'

'Yes. I do. Toro?' She sipped the whisky again. It burned a hot trail right down to her belly. Gave her courage. 'You've helped me at every turn, haven't you? Why?'

He blinked. Turned his head away. 'Christ knows,' he sighed. 'You know, the first time I saw you, you were standing in the street with your mother. You must have been – oh, I don't know – maybe fourteen?'

She remembered the day. Gustav walking ahead of his men down the street, everyone drawing back, afraid. Toro following close behind. She remembered *him.* So dazzling to look at, and she'd despised him on sight.

'I was fifteen,' she corrected. 'I saw you too.'

He gave a smile. 'And you hated me. I could see it in your eyes.'

'And hated you, yes. Did you burn down the Milano? I've always thought you did.'

Toro shook his head. 'My best guess? Victor, for the insurance and for the chance to cause me trouble. I thought you were the most gorgeous thing I'd ever seen.'

'I thought the same when I saw you.'

'You did?'

She nodded, leaned forward, kissed him very softly on the lips. He was completely still for one shocked moment. Then Toro's hand fastened behind her head, holding there for a deeper, longer kiss. He drew back and looked into her eyes.

'I've still only had a small down payment for helping out you and the Blades,' he reminded her.

Diamond felt like her heart was going to explode, she was filled with such joy. Toro bloody Wolfe, of all people. Not Fabien, not Richard. *This* one, who had been her enemy but was now her friend. And soon – please soon, she hoped – her lover. She had lost one man's child, much to her sorrow, but she could start again, with this one. With Toro Wolfe. The future was opening up to her now, and the past was fading.

'You can take full payment any time you like,' she told him.

'You're a very bold woman, Diamond Butcher,' he said, pulling her off the bar stool and into his arms.

Acknowledgements

To all the people – friends, fans, everyone – who have helped in getting my books into the top ten *Sunday Times* Bestseller List time after time, and who have helped me stay sane(ish) while writing this book in lockdown, thank you. It is very much appreciated.

jx